SOUTHWEST
of
HEAVEN

SOUTHWEST

of

HEAVEN

GILES TIPPETTE

A Tom Doherty Associates Book

New York

3 1969 01108 0727

SOUTHWEST OF HEAVEN

A Forge Book
Published by Tom Doherty Associates, LLC
175 Fifth Avenue
New York, NY 10010

www.tor.com

Forge® is a registered trademark of Tom Doherty Associates, LLC.

ISBN 0-312-86048-X

First Edition: March 2000

Printed in the United States of America

0 9 8 7 6 5 4 3 2 1

To Betsyanne, all my love and flowers

CHAPTER
1

FROM BEHIND me a voice said, "All right, buddy, on your way. We don't allow no bums on railroad property, especially at night."

I looked back. A thickset man was standing there with a billy club in one hand and an out-of-patience look on his face. I was sitting on the end of the freight-loading platform in the railroad yard in Galveston, Texas. It made me angry, him calling me a bum like that, but I kept my voice civil. I said, "I'm just waiting around for the late trains to come in. Thought they might use an extra hand. The straw boss off the last shift said I had a good chance."

The man snorted. He said, "Yeah, you look like you're looking for a good chance, a chance to steal somethin'. I been dealin' with you bums fer ten years an' you don't change none, just git younger. Now off with you 'fore I put some lumps on your head!"

And he raised his club as if he meant to strike. I wheeled around, bringing my feet up, and stood up slowly. My anger was stirred, as it had been for some time now, but it wasn't ready to boil over. The man had a gun on his hip, though it didn't look much-used, and some kind of badge on his chest. It wasn't an official badge like a sheriff's deputy or a town constable. I took it to be that of a railroad detective. The railroads handed them out to every yard bully on their payroll. I wasn't afraid of the club or the badge, or even of the gun. And certainly not the man. I was twenty-seven years old and six feet tall and hard as nails from the life I'd been leading. My only weakness was I was underfed for a man of my size.

What I was afraid of was the bottled-up fury inside me. I knew if that got loose I might not be able to get the cork back in the bottle in time. I said to the man, who looked to be in his forties, "Look here, mister, I don't take to being called a bum. I'm here looking for work and I got that right. So you keep the names to yourself and haul your fat ass out of here before you find out what a bad mistake looks like."

That did it. He was a soft-looking man but he'd obviously been used to throwing his weight around among them as was down and out. Now he swelled himself up and reached out and poked me in the shoulder with his club. There was an outside light at the end of the freight shed that reflected out onto the platform. I saw movement step into that light but I paid it no attention. The railroad cop punched me again with his club. He said, "I ain't telling you again, boy! Now, git!"

In the last year or so I'd had about all the shoving-around I was going to put up with. I'd somehow come from being an aerial ace down to being shoved around by some bully with a tin badge and a misconception of his own toughness. I would have admitted I didn't look like no gentleman. My clothes were rough and bought at the cheapest place and they showed the effects of unloading boxcars all day, but I wasn't going to be run off and I damn sure wasn't going to be punched with no club.

He did it again, harder this time, sticking the end of his billy into my left shoulder. I was once again conscious of movement in the light by the freight warehouse, but I didn't care. With my left arm I flicked his billy club away, set my feet, and then drove my right fist into his belly with a hard, hooking motion. I had everything in the punch and I heard him let out his breath in a loud whoosh as I buried my fist in his soft middle. He staggered back a step and I shifted my feet and hit him the same punch with my left. I always could hit about as hard with either hand.

This time he let out a little moan and his mouth formed a little **O** while shock ran all over his face. I was about to hit him another punch with my right when the billy club fell out of his hand and clattered on the platform boards. He took one, two, three quick steps backward like a man trying to catch his balance and then bent over like he was going to lose his supper. Finally, he took one more step backward and then sat down, heavily, like a sack of flour hitting the floor.

I took a step toward him. I wasn't sure but what he might suddenly take it in his head to reach for the revolver he wore at his side. If he had taken that notion I wanted to be close enough to kick it out of his hand.

Our movement had taken us closer to the circle of light cast off by the big bulb at the corner of the warehouse. It was then that the figure I'd been dimly aware of took shape. A voice said, "What the hell is going on here?"

I glanced up. A perfectly ordinary man was standing about ten feet away. He was of average build with a round face and stubby arms and stubby hands. About the only thing unusual about him was how out-of-place he looked in the coat and tie he was wearing. It was a warm June evening, but that wasn't what made him look odd in the dress-up outfit. He was the kind of man who should have been wearing overalls and, as nearly as I could remember, that's what he'd been wearing the last time I'd seen him.

We stared at each other. Finally he said, his voice uncertain, "Lieutenant?"

I leaned forward, studying his face. It had, after all, been three years. I said, just as uncertainly, "Dennis?"

The last time I had seen Dennis Frank had been at a little temporary aerodrome just outside of Rouen, France. We were in the process of disbanding our unit and Dennis and I were in the process of discontinuing a partnership that I figured had gone a long way toward keeping me alive for near on to three years. Dennis had been the chief mechanic who kept the succession of planes I piloted during the World

War from falling apart. I had inherited him in 1916 when I was a wild-eyed nineteen-year-old without a lick of sense. We'd been in the French flying corps then and, together, we'd made the switch to the United States' branch of service when America had come into the war. It had been Dennis who'd tightened my shoulder straps and wished me luck when I'd gone off on those early-morning sorties. And it had been Dennis who'd been the first to greet me and help me from the cockpit when I'd made a safe return. All the time he was my mechanic never had an engine failed me nor a control surface failed to function because of error. Some of them had failed because of enemy bullets, but never from neglect or carelessness.

Dennis had seemed so much older than I in those days. In truth he was only ten years my elder, but, when you are nineteen, a man of twenty-nine seems middle-aged. And, too, not many of us expected to get much older, not in the fragile kites we were flying. When I would limp home in a shot-up aircraft Dennis would walk slowly around the plane, sticking his finger in the holes in the fabric and shaking his head. He'd say, slowly and gravely, "Lieutenant, these here machines ain't built hell fer stout. You got to know when to light a shuck and get out of the way instead of sticking around with the lead flying. One of these days you are going to git somethin' vital shot, like your body."

But now I stared at him in disbelief. As important as he had been to me during my flying days in the war, I'd completely lost track of him. We stared at each other for another second and then both of us took a step toward the other. My path was directly across the fallen night watchman. In the excitement and wonder of seeing Dennis again I had completely forgotten all about him. I stepped around him and took Dennis's outstretched hand. We were glad to see each other. Dennis looked me up and down and I did the same for him. He'd put on a little weight and his hairline had retreated a bit, but, except for the suit and tie, he looked the same.

However, there was a look of distress on his face as he eyed me. I reckoned I didn't make too much of a showing in my rough work-clothes and boots. He was used to seeing me spiffed up as an officer and a pilot. He said, "Lieutenant, what are you doin' around this freight dock in the middle of the night?"

Before I could answer, the night watchman groaned and stirred himself. We both gave him a look. It was plain to see he was about recovered from the pounding I'd given him. Dennis hurriedly took my arm and urged me toward the edge of the platform. He said, "Let's get along someplace and have a drink. We got a world of catching-up to do."

I stepped over the guard and followed Dennis to the steps that led down off the platform. The train depot was nearly in the center of town, as were the docks, Galveston being a pretty important port, and there were plenty of places still open even as late as it was.

We didn't walk far. Dennis was quiet and so was I. I was glad enough to be away from the railroad detective. I had about as much trouble right then as I could handle without taking on a fresh load. But mainly I was overwhelmed at Dennis suddenly turning up. More than once my mind had gone back to him, wondering where he was, what had become of him, what he was up to. About the only thing I knew about him was that he was from Oklahoma and claimed to be part Cherokee Indian. That and the fact that he could find whiskey where none exsisted and could fix anything that was broke.

The place we turned in to was about half cafe and half saloon. It wasn't crowded, but more than a few tables were filled with men taking a late supper or a last few drinks. I found a small table by the wall while Dennis went to the bar to get a bottle and a couple of glasses. I hadn't protested when he'd said he'd get the whiskey. I was nearly as flat as Army pancakes. I wasn't looking for casual labor down at the freight yards because matters were going so well in my life.

Dennis came back with two shot glasses and a passable bottle of French brandy. It surprised me and I said so. He looked pleased and said something about it reminding him of old times. He sat down and we poured out and then looked at each other, waiting for the other man to come up with the appropriate toast. It was kind of an important occasion, two who had shared danger meeting up after such a long time. We could have toasted to fallen comrades or those who had pulled through or even the coquettes that had made life a little easier. But, finally, I just shrugged and said, "Hell, Dennis, let's just drink to the damn brandy. I reckon it was the very blood of life on more than one occasion."

He said, "I hear that, Lieutenant."

Then we knocked them back, draining our glasses. I set mine down on the table and sighed. The brandy was doing a nice job burning a new road down my gullet. I hadn't been doing much drinking of late, what with the price of whiskey. I said, "Aaaah, that hit the spot and no mistake."

Dennis was ready with the bottle, pouring my glass full again. I said, "Much obliged, Dennis. But you ought not to have been buying French brandy, as expensive as it must be here."

He raised his glass. "Don't you worry none about that, sir. It was many a drink you bought me and the other men of the ground crew when we was yonder across the water. Any thanks, they be to you, Lieutenant, sir."

I half smiled. I said, "Dennis, we are a long time out of the flying corps and I'm not a lieutenant anymore and you sure as hell don't have to call me 'sir.' Considering the difference in the way we're dressed might be I ought to call you 'sir.'"

It brought a crease in his forehead between his eyes. I'd seen it before, many times when he was faced with something he didn't understand or couldn't figure out. Sort of a perplexed frown. He said, "Excusing me, Lieutenant, but that wouldn't seem right to me, especially you 'sirring' me. No, sir, you'll always be the ace of the skies to me."

I laughed. Dennis had always had that effect on me, especially when he was trying to be serious. I said, "Dennis, you are likely calling me 'Lieutenant' because you can't remember my name."

He looked scandalized. "Not *remember* your name? Why, I'd forget my own first. You was my pilot. You flew my planes, at least the planes I tried to keep running. Forget your name!—many a time as I've bragged about it in the enlisted men's mess? Huh!"

"Well, what is it?"

"Why, it's Lieutenant Willis Young of Del Rio, Texas. Yes, sir, and that's a fact, and the finest aviator in the whole AEF, Eddie Rickenbaker be damned."

I laughed again and took a drink. "Well, that is fine, Dennis. But now tell me what you've been up to and how you've come to look so prosperous."

He got the crease in his forehead again and he looked at me, frowning. After a pause he said, fumbling at the words, "Well, now, I ain't so sure that that is what is important. I ain't all that prosperous, far as that goes, but I'm a good deal more interested in you and what's come your way since I last clapped eyes on you some three years back."

I shook my head. I knew what he must be thinking; the hotshot young pilot transformed into the laborer in the railroad freight yard. Not only that, but the son of a supposedly well-to-do man, a man that was even famous. So how had I ended up on a loading dock slugging a night watchman in the belly? It wasn't much of a story, and one I didn't care to go into detail about. I said, "Hell, Dennis, hard-luck stories are a dime a dozen these days. It's 1924, the war's over, and five million men are out of work. I'm just one of the five million. What's new? But I want to hear about you. Do you know, I think that is the first tie I've ever seen you in. First suit and vest, so far as that goes."

He had a bewildered look on his face. He said, "But, Lieutenant, I—"

I slapped my hand down on the table, hard enough to make the glasses and the bottle jump. I said, "Damn it, Dennis, I'm not a lieutenant anymore. I got no rank. I'm a civilian now. So either call me 'Willis' or 'Will' or 'son of a bitch' or 'Mr. Young,' but cut out that damn 'Lieutenant' shit. It don't bring back good memories."

It startled him enough so that I could see I had his attention. I think, for the first time, he was starting to see me as I was right there in that place and in that time, instead of as the young aviator he'd mothered. He blinked a few times and then poured himself out a drink and downed about half of it. Then he said, "Well, uh, uh, Mr. Willis, uh, this has all kind of taken me off-guard as you might say. I never expected to see my old commander in such circumstances as I come upon you in. And you know I don't mean no disrespect by that."

"None taken. I imagined it give you a pretty good start."

It put a smile on his face and made him chuckle slightly. He said, "Well, yes, sir, you might say that. Hell, I was coming over to help out the guard. Figured he'd been set upon by some scofflaw. Then I got up close and seen it was you an' my jaw damn near hit my boottops." He pulled his head back and gave me a look. "Hell, Mr. Willis, I damn near didn't recognize you. Took me the better part of a minute."

I took a sip of brandy. "Was it the rough clothes, Dennis? Or didn't you figure to see your old squadron commander on a railroad loading dock in the middle of the night?"

He looked uncomfortable, but he spoke up. "Well, it was a little bit of all of it. Hell, your daddy is a wealthy man! A big shot. You know, when you used to tell us over there in Frenchy-land that he'd been some kind of bank robber I never gave it two thoughts. Then I get back home and I find out that your daddy and Wilson Young the bank robber was one and the same. Hell! And you never let on about it."

I said, "He was pardoned, Dennis. By the governor. When he was twenty-eight years old. He lived straight after that."

Dennis's eyes were still round, a look I was used to when my father's name came up. He said, "Yeah, but he was still knowed as a hell of a gun hand. Didn't many fool with your daddy, and them as did was right sorry about it afterward."

"What's my father got to do with this? I thought you wanted to know how I came to be called a bum by a railyard bull."

He looked nonplussed. He said, "Well, uh, Mr. Willis, I, uh, kind of understood your daddy was in the chips, so to speak. Heard he had a casino and a bar and saloon down along the Mexican border."

I nodded slowly. "So what?" I had been hearing about my daddy for as long as I cared to remember. He was the famous bank robber, the outlaw, the pistolero, the bandit they had to pardon because the law couldn't catch the famous Wilson Young. He may have been a hero to a lot of people—muddle-headed people—but to me he was just a man who'd spent a little more time than I'd reckoned trying to run my life. I figured he was good and scared I'd end up like him so he'd taken a stern hand with me and had judged me guilty when I hadn't done anything. He was never going to get the satisfaction of hearing it from me but I'd headed for the war and France because he'd forbade me to do so, more than for any reasons of joining the right side in a big fight. Of course, I'd always wanted to fly and it appeared the French were willing to give Americans, or anybody else for that matter, all the chances they craved of getting killed in one of those kites. All we were supposed to be was fodder for the Germans while the French aviators snuck around and knocked down the stray pigeons.

But that had nothing to do with my daddy, Wilson Young. I knew what Dennis was getting at; that I shouldn't be on the shorts financially when I had a father with his money. I wasn't going to make it easy for him. I said, "Do I hear you saying you think I'm busted and ought to run to my father?"

He looked embarrassed. It almost embarrassed me, Dennis was such a good-hearted soul. He said, half blushing, "Well, no, I didn't mean you was busted. Not exactly." He stopped, looking uncomfortable.

"Well, what the hell did you mean? C'mon, Dennis, you were always honest with me in the past. What's the matter now, that fancy suit you're wearing got your tongue?"

He simmered for about a half a minute and then he burst out. He said, "Well, hell, Willis, what am I supposed to think? You never had much meat on your bones, but now your jeans is hanging off the points of your hips and your belly is as flat as the top of this table." He gave the table a slap and gave me a frustrated look. "And you ain't exactly buying your clothes at the Emporium and I never seen you with a pair of workgloves in your back pocket! Have you been eatin' regularly? I want a honest answer on that one."

What had brought me low, so to speak, was, by then, a boring story and one I didn't much care to repeat. Some of it was my fault but mostly it had just been circumstances. When the war had ended in 1918, most of the Americans had been demobilized and sent home immediately since it had not been a popular war and the politicians were in a hurry to get the boys home so they could pat themselves on the back and count votes. But I was in no hurry. I'd been offered a job helping to disband the American part of the Allied air force. I'd been told the job might take a year, but there'd be a promotion to captain in it for me and an excellent chance of being taken on as Regular Army. Hell, it looked as good as anything to me. I didn't have any career planned and I liked the military. Of course, you weren't going anywhere as a Reservist, which was what I was, or as a member of the National Guard. You had to be RA if you wanted to get anywhere. So I'd said yes and set to work. The job mostly consisted of sorting out which airplanes belonged to who and shipping home the few I could wrest away from the Tommies and the Frenchies. We'd put a hell of a lot of money and men into the job of flying against the Hun but we got damn little out of it, at least so far as planes and equipment went. The French were the worst. There were some of those planes that I figured we'd paid for a half a dozen times, but the Frogs could always come up with enough paperwork to keep you from sending the airplane back home, and that was true no matter under whose manufacture the machine had been built.

But it was all for nothing. I didn't save us many planes and I didn't come out so good myself. After about a year and a half I could see I was wasting my time. I didn't get made a captain, I didn't get assigned to the Regular Army, and I was finally taken off active duty and sent home. It really didn't make me much difference. I'd had about enough of France and the Army, so I figured a different view wouldn't be hard to take. Not that I was very excited about going home. I was looking forward to seeing my mother, but once you've been in a flying war everything else seems sort of dull.

But, as it turned out, I missed my mother, and my daddy, too, for that matter. They had just left on an extended trip into the interior of Mexico. One of my father's managers told me that my daddy was looking for racehorses, but I figured he was hunting out another hideout. Old habits die hard.

I didn't have much trouble catching on with a flying circus, though I was told the novelty was starting to wear off and that there was more money in giving folks rides at five dollars a head. Unfortunately, I didn't have an airplane and nobody seemed to want to give me one. Besides that, there was the world and all of pilots. It seemed to me that there were more pilots in the entertainment business than had been in the entire war. For that reason, as much as any other, the flying business took a downturn and I was finding myself doing more looking for jobs than flying. But then I had been late getting home. I'd lost a year and a half to my fellow aviators and, in that time, the public had gotten pretty sophisticated and weren't all that much in awe of a plane or a pilot or a flying circus.

I was a little disappointed at the state of affairs. I had thought that having the ability to fly an airplane was a rare and useful skill and one that a man could use to make his living with. I was sadly mistaken. I had no way of knowing the volume of pilots that were trained in the war, and I had no way of knowing how quickly the public would become bored. So a man could fly. So what? It didn't make life better for the boys sitting in front of the barbershop. It didn't get the clothes washed or the hay baled or the timber cut. It didn't build houses and it didn't put the baby to sleep. All it did was get one or two men from one place to another a little faster than a car did. And once you had had your thrill ride in the passenger seat of a Jenny, you were pretty well cured of spending any more money on such foolishness.

I had not expected a hero's welcome or even a pat on the back for a job well done, but neither had I expected not to be able to make a living with my well-honed skill. There was still flying but it was being done by the men who'd come straight home and got in on the ground floor. I had no gripe coming. Just a little regret.

Of course, I had no need to want for money. I could have gone to Del Rio and stayed in my father's house and his managers would have seen to it that I had plenty of money. But somehow I couldn't bring myself to do that. My father and I had quit each other on stiff terms and I wouldn't feel right about his money until it was right between us, and that was an accommodation he was going to have to instigate since I hadn't been the party who'd stipulated as to what terms must be met. It hurt me to know I was grieving my mother by my attitude, but that couldn't be helped.

In the meantime I had to get myself a living any way I could. I'd had a little college, but not enough to count. I had no skills of any account. About all I had to offer the world was a strong back and an ironlike constitution. As a result I had become a day laborer, working wherever and whenever I could.

An amazing amount of time passed that way. I hadn't meant for it to, but two years and a little better passed in that aimless fashion, so that it was September of 1924 when Dennis and I ran up against each other. I was twenty-seven years old and didn't have a damn thing to show for it. Hell, by that age Wilson Young had robbed a string of banks. And even though he later claimed he wasn't proud of the deeds, I was pretty sure that Father had counted coup on each one and considered the forced bank withdrawals as stepping stones on his rise to fame and fortune. Sometimes I wished that my father and I had been able to talk more. There was a good deal I wanted to understand and a good deal I thought I could learn from the old man. But those days were long past, lost in the fight we'd had over my going to Paris to a war my daddy had reckoned wasn't any of my affair or business.

CHAPTER 2

DENNIS SAID, "Have you got a place to stay? You are so damn close-mouthed about your business I'm nearly scared to ask anything."

I smiled slightly. I was standing under a streetlight just outside the bar where we'd been drinking brandy. The light from the street lamp highlighted my complexion and hair and features. I had inherited my father's wide-shouldered build, but had taken my mother's blondeness and golden skin coloring where my father had been dark. I had also taken her green eyes and her even features. I was tall at six foot, but light for my size at a hundred and seventy pounds. Days of hard work in all kinds of weather had given me a lean, almost gaunt look. I was very strong for my size and not a man to be fooled with when I had my mind set. I said, "No, Dennis, I haven't found a room yet. Hell, I just got to Galveston this morning. Rode a freight down from Houston that looked like it was going to need some unloading. Made four dollars. So I got money for a room. I reckon there is a rooming house around here somewhere."

Dennis said, "Listen, I'm staying in a hotel. Got plenty of room. Two beds in the place. Why don't you come along and put up with me? Give us a chance to have some more talk. I want to tell you some about this oil-drilling business I'm in."

I said, "Well, I wouldn't say no to a free bed. Though before I had that little run-in with the depot watchman I was planning on bedding down in a boxcar. What hotel you staying at? Not that it matters."

He got a kind of funny look on his face and cleared his throat a couple of times before he said, in a sort of squeaky voice, "Uh, the, uh, Galvez."

Dennis had always had a bit of a high voice, especially for his bulk, but when he said the name of the hotel it went up even higher. I had to chuckle. Dennis had come a long way to be staying at a hotel like the Galvez. I said, "Dennis, are you crazy? They ain't going to let me in a place like that the way I'm dressed."

But he gave his head a hard shake. We were walking along the streets past the wharfs and warehouses of the port. He said, "There's a bunch of oil drillers in town and some of 'em with a pocketful of money ain't dressed no better than you are. Naw, we'll be all right. Hell, I feel like I could talk all night, get caught up on matters."

The Galvez was down on the road that ran along the beach just behind the seawall. I could hear the Gulf of Mexico even when we were several blocks short. I always liked the sight and the sound of the sea. It had a soothing effect on me. I suppose I'd come by it naturally since my daddy had been raised farther down the coast at Corpus Christi.

We got to the beach road and turned left. Even as late as it was, there was still some traffic running up and down the bricked street. Most of the vehicles were Fords or Chevrolets, but now and again you'd see a Packard or a Hupmobile or a Stutz Bearcat. It was a good warm evening and the breeze off the gulf felt refreshing and pleasant. There were several ritzy hotels all in a row, but the Galvez was by far the biggest and the fanciest. Big-time singers and bands came down and played its ballroom, and the richest and toniest people wouldn't stay nowhere else. I could just imagine the sight I was going to make walking through the marble lobby in my work-stained clothes.

But I was glad to see Dennis again. Hell, I was glad to see anyone

I knew. For whatever reason, it seemed that I'd cut myself off from my old friends and what little family I had. There was my mother's sister, my aunt Laura, and her husband Warner Grayson. But they lived way the hell up in the piney woods of east Texas. I'd written them a letter when I'd first got back, but I'd moved on before a reply could reach me. And there were other friends, but mostly they seemed to be friends of my daddy's. In fact, thinking on it, it seemed that nearly everything was in some way part of ol' Wilson Young. I didn't begrudge him, but I wanted a few items on my own. Dennis, at least, fit that bill.

Just down and to our left were the brilliant lights of the Galvez Hotel, eleven stories and every one of them going strong. Off to our right the surf made long, silvery streaks as it rolled up on the sandy shore. The air was warm and a touch on the moist side. I didn't know what the hell I was doing except going to have a visit with an old comrade and maybe a good night's sleep. We came to the hotel and turned in at the long entrance that was bowed over with a stone colonnade. It was an impressive sight all right, and when we got to the steps that led to the front door I got a good look at the doorman in his maroon uniform, and I whispered to Dennis that there was no chance the man would let me in.

Dennis said, as we started up the concrete steps that was about twenty feet wide, "Oh, don't be silly. Hell, I'm a paying guest of this hotel. I'll brang in anybody I'm a mind to."

About that time the doorman shifted from his position at the corner of the big doors and got right in front of me on the top step. He said, "One moment, if you please, sir. Are you a guest of the hotel?"

I heard Dennis raise his voice. He said, "Hell, no, he ain't no guest. And neither am I. Guests don't pay, or didn't you know that?" He dug his hand in his coat pocket. "But we are damn sure renting a room in this joint, and I reckon that gives us the right to come and go without no bother and commotion." He jerked his key out. "You see this? What does that tell you? Does that make us guests enough to suit you?"

The doorman stepped back. He said, "I'm sorry, sir. I got my orders."

Dennis said, "You ought to get *yourself* some working clothes instead of standing around here in a purple uniform insulting hard-working folks that can pay the rates this overpriced rooming house charges."

I got him by the arm and steered him through the door and into the big, high-ceilinged, brilliantly lighted lobby. It seemed as if they had a hundred overhead fans stirring the air around and there seemed to be no end of well-dressed men and women milling about among the big, overstuffed furniture and big, brass-framed gilt mirrors. I said, "Dennis, don't be picking on the hired help. It wasn't you he was going to keep out. It was me, and I ain't mad."

He said, "Well, you ought to be."

We headed for the elevators to ride up to Dennis's room on the fifth floor. I didn't get to ride in so many elevators that I took it as a commonplace thing. You'd think, me being a pilot, it wouldn't be no thrill, but that elevator didn't have any wings.

What I knew about the oil business, much less the oil-drilling business, you could have stuffed in a thimble and had room left over for what I didn't know about women. When we got settled in his room Dennis tried to explain that it all got started at Spindletop, which was a salt mound or dome right outside Beaumont, Texas. It seemed that that was where the first big strike was made, which caused the boom in gasoline engines and made cars go and planes fly and got us into the modern world. Dennis said, "If it hadn't've been for Spindletop you couldn't've had a World War like we did. Before that there wasn't enough oil and gas around to have a good skirmish, let alone an all-out mechanised war."

I said, "But, hell, Dennis, wasn't Spindletop way back there?"

"Oh, yeah. They made the discovery in 1901, but it didn't really get cranked-up for another five years. Of course, there have been a bunch of discovery fields since then, but it was that one jerked the plug out of the jug, so to speak. It was going strong when I come home from the war and was where I got my start."

While looking for work, Dennis, not knowing any more about

the oil business than me, had heard they were looking for men good with their hands and tools at this place outside of Beaumont. The wages as a mechanic on a drilling rig had been more than fair and he'd settled in and gradually learned what it was all about. Then one day the driller had shown up too drunk to work and the drilling superintendent had given Dennis the job. "Lots of drinking goes on in the oil patch and if you can handle yours, you got a leg up on the other man. I'd probably still be a mechanic if it wasn't for whiskey. I damn shore wouldn't be staying in no swell joint like this." He waved his hand around his room.

It was a spacious layout, all right. There was two beds, just as Dennis had said, and they weren't a couple of cots, either, but regular-sized beds where you could put the kids in one and Mom and Dad in the other. There was a big, overhead ceiling fan and a picture window that faced on the beach. You could look out it and see the waves and the occasional lights of passing ships. Me and Dennis was sitting opposite each other at a wooden table that had four chairs to it. Dennis said you could telephone down to room service and they'd serve you right there in your room. Of course, I knew that, but Dennis acted so in awe that I never let on. Dennis had more money, but I reckoned I was the more traveled of the pair of us.

Not that it mattered that Dennis had more money. Hell, anybody had more money than I did. I was just glad to see my old friend and glad for a good bed for the night. I knew I was drifting. I knew I had been drifting. I knew I didn't have any plans or ambitions to stay my aimless path. But the fact of the matter was, I didn't particularly give a damn. Something had gone out of me, something vital, something that made me care. I didn't know how or when I'd lost it, but I knew it was gone and I didn't have the first idea of how to get it back.

Dennis said: "So I hung on there at Spindletop for a few years, making more money than I could spend, then I drifted down to a new field that had opened up in Corsicana. They was paying higher wages because the rock structure was different and nobody knew how to drill through it. Neither did I, but I got the reputation for being lucky, which is even more powerful in the oil patch than whiskey. Pretty soon

I was hiring on for a share of the well, taking an eighth or a sixteenth or whatever. I tell you, Willis, you don't have to do that many times until you got to go hunting a bank, and a big bank at that, to hold your money. Finally come a day we drilled a duster and this bunch I was working for couldn't pay me off so they offered me their string of tools as payment. First thing I knowed, I was a drilling contractor with a good rig and mighty good prospects. Drilled two wells in Corsicana and brought both of them in and decided the field was playing out and I ought to look elsewhere." He raised his eyes. "Hell, I believe there be oil all over this state."

But I was still mystified. I knew all I needed to know about airplanes and machine guns and aerial maneuvers, but I didn't have the slightest idea what it was that Dennis kept referring to, "a string of tools." I said so.

We had some drinks that Dennis had sent down to room service for, more for the pleasure of the thing, I thought, than any desire for whiskey. He took a pull from his glass and said, "Yeah, I reckon the expression don't make a lot of sense. But it's the equipment you need to drill an oil well. Everything but your derrick, which you buy the lumber for wherever you are and build it on the spot. A string of tools is your drill stem and your pipe and your drilling bits and your cable tool, if it be a cable-tool rig, and your rotary table and all your tools like your chocks and blocks and your tongs and so on. And that ain't counting your boilers or your draw works, which is the main thing, or your cable or your crown block. It's a sight of stuff and pretty damn expensive. You go to drill a two-thousand-foot well, which ain't shucks these days, and you got to have that much drill pipe, not to mention your casing and your drilling mud. I tell you, you go to spud a well in, you better have some heavy cash behind you. This wildcatting is pretty risky business."

I said, "You said you thought there was oil everywhere in Texas. Is that what you come to Galveston for, to drill an oil well?"

He shook his head. "Not really, not unless I run across somebody with a lot of money that just wants to. No, I'm down here hunting investors. There's a power of money in this town and I'm looking for somebody that wants to foot the bill to stick some iron in the ground. This hotel right here has probably got a dozen of the very sort I'm after. This time of year lots of the well-to-do come here to cool off."

"Then what you got your drilling rig with you for?"

He shrugged. "It's got to be somewhere. I had it stacked in the North Dayton field after that place played out. All shallow production, though I think there's some real oil down deep. Naw, I just brought the string along in case any prospective investor might want to look it over. I got heavy equipment and I can go deep. That's getting important now since nearly every dome like they discovered in Spindletop has had a hole dug in it."

I said, half teasing, "Hell, Dennis, way you look and talk I didn't figure you'd need an investor. Why don't you finance it yourself?"

He gave me a serious look. "Lieutenant, I ain't bragging when I say I could pay cash for a ten-thousand-dollar house and have enough left over to court a damn pretty woman to fit in the place. But when you are talking about wildcatting you are talking a jolt of money. I'm a drilling contractor. I drill on the other man's money and I drill where he wants me to. That's another reason my rig is here; so I can be ready to ship it wherever I'm told. But listen—Even though I ain't got oil-drilling money I don't intend to leave here without seeing your circumstances considerably improved."

I gave him a quiet look. "It's a pretty good walk back to that freight yard and a bed in a boxcar, but I'll make it if there's any more of that kind of talk from you."

He grimaced. "I knew I shouldn't've said it the second the words was out of my mouth. But I was building up to another something else and I kind of wanted to slip up on its blind side."

"What?"

He leaned forward confidentially. "Well, it wasn't a minute after we met back up that it come through my mind."

"What?" I had a half a mind where he was heading and I was hoping he wouldn't.

He said, "Well, I don't see nothing wrong with you coming in with me, throwing in your lot. I mean, it ain't like you've—" He stopped. I knew what he'd stopped himself from saying. He changed tack and went on awkwardly. "I mean it ain't like you had got yourself settled into a steady profession, something you'd have to chuck. So I figured maybe you'd come in with me on the partners."

I took a slow drink of whiskey. The little I'd had that night was starting to get to me. I hadn't had much money to stay in whiskey-drinking condition. I put my glass down carefully on the table. "Dennis, are you crazy? I've got about four dollars to my name. You figure that buys half a drilling outfit? I—"

He was holding up his hand and saying, "Wait, wait. Wait now. Just a minute. Let me explain."

"You better let me—"

"Naw, naw. Hear me out. It ain't a matter of money. You don't need no money. But I need somebody high-class who knows his way around this old world, somebody I can trust. I tell you, Willis, this oil bidness is a wonderful way to make money but it has got more snakes in it than a south Texas brier patch."

"Dennis, I'm not your man. In the first place, I don't know the first thing about the oil business and—"

He waved his hand at me again. "Hell, you don't have to know nothing. I can teach you how to *talk* the business in one night and that would be your part. No, no. I need you to front for me. Hell, you're all elegant-looking, even in them clothes, and you talk like you been to a university, which you have, and you was an officer and—Well, hell, that's plenty. I don't need no money off you. I know how to get that, and with your help I'll make an easy job of it." He leaned forward earnestly. "Come in with me, Lieutenant. Throw your gear in with mine. Hell, we'll get rich."

I looked at him sadly. I didn't know if I had the words to explain myself. I didn't want to get rich. I didn't want to get anything. I had no ambition. I had no drive. I had no desire. All I felt was sort of empty inside. I worked at the laborer's tasks that I could get merely for food and clothes and shelter and because they didn't require me to think. At some point, at some time, at some crossroads inside myself I had run empty. I didn't know what had caused it, whether it was the war or the disappointments that had come after, or finding my parents gone, or just what. But it didn't seem to matter. When you didn't care you didn't care. And you didn't care that you didn't care. So it made no difference. But I didn't want to try and tell Dennis all that. Hell, if I couldn't understand it myself, I damn sure couldn't explain it to another person, especially one as level-headed and down-to-earth as Dennis. To Dennis, things either worked or they didn't. If they didn't, you fixed them or got a new part that would work. I didn't want him to know I was broken, in spirit at least. I expected I could describe myself that way except I didn't know what in hell was the matter except I couldn't find anything I cared about. I said, "Dennis, I'm much obliged for the offer and I know you are doing me a kindness, but I reckon I'll keep on like I been going."

He looked at me in amazement. "Keep on like you've been!" He threw his head back as if to get a perspective on me. "Hell, have you noticed where you been? Roustabouting in railroad freight yards? Doing the odd job for the odd dollar? I reckon this sounds like I'm sticking my nose in where it don't belong, but, hell Lieutenant, you was cut out for a good deal better hand than the one you are playing at. You can't say no to me. It's too important. It was meant we was to meet up like we did."

I shook my head slowly. "Dennis, you don't want no part of me. Take my word for it. I lost something somewhere and I ain't quite whole."

"I seen that, Willis. I seen it and I seen it was my duty, my willing duty, to help you get fixed back up."

I had to laugh slightly. I said, "Dennis, you don't know what kind of a game you are trying to buy your way into. Might not be as easy as you think. It's bad enough that I'm missing something; the hell of it is that I don't even know what it is. You can't fix something if you don't know which part is broken."

He gave me a firm look. "Hell," he said, "I wouldn't have hired on if I didn't expect to work. I ain't asking it to be easy. But somebody has got to get you back on track and I reckon it is right that it be your old mechanic."

I gave him a shrug. "Dennis, I'm just pulling your leg. Nothing wrong with me that a good night's sleep won't cure. You save your worry for somebody that needs it."

He pulled a face at me. "Lieutenant, it don't look good on you, lying. Ten minutes after we got talking I knew your engine was missing and sputtering and before we finished the first glass of whiskey I knew you was losing altitude faster than you could get it back. I took as much care of you as I did them kites you flew, and they ain't much I don't know about the way you fly. And right now you are out of rig. You are out of trim and flying one wing low, and missing on two magnetos." He looked at me steadily. "Deny it."

Dennis was just a good man and he couldn't help himself. Here he'd found this poor crippled waif, and matters had to be put right. Might as well tell water to run uphill as tell Dennis it was none of his affair and no help was wanted or needed. I said, "Dennis, if fronting for you involves convincing people, I am the wrong man. I'm no salesman. If it involves any form, and I mean *any*, of engineering talk, I am not your man because I have absolutely no mechanical aptitude, which you should remember from France. And if it involves getting dressed up and acting wise, I will have to pass. So you see, I am a lost cause."

He said, "Willis, quit trying to complicate this here situation. A wildcat oil well ain't nothing more than a hole in the ground surrounded by liars. Ain't no man, unless he's drilling on proven ground, can tell you if there's oil where he means to spud in."

"Is that what a wildcatter is? Someone who drills on unproven ground?"

He nodded. "Out of a proven field. The odds are a thousand to one against him, maybe more."

"But if that is the case, why should he have to lie?"

"Because he wouldn't get any backers if he didn't. And they would be considered damn fools if they didn't lie and say they thought the well had a damn good chance. They know it doesn't, but they can't put their money in and then admit what a wild gamble they're taking. They be businessmen, not gamblers."

I had to smile. "So, everyone really is lying. But why do they do it? Why do they back a well if they know it's such a long shot?"

He gave me the eye. "Same reason anybody backs a long shot. There can be a hell of a payoff if just a little oil is found. You strike a good producer, let alone a gusher, and there is a barrel of money. You develop a field—a piece of ground on an oil-bearing structure, a reef— and you can figure to buy yourself two or three pretty good-sized cities. I tell you, ain't nothing quite as exciting as when that drill bit bites into a piece of unproven ground. And you can do it and not call it gambling. Hell, I've knowed a Baptist preacher to even take a share in a drilling prospect."

I stood up and stretched and walked over to the big windows. I still didn't feel alive, but a little of Dennis's company was causing a stirring in my veins. If there were still men such as Dennis, the whole world wasn't rotten.

I stared out into the darkness, thinking. Just in front of the hotel was the seawall road and an occasional car passed by, even as late as it was, its headlights searching through the dark like probing fingers. Just beyond the seawall the surf was luminous as it rolled up on the shore in long, wavering white lines. I half turned and said, "You just want me along."

He nodded vigorously and said, "I *need* you along."

I leaned against the windowsill. "What for, Dennis? I think it is plain and simple charity."

He shook his head. "No, sir! No sir! Not by a long shot. Willis, you got something can't be bought in a store. You got that breeding. You got that, that, class! Yessir, that's what you got. And some of it will rub off on me and impress the hoi polloi I'll be trying to get interested in a well."

I raised my eyebrows. "That's all I got to do? Hang around?"

"You don't even have to open your mouth. 'Course, I hope you will. You sound mighty cultured when you talk."

I waved my hand down my body. "In these clothes?"

He almost frowned but he caught himself in time. "If it has got to be. Of course I got the money to get you a whole new rig. White shirt and stiff collar and tie. Regular suit of clothes."

I poked at him. I said, "You don't mean off the rack, Dennis? Surely not. Why, in France all my clothes were tailor-made. Even my uniforms."

He scratched his head. "You reckon we can find a tailor around here will come up to your standards? And can get the job done quick enough?"

I laughed. I said, "Don't worry, Dennis. I've still got some good clothes that I haven't sold. They're in a big suitcase checked down at the depot. I never thought I'd be needing them this quick."

Dennis jumped up. He said, "Well, hell, let's go down and fetch your grip. It ain't all that late."

I put my hand up. "Hold on, Dennis. I ain't agreed to nothing yet. Let's sleep on it. Besides, I still got quite a few questions."

Next morning we ate breakfast in the elegant restaurant right there in the hotel. The linen was snowy and crisp and the silver shiny and real. I hadn't been in such surroundings in some time. In my rough clothes I drew more than one frown, mostly from the head waiter and some of the other help. But I saw Dennis slip the head waiter a bill of some denomination. It was obviously large enough to sweeten his disposition because he brightened right up where I was concerned. I really didn't give a damn what the man thought, but I reckoned it was important for Dennis to keep up his front so I never said anything about him bribing the man.

We had finished our steak and eggs and were sitting back drinking coffee. Dennis had lit a cigar and was puffing away. I didn't smoke and didn't much like the smell of the stogie, but Dennis was too good a man to hurt his feelings. He took the cigar out of his mouth and stared at me through the smoke for a few good many seconds before he spoke. He said, "Willis, what are you, twenty-seven?"

I nodded slowly. "Yeah, about that. Why?"

He said, " 'Cause I know a case when I see one." He hunched forward across the table. "Likely you don't know it, but I've been married three times already and I still got a few years to go before I'm forty. And the marriages ain't nothin' to the number of females I've squired around. So I know of what I speak when it comes to the fairer sex. So you might as well break down and tell me about it, It'll come out sooner or later."

I gave him a bewildered look. I hadn't the foggiest idea what he was talking about and I said so.

"Now, don't come that on me, my son. I find you looking all down-in-the-mouth and bedraggled in soul and body and I says to myself right off, that there's a woman mixed up in it somewhere. Now, who is she, Willis, this woman that done broke your heart?"

I laughed so loud that one of the waiters glanced my way. "Dennis, you are off the mark. There's no woman involved here. Why would you even think such a thing?"

"Why, because of the way you are. All drug-down and browbeat. Got the jimjams, off your feed, don't give a hoot about nothin'. Only one thing will make a healthy man act like that and that is a female. Come on, now, did one throw you over for another fellow? She must be blind if she done so."

I shook my head sadly. I didn't want to explain to Dennis Frank. Hell, I didn't want to explain to anyone. I said, "Dennis, take my word for it. I ain't been forsaken in love."

"Then what do it be?"

I waved my hand. "Let it go, Dennis. You wouldn't understand."

"Listen . . ." He pointed a stubby finger at me. "How many early mornings did I strap you into an airplane, seeing you nervous and near scared to death but still determined to go, to do your duty. And how many times was I there to meet you when you got back, sometimes with the plane a little shot-up and bruised, but you just completely exhausted, wore out, and down? Down because you'd been near all that death and destruction. And maybe you'd had to kill, to take the life of an enemy. You never had to tell me. I could always see it in your eyes. So now I want you to recollect who you are talking to. I reckon I know you better'n anybody in the whole world, including your momma. So if it ain't a woman, it has got to be black-hole serious. You on the run, Willis? The law after you?"

I said, grimly, "It was my daddy was the bank robber, remember?" It always had to be something easy to understand for most people. Trouble with your wife. You've lost your job. You've run afoul of the law. People didn't seem to understand that a man could be disillusioned to the point of despair just by the way he perceived the world around him. So far as it being a woman, Dennis was way off the trail. My last contact with a woman that had been anything more than casual had been better than a year past, when I'd been working on the docks in Corpus Christi. She'd been a girl I'd known before the war, when I'd been going to the university. But her father hadn't liked my ideas, so that ended that. Of course, there had been the occasional liaison with this woman or that, but that had been no more than fulfilling a physical need. I said, "No, Dennis, I'm not broken-hearted. As a matter of fact I haven't had anything to do with women in I can't remember when. They don't much care for day laborers."

He sat up straight. "Then right there is the problem. We got to get you laid. No wonder you be going around with your dauber down. We'll find out where the most select salon is and I hear they got some honeys in this town, and get this piece of business tended to proper."

I sighed and shook my head. "Ain't what I'm saying, Dennis. I can get laid if I need to. You got the wrong idea."

He stared at me, perplexed. "Then what in the hell ails you, son?"

I got up, signaling I was through with breakfast. Dennis picked up the bill. I made no protest about that since I knew I damn sure couldn't pay it. Besides, I was a prospective employee. Or partner. Or front man, whatever that was. The only front men I'd ever heard of had been barkers in a carnival sideshow.

I said, "Before we go down to that depot and go to all the trouble of lugging my suitcase back, I think I need to know a little more about what you expect out of me except standing around looking wise."

We were standing out in front of the hotel. He said, "Well, hell, you're coming back with me anyway. I ain't leaving my old squadron commander, out here wandering around in worn-out jeans whether you call it charity or not. But so far as what you do, I reckon we'll say you're the land man. Remember I told you we needed money and a piece of land to drill a well? Well, you are the land scout that finds that drilling prospect."

I gave him an amused look. "I'm supposed to know which is the kind of land you drill wells on?"

He grimaced. "Hell no. And don't nobody else know, neither. What everybody does is signs over a one-eighth override to some farmer and then you set up in the most likely-looking place in his pasture. The salt-dome theory was the only one we knew for sure, but they ain't no more of them. But don't worry. When it comes time, I'll be the one talks about the surface indications. I just want you around as part of the operation. Besides, didn't you have some science in that university you went to?"

I cocked my head at him. "Ain't this just a touch on the immoral side?"

He shook his head. "No, I wouldn't do it if it was. We're all just playing at business. I want to drill a well because I want to strike oil. Crude oil, not snake oil. I've done it before. Several times. And the backers want to get in the oil business with their money. Nothing immoral about that."

I couldn't disagree with him, though I still couldn't say I wanted any part of the oil business. I had that aunt and uncle up in east Texas. She was my mother's sister so I felt pretty close to Aunt Laura. My uncle was in the racehorse-breeding business, and I'd had a hankering for some time to go up and see them. It was one way to maybe get some sense of family again. Not that I'd ever really had much to begin with.

We walked to the depot but took a taxi back. Soon as we pulled up in front of the hotel one of the bellhops come running out and grabbed my suitcase and started lugging it up the steps. I reckoned he was sorry to be so helpful. I figured that grip must have weighed seventy or eighty pounds. It had everything in it that I owned.

First thing, up in the room, Dennis had my bag open on the bed, going through it to see how I was going to shape up. I had a good

garbardine suit that hadn't been worn more than a few times. All it
needed was pressing and I thought sure that was what Dennis would
see a land scout wearing. But I had the picture all wrong. He come out
with a pretty sharp houndstooth jacket and a pair of corduroy jodhpurs, flared riding pants. He laid them aside and pulled out my boots.
They were pretty sorry-looking. They were brown calvary boots that
went with the riding pants. It was an outfit that all the pilots affected.
And still did, for all I knew. He said, "You be going to need some new
boots. And some new white shirts."

I said, "Hell, Dennis, what do land scouts dress as, steeplechasers?"

He said, "They try to look like a cross between a Ranger and a
man going to a ball."

"Have you got any land in mind that I'm supposed to have scouted
out?"

"Got a good prospect down in Matagorda County. Surface signs
of oil in a sour lake there. Onliest problem is the land owner ain't that
easy to close with. He's running a pretty good cattle operation and he's
afraid oil-well drilling will interfere with that. He wants more cash
money than I'm willing to put up to insure against damaging his damn
cows. That's why I got to get a backer from the git-go."

I sat down on the bed I'd slept on the night before.

It didn't feel right to me. "I don't know, Dennis. I don't think you
need my help and I'd just as soon not get on your charity list. Things
could get uneven right quick."

He was busy hanging my clothes up in the closet. It was an odd
thing for one man to do for another, but Dennis had been more than
my mechanic in France, he'd also sort of been my valet—though he
would have been offended at the word. He thought of himself as a
friendly helper. And, in truth, when I'd returned from some long flights
it was all I could do to get myself to my room while Dennis saw to my
other needs. Now he turned around and spoke. "Lieutenant, I need
your help. I ain't been doing so good at this contract drilling business
and I think it's because I can't talk these swelled-up gents' lingo. If
there is any charity here, it's coming my way."

I hung my head and looked at the carpet pattern on the floor.

He stood, staring at me, wrinkling his brow. Finally he burst out, "What in hell ails you, son? I thought a good supper and a good night's sleep would fix it. What is all this? Tell it to me like I was an idiot, which is the way I feel right now. You got me all flummoxed."

I waved my hand at him in dismissal. "Forget it. You wouldn't understand."

"Try me. I ain't as dumb as this mug of mine would make you believe."

"Listen, Dennis, you were doing fine before I came along. Why don't you continue as you were?"

"Willis, I got about two thousand in cash left. My string of tools is worth about twenty thousand, but it ain't worth nothing if it ain't working. I could sell it, but what would I do then? I'd have a wad of money, but it would be gone before a man could blink. No, I got to drill oil wells. I got to bring in oil wells. Now, tell me what you got that is so damned important you can't give me a hand."

I got up and went over to the big windows and looked out at the Gulf. I said, "Well, for one thing I went and fought a war. I killed men who were trying to kill me. But I also saw an awful lot of other men trying to kill each other. And I saw an awful lot of men that had been killed. I was just a kid, and, at first, it seemed like some sort of game, one of those games you play when you're a kid, like hare and hounds. Only I noticed that after the game, all the players didn't get up and start over. They stayed dead. That's when a hell of a lot of fun went out of it." I looked around at him. "I know you stayed at the rear, Dennis, but you had to have been aware of all the death that was all around. Hell, we saw hospital trains of infantry being taken to the rear."

He nodded. "Yeah, I saw it. But there wasn't nothing I could do; none of us could—except what we was told. Willis, they was a whole bunch of young men went through what you did, but they ain't throwed their hand in. They've come back and picked up their lives and gone on."

"And I'm happy for them," I said. And I meant it. "But maybe they can't see as good as I can."

"What are you talking about?"

I said, "Have you taken a good look around you, Dennis? Have you taken a look at this so-called civilization we risked our lives to protect?"

He furrowed his brow. Dennis had a lot of forehead, so when he was perplexed it wasn't hard to tell. "What in hell are you talking about?"

I didn't want to get melodramatic about it and, besides, maybe the rest of the country didn't see things as I did. They sure as hell didn't act like it. But I said, "Dennis, where in hell is this great democracy we fought for? This goddamn country is about as shallow as a tin plate. The damn women are busy tying down their breasts and rolling their stockings and having their hair bobbed and dancing on tabletops. And the men are urgently carrying silver flasks of whiskey and wearing raccoon coats and joining the right clubs and getting jobs where they don't have to work. The whole damn country is off on a cheap drunk, and it's Prohibition, which nobody is paying the slightest attention to. I ain't in favor of the Volstead Act, but it is the law. You ever had any trouble getting a drink?

"But that ain't what I'm talking about. I'm talking about a whole society that is just plain worthless. I never seen such a bunch of people so damn concerned with nothing but their own fun. They even dance silly. And you never heard such music. Rudy Vallee is the big heart-throb. Can you imagine listening to Rudy Vallee unless you were tied in a chair with a knife at your throat?"

"Willis, you are taking on a bit more than is called for here. I mean—"

"Am I? Hell, the damn stock market is going up and up and up, and that without any visible means of support. Dennis, nobody is working! I know. When I show up with a pair of willing hands to do menial labor I am welcomed with open arms. Nobody wants to lay bricks, plumb, carpenter, roof, paint, or anything else that gets things done with a little muscle and a little sweat. What in hell is a 'flapper'? What in hell is a 'jellybean'? Why is a woman named Gertrude Stein telling us how to live."

"Huh? Gertrude who?"

"Never mind. Somebody is calling this 'the Lost Generation,' and I damn well agree with them. But if they were going to get lost anyway, why in hell did all those men have to get killed to give them the chance? I—"

I stopped suddenly. I could feel the tears welling up in my eyes. I turned away from Dennis. The tears had happened before, though not in front of anyone. I didn't even know why I was moved to such emotion. I could never recall being reduced to such utter despair while the fighting was going on. It was only in the last year that the disillusionment had set in. Maybe it was that I hadn't been able to come home to my parents, to see my mother and to fight with my daddy for his bullheaded stand. He and I had always butted heads, but nothing like the melee that had occurred when I'd announced I was going to France.

I felt a hand on my shoulder. From behind me Dennis said, "Willis, I don't understand all of it but I can see that you are troubled."

I wiped at my eyes with the back of my hand. "Forget it, Dennis. Just forget it. Sometimes I get wound up and can't stop myself. Reckon I been spending too much time alone."

He said, "No. I can see you are truly troubled. I can see that you need help. I ain't the one to give it to you, but I know someone who can."

I was at the window, gazing out at the bay. "Who?"

"Have you ever tried Jesus Christ? It appears you got a big hole in your heart, and He's mighty good at fixing such matters."

I gave a slight groan and put my hand up to my face. "Not you, Dennis. That was maybe the only thing my daddy and I agreed on. And it was a good thing because it took both of us to hold my mother off. So, listen, don't you start. I've 'churched' just about every way there is."

But Dennis shook his head. He said, "I ain't talking about church. I'm talking about the pure Spirit of the Lord."

I waved a hand at him. "Dennis, I never would have thought of you as one of those Bible-thumping, psalm-singing so-and-sos, but we are going to have to part company if we got to agree on this."

He put up his hand. "I won't say another word, but I had to offer. I know it works. I know in my own case."

I gave him a surprised look and he stepped backward, shaking his head. "Never mind. Why don't we go down and buy you them boots and some new shirts?"

I said, "Dennis, I ain't real sure about this. I don't want you laying out money on me that might go to waste."

"I'll chance it. I'm in the wildcatting business, remember?"

We went on about our business of getting ready to go but I could tell that Dennis hadn't quite emptied his pitcher. He was over at the closet and he said something in a muffled voice.

"What?" I said loudly.

"Nothing, nothing. I didn't say nothing."

"Oh, yes you did."

He turned to face me. "Appears to me that if anybody is shallow it might be you. You're the one feels empty and don't care about nothing. That's what you said."

"And you've got the answer."

"Man has got to have something to believe in. And Christ is the only answer."

I gave him a disgusted look. "Dennis, you said you were going to lay off that. We ain't going to get along if you don't."

"That's fine, that's fine." He turned back to the closet. "Onliest thing—I can't understand how a man who's been as close to heaven in an aeroplane can't see something so obvious."

CHAPTER
3

DENNIS HAD a meeting that next morning with some "moneymen" to discuss financing an "oil prospect." He was going to get the lay of the land from how they sounded before he brought me in. But these men, he was at some pains to explain, were not the pick of the litter. He said, "These are shallow-well folks. They think investing a hundred dollars a foot in a thousand-foot well is high cotton. But I got a rig that can drill through caprock, drill to five thousand feet. There's big oil down there deep, sonny boy, and don't you doubt it."

I didn't doubt it. There might have been sorghum syrup five thousand feet down, for all I knew. But what I couldn't really get hold of was this land business. You went up to some farmer or someone who had a piece of land you wanted to drill on, and you offered to buy his mineral rights. You gave him some cash, as little as you could, and a one-eighth royalty on any oil you produced. I couldn't see where a man could lose with that kind of proposition, but Dennis said that oil fever was sweeping the country, and every backwoods nabob wanted top dollar and was unwilling to sell at less than a one-sixth royalty. He told me, "Too damn many fools have ruined it for the rest of us. They went charging out expecting to hit oil everywhere they sunk a drill bit. They'd pay any price to the land owner. Now it's got to where you've got to hock your soul just to get ground to throw up a derrick and drilling platform."

I took my breakfast at a different place than where Dennis was meeting with his high rollers. I was back at the room first and was standing at the window looking out at the breakers when he came in. I turned around and he sat down at our little table. He took his hat off and laid it down and furrowed his brow. Then he shook his head. "Same story. 'Have you got the mineral rights tied up?' I couldn't lie about any one specific place and they weren't interested in hearing what a hell of an oil contractor I was without a specific prospect in mind. They want to see a contract with the deed holder. But shucks with it. These was small fry. They weren't interested in nothing but shallow drilling along the Gulf Coast somewheres. People seem to have forgotten that the first drilling in this country took place in the interior. Places like Pennsylvania and Ohio and Virginia. Spindletop knocked all of that out of their heads. You make a good breakfast?"

"Yeah, I found a little cafe on a street a few blocks back toward town. Eggs and ham and toast for sixty-five cents. Could have had a glass of milk for a nickel more, except I don't like milk."

He passed his hand over his face. "What I think we ought to do—" he said, "is maybe run down to your part of the country. Surely you know somebody that would sell some mineral rights cheap. You must know a trainload of folks there."

I shrugged. I said, "If you are just looking for somebody who owns some land and will convey the mineral rights, well, hell, I got a parcel of land. Pretty good-sized piece, at that."

He slowly turned his head toward me and took his hand away from his face. "You got *what*?" He said the words slowly, but they seemed to weigh a great deal.

He said, "Now, let me get this straight. You got a big plot of land out in west Texas that your daddy gave you. I thought you and him weren't on them kind of terms. Where he'd give you a deed like that?"

"That was just the point. He gave it to me right before I got on the boat to go to France. Must have planned it in advance and brought it along with him. You know I told you that him and my mother came to New York with me where I was to ship over to Europe. They were still trying to talk me out of it right up to the last."

He nodded his head impatiently. "Yeah, yeah. Get to the part about the land. Get to the part about the deed."

I shrugged. "Well, we was in my cabin, him and me by ourselves. My mother was somewhere else. He'd seen my mind was made up. So that was when he pulled out this deed of title and handed it to me. He said, if I was set on my course and set on breaking my mother's heart, that—the land—was all I'd better ever expect from him. Said he'd won it in a poker game. I took it and I looked at it and I saw how many acres it was and set in to thank him but he shook his head at me. 'Don't bother,' he said. Just like that. Good and dry. 'Don't bother.' He said the land was worthless. He done everything but tell me that was the reason he was giving it to me, worthless land to a worthless son."

Dennis's voice got a kind of squeal in it. He said, "Two *hundred thousand* acres? *Two* hundred thousand *acres*. Son, two hundred thousand of anything ain't worthless, especially if it's acres of land!" He was sitting bolt upright in his chair, staring at me. "Why ain't you mentioned this before? Hell, now who's giving the charity?"

"Dennis, it's in west Texas, *far* west Texas. It's up on the Edwards Plateau."

"I don't care if it's on the moon. If we can get a drilling rig to it, we can get somebody to finance the drill." He paused, and a shadow flitted across his face. "The deed does convey the mineral rights, don't it?"

"I don't know." I said. I started across the room to where my suitcase lay on the bed. "I got a portfolio of papers in my grip, Army stuff and personal effects. I think it's in with that lot. Least, that's the last time I remember seeing it."

"Let us hope," Dennis said. "If it ain't spelled out on the deed it is hell to prove up, and make no mistake."

I sat down on the bed and rummaged around in the big piece of luggage until I found the accordion portfolio. I got it open. The papers were just jammed in there in no special order. There were even some letters from my mother, sent to me when I was over in France. There were none from my daddy, as he hadn't written. But it gave me an odd pang to recognize her writing and remember how alone and frightened and homesick I had been when I'd received those letters at the lonely little aerodrome on the western front.

Dennis said, "What's it say?"

"Haven't found it yet," I said. But I'd no more than spoken the words when the stiff piece of legal-looking paper came to hand. I just turned and handed it to Dennis. "Here. You're more used to reading these things than I am."

He looked at it for a moment and then began nodding his head. "Yep. Yep. Yes, sir! All mineral rights included just as slick as a Lewis machine gun." He handed me back the deed. "Willis, my son, you might just be holding yourself an oil well in your hand. All we got to do is find some backers."

I shrugged my shoulders and put the deed back in the portfolio. I said, "I find that strangely unexciting, Dennis."

He looked at me closely even though there was very little space separating us. He said, "What? Drilling an oil well?"

"Naw, I'm willing to go along with that. I don't much want to be involved, I must say. That is, on the actual drilling part. I just don't find sticking an iron pipe into the ground very exciting, that's all."

He was getting anxious. He sat up in his chair and pointed his finger at me. "Willis, you don't know what you're talking about. Why, when that pipe starts going deeper and deeper into the ground and you realize that almost anything can happen at any time—anything! at any second—why, you could strike a gas pocket and *whoosh!*, up comes everything out of the ground, drill stem, pipe, casing, everything! And then the oil comes gushing out. High as your derrick top. What a sight! My word, it will stir the blood of a dead man!"

I gave him as good a smile as I could work up, but I still didn't give much of a damn about drilling an oil well. I said, "I guess, Dennis.

Whatever you say. But you don't need me. Hell, you can have the mineral rights. I'll sign them over to you."

"Are you crazy? Are you plumb loco? Two hundred thousand acres to drill on? Hell, a man could hit a thousand wells. And nobody has really tested out that western country yet. For all we know, it's the mother lode."

"I just can't seem to get all fired up about it."

"Fired up?" He hunched toward me. "Son, have you got any idea what kind of money we might be talking about here? Son, you could get rich. I mean *rich*. I mean *big rich*. Big, big, big, BIG rich!"

There wasn't much use in talking about it. He'd never understand. I just said, simply, "Dennis, I don't want to be rich. I don't want the bother of it."

He stared at me openmouthed. "The . . . the 'bother of it'? Hell, we'll hire somebody to handle the bother. Being rich ain't a bother. Being poor is a bother. What is the matter with you, Willis?"

I smiled to show I knew I was talking like a damn fool. I said, "Oh, I never put much stock in it. I've seen rich folks and I've seen them poor. They all seem to do about the same."

"Here you go again. You ain't making no sense."

I said, "Look here, you was talking to me about that religious stuff. Don't it say in the Bible that it's easier for a camel to pass through the eye of a needle than for a rich man to make it into Heaven?"

He pointed that stubby forefinger at me again. He said, "It also says that all things are possible through God. But I ain't here to argue theology with you. It don't say a man can't make a little money. You get enough, you can do some good with it. But I never heard a young-'un your age say he didn't care nothing about money. What is the matter with you?"

I gave him an answer I thought would satisfy him. I said, "I figure that one in my family that cared enough about the stuff that he went around robbing people was enough. Let's just say I don't care to follow in ol' Wilson Young's footstep."

He shook his head at me slowly. "Why don't you give your daddy a little rope? You got him snubbed up nose-to-the-post. Hell, the government forgave him. Couldn't you do the same?"

"I haven't got anything against my daddy."

Dennis changed the subject. "We got a meetin' with a couple of gents this afternoon. They are a little higher on the money scale. I reckon, you being the land owner, that it's about time for you to make your appearance as the land man."

"Won't that sound kind of fishy, me being the land owner and coming to them for money? Sounds like I got a personal stake in it."

Dennis shook his head. "No, it ain't like that. A lot of land men get the prospect conveyed into their name when they are out in the field. You don't necessarily own the land, just the mineral rights. Lot of times, out in the field, the land has to be conveyed to someone that is right there to receive it. So the land man just has it conveyed into his name and when he gets back to headquarters he has it put in the company name."

"What's the name of this company I work for? If I work for them."

Dennis smiled benignly. "You'll like it. I call it the High Flyer Oil and Exploration Company. Sounds like I sorta named it after you."

I made my best attempt at a smile. "I don't think it is quite appropriate here lately."

He got up and slapped me on the shoulder with his heavy hand. "Hell, Willis, we get us a drilling contract and we'll have you rich and sassy in no time. You'll have to hire a man to keep the girls off you."

I said, softly, "I kind of like things the way they've been. I don't think I'd care to be sassy, and you already know what I think about rich. The girls? Other than a quick romp in the hay, I ain't got much to offer the girls."

The men we met that afternoon were named Butler and Grimes. They owned a string of nickel-and-dime stores, sort of like Woolworth's only nowhere near as big. Butler was Abner, a tall, thin man in his middle age. Grimes was Joe, a little younger and wearing a red velvet lining to his vest, as well as a big Windsor knot in his tie. We met them at a place called Gallatories, which was a very tony drinking club out on a pier that stuck into the Gulf. Walking out on the pier, with the surf breaking some twenty or thirty feet below us, felt very strange. I glanced down once but it almost made me giddy. An odd sensation for a man who'd been locked in mortal combat with another pilot at ten or twelve or even fourteen *thousand* feet. Fourteen was about as high as our biplanes would fly and handle well. Over that, and the air got too thin. There was also the danger, because of the cold, of our machine guns seizing up because of the lubricating oil getting too thick. You didn't want anything to happen to your machine gun when you were in an aerial fight. You either killed the other man, or he would kill you. It was a situation that reduced life to very simple terms. It didn't help if you knew the latest fashion or belonged to the right clique or had credit at the bank, or even how good you looked in a lounge suit. That other pilot didn't care anything about that. He wanted to kill you before you could kill him. I could look back and remember, in some amazement, how I, as a young man of nineteen, had found it all very exciting and glamorous. I'd looked at the old, haggard faces of the pilots who'd been there for some months, and wondered how they could not find aerial combat the most thrilling adventure a man could want. They only looked back at me wearily with eyes that had said, *Wait. You'll learn. If you live that long.*

And their eyes had been right. You could get giddy looking down thirty feet at breaking surf, but you couldn't hanging upside down in an aeroplane at ten thousand feet with an enemy shooting at you. It was too serious for giddiness. And it wasn't long before your face began to look like the others'. And all the fresh, eager young men that arrived in their new uniforms looked at you with those same excited eyes you'd once looked out from.

We sat down at a table that had a view of the Gulf. Mr. Butler and Mr. Grimes sat on one side of the table, and Dennis and I sat on the other. This, I had found out, was an appointment that had been made some little time in advance. Mr. Butler and Mr. Grimes were from St. Louis and they had brought their families to Galveston on a holiday. They had been put together with Dennis by a mutual acquaintance

who knew they were looking to invest in a well, and had recommended
Dennis as the drilling contractor. Dennis had explained it all to me on
the walk over from the hotel. There was something about taxes, income
and corporate, that was involved, but I hadn't understood much of
that. But Dennis had insisted it was an important point. He'd said,
"Even if we drill a dry hole they come out ahead, because it's a business
loss and they can deduct it, write it off."

I didn't know what in hell he was talking about. I didn't see how
they could lose and still win, but Dennis assured me it was a fact. He'd
screwed his big face up and given me a wink. "Don't worry about it,
son. I got it covered."

Mr. Butler spoke. He spoke, and I nearly jumped a foot. He was
a tall, cadaverous-looking man, skinny as a rail, and about as solemn-
looking as a Baptist preacher asking for money. But he had a voice like
a bass drum. His Adam's apple in his skinny neck jumped and then
out came this loud, booming voice. I couldn't have been any more
surprised if he'd fired off a pistol. He said, to Dennis, "Let's get some
drinks ordered and get down to business. The wives expect us back
in quick-march time and I can tell you in ten minutes of talk whether
we are gonna do business or not."

And all the while, Mr. Grimes was beaming on, in his red silk–
lined vest, like he was the guest at an afternoon tea.

Dennis said, "Well, I'm for that." He looked around, and a waiter
wearing sleeve garters and a bow tie arrived at our table and asked
what ours would be. There was no discussion. Mr. Grimes wanted
sweetened seltzer water with a cherry and a squeeze of lime. I said that
I would have a beer though, truth be told, I'd have rather had the
cherry seltzer water, but it didn't seem to fit the role of land scout.
Butler and Dennis both went for the hard stuff. Butler had brandy and
Dennis ordered a shot of what I knew was a particularly expensive
brand of bourbon. I wondered where he'd developed a taste for such.

When the drinks came, Butler took a good sip of his brandy and
then said directly to Dennis, "All right, what have you got? Joe Grimes
and I don't mess about. If you've got a workable proposition, let's
hear it."

My old mechanic, looking and sounding every bit the business-man, said, "I've got the proposition. I've got the mineral rights on a prime drilling prospect, I've got a first-class drilling rig capable of going over five thousand feet deep. And it's a rotary rig, none of your cable-tool gimcracks. And I've got a good crew of men, who've worked in every part of the oil fields. I've come to meet you and your partner because I've been told you were the kind of men didn't let grass grow under your feet. I'm glad to meet you here in Galveston because if the proposition ain't to your liking, there are plenty of backers here. I understand the island is running knee-deep in them."

I was slightly amazed at the self-assured and confident manner in which Dennis came across. You'd have thought he was holding four aces and was impatient for the showdown. If he had other backers lined up, he hadn't said anything to me about them.

Butler said, "Just hold on, Mr. Frank. I'm a little surprised to hear you have drilling rights on a prospect. Last we heard, you were still scouting around."

Dennis turned and clapped me on the shoulder. He said, "In case you didn't get the name, this is Mr. Young, Mr. Willis Young. He's my land man. My scout. And he's just come to town with a lovely deed of conveyance of mineral rights on a piece of property that will be in the hottest zone around in six months. I feel like, for once, I've beat the crowd to the bar." He clapped my shoulder again. "Ain't that right, Willis?"

"Whatever you say, Dennis," I said, a little coolly. I'd already warned him I wouldn't lie or misrepresent anything.

Mr. Grimes leaned back in his chair and hooked his thumbs in the watch pockets of his flamboyant vest. Around us was the low hum of earnest conversation. Most of it came from men who resembled Butler and Grimes, but here and there were the bright colors of a pretty frock and the sleek, slim form of a delicate flower of womanhood. It appeared that all kinds of deals were being struck in Galatories. Grimes said, "Now, just where is this drilling site, Mr. Frank? All the drillers we've talked to want to hang along the coast, but they say drilling rights are coming mighty dear in these areas."

Dennis nodded with conviction. "Quite so, Mr. Grimes. And why not? That's where most of the oil has been discovered. But nobody has taken the time to stop and realize that is also where most of the oil has *not* been discovered."

"I don't get you."

"Mr. Grimes, there ain't oil under every acre along the Gulf Coast. I'd bet you there's been more dry holes drilled from Brownsville to Beaumont than the rest of the country together. Hell, it's time to look elsewhere, it's time to know your geology and your oil signs and spud in on land you've got better odds at."

"Where, Mr. Frank? Where?"

Dennis leaned back in his chair and managed to look triumphant, like he was about to pull a rabbit out of a hat. "West Texas, Mr. Grimes. *Deep* west Texas. Do you know the country?"

Grimes and Butler looked at each other and it was not an encouraging glance. Mr. Butler, who obviously handled the heavy work, said, "Mr. Frank, west Texas is a good ways off. I don't know what you mean by '*deep* west Texas,' but I can only guess it is farther away. Yes, I've had a glimpse of the country. I went out to California on the train and got a vision of the place. I was not impressed."

Dennis give him a severe look. "I ain't proposing, Mr. Butler, that we try and sell town lots on the place. I don't care what it looks like on top. I care what it looks like about two thousand feet down and I smell oil, gentlemen. I think we'll hit a discovery well and open up a field. I don't have to tell you what that means. I understand from our mutual friend that you've been nosing around the oil patch long enough to learn your way around. Well, I've got the mineral rights to two hundred thousand acres. Even if it is in west Texas. I'd nearly bet my wife I'll strike oil on that much land in no more than two tries."

I looked at him in amazement. He didn't know anything at all about the land in question. Furthermore, he wasn't married, so he had no wife to bet. But I kept my mouth shut. My deal was, I wouldn't say anything either for or against.

But Mr. Butler looked over at me and narrowed his eyes and went way down deep in his throat and asked me what I thought. "You are the one who made the lease—and by the way, I'd like to see that document before we get much farther down the road—but you've been on the ground, so to speak. What's your opinion?"

I could feel Dennis looking at me. I took a slow sip of beer. I wasn't going to lie, but Dennis was an awful good friend to me. I said, "Well, you are correct that it is rough country. And sparsely settled. Not many ways for folks to make a living out there."

"No, no, no. I mean, what do you think of its chances as an oil prospect?"

I didn't look Dennis's way. I said, slowly, "Well, Mr. Butler, as you know, you can't see oil through the surface of the earth." I knew that sounded pretty dumb, but I didn't know what else to say.

Mr. Butler said, "No, no, no. I mean, did you see any surface signs? Did you see any water, any lakes where oil might have rizz to the surface?"

"To begin with, there ain't no lakes out there. Surface water is about as scarce as money. So, no, you ain't going to see nothing of that kind. What you got in the way of lakes is salt flats."

Dennis jumped on that one. I doubt he'd even known there were salt flats out in that country, but it was all he needed to build a story around. He said, "You well know the story of the salt domes. That was what led to the discovery at Spindletop. And Mont Bellvieu and North Dayton and Coriscana and I don't know how many places. But those salt domes are gone. Every one has had more holes stuck in it than Swiss cheese. I say a salt flat is just another way of indicating that there is oil below. I admit it ain't a tried theory yet, but neither was the salt dome until money and nerve enough was got together."

Butler and Grimes jumped in and I looked down at my beer while they talked. I never really had been much of a drinker until the last of the war when I had taken on a pretty strong affection for French cognac. It seemed like you didn't feel as much when you were about half sloshed. Some of the pilots wouldn't drink and fly. They said it slowed you up. Hell, that was fine with me. I wanted things slowed down. Men and planes were disappearing entirely too fast. Sometimes the only way I could nerve myself up to climb in the cockpit and take off, dawn or evening patrol, was with the help of a French seventy-seven which is what we called the cognac. Sometimes Dennis worried that I'd overdone it and maybe ought to drink some coffee before I left, but I'd just tell him the hell with that. It got cold up there at ten thousand feet. Hell, it got cold at any altitude with people shooting at you. Toward the very last, I started taking a bottle along with me in the cockpit. It made for some interesting landings, when I was able to find my way back to the field. It made for some even more interesting landings when I couldn't find the field, or found the wrong field. Once, I landed at a German aerodrome by the mistake of getting completely confused on direction and heading. Fortunately, they were as surprised as I was and I was able to gun my engine and take off before they could riddle me with ground fire. That did a considerable job of sobering me up. But the war ended before I could drink myself to death one way or the other.

Mr. Butler said, "This rotary rig of yours—what does it cost to operate a mechanism like that? I ain't asking for specifics. Just round it up to a sum a man can understand."

Dennis gave me a wink. Apparently some sort of high point had been reached. He said, "Mr. Butler, I'm sure you know that drilling contracts are let on how deep the well is and what you are drilling through. Dirt and sandstone and conglomerate—kind of like gravel— is pretty easy going and you can make a pretty good number of feet a day. But you bust into a granite ledge or a long stretch of limestone, and progress is gonna slow down right sharply."

Grimes said, "Talk so we can understand you, man. Give us some figures. Hell, we are businessmen, not petroleum engineers. Talk dollars, man."

Dennis creased his face. He said, "Well, it ain't all that easy to get down to specifics, Mr. Grimes. They is a lot of unknown factors involved." He held up his hand. "But if you want me to round you off some numbers, I will. Through the soft stuff will cost about twenty dollars a foot. When you hit country rock you can double that. Maybe a little more. Depends on how much equipment you tear up and how your workers hold up. It's terrible hard work."

Butler and Grimes looked at each other and then Grimes leaned over and, holding his hand over his mouth, whispered something in Butler's ear. After a moment they both looked at Dennis. Butler said, "You say your drilling apparatus can go to five thousand feet?"

Dennis nodded silently.

"What happens if you haven't struck oil by then?"

Dennis shrugged. "Pull the string, out of the hole and try somewhere else. If they ain't no oil by that depth, then there ain't no oil."

"What if we want to limit our investment? What if we don't want to go on if the first hole is fruitless?"

"Mr. Butler, I'm trying to put together a syndicate of investors so we won't have to quit on one try. I'm hoping to get several backers interested. What would you say would be the outside of your interest? Could you be counted on for, say, seventy-five thousand?"

Mr. Grimes said, "Seventy-five thousand dollars! That is a hell of a lot of money, Mr. Frank."

"Yes, but if we hit, we're talking millions. You and Mr. Butler know that, Mr. Grimes. And I know you are mainly interested in this business as a deduction from your taxes. If you lost seventy-five thousand it wouldn't be real dollar bills."

They looked at each other again, and this time it was Mr. Butler who leaned over and whispered in Mr. Grimes's ear. When their private conversation was finished Mr. Butler said, "We're not interested in being in with other parties." He waved his hand. "We might be willing to commit to, say, fifty thousand but no more. And that would make us the sole proprietors, with you as the drilling contractor."

Dennis said, quickly, "Of course, I'd get a royalty. A drilling contractor automatically gets a one-eighth royalty. That's a known fact."

Butler said, in his heavy voice, "That's a detail. What is more important is if you feel you can drill a well that's got more than half a chance on the money we're willing to risk. We have been talking around. You are not the first contractor we have talked to, by any means."

"And you and Mr. Grimes are not the first backers to be seeking my services."

Mr. Butler ignored that. "And we have come to understand that a well with a high prospect of success can be drilled for twenty or twenty-five thousand dollars."

Dennis leaned back in his chair and looked amused. "Of course it can. But that's drilling on proven land, and the cost of the lease and the royalties to the land owner and the lease owner will suck up every bit of profit you can ever hope to make. And if oil was to drop two bits a barrel you'd be stuck for storage that you couldn't write off. Mr. Butler, I know why y'all want to drill an oil well and it's not on proven ground. You want a real wildcat and I think I could just about hand you one on this land out in west Texas."

Mr. Grimes said, "You seem to know our business better than we do, Mr. Frank."

"I know every reason there is to drill an oil well, Mr. Grimes. And unless you and Mr. Butler are crazy, that don't leave but one reason: that it's good business."

I looked over at my old mechanic. I was frankly amazed at Dennis's composure and business acumen. He'd come a long way from patching up my planes. They talked on, though I didn't pay much attention to what was being said. The club was built in an octagonal shape with windows all around so you could see the water in any direction. Off in the distance I could see a big steamship headed for our port. I couldn't tell at that distance if it was a passenger liner or all cargo. I'd been on two of them in my time, and I had no desire to repeat the experience in the near future. Now, actually, I wanted to go inland. I was anxious, suddenly, to see the plains and rolling prairies of my younger life. It had been a long time since I'd sat a horse, and I wondered if I still had the skill. It would be a hell of a joke to be able to fly a plane but not ride a horse anymore. I supposed that the unexpected rush of nostalgia had been brought on by my bringing out the deed for Dennis's use. I guess it had brought back all those times before the war.

My wandering mind had taken me further than I thought, because Dennis was getting to his feet along with Butler and Grimes. I rose also. Apparently the meeting was over, though I was fried if I knew what had been resolved. We shook hands all around and then Dennis and I left. Once we got outside he slammed one fist into the palm of his other hand and said, "Boy oh boy, I think we got 'em, son! What do you think of that?"

Since my contribution to the effort had been to show the deed and talk a little about the terrain, I didn't know what I thought about it. I knew Mr. Butler and Mr. Grimes—and Dennis, for that matter—didn't have the slightest idea of just how rough and raw the west Texas country was. Ol' Wilson Young hadn't been far wrong when he'd called it worthless. Now, if Dennis had persuaded Butler and Grimes into financing an oil well on the site, he was in a good deal more trouble than he thought he was. If he was real lucky he might get back alive— forget about finding any oil.

I said, "Ya'll reach a resolution?"

"If that college word means, 'Did we make a deal?' the answer is maybe. They are going to sleep on it and we're gonna have a meeting right at the hotel for lunch. But they as good as committed to advancing twenty thousand."

"I thought you needed fifty."

He rolled his eyes at me. "Son, when it comes to drilling oil wells nobody knows how much you need. The rule of thumb is get all you can and then ask for more. It ain't real money for them anyway. The way the government has put a bite on the income tax and the corporate tax to pay for the war, I bet it wouldn't be costing them twenty cents on the dollar to lose money on an oil well—and that stacked up against the chance to make millions. But never mind about the twenty thousand. If they advance that, they'll come in for the whole fifty. I can guarantee that."

We went down to the main dining room that night for dinner. Dennis had on a fresh black suit, and I was wearing my best of elegance, a gabardine suit that was sort of a military tan. It had been hand-tailored for me some several years back, but still fit very well. I didn't have a vest, but Dennis loaned me one of his black ties and I wore my new boots which I'd shined. Except for needing a haircut, I reckoned I looked nearly civilized. It was strange, after my existence of the last two years, to be civilly dressed and to be going into such an elegant supper club to eat well and to drink alcohol that, while it wasn't legal, would be damn potable.

We walked across the echoing marble floor of the lobby and paused at the entrance to the dining, salon while the maître d' ran his list to see about our reservation. He found our names just about the time a two-dollar bill landed in his palm. Of course, such activity was nothing new to me. I'd done it myself in Paris and London and New York, but I was damned if I was ever going to get on to the idea of paying someone to come into their place to pay to eat their food.

But if Dennis didn't mind, I didn't. A waiter showed us to a table near the dance floor. A good small band was playing popular tunes of somewhat recent vintage: "Lady of Spain" and "All By Myself" and "'Till the Clouds Roll By." The band was a piano and violin and bass with a banjo beating time. I felt immediately out-of-place.

On the dance floor were some young couples. The women appeared to be what were called flappers. They were wearing slim-fitting, short-skirted outfits that made them look boyish, especially with their bobbed hair and their sailor tops. The men were dressed in pinch-backed tuxedoes with wide, satin lapels. As the waiter brought our round of drinks, the band struck up, and the couples began to dance the Charleston. All of the women had on long strings of beads, and the baubles bounced and swayed as the girls moved with the music. One of the women was dancing, holding a long, ivory cigarette holder with the cigarette still burning. They all adopted a very cool, very casual attitude. I thought they looked a little silly, but, after all, they weren't doing me any harm.

Dennis said, "Looky yonder."

I followed the nod of his head across the room to where a woman sat alone at a table. The floor surrounding the dance floor was slightly tiered and the woman was at a table above us. The lighting was dim except for the odd shaft of light that probed down from the ceiling. One of the spotlights had fallen on the woman, giving me a clear and vivid view of her. I had her three-quarter profile, but it was enough to see the soft, white beauty of her face. Her brows weren't plucked and her hair wasn't bobbed. Instead, it fell in soft reddish curls down to her shoulders. Her dress was some sort of layered, fragile affair made of the softest diaphanous silklike gauze that could be imagined. She had on a single strand of white pearls that went perfectly with the light-gray of her dress. I stared at her, fascinated. I hadn't seen anyone like her since I'd left Paris. The band was playing the famous Irving Berlin melody "A Pretty Girl Is Like a Melody," and the swelling notes of the music as they rose and fell and weaved their magic seemed to go perfectly with her as she sat there. The delicious-sounding music, the delicious-looking woman.

Dennis said, "Why don't you go ask her to dance with you?"

His words startled me because that was exactly what I had been thinking, about walking across the open dance floor, stepping up to the level of her table, leaning down and, in a velvet voice, asking her to dance. But of course, I had just been daydreaming. Dennis's words were real and they startled me back to myself. I said, "Of course not. Are you crazy?"

"Hell, she won't bite you."

"No, but her escort, who may turn out to be her husband, might. Or worse."

He was shaking his head. "She hasn't got no escort. We been sitting here half an hour and she was alone when we came in."

I shook my head. "Dennis, you are off base. Women like her don't come into supper clubs by themselves."

He laughed. "Boy, you have been out of circulation. The female population has changed since you shipped for France. Now they do just about anything they damn well please. And you better not remark on it, either, especially with these younger ones. If she wants to dance, she will."

"How come she hasn't been dancing before?"

"Look around. There ain't that many single gentlemen in her

league. Besides, I haven't seen anyone ask her. I reckon they all got
cold feet like you. Mighty pretty lady. If I was about ten years younger
and thirty pounds lighter and knew how to dance, I'd be up and giving
her a go."

"I don't have cold feet. It's just been awhile."

He smiled. "That's what you said about the whiskey, but I noticed
you managed to get that down."

"Yeah, but I didn't like it."

"Go on. We got to order our supper pretty quick. And she might
get up and leave. I don't think she's here to eat. Look. She's fixing to
light a cigarette. You better get up there before she can get lit up."

I was half tempted, but I said, "I'm a little rusty."

"Oh, hell, Willis. I've seen you waltz an airplane all over the sky.
You going to tell me you can't handle a two-step?"

And by then the band was starting to play "Stairway to Paradise."
Dennis was right about the cigarette. As I watched, she was fitting a
cigarette into an ivory-and-silver holder. I could see she was wearing
gloves. Altogether, she did make a very fetching picture. I felt a sudden
hunger, the kind I hadn't felt in a long time. I stood up and rounded
our table and stepped onto the dance floor. Behind me Dennis said
something but my eyes were riveted on the woman. She had the cigarette holder between her lips and was playing with a lighter as she
watched the few dancers on the floor. Barely a bar of the song had
gone by.

I was at her side. Slowly, very slowly, she turned her head to look
at me. She was even better-looking up close. Her eyebrows were arched
and her almond-shaped eyes were wide and dark. I could see just the
faintest trace of lip paint on the cigarette holder. Her lips were a ruby-
red and her cheeks were lightly rouged. I made a slight bow, aware
that my gabardine suit fit a little tightly and that my riding boots
weren't exactly dancing slippers. But it didn't seem to matter. I wasn't
altogether sure that she was real. I said, "My name is Willis Young. I'm
a stranger in town. Would you care to dance?"

She didn't hesitate. With a swift motion she laid her holder and
cigarette in an ashtray and stood up. She took away a small bejeweled

handbag from the table, holding it in her left hand. I held out my hand
and took her other. It rested lightly on my upturned hand, her fingers
slim and cool and without jewelry. I led her down the few steps to the
floor and turned and she came perfectly into my arms. From my height
I guessed her to be about five foot eight or nine. It was a perfect fit.
She danced close enough so that I could smell her hair and the musky
perfume of her neck. I could not quite feel her breasts against my chest,
but I knew they were there. I had my arm around her waist, with my
hand resting on the top of her hip. Just as we began to dance she
pulled her head back and said, "Genevieve."

I nodded. I didn't need to know any more. It was enough.

We caught the music and began to move with it. It was like dancing with someone in your dreams. She was so close with me on every
step that it seemed as if nobody was leading. We moved and we twirled
and dipped and counterstepped as if we had been dancing together
for a lifetime. Neither of us spoke. There was no need to. Our rhythm
to the music was speech enough. I knew there were other dancers on
the floor but I was unaware of them. We turned and circled and wove
our way without a care for any interference. And there was none. I
could feel eyes watching us, but I didn't see them. My own were half
shut and tuned only to the circuit of our dance.

But then the orchestra began the last bar and the song wound
down, and then it stopped. For a second we stayed in the dancers'
embrace, but then I felt her move and I dropped my arms. She turned
and I followed her back to her table. I got her chair out and held it for
her until she was seated. Then I stepped back and said, "Thank you.
I enjoyed that very much."

She picked up her cigarette holder with its unlit cigarette and put
it to her mouth. With a gold lighter she lit the end of the cigarette.
She blew out a thin veil of smoke and looked up at me. She gave me
a slight smile. She said, "So did I."

I turned around and went back to the table where Dennis was
sitting. He said, "Wow! You two looked like Irene and Vernon Castle.
And boy is she a looker! But what are you doing back here? Hell, I'd've
understood."

I picked up the menu. I said, "Let's order. I'm hungry."

"But don't you want to get in a couple of more dances with her before the food comes? You need to make your play before someone gets in ahead of you. Hell, woman like that ain't going to be alone very long."

"How is the steak here? I'm getting a little tired of seafood, though I wouldn't mind one of those shrimp cocktails to start off with."

"Are you crazy? The band is nearly through with another number. You better get up there and ask her to dance again before somebody cuts you out."

I was still studying the menu. I said, "I'm not going to ask her again."

"What? Have you lost your reason? You made a perfect couple. Why, everybody in the place was watching you. You danced like you was glued together. Why not?"

I put the menu down. "Dennis, you won't understand this. I was getting back a few moments of the youth I didn't have. It wasn't a dance, it was a sort of a visit to a place I didn't get to go."

He crowded up his face again. "That don't make a damn bit of sense. Here you are and there's that damn good-looking woman. You're not going to let her slip through your fingers, are you?"

"Exactly where do you expect it to go? I'm a day laborer. Does she look like she steps out with day laborers? I'll be gone in a day or two."

"You're not a day laborer. You're in with me now."

I shrugged. "However you want to say it. But she's here and I'll be gone. One way or the other. It doesn't matter, Dennis."

"But you might, you know, hit it off real quick."

I gave him a look. "She's not real, Dennis. Understand that. You don't, as you say, 'hit it off real quick,' with a dream."

"Hell, it's all pink on the inside."

I looked at him. Sometimes Dennis could be crude at the wrong time. After a moment I said, "Dennis, did you ever wonder why it was you that stayed on the ground and fixed the airplanes and it was me that flew them high up in the sky?"

He shook his head. "No."

"Why not?"

"Because that was just the way of the matter."

I nodded. "Now you understand why it wouldn't be right for me to dance with the girl again."

CHAPTER 4

I TOLD him the next morning at breakfast that I didn't want to be part of the oil-drilling effort. I told him he could have the mineral rights to the land, but I didn't think I was cut out for a big operation like sticking holes in the ground looking for oil.

He was immediately distressed. He said, "Aw, hell, Lieutenant, I thought we done had us a deal. When you trotted out that deed on that land your daddy gave you, I figured we was all set. Now you are changing your mind."

I shook my head. "No, Dennis, I never said I was for it. You needed some land to drill on to sell your prospects. I had that worthless stuff from old Wilson Young. But that was as far as I was willing to go."

He got a pained look on his face. "Hell, Willis, you got to do something. You can't keep on bumming around like some low-class tramp. You be an educated gentleman. You need a higher calling of work than catch-as-catch-can."

I put my knife and fork down and pushed my plate of ham and eggs away. I said, "Dennis, I have enjoyed the little rest you've given me by taking me in and giving me board and room, but it ain't for me.

I figure giving you those mineral rights makes us just about square on what you've laid out on my account."

He pulled his head back. "Are you crazy? Those mineral rights could be worth hundreds of thousands, maybe millions of dollars. Shoot, old son, I ain't done you no favors. You was good company as it was. But I didn't need the mineral rights without you in the bargain."

"We ain't a package, Dennis."

"But you got to be doing something. Why not drilling for oil? Hell, it's got adventure, danger, good-looking women involved. All the things you like."

I gave him a furrowed brow. "Where do the good-looking women come in?"

He gave back a half smile. "I just throwed that in there to see if you was paying attention."

I shook my head. "Well, even if it was true, it wouldn't make any difference. I think it's about time I got back to my own business."

"But I still need you as my land man. Hell, Will, I—"

I raised my head quickly. I said, my voice hard, "Don't ever call me that again."

"What?" He looked puzzled.

" 'Will.' That was my daddy's nickname. Willis is not Wilson."

He put a hand to his head and made a scratching motion. "Sorry. I didn't know I was in the briars."

I calmed down. "That's all right. It's a mistake that's been made before. I don't care for it."

"Of course, of course. But what I was trying to say was that the lease ain't no good without you. I ain't never been in that country before. I don't have the slightest idea where the prospect is located."

"You've heard of maps."

He sighed. "Yeah, but a map can't tell you what conditions are like. You been on the actual ground. You know the country. Hell, you be part of the package I'm trying to put together."

I said I was sorry about that but it couldn't be helped. He argued back and we kept going around like that until it became clear to me that it was going to take some strong language to get Dennis to understand what I thought. I said, "Look, Dennis, maybe you don't mind hanging around folks like that Butler and Grimes to get them to invest in your scheme, but I just ain't built for it. There's not enough good reason in this world to get me to put up with their kind for any longer than it would take to shake the dust off my boots."

It hurt him. I could see that. His face went sort of pale and he looked down at the table. After a second he said, "You ain't got to say ugly things to me, Willis. If you don't want no part of it, why, that's all right. I can understand. But you ain't got to make it sound like I'm bootlicking to raise money." He lifted his eyes sadly. "That's just the way business has to get done. I wish I didn't have to ask nobody for nothing. And maybe someday I won't. I need speculators like Butler and Grimes. I know. They are a couple of stuffed shirts and over in France we'd have laughed them out of the squadron. But times are different now."

I felt bad. I said, "Aw, hell, Dennis, I'm sorry. I shouldn't have spoken like I did. Here you been feeding me for the last few days and this is the way I thank you. I just said it so you'd know how I really felt, so you'd quit arguing."

He gave me a long, appraising look. "I ain't altogether convinced. I think you don't want to go out to west Texas on account of your daddy. He give you that land and you are damned if you are going to profit by it. You don't want nothing to do with anything bearing on him. I believe that's the truth of the matter. I don't believe it is the oil business or anything else. I think you got a mad on against your father."

Now I was the one that was stung. I jerked back in my chair as if to get as far away from Dennis as possible. I could feel my face flaming. I said, "How dare you say such a thing to me! My father ain't got no influence over my life one way or the other. I decide what I want to do on my own and by my own. I wanted to go to war. He didn't want me to. You saw where I went. Don't you ever say anything like that to me again!"

He narrowed his eyes. "You seem to be getting considerably upset about a matter that ain't of no importance to you. Maybe he's still more your daddy than you like to let on."

I was nearly angry. I threw my napkin down on the tabletop and said, "You think what you want. But I'll tell you this much—Wilson Young is too much of a man to go around peddling his little schemes like some barbed-wire salesman. I left a pretty good country when I went to France. Wilson Young was an iron ass then. Still is, I'd reckon. And there was a bunch of others just like him. But at least they were their own men. I come home to this damn place and it seems like it has all been painted one color. Everybody dresses alike, act alike, and, for all I know, thinks alike. Wilson Young might be a son of a bitch but he is an individual son of a bitch. And if you bring him up to me again like you just did, you are liable to get to eat your words. Understand?"

Dennis took a minute. Then he said, "I reckon our coffee has done got cold." He raised his arm and signaled for the waiter. "We better get it warmed up."

"I don't want any more."

"Don't make your mind up, Willis. Not just yet. I've got another party to see tonight. Man named Teddy Atlas. I think you'll like him. He ain't a Butler nor a Grimes."

"Yeah? How come?"

"Well, he's got a different view on matters. He's a spoiled rich man, but he's got some sporting blood in him. Owns a stable of prizefighters. As a matter of fact, he's got a heavyweight going in a bout in the Civic Auditorium tonight. Supposed to be a pretty good boy. Mr. Atlas has invited me down for the bout and then to talk business. Why don't you come along?"

"I don't much care for fighting. Of any kind." I especially didn't care for two men getting in a ring trying to brain each other for the sake of money. Especially with a lot of idiots looking on.

He waited while our cups were refilled. Then he said, as he raised his to his lips. "You appear to be in good supply of strong opinions, especially for one of your age."

I said, in a flat voice, "You age faster the higher you go and the more bullets they shoot at you. I don't care for prizefights because I been in too many of them. The kind where the prize is you get to stay alive if you win."

"Aw, Willis, don't be like that. Listen, I really need you along tonight. You and Mr. Atlas are going to speak the same language. He's a classy young gent and you two will hit it off. Hell, what have you got to lose? Another day or so of hanging around in a swank hotel? That ought not to be too hard to take."

We kicked it around a little more and, in the end, I agreed to go. I was somewhat surprised to find a fight of such magnitude was being held in a city the size of Galveston, but then, there was a lot of money around. Dennis said ringside seats were going for a hundred dollars apiece and in short supply.

Teddy Atlas turned out to be a short, athletically-built man of some thirty years. He was blond, both in hair and in complexion, and was wearing a turtlenecked sweater under a sports jacket, a combination I hadn't seen before. Even before you shook his hand he looked at you with his cold blue eyes and his whole person seemed to say, *Hello, I'm Teddy, and I'm rich and used to getting my way.*

At least that was what I read, which was sort of unfair to a man on a first meeting. But he did look all-fire cocksure of himself, though the smile he put on when he stuck out his hand was friendly enough and his manner of greeting us was hospitable. For all I knew, he might turn out to be a prince of a fellow, but there was just that little flash and ease about him that put me off. Admittedly, that was one of my faults; I was too hard on people. I expected them to either come up or down to my measuring stick. It was a bad habit, and an unjust one, and I knew I needed to rid myself of such an attitude.

Mr. Atlas received us in his fighter's dressing room. The place was hot and crowded and full of men smoking cigars. Mr. Atlas's fighter was a big Negro. He was sitting on a dressing table in his ring shorts with nothing else on but his boxing shoes and the tape a little man wearing a beat-up bowler hat was applying to his hands. The Negro was hard-faced and hard-muscled. He wasn't wearing any hair, and I figured he'd shaved his head. On the way to the auditorium, Dennis had told me the fighter was a heavyweight, which meant he had to weigh over 184 pounds. The Negro looked like he weighed considerably more than that. As I understood it, Atlas's fighter was the heavy favorite, another Jack Johnson, and the fight in Galveston was against an inferior opponent and intended to give him a good workout and some more publicity.

But it wasn't a fight that we had come to see. I didn't know why Dennis was trying to do business under such conditions, but he'd said that was the way it had to be. He'd said, "Mr. Atlas told me I had fifteen minutes to tell him my story, while his fighter was getting ready. I know it sounds like I'm a chump, but it was the best shot I had and I took it."

I was fascinated by how clean Teddy Atlas looked in the grubby dressing room. His jacket was white linen and his turtleneck was white also, made out of some kind of finely woven cotton. Even his shoes were white, though his pants were gray flannel. It wasn't his clothes so much that gave that glowing sparkle, as the man himself. He looked scrubbed and buffed and combed and brushed within an inch of his life. He looked like he'd never had a speck of dirt under his fingernails.

Dennis and I stood back against a wall by the entrance door while Mr. Atlas was busy talking to his fighter whose name I had come to understand was Sam Crawford. He had another fighter going in a preliminary bout, but Crawford was the main attraction.

Dennis leaned over and whispered to me, nodding his head toward the business around the fighter. "Look at him, Atlas. Look at how he tends to business. He's got a manager and a trainer for that boxer, but he's calling the shots. He's right in the middle of it, making decisions right and left. I tell you, Willis, this is the man we need. He's the real goods."

Dennis had told me that Atlas was a plunger. He'd said, "If he comes in he'll come all the way in. Won't be no talk about drilling one dry hole and quitting. If he throws his hat in, it'll be for no less than a hundred thousand. If he's my man, Willis, I'm home free. He ain't no nickel-and-dimer like Butler and Grimes. He's a sportsman."

I noticed Teddy Atlas glance over my way several times while he was getting his fighter ready. I was wearing my jodphurs and boots, looking like something halfway between a polo player and a damn fool, but Dennis had insisted on it. He'd claimed it made me look upper-crust.

Now Teddy Atlas was coming toward us, wiping his hands on a clean towel. He tossed it aside as he came up to us. We'd shook before, but he put out his hand again. I took it, since it was aimed in my direction, and we shook. He said, "You're a flyer, aren't you?"

I nodded slowly. "Yes. I guess you could say that."

"In the war?"

I nodded again. "Yes. In France."

He looked at me for a long time. "In combat?"

I smiled slightly. It wasn't a very smart question. "That's about the only kind of flying they had."

He cut his fist through the air. "Damn! I would have loved to have done that! I'll bet you were there before the country got involved in the War."

Dennis decided to answer for me. He said, "You betcha, Mr. Atlas. Willis here was a double ace. Eleven kills. And a couple of probables. He was hell on wings."

Teddy Atlas looked at me with his intent blue eyes. "I can't tell you how much I envy you."

That marked him down, for me, as a damn fool. But he was Dennis's pigeon, and I wanted to stay out of the way. I jerked my thumb in Dennis's direction and said, "I'm just kind of tagging along here. I'm not the man you want to be talking to."

Dennis said, "You remember I approached you about a possible drilling prospect? Well, I got one now and it is a good one."

Teddy Atlas looked behind him at the little knot around his black fighter. He opened the door into the hall. He said, "Let's step outside where we can hear ourselves think." He glanced at his wristwatch. "I can give you ten minutes, Mr. Frank."

I wanted to ask what happened to the fifteen minutes, but I kept my mouth shut and followed them both out the door. We walked down a hall that was crowded with fight fans waiting to get into the arena, and went out a side door and stepped into the warm, humid night. Even so far from the beach we could still hear the faint sound of the breakers washing ashore.

We stopped after a few feet and Teddy Atlas got out a cigarette and lit it. He said, "All right, what have you got, Mr. Frank? I know a little of your reputation and that is important, but the business deal is more important."

Atlas had a rapid, forceful way of speaking, almost as if he was jabbing you in the chest with every word.

Dennis started in telling his story. He was a little nervous and got slightly confused about where the property was. He placed it south of El Paso, which, of course, would have put it in Mexico. I stepped in and, as gently as I could, corrected him by putting the prospect in the Pecos, Monohans, area. It was only a matter of a hundred miles or so, but a hundred miles in that country was nearly off the face of the earth.

Atlas whipped the cigarette out of his mouth and turned to me. "So it is your property? You are the landowner."

I nodded, not quite certain if I was supposed to say anything.

"So you are coming in on this proposition?"

I said, "Well, I—"

Dennis broke in. "He's in for a one-eighth royalty for the mineral rights and the right to drill. By the way, that's over two hundred thousand acres. That's a power of land and a power of drilling prospects."

Atlas said, quickly, "Not for west Texas it isn't. All that is out there is land."

I said, "Then you know the country."

He gave me a curt nod. "Yes."

I nodded at my old friend. "Dennis has never seen it. He doesn't know what rough country it is."

Atlas gave Dennis a brief look. "It's rough." Then he swung around on me. "You think there's oil there?"

I shrugged. "I don't have the first idea where any oil is. I've got that property and Dennis thinks the salt flats out there might be the same as the salt domes that have been so successful."

Teddy Atlas pursed his lips for a moment. He said, "No one knows where oil is. Everyone thinks it is along the coast, but that is only because that's where it's been found. If oil were to be found in west Texas, everyone would go rushing in that direction. It's a gamble." He turned back to Dennis. "How much will you need?"

Dennis said, "Understand one thing—I'm not looking for capital to drill one test hole. I don't know what the strata is out there and I don't want to miss an oil reef by a quarter of a mile and regret it ten years later. I want to drill at least four holes, maybe five."

"I asked you how much you needed."

For a minute Dennis pulled a face though I knew damn good and well he wasn't thinking over the arithmetic. He knew how much he was hoping for. He finally gave a kind of sigh and said, "About thirty-five thousand the hole. Say one hundred twenty-five thousand for four holes. Might stretch that to five if we don't have to go deep on every one. But then there's the matter of getting my equipment out there. And a crew. And supplies. Say another ten thousand."

Teddy Atlas didn't hesitate at all. He said, "Now I've got to get back to my fighter. I think I've got the next world heavyweight champion there. Dennis, you come around and see me in my office tomorrow afternoon. I'm in the Cotton Exchange, but then you know that." He suddenly clapped me on the shoulder. "I think our young flyer here is going to bring us luck. And you caught me at the right time. I was tired of hearing about salt domes along the Gulf Coast. You are welcome to come in and see the fight. Sit down in the press section right at ringside. I'll be kind of busy so don't bother trying to talk to me anymore."

I looked at Dennis and he looked back. Finally I shrugged. Dennis said, "Why sure, Mr. Atlas. We'd be much obliged."

We filed back into the auditorium, following the white coat of Mr. Atlas. He had made it clear he was through talking to us for the night. His last act in our direction was to shove a couple of press passes in Dennis's hand.

The auditorium was crowded and hot and loud. We found our seats down by ringside among a gang of men, some with typewriters, all of whom were wearing hats with cards that said PRESS stuffed in their hatbands. They gave us looks, and one or two asked what paper we were with. When we said we were only guests they pulled away and gave us a good letting-alone.

A preliminary bout was going on when we got seated. The fighters weren't as big as Sam Crawford, but they were still good-sized and could hit hard enough that the blows were plainly distinct. Once one caught the other in the face with a hard right hand and a stream of blood stained the canvas right in front of me. Both men looked utterly spent and seriously hurt. But they kept on fighting, rising from their stools at the summons from the bell and only stopping when the same bell gave them a brief rest.

It was hard to talk normally because of the noise. I leaned over and yelled in Dennis's ear, "Why do they do it?"

He gave me a grim look. "Same reason I go around begging for drilling money. These are hard times and a living is hard to come by. Ain't everybody got a million dollars like Mr. Teddy Atlas."

I thought that was a poor measure of the man, bad or good, but I let it go.

The preliminary fight finished and one of the fighters raised his arms in victory while the other looked downcast. To my eye they both looked like they'd had the hell beat out of them. Picking a winner off the remains looked like quite a job.

Now the ring announcer had his megaphone to his mouth and was walking around the area between the ropes, and proclaiming the coming of the principals for "the Main Event."

Mr. Atlas's fighter got the larger applause by far, and it was easy to tell he was the comer with a shot at the championship if all went well. I turned in my seat and looked to see Mr. Atlas and his party proceeding up one of the aisles toward the ring. The fighter was first, with a purple robe over his shoulders, his skin black and glistening where it showed. He had his head down and was pounding his gloves together, working himself up. Behind him came the little man in the bowler hat wearing a vest and a white shirt without a tie. I had understood he was the manager. Then, clustered in there, were three other men, one carrying a stool and the other two carrying buckets and bottles and towels. I understood they were called "cornermen." I didn't know what they did, but I expected it was necessary or Mr. Atlas would not have had them on the payroll. Dennis whispered to me that one of them, somebody named something-or-other, was the best cut man in the business though Crawford didn't need him because Crawford never got cut. I was amazed that Dennis knew as much about the fight game as he did. I wondered when he'd gotten time to study it in between drilling oil wells and hustling money.

The opposing party climbed through the ropes as Mr. Atlas and his crew made their way up the steps and entered the ring. The crowd was keyed-up and anxious and it was clear the two fighters were also, especially Crawford's opponent, who was no less a physical specimen but somehow didn't have the look of destruction about him that Sam Crawford did. The calmest man in the ring, to my eye, was Teddy Atlas. The referee called the two fighters to the center of the ring, the seconds climbed back out through the ropes, and the fight began.

I found myself watching Teddy Atlas more than the fight. It had become clear very early that Crawford's opponent was no match. Crawford spent the first round hitting him with straight lefts, snapping his head back with each one, and then switched to hooks to the body in the second round. I didn't figure the man to last four rounds, if that.

But I was curious about Teddy Atlas's activities. He was up on the ring step at the end of every round and talking in his fighter's ear for the entire rest period. I could see by his gestures the kind of punches he wanted Crawford to throw. I leaned over and cupped my hands toward Dennis's ear. The auditorium was bedlam. Crawford had rocked his younger opponent with two straight lefts and then knocked him down with a short, hard right hand. He had barely made it up before the count and only the bell had saved him further punishment. I yelled, "Dennis! Ain't the guy in the bowler hat Crawford's manager?"

He looked around at me and nodded.

I still had my hands cupped and was talking loud. "Then how come he ain't telling Crawford what to do instead of Atlas?"

He rolled his eyes. He yelled back. "Mr. Atlas owns the fighter. He owns the trainer. I guess he can do whatever he wants to do."

I said, loudly, "Then what is going to keep him from telling you how to drill an oil well if he buys you?"

Dennis frowned. "He ain't buying *me*. He's investing in a wildcat scheme."

"All right. What's to keep him from telling you how to run the business, the drilling?"

The crowd let out a roar as Crawford knocked his opponent down. Dennis let the noise subside before he said, "It's different interfering with the management of a fighter and the drilling of an oil well. Most every man thinks he knows how to fight. Damn few know the first thing about the oil business." He gave me a look. "You are determined to try and get at me, ain't you, Willis?"

In the ring the referee was trying to push Crawford toward a neutral corner so he could begin counting over his fallen foe. I said, "Where do you get those kind of ideas?"

Dennis stood up. He said, "Let's go. This thing is over with. They let it go on, they'll have to have a funeral for that kid in there against Sam Crawford."

I said, "Ain't you going to hang around and congratulate Teddy Atlas?"

Dennis gave me that same look again. He said, "I reckon not. Might be somebody would accuse me of bootlickin' and apple-polishing."

I gave a laugh and followed Dennis out of the auditorium. As we went out the double doors at the front I could hear the crowd roaring. I reckoned that meant that Sam Crawford's adversary was sorry he'd come to the party.

We went up the wide hotel steps and through the brass-and-glass doors. This time the doorman didn't try and stop me.

We halted just inside the lobby and stood for a moment looking around. Almost as if my eyes had been drawn there I looked toward the elevators. There she stood, the auburn-haired lady I had danced with. She was wearing some sort of sleek, metallic-looking dress. I had not really seen her figure before. Now I did and it made me catch my breath. If anything, she was more enticing in the bright lights of the lobby than she had been in the dim glow of the supper club.

It was a little before ten o'clock in the evening and I assumed she was heading upstairs to her room. But it was still early for a woman like her to be calling it a night. If I hurried I might catch her before the elevator came, and invite her for a drink and a dance. God knows I looked dashing enough in my polo outfit that she might think I was some rich nabob just coming in from the fleshpots of town. Dennis hadn't seen her and I was about to take a step in her direction when an elevator door opened and she stepped inside. As she did she turned and faced in my direction. I looked into her eyes and slowly raised one hand. Even at the distance I thought she recognized me. She raised her hand slightly and smiled. Then the elevator door closed and she was gone. Dennis said, "Say, wasn't that that lady from the night before?"

I said I didn't know what he was talking about.

"Aw, you know the one. The lady you danced with. Real good-looking."

"Let's go and get a drink. And you better get your mind on the oil business. You got to see Teddy Atlas tomorrow. Remember?"

The lobby bar was doing a brisk business and, while we waited for a table, I thought about the woman and felt a vague sense of disappointment. She might have been very willing to go to the supper club and have a dance or two. It had been good chance to have seen her like that. *Bon chance,* as the French said. But the whole idea was silly of me. I had told Dennis that meeting the woman and dancing with her hadn't been real, it had been a dream. You didn't go from being a day laborer one night to dancing with someone like her the next. More than likely I'd never see her again and, if I did, it wouldn't mean anything.

We got a table and ordered a drink. I said, to Dennis, "You better get your bargaining cap on. I got a feeling Teddy Atlas is about as tough as that fighter of his."

Dennis spread his hand. "A hole in the ground don't bargain. You never know what is down there. Ask for money to get through granite and hope for limestone. That's the way the oil business works."

"You like Teddy Atlas for a partner?"

Dennis shrugged.

I was sleepy. Oddly enough, I was more tired of a night when I hadn't been doing anything all day than when I'd been doing hard physical labor. I think the strain of hoping things worked out for Dennis was what did it. I said, "I still think you are going to have Teddy Atlas in your back pocket if he goes in with you."

"That is where you are wrong. Or that is where you ain't got no experience. Atlas is the kind of man who will forget the oil well as soon as the papers are signed. Next time it crosses his mind will be when I come in to tell him we've made a well or drilled a duster. I know who is a plunger and who ain't. No, I'll be comfortable with Mr. Atlas."

The waiter brought us our drinks. I took a sip and then said, "Dennis, I can't shake the feeling that you are willing to drill out in west Texas just because you want to drill. Hell, you've never even seen the country. It's awful. Hot as hell in the summer and freezing in the winter. No water, no trees, no grass, damn near no people. I think if I had two hundred thousand acres on the moon you'd be willing to drill there."

He hunched forward across the table toward me and his voice took on an earnest tone. He said, "Willis, it's the chance to discover a new field. A *field*! Don't you understand? It can make a man immortal. Forget all the money, just think what it would be to hit a new field, a new pool of oil. Hell, people would come from all over, towns would rise, there'd be new industry. I don't want to drill an oil well, I want to get famous!"

He looked so sincere I had to smile. I said, "Well, you've got Mr. Atlas to get through first before you tackle my land. He's already famous. He's got the next world-champion heavyweight. He might not have your same need to drill."

He gave me a wise look. "I know my man. We'd have done the deal tonight except he wanted to celebrate about his fighter. He'll come through, all right. I reckon an easy hundred fifty thousand dollars for the drilling, with me getting a one-eighth royalty, and at least twenty-five thousand to move the rig and get set up. You watch, we'll be going first-class, my young friend. If there was ever a match, it is your land in west Texas and Teddy Atlas. He's a man likes a challenge."

I was sitting in the room when Dennis came in about a half hour before noon. He just walked in with his face down around his ankles, and bottomed out in a chair and stared out the window.

It was clear he was not in a jubilant mood. He also looked as if he wasn't going to talk. I figured I'd have to get him started. I said, "I take it he backed out of the deal."

Without taking his eyes off the window he gave his head a slow shake from side to side. "Nooo," he said slowly, "he didn't back out. Not altogether. He broke my heart, but I reckon that's my own fault." He looked over at me. "It don't pay, Willis, to count your chickens before they hatch or your oil wells before you drill 'em."

"You ain't making a hell of a lot of sense, Dennis. You look like your last milk cow died but you say he didn't back out. What the hell is going on?"

"That's another thing you don't want to count. If you got a fighter in a ten-round bout, you don't want to declare him the winner in the sixth round and get up and leave."

"What has the fighter got to do with it?"

Dennis got up suddenly. He said, violently for him, cutting his hand through the air, "Everything! Every blessed damn thing! That so-and-so Crawford had that other pugilist beat all to hell. Only thing holding him up was the starch in his drawers. Then Crawford has to get cute."

"What happened?"

"What happened?" Dennis took a step toward me and jabbed out his stubby forefinger. "I'll tell you what happened. The son of a bitch lost! That's what happened."

I was startled. If ever a fight was decided, that one last night had been and by the second round. "Crawford lost? How?"

Dennis put on a very sour face. He said, "By acting like a damn fool, that's how. Crawford went to playing around, mugging for the crowd, cutting up little didoes, dropping his hands to his side and daring his opponent to hit him." He stopped and looked sadly out the window. "Well, he did."

"What?"

"Hit him—Crawford. He had his gloves down and he went and looked out at the crowd to make sure they could see how cute he was and that other boy reached way back yonder and hit him a lick that put him down to stay. And it was a guess if the other fighter was going to make it to a neutral corner. That last swing had nearly done him in. At least that's the way the manager told it to me. He was pretty bitter about the whole thing."

"The guy in the bowler hat? The little skinny guy?"

"Yeah. As you can imagine, Mr. Atlas didn't want to talk none about the fight or about his fighter."

"How about his interfering with the manager and handling the fighter himself?"

Dennis got that sour look on his face again. "We didn't get into that."

I leaned back in my chair and put my hands behind my head. "It appears to me that you are not the happiest of men. But yet you tell me that Teddy Atlas didn't back out on your deal."

He turned back to the window and grimaced. "No, but he cut the heart out of it." If it had been another man he'd have added, *Damn him!*—but not Dennis. "That durn fighter had to get cute and get hisself knocked out and lose the fight. It put Mr. Atlas in the most god-awful mood. He was just plain irritated and was taking it out on everyone around him. He even ate that manager out for letting him, Mr. Atlas, get up and get in the way when he had no business being there."

"I'm amazed you come away with a deal."

"I durn near didn't. He got to cutting up at me pretty sharp and I said to him he had me confused with someone else. I told him I was the man that drilled oil wells and my oil well hadn't gotten knocked out. I said I was sorry about his fighter but I'd understood that we had a deal and I'd come over, like he'd told me the night before, to work out the details."

"Good for you, Dennis."

"And I said I didn't see where the one mishap had aught to do with our business."

"What'd he say to that? He looks like a man with a short fuse. Did that set him off?"

"No, just the opposite. He calmed down right quick and said I was right. Said all we had to do was work out the details and get the contracts drawn up."

I clapped my hands. "Then you ought to be ready to celebrate."

He looked gloomy. "Not quite. He cut our deal practically in half."

"What? He's not going in for four test wells?"

"Oh, yeah. He'll go for four wells. Or five or a dozen. Long as I do it on seventy thousand. And fifty-five thousand on the balance."

"That's no good," I said. "Not considering where we're talking about. Will he pay for moving your equipment and getting you set up?"

He shook his head again mournfully. "No. Nothing more."

"Then you'll have to take in some more partners. Butler and Grimes, maybe. I know they ain't your first choice, but—"

"Can't be done. Mr. Atlas is to be the sole backer. He won't put his money in with anyone else. Says it makes things too crowded. I think he likes to be the lone wolf. Don't want to share."

"What are you going to do?"

He shrugged. "Drill. That's what I do. I drill for oil."

"But you said you wouldn't take a deal unless it allowed you to drill four wells so you could give the field a good test."

He looked over at me. "When you can't get what you want, you got to want what you can get."

CHAPTER
5

I WAS considerably worried about the start that Dennis and Teddy Atlas had made together. I didn't know anything about the oil business, or what was customary, but I figured it was like any other endeavor—if you made an agreement you were supposed to stick to it. And it appeared to me that Mr. Atlas was changing the deal before the water got hot, much less the coffee made. And it appeared to me that he was doing it in a childish fashion; his fighter had lost so he was taking it out on Dennis. I couldn't see how that kind of attitude was going to make for a very good partnership. Dennis was as capable a man as I knew at certain matters, but handling people wasn't one of them, especially people of Mr. Atlas's ilk. I lay awake that night after Dennis had told me the deal, worrying about him. Even though I'd said I wanted no part of drilling an oil well, and no part of west Texas, I couldn't help remembering how Dennis had looked after me in France. I could almost say I owed my life to his hands and brains, the hands and brains that had kept my airplanes in top condition. Could I let him down now? Didn't he need me now, if for no other reason than that I knew the country and the lay of the land and he didn't? And couldn't I help him with Mr. Atlas, if it should become necessary?

I had to answer yes to those questions I was asking myself. Dennis thought Mr. Atlas was simply going to hand him the money, short money at that, and walk away. I didn't think so. I'd seen how Mr. Atlas kept his hands off his fighter. What he wanted with a manager was anybody's guess since he hadn't let him do his job. I had the uneasy feeling he might set up to do Dennis the same way. But what I hoped to do to prevent that happening in Dennis's case was open to guesswork. But I did know that I'd inherited several traits from my daddy, and one of them was the ability to talk to people in such a way that they would become agreeable to the way you wanted matters handled. If Atlas was to come to the drill site to take over, I might be of some help to Dennis. I'd also be in deep west Texas with no desire to be there. The only way I could see my life being more barren was to be on that two hundred thousand acres of dry hell. Did I owe Dennis that much?

He more or less took the guess out of it the next morning at breakfast. He said, looking down at his plate, "Lieutenant, I ain't got no right nor want to call upon you for a big favor. I . . ." He let his voice trail off.

"What is it, Dennis?"

He coughed a dry, nervous kind of cough. He said, "Well, without hemming and hawing around about it, Mr. Atlas has done put me in a kind of position. And it kind of involves you. I know you said you didn't want no part of the oil business and didn't have no want-to about going to deep west Texas, but . . ."

He did quite a bit of hemming and hawing before he finally got down to what he had to say. I didn't blame him. He was taking enough for granted to build a mountain. He said, "See, Mr. Atlas has got this idea that it would be nice if he had an airplane out yonder in west Texas. A plane and a pilot. See, he just kind of got it in his head that you would be going along and helping out. He's taken quite a fancy to you, just like I told you he would. Thinks you are quite a gent. So naturally he figured you'd be his pilot, you already being there and all."

"I would, huh?"

Dennis had his head down, not looking at me. "Yeah, you know how it is."

"Yeah. Oh, yes. I know how it is."

He lifted his eyes and gave me a quick look. I guessed he didn't care for what he saw because he dropped his eyes back down. He said, "You ain't got to make this no harder than it has to be, Willis. It was Atlas's idea, you being the pilot. In fact, the only thing he'd allow me any extra money on was the plane."

"The plane?"

He nodded. "Yeah. He wants you to buy an airplane and we'll ship it out there on the same train with the rig. Ought to be some planes for sale in Houston. Big town like that got a airport. Ought to be able to pick up something."

I leaned back and looked at him. "What does he want a plane for? To chase buzzards?"

Dennis shrugged. "He's got some kind of idea he can fly around and look the terrain over and figure where the best place is to drill."

I laughed, but without much humor. "So he's starting to tell you your business already."

He said, a little grate in his voice, "I can straighten it out later. But right now I got to have the money. You can't drill without the money. And I ain't like you, I ain't empty and I care. I care about my work. I got something I want to do." He looked at me again. "I wish you wouldn't make me ask you. Hell, just go and come right back. Make him think you are part of the deal. I'll find another pilot. Hell, they're a dime—" He stopped.

I laughed again. "Don't spare my feelings, Dennis. I know they are a dime a dozen. But you don't want me to make you ask me to go along. Is that the ticket?"

"I know you don't want to go."

"But if I can't get what I want, I need to want what you get. Is that the way it goes?"

"Aw, hell, Willis." He got up and walked over to the table and poured himself a drink. "Just forget it."

I didn't know why I was tormenting him. I'd known from the night before that I was going. I said, "Okay. Why not? Let's get it off the ground."

He said, "Well, they is a few legal steps before we are ready to fire. Atlas is having some agreements drawn up between the principal folks, which is you and me and him."

"I never have quite known—what does he get out of this?"

Dennis smiled slightly. "You and I each get an eighth. You for your land and me as the drilling contractor. Mr. Atlas gets the rest."

I blinked. "I must say, he does himself mighty handsome. Just the three-quarters of the pie? Is that all he takes?"

"It seems like a lot, especially when you are going wildcatting. The odds are that all we are going to strike is dust. In that case it doesn't matter who owns how much of how much. And he's the one risking the money. He'd have a better gamble at the racetrack."

"Then why is he doing it?"

Dennis shrugged. "That question gets asked a lot. I guess because there's a lot of men who want to be John D. Rockefeller. Hell, I don't know, Willis. I'm just glad there are men like Teddy Atlas who are willing to take the chance. If there weren't, we'd all still be riding mules and you'd never have gotten off the ground. Oil makes gasoline, and that makes the world go round. It also gives me a job."

I looked at the far wall, thinking about some things my daddy had said. "Maybe we'd all be better off. Maybe not so comfortable, but more content."

Dennis cocked his head at me. He was wearing a salt-and-pepper suit that was a little too tight for his expanding bulk. "What are you talking about?"

"Maybe we'd all be better off still riding mules. Who knows where all this so-called progress is going to take us? I bet we'd have killed a hell of a lot less men in the war if there hadn't been any gasoline."

"You are a strange duck, Willis. Was you this way in France? I can't remember. Well, you can't fight progress so you might as well not try. Besides, without gasoline, there'd have been a hell of a lot more dead mules in the war. Now, you better put you on a shirt that will accommodate a necktie. We are due over to the lawyer's office at half past three this afternoon."

I started to get up, but then I stopped. I said, "Dennis you made the appointment before you talked to me. How'd you know I'd go along?"

He was silent for a couple of seconds. "I was hoping, Willis. Just hoping and praying."

I chuckled. "Praying, huh? You reckon that's what done the trick on me?"

He reddened slightly. "All I know is that you are going, for which I am much obliged."

"Dennis, could it be that I'm going simply because I didn't have anything better to do and all the praying in the world didn't have an ounce to do with it?"

"It can be anything you want it to be. You and I ain't got that much say about it anyway. Now you better get to stepping or none of us will be going anywhere."

I saw my dancing partner later on that afternoon. My business at the lawyer's had taken only a few moments. I'd signed the necessary papers and left Dennis and Mr. Atlas to the rest of it while I'd gone back to the hotel. I'd gone into the lobby bar and there she'd been, sitting at a small table against the wall, looking just as cool and beautiful as she had the night we danced. In other days a woman would no more have thought of going alone into a bar then she'd have ridden a cow down the street. But these were different days and different women. I'd even seen a few, in our nightlife around Galveston, smoking cigars. And looking quite pleased about it. Generally I was against that kind of feminism, the kind that got in your face and dared you to make something out of it. I called it "the chip-on-the-shoulder approach," but in the case of the beautiful lady I was very glad indeed to see her sitting alone in a bar in the middle of the afternoon. Without thinking about it and without much hesitation I made my way over to her table, racking my brain for her name as I went. It had been something that started with a G, but I couldn't think of it for the life of me. But who remembers every detail of a dream?

Yet here sat that dream and I was about to make a fool of myself. I arrived at her table and smiled. She looked up with nothing in her face. For a long heartbeat I thought she wasn't going to recognize me. Admittedly I was dressed different. I was wearing the riding boots that Dennis had bought and my aviator's jodphurs and a white shirt opened at the collar. All I needed to complete the picture of a hero just returned from battle was a silk scarf and a leather helmet complete with goggles.

But then recognition came into her eyes and she smiled. "Oh, hello," she said. "I almost didn't recognize you in those clothes. Have you been playing polo?"

It made me laugh. I said, "No, I'm dressed as an aviation hero this afternoon. But I can see the similarity to someone taking a rest between chukkers, or whatever they are called. The costume is purely for business reasons. My partner is using me to impress an investor."

She looked amused. "He must be easily impressed."

"That's what I thought," I said. I made a motion with my hand toward the empty seat across from her. "May I join you? Or are you—"

"No, no," she said, "I'm not waiting on anyone. Please do. Sit down. I'm only waiting for them to make my luggage ready."

My heart sank. "You're leaving?"

She nodded. "Yes, on the six o'clock train."

I could see by the wall clock that it was about four-thirty. I said, "Well, that will at least give us time for a drink together."

She shrugged and held up her half-empty glass. "I'm only drinking seltzer water. Not very exciting."

My mind was racing. I said, "But we can do better than that. How about we have a bottle of champagne to celebrate our almost meeting?"

Her gray, green-flecked eyes looked amused and then she shrugged. "Why not? Why not indeed."

I said, putting out my hand, "By the way, in case you've forgotten, my name is Willis, Willis Young."

She smiled again. She had such beautiful creamy skin that went so well with her soft, auburn hair. Her lip rouge, all her makeup, was subdued. And, there was really no need for what makeup she was wearing. But I could see what I hadn't realized during the evening we'd danced; she was older than I'd thought. Not that she was old—even in my young eyes—it was just that she wasn't a girl, I guessed her to be somewhere around thirty. It made her that much more desirable in my eyes. She had a certain something in her movements and in her speech and in her eyes and the way she moved her hands. She was wearing a lightweight gray outfit that permitted her coloring to express itself to its best advantage.

She said, "I think it is you who have forgotten my name." She looked amused. "But I won't torment you. It's Genevieve."

Then we both laughed and the waiter came and I ordered a bottle of Cliquot and hoped I could put it on Dennis's room because I still only had about four dollars in my pocket and the champagne was going to be a good deal more than that.

I didn't let that stop me from enjoying that first glass with her. I didn't much care for champagne, but it had been the first thing that had popped into my head, and now it seemed appropriate. She wanted to toast to poetry with that first glassful, and I to luck. We ended up by compromising on Irving Berlin because we both liked his music very much. She said, "He's going to have a revue in New York. On Broadway. Why don't we go?" Her eyes danced, but I halfway thought she was serious. Even the notion of doing something like that with such a woman made my heart tug. I said, ruefully, "I wish I could. Unfortunately, I'm going the other way. To west Texas. Got a date with an oil rig out there."

She looked startled. "Are you in the oil business too?"

"No, just helping out a friend. But you said, 'too.' Who did you mean by that?"

Her eyes lost their spark. She looked away. She said, "Oh, no one in particular." She shook her head. "I don't know why I said that."

I looked down at her left hand. There was a pale band of skin where a ring might have been. It was clearly visible against the tan of her hand. I said, gently, "May I ask you something that is absolutely none of my business? The odds are that I will never see you again and

I don't want to spend the rest of my life tormenting myself about the questions I didn't ask the mystery woman. May I do that? May I ask questions that are absolutely none of my business?"

She looked at me for no more than a split second. I was very conscious that it was quiet. The lobby bar was a small, rectangular alcove just off the main part of the lobby, right before you entered the restaurant. The real bar was at the end of the lobby floor and gave off to a vista of the waves coming in from the Gulf. The main bar was for people settling down for a good time, several drinks and maybe a dance or two to the little combo that played in the afternoon. The lobby bar was for people who wanted a drink or who wanted a quiet place to sit. I waited in the quiet for her answer. There had to be a reason why a woman like her was alone. If she'd have been mine I wouldn't have let her wander around alone.

She said, bluntly, "I'm in the process of a divorce. I came down here for a few weeks while my ex-husband gets his things out of the house and smooths off all the jagged edges you get with a thing like a divorce." She gave a throaty little laugh, "He's very good at that, my ex-husband. Filing off rough edges. But it does make matters dull if carried to extremes, don't you think so, Mr. Young?"

I didn't know what to say. Her frankness had taken me off-guard. What do you say to a woman who is getting divorced? "Hooray"? *Congratulations. You're well out of it.* Divorce was a failure. Even I knew that. I finally said something about being sorry to hear of it.

She took a sip of her champagne. "Don't be, Mr. Young. And you are, aren't you?"

"What?"

"Young. In age."

I pushed back a little from the table and glanced over at the waiter who was standing by with a towel folded over his arm. I said, "That all depends on how you look at it. Do you know anything about airplane engines?"

She looked puzzled and shook her head. "Of course not."

"Sometimes you can get in a tight spot in the air and have to pour the throttle to an engine. It causes you to overrev the engine, run up the revolutions higher than the engine is built to stand. If you have to do that a few times you can make that engine old before its time. The paint might still be bright and new on the outside of the metal but, inside, that engine has aged. Do you understand what I mean?"

She had a beautiful soft smile and now she put it on. She said, "And are you like that engine, Mr. Young?"

I said, "It's not the years you've lived, but how you've lived them, Mrs. . . . ."

I stopped because I realized I didn't know her last name and I didn't feel comfortable calling her Genevieve. I looked at her questioningly.

She sighed. "I haven't really given it much thought. His name was Maxwell and I registered at the hotel under that name, but now that the divorce is final I suppose it's not appropriate." She frowned, putting the slightest furrow in her forehead. "And I've never really cared for my maiden name, my family name. It sounds so, so pretentious. Perhaps I'll just call myself something like Smith until I can come up with something I really enjoy. Something that fits."

She fascinated me. Everything about her fascinated me, and not just her abundant beauty. But I said, "Can you do that? Pick your own name? Is that legal?"

She turned her level gaze on me. "But it wasn't names we were speaking of, Mr. Young. It was age. Were you saying that you were like that airplane engine—old before your time?"

I thought a moment. I didn't want to talk about the war and I didn't want to get into my adventurers as a knockabout bum. Finally I nodded slowly. "Yes, I think so. I think perhaps you are older than me in years, but I may be as old, if not older, in other ways."

She gave me her soft smile. "And how did you get to be so old, Mr. Young? Were you in the war?"

I nodded, but without much enthusiasm. "Yes."

"You were a pilot but you'd rather not talk about it. Is that correct?"

I nodded again. "Yes, Mrs. Smith, you have that part right." I smiled. "Do you want to talk about your divorce?"

She laughed out loud. "Touché."

"I'm afraid I've forgotten my French. Deliberately."

"But now you are to be an oil man."

I shook my head. "No, and no again. I am allowing a friend to drill on some land I own. Though how he expects to find anything besides rocks and rattlesnakes is beyond me."

She sipped at her champagne, eyeing me over the rim of her glass. "You never did say how old you are, Mr. Young."

I thought of telling her the truth and then I decided to lie. If she could call herself Mrs. Smith I could play fast and loose with the truth. "I'm almost twenty-eight," I said.

It made her give that throaty chuckle again. "Yes, of course you are."

"Why did you get divorced?"

"That's none of your business."

"Of course it is. I am greatly attracted to you and I have every right to know what kind of person I'm getting mixed up with."

She frowned at her champagne glass which was almost empty. "I swear," she said, "I must be getting tipsy on this stuff. I thought I heard you say you were getting 'mixed up' with me. We've had one dance and one drink. That hardly constitutes a liaison of any kind and certainly couldn't be so vulgarly described as being *mixed up* together. Heavens!"

She made me feel good with the cool way she said things. "All right. Without the 'mixed up.' Why are you divorced?"

She took a drink of champagne and set her empty glass down on the table. The waiter instantly appeared and refilled it from the bottle in the ice bucket. When he was gone she said, "Because he was in the oil business. You see? That's why it's no good you lying about your age. We are doomed no matter what your age because you are in the oil business."

I saw that it was a hopeless cause to convince her I was not in the oil business. I said, "Where do you live? Not west Texas by any chance?"

"Not while I am able to protest." She pushed her chair back from the table. "It's been delightful, Mr. Young, but I really must go. I've got that train to catch."

I indicated her almost-full glass. "But you haven't finished your champagne."

She smiled. "And I'm not going to, either."

"Won't you tell me where you live?"

She shrugged and reached for her purse. "I suppose Houston. My husband, my ex-husband, was good enough to give me the house. And since it is quite nice and I don't have another, then that is where I'll live." She stood up. "I've enjoyed myself."

I stood up. I was taller than her, it seemed, than when we'd danced. "But how will I find you? Look in the city directory under Smith?"

She smiled and opened her purse. She took out a small white card and passed it to me. "Now I must go." She put out her hand and I took it in a kind of limp, tender handshake. "Good luck, Mr. Young. If that is really your age."

"And the same to you, Mrs. Smith. If that is really your name."

We both laughed and then she disengaged her hand and walked away. I watched her trim figure for a few seconds and then I sat back down. I was going to finish the champagne. At such prices it was necessary. I looked at the card she'd given me. It had obviously been printed while she was still married since it referred to her as "Mrs. Genevieve Maxwell." But it gave a street address and a telephone number. If it was correct, finding her in Houston wasn't going to be any chore. Though I had to admit to myself a grave misgiving as to whether she wanted me to find her. Her card was embossed and she looked about the same, certainly her clothes and the way she was made-up. She'd been used to money. I didn't have any money and was not likely to get any on some oil-drilling scheme.

I finished the champagne, signed the ticket with Dennis's room number, and went on up to see if he had returned. The place was empty and I took a seat in front of the window and stared out at the Gulf. I was just in time to see Genevieve being helped into a cab along with a mountain of luggage. Hell, I couldn't afford to keep the lady in suitcases, let alone what went in them. About the only place I could see myself as being in the picture was that I wasn't in the oil business. Seems her ex-husband had been. Of course I didn't know if that was how he'd come to be her ex, but it certainly seemed an occupation to avoid if you wanted to make time with the lady.

Not that I expected to. As I'd told Dennis, she was just part of the dream.

We took the one-o'clock train the next day, riding in the chair cars since it was only about a two-hour trip to Houston. Dennis had a big leather wallet that he carried in the inside pocket of his suit coat. In it he had several checks from Teddy Atlas and a copy of their contract. He'd shown me the lot before we'd left the hotel. He had one check for forty-five thousand dollars. That was supposed to get him rigged up to drill the first well. He'd grumbled that it was about ten thousand dollars short if he had to go as far as two thousand feet and ran into any hard rock. The other two checks were for twelve thousand five hundred dollars each and were postdated two and four weeks into the future. They were to be for future wells.

I'd mentioned the way the two other checks had been postdated in advance. "Hell," I'd said, "he can back out on those in a second. Stop payment. Don't seem like he trusts you overmuch, Dennis."

"Don't nobody much trust anybody in the oil business. Place you want to protect is your back."

It made me think of Genevieve and her ex-husband. Maybe he'd brought home the tactics of the oil fields to his marriage.

But Atlas had relented slightly. He'd given Dennis an additional five thousand dollars to ship his equipment and to buy what additional supplies and apparatus he was going to need. He was pretty sure he could use about ten more stands of casing, the big pipe that went outside the drill stem. First you drilled down a ways, then you came out of the hole and set your casing. After that you ran your drill bit and your drill pipe down inside the casing. If you didn't have that casing holding the hole open, it would collapse.

And, figuring to run into hard rock, Dennis wanted to take plenty of drill bits. "Granite or country rock will chew them up like the blazes," he said. "We don't want to be a thousand miles from nowhere and out of drill bits. We got to figure out everything we are going to need and take it with us from Houston."

Houston, I had discovered, was the center of the oil industry for the Southwest. Most of the big companies had their head offices there. It was a natural condition since Houston was the nearest big town to most of the early oil activity. As a result, Houston was where you went if you needed anything in the oil line, either men or materials. Teddy Atlas had a home and an office there. Of course, he also had others in New York City, Lexington, Kentucky, and New Orleans. Besides trying to develop the heavyweight champion of the world, he also had racehorses, and was said to own a small piece of the St. Louis Browns baseball team. And that was not counting his interest in the wildcat oil business. He struck me as a man who liked to gamble.

When we were about halfway to Houston, Dennis got to thinking out loud. He said, "Far as hired hands go, the first thing I got to find me is a good fireman. He is damned near as important as the driller, but, since I'll be the driller myself, that's taken care of. We got to take a fireman with us. They is other jobs on the drilling rig that can be taught to the locals, but a fireman ain't one of them."

I was mystified. I was seeing a man in a fireman's red hat with a hose in his hands and a burning building in the picture. I said, "What the hell do you need with a fireman? We going to have a fire?"

Dennis laughed with good humor. He said, "Son, a fireman around a steam-driven oil rig tends to the boilers. He keeps the right amount of steam up. Too little and you ain't got the power—too much and, why, BOOM!" He waved his hands in the air causing several passengers to look around at him.

"He tends the boilers?"

"Yes. Keeps them stoked, keeps the water level right. What'd you think he did? Watches his gauges. A good fireman can stay ten minutes ahead of a boiler. Knows when it is rising too fast even before the boiler does."

"Look here, what do you plan to burn in those boilers?"

He shrugged. "I don't know. I doubt if we'll be able to lay our hands on much coal. I reckon how we'll cut down a bunch of trees and fire them with wood. It ain't as good, but I've made do before."

I rolled my eyes. "Dennis, they put trees in deep west Texas in museums."

He stared back at me for a half a moment. "You are not going to tell me there's not any trees."

"No, nor water to boil, either. I already told you all this. You didn't listen."

"No water?" He looked disbelieving. "I don't mean piped-in water delivered right to the well. I just mean water: a pond, a river, a good-sized creek."

I looked out the window at the landscape hurrying by. It was coastal plains with a lot of salt grass and trees permanently leaning away from a constant onshore breeze. "No, Dennis, no water. Look, you lived in Oklahoma. Didn't you ever see any badlands?"

"They is trees all over Oklahoma." He gave me an unhappy expression. "How the hell you think the place got settled? How you think it got to be a state? How *did* Texas get to be a state, with no water?"

There were a few cattle grazing on the waist-deep grass. "We got in the Union before they got firm on the water rule."

Dennis said, "You may make your jokes if you want, but you can't drill for oil without water." He looked very disturbed.

"Dennis, I don't know how many times I told you how desolate the country is. You didn't listen. But I guess you can get water. There are several towns in the area, and they have to have wells or some source. I imagine you can get water hauled, though I'd hate to think what it would cost. And, as well as I remember, the railroad is pretty near. They have water tanks ever so often."

Dennis now looked considerably cheered-up. "Yes," he said, "and they also have stockpiles of cross-ties ever so often. A cross-tie will burn as good as coal."

I looked back out the window. Mr. Atlas hadn't given me any checks, even though he wanted me to buy an airplane and ship it to the well site. He'd even thought of having me fly it out to west Texas but I had assured him I wasn't about to try and make it across hundreds of miles of deserted badlands in a not-too-dependable plane. Planes needed gasoline and maintenance, and their pilots needed to know they weren't going to end up in the desert with no water and no one knowing where they were.

I was to locate an airplane while we were in Houston, negotiate a fair price, and then contact Mr. Atlas's Houston office. They'd handle the paying end. Mr. Atlas wasn't at all sure he'd be in Houston while we were still there—he had to take his fighter to New Orleans—but if he was, he wanted me to start his flying lessons. I had protested, in vain, that I was not an instructor pilot. It didn't matter to Mr. Atlas. He had decided I could give him lessons and that was that.

I was carrying Mrs. Smith's card in my shirt pocket, and I got it out and took another look. She lived on a street called River Oaks Drive. I knew Dennis was familiar with Houston and might know where the address was, so I asked him. He rolled his eyes like he always did when he was trying to make a point and said, "*Now* you are talking about high cotton, young man. Who you know lives on River Oaks Drive? That's big money. Is that Mr. Atlas's address? I got it around here somewhere but I forget what it is." He saw me holding Genevieve's card in my hand and said, "Is that Mr. Atlas's card?"

"No," I said. I quickly put the card back in my shirt pocket. Dennis never had asked me about charging a bottle of expensive French champagne to his account at the hotel. I guessed he figured I'd gotten homesick for the war.

The train pulled into Union Station in the middle of downtown Houston. We got off, hired us a porter with a cart, collected our bags, and then walked two blocks down the street and checked into the Ben Milam Hotel, which was nearly brand-new. It wasn't a fancy place like the Galvez in Galveston, but was straightforward and businesslike, just like the trade it catered to. Dennis said, "We'll see a lot of oilmen around the lobby. They damn near built this place for folks running back and forth between Houston and Spindletop. I ought to be able to pick up a crew here. Well, not a crew, because roughnecks don't stay in places like this. Little out of their price range. But I ought to be able to get a line on who is looking for work—though I'll probably have to pay top wages to get hired hands to go so blamed far. Why couldn't you have had that two hundred thousand acres close to Dallas or some such place? Hell, why not just right out of town?"

I didn't bother to answer him. If I'd've had two hundred thousand acres in that kind of real estate, I damn sure wouldn't have been messing around with the oil business.

I knew that a roughneck was someone who worked on a drilling rig. And I knew that a roustabout was a man who worked in the oil field, doing general work, but I didn't know why they were called such, nor did I know much more about the personnel involved in the scheme of things where the getting of oil was concerned. But I did have one question about the oil industry I wanted to ask Dennis. I waited until we'd got a room, got upstairs, paid off the porter, and were settling down with a bottle of whiskey to wash some of the train dust out of our throats.

When I thought the time was right, I asked Dennis if he knew anybody in the oil business named Maxwell. I said, "I don't have a first name and I don't know what he did, but I would imagine it was something big. Seemed well-off."

He gave me a frown. "Maxwell . . . Maxwell . . . Maxwell?" He stared down at the carpet for a second. "Well," he said finally, "a couple of names come to mind, but I couldn't say for sure without I knowed more. I knew a Donald. Well, not a Donald. Everybody called him Billy Don. Was a driller for the Liberty Hill bunch. Then I knew a J. B. Maxwell in Corsicana. He was a landman for Humble Oil. You remember, I told you what a landman did."

"Yes," I said, "but I don't think either one of those is my man."

He gave me a puzzled look. "Just where did you meet this here mystery Maxwell?—or hear of him?"

I didn't mind telling Dennis except I didn't want to answer a lot of questions. I said, "You remember that lady I danced with at the hotel that night?"

"The one you kept telling me I imagined?"

"I didn't tell you that. I said she was all part of a dream I was having, that she wasn't real. Except I saw her again. A couple of times. She's the one lives on River Oaks Drive."

"What do you mean, you 'saw her'? In the lobby? In the elevator?"

"Never mind that. Try and think of someone of substance named Maxwell."

He suddenly snapped his fingers. "It just come to me. They is a big shot works for Texaco named Maxwell. Douglas Maxwell, I think. I believe he's a field superintendent. Might even be a vice president."

"Texaco? That's a big company, right?"

He looked disgusted. "Yes, and it's just another way of saying John D. Rockefeller. Or Standard Oil."

"That's bad?"

"Hell, yes. Where you been? Standard Oil is the most monopolistic bunch of sons o' bitches in the world. When Spindletop blew in, everybody knew that Rockefeller would be down here taking control. So the legislature passed some antitrust laws that Standard couldn't hack. Except that John D. got around them by having Texaco formed by men from Texas, and they can't prove he's got a hand in it, but he does."

"What does Standard Oil do that is so bad?"

"They squeeze the little man. Oil right out of the ground ain't worth nothing. It's got to be refined, and Rockefeller owns all the refineries. You can drill all the oil you want, but you can't ship it or sell it unless you pay John D."

I said, "I know this is going to sound like me asking you in France if the enemy pilots are using real bullets, but is the oil business kind of a rough game? A little cutthroat?"

He gave me a brief look like I'd fell out of a tree. "You're right. Yeah, they are real bullets. I'd say the only practice for the oil business is to actually be in a war. Get shot at like you done. You ought to do a lot better than me. Hell, I'm a babe in the woods with the sharks swimming in these waters."

I thought of Genevieve. It would have been nice to think that she'd divorced her husband because she'd disapproved of his morals or his business practices. Somehow, I doubted that. I imagined it had, more

likely, something to do with staying out too late or working too much
or even being stingy with the household money. But it was good to
know that her husband had worked for what Dennis regarded as the
enemy. Not that any of it mattered to me. I couldn't guess when I'd
see her again. But I couldn't forget the cool, brief touch of her fingers
as she'd handed me her card.

Dennis had rented an automobile, a Dodge Brothers touring car. He
had to get around and get his equipment together and try and assemble
a crew. And I had to find a plane.

The second day we were in Houston I took the Dodge and set off,
with a set of directions written out for me by one of the desk clerks,
to find this River Oaks Drive and the house Genevieve lived in. I wasn't
going to see her, didn't even plan to slow down if I could find the
house, but I did want to see how she lived. I thought it would tell me
more about her.

It was farther out than I thought, some two or three miles from
downtown. I seemed to be getting almost into open country, and was
wondering if I'd made a mistake when all of a sudden I came upon a
big, bricked entrance that had the name RIVER OAKS spelled out in
wrought iron. Straight off I could see that it was a new development,
and a pretty swank one at that. The neighborhoods I'd been passing
through had been okay, but they'd showed the descending side of the
economic order. This River Oaks section was a different matter entirely.

It was a pattern I had noticed in other towns. A town grows into
a city and begins to decay around the edges as it gets bigger. But then
suddenly something comes along to put fresh blood in the place and
you find a brand-new circle of prosperity springing up a distance from
where the town started. Of course, the old parts had become run down
by then and it was like the new money wanted to put some distance
between themselves and the ones on the way down.

I turned in at the big, grand entrance and noted, by a street sign,
that I was on River Oaks Drive. Now it was only a question of finding

2110. I spotted a house with a number on it and saw I was in the 500 block. That meant, to me, that the street was going to be a long one, but presently little side streets commenced cutting in and the house numbers started jumping up. Before I knew it I was in the 1900 block. I slowed down and began having a good look. All the houses were big, most of them two-story affairs, and most of them brick. They were all set on good-sized lots, at least an acre or two, and were all well-tended. You could see the hand of the professional gardener at work, especially in the hedges and the trees. There were sycamores and birches and some breeds of oak trees that weren't native to that country. It told me that Genevieve's husband had been doing all right, but she hadn't hesitated to walk out on him. She wasn't a woman who cared all that much about money.

Except I was forgetting one thing. I didn't know if she'd left him, or the opposite. But she'd gotten the house. I was no expert, but I figured if a man done the divorcing, he had cause and the judge would lean his way when it came to a property settlement.

At least, that was the way I put it together. If he'd caught her out and had reason to sue for divorce, then she ought to take nothing except what she brought with her. That seemed the right and sensible thing to do.

I did not know why I was driving slowly along a road thinking like that. Hell, I knew waitresses in cafes I'd taken my meals in better than I knew this woman. It was a damn silly way to be thinking. And pretty forward on my part.

And then I saw her just ahead. She was standing in the yard of a two-story red brick house looking up at a live oak that was in full foliage. I was too far away to see her face, but there was no mistaking the lissome, willowy figure. She was dressed in a yellow frock with white lacing and was wearing white-and-brown medium-heeled pumps. Her hair was even more amber in the sunlight and it still fell to her shoulders in natural, cascading waves. I had seen bobbed hair and compressed breasts and rolled hose and skirts above the knee until I was sick of women trying to look like boys. Mrs. Smith, as she styled herself, looked like someone who was glad to be a woman. Her hair was natural and her breasts were free to express themselves, and where her hose ended was her business and the hem of her skirt was at a demure midcalf heighth. It left something to the imagination.

I didn't know what to do; whether to stop or to go on. She had her back to me and, probably, if I coasted on by, she'd never notice it was me.

But a great longing to see her was overcoming me. I did not know what kind of reception I might expect, but she had given me her card and invited me to drop in. Of course, she'd done that after several glasses of champagne, so it might not be considered a proper invitation in polite company.

I didn't see what I had to lose. All she could do was make it clear I was unwelcome and I could leave. And I'd be meeting her outside in her yard so it would be informal, to say the least. I didn't figure to pass up the opportunity. I took my foot off the accelerator and steered for the curb, pushing in the clutch as I did. I drew up just even with the walkway up to her house and switched off the engine. It was then she became aware of me. She turned slowly and looked my way. Her house faced west and she put up a hand to shield her eyes from the sun. I opened the car door and got out and started toward her. When I was some fifteen feet from her I said, "Hello. Willis Young, Mrs. Smith. Come to pay a call." She certainly looked good. It made me wish I wasn't going off to west Texas to fool around with oil-drilling. But if I stayed, I'd just be a day laborer courting a lady who was out of my social circle. I said, "It's good to see you again. I hope I didn't take you unawares or catch you at a bad time." I found myself wishing I had a hat or cap that I could doff.

CHAPTER

6

SHE TOOK her hand away from her eyes and looked at me, a faint smile playing around her lips. She said, "I must say, Mr. Young, this is quite a surprise. Didn't I just see you in Galveston yesterday?"

I stood awkwardly. I could tell her lawn had just been mown by the smell of the grass. I said, "Well, yes, but I thought I mentioned that we were coming to Houston today."

" 'We'?"

"Me and my partner." I looked past her at the house. From closer, it was even more imposing. "I told you he was an oil driller and we were going to drill on some land I've got out in west Texas. Deep west Texas."

Her face seemed to take on an expression of distaste. Or maybe it seemed that way to me since I'd decided why she'd left her husband. "Oh, yes. Now I remember. You told me you were in the oil business."

I shook my head violently back and forth. "No, ma'am. Not a bit of it. I ain't never been in the oil business in my life. Don't know anything about it and don't want to learn. I'm involved because I own the land and my friend needs a place to drill. If you've got to put me in a business, I guess you'd have to say that my most lengthy experience has been the flying business. I've been a pilot more than anything else and I'll be taking a plane to the west with me." Not being a complete fool I knew that there were still a few women attracted by the supposed thrills and glamour of flying and pilots. I didn't know if she was one, but I wasn't going to pass up the chance.

She gave me her faintly amused look again. "Well, I don't believe we have any airplanes around here, Mr. Young."

I gave a little laugh. It appeared the lady was going to have a little sport with me. I said, "I didn't come out this afternoon to do any flying, Mrs. Smith. Or is it Jones? I get confused."

She smiled fully. "Well, then, I must assume, since you are not flying, that you've come to pay me a call. Is that the business we are about here?"

For some reason it made me feel slightly embarrassed, like I was pursuing her. I certainly didn't want her thinking that. I said, "No, not actually. I was out driving and I saw the gate to your development and then your street that I had remembered from your card, and I turned on it and came along to see where you lived. I hadn't expected to see you."

"But yet here you are."

To me it sounded as if I were intruding and she was calling it to my attention. It made me even more uncomfortable. I took a step backward toward the street, still facing her but putting a little more distance between us. "Yes," I said, "here I am. I had no right to come calling without an invitation." I half turned toward the street and the Dodge.

She said, quickly, "But you had an invitation. I gave you my card in Galveston, at the Galvez."

I hesitated. "Yes, but I didn't have an appointment. I don't want to just be dropping in. You don't strike me as the casual, drop-in-on kind of lady."

"Oh, now don't be silly. I shouldn't have teased you. No, I'm glad to see you, Mr. Young. It's Willis, is it?"

I nodded.

"I had never before enjoyed that marvelous French champagne you ordered. I suppose you were in France during the war."

"How do you know I'm not a World traveler? How do you know I'm not rich? Why do you think the only way I could get to France would be to fight in the war?"

She looked at me and I stared back. She sighed. She said, "We've had one dance and one drink together and now we are being rude to one another."

"Rude? Who?"

"Us. You and I. I made it seem like you came hunting me up the first day back in Houston when you said you were just riding around. Then you took an innocent remark about France, that I was being some sort of snob, so you got sarcastic. Wouldn't you say that was rude?"

I halfway wanted to smile and I felt like she did, too, but I said, "I did come looking for you. But on the second day, not the first. And I was in France because of the war, but I didn't want to be reminded of it."

She lifted her upper lip and her painted mouth rose at the ends. She said, "Willis, I think you are sort of a hard case. Where did you get such a silly first name, anyway? It sounds very country."

I shrugged. "My daddy's name was Wilson and they wanted something close to that."

"Why didn't they just name you Wilson Junior?"

I gave her a grim look. "Probably because they knew I'd change it first chance I got."

"Oh, so it's like that. A rift between father and son. Listen, this is a fascinating conversation and I—"

"I was just leaving." I said quickly. I turned again for the street.

She gave an exasperated half shout, and slapped herself on the thigh with the flat of her hand. "No, damn it. You seem determined to leave. What'd you come all the way out here for?"

"It sounded like I was being shown the gate."

"I was going to ask if you'd like to come in the house and have some coffee or something. It would be better than standing out here talking under a tree."

I frowned. I was not sure of myself with this woman. I said, "You are inviting me in?"

"Are you troubled with poor hearing or are you being difficult and shy? Yes! Come in and we'll have a talk."

I shrugged. "All right."

Her maid served us coffee in what I took to be the front parlor. It was a big, airy, light room that seemed like her. Over some wide French doors were gauze curtains that moved and waved in the light breeze that was blowing in. There were a number of paintings on the wall and the ceiling was high, like they were in houses in Europe. She and I sat opposite each other on divan sofas with a low glass-topped table between us. The maid brought the silver coffee service in on a tray and then Genevieve did the honors.

I wasn't particularly interested in the coffee. Once breakfast was over I didn't see much benefit in having coffee. I suppose it was all right to discuss the news of the day over, or for something to warm you up on a cold winter's day, or maybe a drink to be shared by a couple of strangers in a train depot. But as a structure to build a social meeting around, and especially a social meeting between a man and a woman who might find romantic feelings, I thought it a damn poor substitute for a glass of cognac or a bottle of wine or, hell, even lemonade with a little bourbon in it.

But I dutifully told Genevieve that I took cream and one sugar. She fixed my cup and then handed it over, saucer and all. I was obliged to quickly set it down on the tabletop to keep it from spilling. I had picked up a slight hand tremor in the last days of the war and it hadn't gone away completely. Normally it didn't matter because I didn't ordinarily handle dainty china, especially in the company of a woman who made me more than just a little self-conscious. I had forgotten about it until I held the cup and saucer and heard the first telltale rattle of the porcelain. I set the whole affair down as quickly as I could, but she had noticed. She said, "What's the matter?" She was holding the silver coffeepot in her hand, about to pour her own cup, but she took the interval to look across at me.

"Nothing," I said.

"Was the cup too hot?"

"No. No, no."

"Don't you care for coffee?"

"It's fine. It was just so light, the cup and saucer, that it surprised me. I nearly dropped the whole thing."

She gave me another look, but finished pouring her coffee. She took hers black, which I had come to recognize as the sign of a sure coffee drinker. Ol' Wilson Young had been that way, though he liked a dollop of what he called "sweetening"—whiskey—in his.

I sat there wishing mightily for the same. A couple of shots of whiskey was the fastest cure I had found for the tremor. The hell of it was it always came at the most inconvenient times, most often when whiskey wasn't available.

She sipped at her coffee and watched me with those gray-green eyes of hers. "What's wrong? Something is. You deceive very poorly, Mr. Young, which is, I suppose an attribute."

To hell with it, I thought. I wasn't going to go on letting this girl make me feel uneasy. I wasn't the first to come out of aerial combat with a hand tremor. Some came out much worse. One of my squadron-mates had developed a horrible facial tic that pulled down his eye and half his face. Another had such a nervous stomach that he was liable to throw up nearly anytime. I held out my right hand so she could see the slight shakiness. "A little souvenir of the air wars. It's not much of a bother, except I fear my days of balancing china on my knee are over with for a while."

She suddenly looked embarrassed. "Oh, I'm so sorry. Is there anything I can do?" She put her cup on the table, out of sympathy with me.

I said, "A shot of brandy will usually do the trick. Or any kind of whiskey. My hand is not particular so long as it is alcohol."

She turned her head and called her maid. "Marie! Marie!"

When the maid had come with the brandy I took a good belt and felt it going to work. Just to be on the safe side, I poured some in my coffee.

Genevieve said, "Oh, that smells wonderful. I think I'll have some."

Then we both sat there, sipping and looking content. Genevieve declared that the brandy and coffee was a wonderful combination. It amused me. I doubted it was anything new to her, but she'd been flustered by my sudden revelation and she was trying to cover it up.

We went ahead, talking of the weather and the world economy and other pressing matters of personal interest to both of us. Presently she asked if I had seen a great deal of air combat. She said, "We saw some newsreels about it and it looked absolutely terrifying. Way up in the air like that."

"It was scary. But usually you were into it before you had time to think. After that you were on instinct. You got scared later." I held up my hand, which had stopped trembling. "That's when you picked up these little mementos, when you had time to think and remember the close calls. That's when the sweat popped out on your brow." She was being very personal and I wanted to encourage her because I planned to get very personal myself in a short while.

She said, "Were you ever wounded? I mean, besides your hand." She stopped and looked confused. "I don't mean you were wounded in your hand. Even though you were." She looked appealingly at me.

"I know what you mean. Yes. I was shot in the leg. In the calf of the leg. Nothing very serious. I think it kept me out of the air only three or four days. It missed the bone and just bored through flesh."

She shuddered. "You say that so matter-of-factly."

"It wasn't that important when you consider what could have happened." I paused. "Why did you divorce your husband?"

The question startled her. For a second she stared at me and I didn't think she was going to answer. Then she gave a rueful laugh. "I suppose I left myself open for that one."

I nodded. "Yes, you did."

"Then I'll have to answer honestly. I didn't divorce him, he divorced me."

That caught me off-balance. The man must have been out of his mind. I said, "You mean he asked for the divorce?"

She gave a little shrug. "It was more complicated than that. It's not something I want to discuss."

"No, but I would."

She gave me an amazed look. "*You'd* like to discuss it. And who are you?"

"Someone who is interested."

"Well, it's none of your business."

"I think it is."

"Why?"

I picked up my cup and drank off the last of the coffee-and-brandy mixture. I didn't look at her. I said, "Because I might be interested in you. I think that gives me the right to ask. Did it have anything to do with him being in the oil business?"

Her face had softened from its amazed and irritated expression. "Willis, I thank you for the compliment, but I'm not ready for anyone to be interested in me. Certainly I'm not ready to be interested in anyone. Not in the near future."

I was stubborn about the matter. I said, "Then just answer the question about his involvement in the oil business. Did that have a bearing on it—the divorce?"

She sighed. "It's so unfair for you to ask me like that. It's all mixed up with a lot of other matters, matters I'm not ready to go into right now."

"It's a simple question. I'm asking it because I'm closer to being in the oil business than I care to be. I know I said I was just connected through my land, but the oil driller is an old friend of mine."

She did not look happy. After thinking for a moment, she sighed and laid her head on her shoulder. It was easy with her slim, graceful neck. "Yes," she said, grudgingly, "I suppose you could say his profession contributed to the breakup. But I want to hasten to add that the oil business was just the fuse that lit the bomb. It wasn't the bomb itself."

"Away from home too much? Late hours?"

She gave me that amazed look again. "Mr. Young, why are you asking me all these questions? You're inquiring into areas I haven't talked about with my best friends, not even my parents."

I was uncomfortable, but I was dogged in my determination to find out what I could about Genevieve. In a few days I'd be gone and I might never see her again unless I made a hell of an effort and I wanted to be sure she was worth that effort. I said, "I am much taken with you. In fact, I am smitten."

She blinked and then she put her head back and laughed. "Smitten. Willis, they don't say 'smitten' anymore. Let me guess. I think it has been some time since you've been courting. Would that be right? Little out of practice with the ladies?"

I gave her a flat look and said, with just a tinge of sarcasm, "Yeah, pilots in France have a hell of a lot of trouble getting dates. Especially if they are American and got a lot of money. And then, back here in the States when you are barnstorming with a flying circus the girls just don't want no part of you. I'm sorry I told you straight-up about my feelings. Maybe you are not used to that. My daddy used to be a bank robber and he had this habit of going directly after what he wanted. I must have inherited some of his bad habit. I'm sorry."

"Wait!" she said, putting out her hand. "Don't get up." She pulled her hand back and ran it through her hair. "Now I'm the one who's sorry. You're right. I'm not used to such plain speaking. And I was only joking about you being out of the habit of girls. As good-looking as you are, I would imagine you have had to flee for your life on more than one occasion."

I said, gravely, "That's why I took up flying."

"Now who is being mean to who?"

"You still haven't answered my questions about your divorce."

She gave her head an annoyed little toss. "I'm not at all sure I want to answer your questions. I still don't think they are any of your business."

I poured a little more brandy in my cup but didn't bother with the coffee. I said, "I'm kind of doing this courting on the fly. In a few days I'll be gone for west Texas. I won't have any idea when I'll see you again. I don't want to make a big effort to find you and pick up where we left off if you aren't the kind of woman I want."

She gave a short chuckle. "Don't ever let anyone tell you that you speak in riddles. Not curious, you understand, but what secrets of my past would disqualify me for pursuit of your hand?"

Teddy Atlas's boxer hadn't sparred any more than we were. I said, "He's divorcing you."

"Divorced. Past tense. All over with."

"All right, divorced. Suppose he divorced you because he caught you running around with other men behind his back. I wouldn't want that kind of woman."

She looked like she was about to grab up something and heave it at my head. Instead she said, "Why, you sanctimonious little prig. Who the hell do you think you are talking to?"

It hurt, but I didn't let on. I said, "I'm none of those things. Would you want to marry a man who'd been running around on his first wife?"

She was good and angry. She said, "I'd like to think I'd be enough woman he wouldn't want to do that. How about you? Do you think you'd be man enough to hold a second wife's interest?"

"I don't have a history of marriage. In fact I don't have a history of being constant with one woman. That's what makes me so awkward in this kind of talk. I don't know what to say or what to ask or how to go about it."

She put her cup down. She'd been holding it tensely with both hands. She said, "I think I have already told you that I was not interested in becoming involved with anyone. It's too soon. Didn't you understand that?"

I nodded. "Yes, I understood. But I also understood it might not be a permanent situation. And if you ever come back on the market I wanted to be primed and ready to go. I wanted to know that you were what I was after."

She shook her head slowly and laughed. She said, "You are the damnedest man I think I have ever met. You are so solemn, so serious. And you're so young. You talk to me about being suitable to marry and you know very little about me. And I know even less about you.

Just now you popped out and said your father was a bank robber. You don't hear that every day."

I smiled stiffly. "I don't say it every day. Look, I've gotten off to a bad start here and I'll be going." I stood up. "But I would like to see you one more time before we leave."

"When would that be?"

"I don't really know. A week, I'd guess. I've got to get busy and buy an airplane so I can ship it out there on the train."

She got a mischievous look in her eyes. "Would you take me flying? I've always wanted to go."

"Sure."

"If you do, I'll tell you about my divorce."

I said, quickly, "That's not necessary. I got carried away with my myself." I smiled slightly. "It'll be a little while before I ask you to marry me."

"Now you're backing out."

I smiled again. "No, just backing toward the door."

"Where will you go now?"

"Back to the hotel. We're staying at the Ben Milam. Near the train depot."

"Where do you come from? Who are your people?"

"Down along the Mexican border. Town of Del Rio. My folks are staying in the interior of Mexico right now."

We were at the door. I reached out and turned the knob and pulled the heavy wooden door back. There was a screen, but it had been propped back. Houses like hers didn't really use screen doors. I stepped outside and then turned to face her. I said, "Thank you for the visit and the brandy. I made a damn fool out of myself, but it has happened before."

She leaned against the doorjamb and looked at me. She looked so cool and pretty I wanted to snatch her up and kiss every inch of skin I could reach. She said, "You can call me."

"I'd like that. And as soon as I get a plane I'll take you up. No kidding."

"That would be thrilling. Flying with an ace. Were you an ace?"

I turned down her walkway. "I'd better get along. Thank you again."

I had taken maybe four steps when she called out, "He didn't really divorce me. It was an arrangement. I wanted the divorce."

I turned back to face her, but I kept walking slowly toward the car. "Then why do it backwards?"

"It was better for his business. He said it would not seem so bad at Texaco."

"Why'd you want the divorce?"

She shrugged. "It wasn't a match. It never was. He was an older man and I suppose he seemed sophisticated. It seemed like a good idea at the time. I wasn't going anywhere."

I said, dryly, "You give all your important decisions so much thought?"

She stepped off the low, stone porch that led to her front door. She said, "At least I don't go around asking strangers why they got divorced."

I had come to the curb. I stepped down on the street. "I had to know if it had to do with the oil business. I told you. If it did I was going back to the hotel and tell my friend I couldn't go with him, that I didn't want to be in the oil business."

She said, "Oh, that's a lie. You weren't going to do any such thing."

I jerked my head in a gesture of annoyance. "I don't lie. Anybody who has ever known me knows I don't lie. I'm too damn proud to lie. And also, for your information, I ain't anything like the hick you think I am. I know I asked some questions that seemed pretty dumb this afternoon, but they were well thought-out. They got results, didn't they?" I reached out and opened the door of the car. I said, just standing there holding the door with one hand, "I might turn out to be as sophisticated as your ex-husband."

"Wait!" she said. She suddenly came rushing down the walkway from her house. She ran with a good, loose gait that seemed light and springy. Before I knew it she was beside me. She put both her arms around my neck and kissed me. I never moved. It was a good long kiss, maybe five seconds. Her lips were very soft and moist. I felt just the tip of her tongue caress mine.

And then she was running back up the walkway. Over her shoulder she called, "How do you like that, Mr. Sophisticated?"

"I like it fine," I called after her. "I wish I hadn't been so taken off-guard."

She paused at the door to her house. "Call me." Then she slipped inside and was gone. I was aware of the light and shadow of the sun shining down through the trees onto the street. It made an impact on me. I got in the car, started it, and drove away. That woman, I thought, was starting to have a powerful influence on me.

Dennis said, "You find an airplane?"

I shook my head. "Ain't going to be easy."

"I doubt they sell many out in that River Oaks area."

We were up in our room. I was sitting on my bed looking at a list of planes that might be available. I'd gotten it from an aero company out at Hobby Field, who made it their business to keep up with such matters. I didn't bother to glance up at him. He was so scared something was going to come along and queer his deal with Teddy Atlas that he was jumping at shadows. I said, "Dennis, you have been out of the airplane business for some time. Take my word for it, there ain't that many around. Airplanes are in short supply."

"Aw, hell. I don't believe that. Why, you couldn't walk, they were so thick over in France."

"That was over in France, and all of them planes were built in France or England or Germany. Damn few got turned out in the United States. All we had over here was the Jenny. For a trainer. And it was built in Canada."

He gave me a surprised look. "It was? I didn't know that."

"Yeah, by the Curtiss Company. They also made the engine, the Cyclone."

"Well, what is wrong with one of those?"

"Hell, Dennis, it was mostly the JN-4D model that got built and they are nearly all worn-out."

"I can't believe that some new airplanes haven't been built since the war. Good heavens, as popular as aviation is!"

"As popular—" I almost strangled. "If it was so damned popular, what was I doing digging ditches for a living? No." I shook my head. "No, no one has built any new airplanes since the war. The Army doesn't even want them. What little there is left of the Army."

He sat down on his bed, facing me, and rubbed his jaw. He needed a shave and his whiskers made a bristling sound. He said, "But you've just got to find a plane. Mr. Atlas is counting on it."

"Oh, I can buy a plane tomorrow, but I don't want to be out in west Texas with it breaking down every five minutes. I know you are a good mechanic, Dennis, but we'll have to take enough spare parts to damn near build another plane."

He looked worried. "What are you going to do?"

He was about to exasperate me. I didn't feel the same duty toward Teddy Atlas as he did. I said, "I'm going to find an airplane if I can, Dennis. But I'm not going to pick out just any old junker in that line."

"Ain't you still got some buddies in the airplane business?"

I laughed. "Yeah, but I'd never get close enough to them to ask anything. They see me coming, they'd take off, afraid I'd be looking for a flying job. Quit worrying, Dennis, I'll get it done. I got a line on a model JN-6H, which is the last off the factory. It's a much-improved airplane over the JN-4D. In fact, the one I hear can be bought is not much over a year old and ain't got more than a hundred hours on the engine, and that new Cyclone, I believe, is a five hundred–hour engine."

"Well, I wish you'd get high behind and tend to business. There'll be plenty of time for River Oaks when we get all set."

I gave him a warning look, but didn't say anything. Instead, I asked him how he was coming on his end. "You got quite a shopping list. You put a dent in it yet?"

"Listen," he said, looking eager, "how'd you like to be a derrick-man? I'm telling you, experienced roughnecks are scarce as hen's teeth right now. But you're young and strong and smart. I could show you the ropes in nothing flat. Give you something to do and make you feel more a part of the game."

I didn't really care to know, but I said, "What is a derrickman?"

"That's the feller up top of the rig that handles the stands of pipe as they come ready to be made up to go in the hole. He fetches up a stand where they are racked and works it into position so the hands on the drilling floor can get hold of it. 'Course, he don't actually have to manhandle the pipe himself. He's got a cable up there working off a draw-works. He gets a loop on the pipe and lets the machinery do the hard work."

I stood up and started to change clothes. I figured we would be going out, and I wanted some fresh duds. I said, "You mentioned the derrickman was in the top of the rig. Is that right?"

"Yeah. That be so. He's up there on a little platform. Of course, he wears a safety belt."

"Just how high is the top of the rig? You going to use the bathroom? I just decided I'd take a shower bath."

"No, you go right ahead. Well, top of the rig . . . Drilling floor is about eight or ten feet off the ground; derrick is about thirty feet high. Say, forty feet up there. Why?"

I laughed. "You don't want me, Dennis. I wouldn't go up there without a set of wings."

"What are you talking about?"

"I've got acrophobia. Or did you forget?"

"What the hell is that?"

"Fear of heights."

Now he laughed. "How in hell can a pilot have fear of heights? Hell, you've been fourteen thousand feet in the air. That's damn near three miles. Tell me another funny one."

"I'm not kidding, Dennis. You have no sensation of height seated in an airplane. Ain't no different than sitting in your own living room. But you couldn't get me up on a stepladder for no amount of money. When I was a kid, I climbed up on the barn roof, not knowing any better, and took one look down and froze. They liked to have never got me down."

"I think you are feeding me a line because you don't want to work."

I got the last of my clothes off and started for the bathroom. I said, "Listen, you can forget about getting me up in the air in anything that hasn't got two wings and a propeller. I get the clammy damps just thinking about standing forty feet in the air on some little platform. Hell, Dennis, forty feet is high as the roof of a two-story house." I stopped at the door to the bathroom and worked a towel around my neck. "What is this? Are you having trouble finding a crew? You told me experienced hands were crying for jobs."

He looked worried. "Well, they are." He paused and looked down at the floor. "Except out in west Texas. I need to find some good roughnecks that ain't never heard of the place. And even that don't help. Soon as I get a good man lined up who don't know nothing about west Texas, he goes to asking around and next thing I know, he comes and quits—quits before he's ever done a day's work."

"I'm in no hurry," I said. And I wasn't. I was no more eager to go to that barren country than any of the hired hands Dennis was trying to pay to make the trip.

He gave me a look. "I know *your* situation, mister. You'd be content to sit in Houston and do your courting out at River Oaks. But Mr. Atlas's money ain't going to last forever and I better be able to show some progress before he pops back into town."

I said, "I guess you are going to have to offer them combat pay like they done us in France."

"I got to do something," he said. He looked plenty worried. "It's bad enough to go off and drill in an unknown part of the country. I'd hate to do it with a green crew."

CHAPTER

7

I WAITED two days to call her, worrying all the time that I might be cutting it too thin. She had surprised me by suggesting we go to dinner at her country club. I knew what a country club was, but I was a good deal taken off-guard by her suggesting she was willing to show me off to her diamond-grade friends.

Dennis took it right in stride. He said, "Hell, you clean up real good. Why shouldn't you be put up with the best? I'd reckon she's trying to make herself look good. But for God's sake, don't order the French champagne. I ain't ever going to tell you what that cost at the hotel in Galveston, but I got an idea what they'll charge in that club for the ladies and gentlemen of the Houston gentry. That'll eat that C-note I gave you plumb up."

Sitting in the country club, I had the hundred dollars Dennis had given me and two remaining from the four I'd started out with in Galveston before I'd run across him. I had bought some new clothes, but I had bought them in a shop in the hotel and had charged them to my account. I was wearing my purchases. On the advice of the clerk I'd bought a pair of lightweight white flannel slacks and a blue blazer with brass buttons. I'd also bought another white dress shirt and a necktie with regimental stripes. I'd bought a pair of black dress shoes that shone like polished glass, and had just barely turned down a straw skimmer with red, white, and blue hatband.

Genevieve looked at me across the table, her head cocked at a critical angle. "You look pretty good," she said. "Those are new clothes."

You hate to get caught out like that, like you didn't have the proper attire to wear to such a swell place and had to go out and outfit yourself, but there it was. I made a little motion like it didn't amount to anything and said, lying at sixty miles a hour, "I needed some new evening-wear. We've been jumping around so much I've got clothes scattered from here to Beaumont."

She said, "You've got the kind of build that clothes hang right on. I bet you don't even have to have alterations."

I pulled at the waist of the white flannel pants. "They had to take this waist in."

"Douglas couldn't buy clothes off the rack. They couldn't be altered to fit him. All his clothes had to be tailor-made. He liked to pretend he did it out of a sense of style, but he didn't. To say that he was portly is being kind."

"Who is Douglas?" I was having a hard time keeping up with her.

She yawned daintily and touched her lips with her fingertips. "I'm sorry, I thought you knew. Douglas is my ex-husband. Douglas Maxwell."

"Oh." I looked down at my plate.

"What's the matter?"

"Nothing."

"There is too. Now what is it?"

"Before I was only vaguely jealous. Now I've got a name to be jealous of."

She said, amazement in her voice, "You're jealous of my ex-husband? I don't believe that."

"Nevertheless."

"You don't have the right. I forbid you to be jealous of anything to do with me. It's damned possessive of you and I don't care for it one bit."

I looked up at her, locking her eyes with mine. She was wearing a sequined white gown that just fell off her shoulders, and she looked like all I'd ever want. I said, "You haven't even told me how long you were married."

"No, and I'm not going to."

"Why not? Was it that long? I wouldn't be surprised if there were children."

"There weren't, but I'm beginning to feel like I'm sitting with one now."

I gave her the slow, crooked smile I'd inherited from my daddy. "No you don't. You can tell when a kid is kidding. You're not sure about me."

She put both her hands on the table, palms down. She had on two diamond rings that probably would have drilled an oil well according to Dennis's figures. She said, "You really lean on that smile of yours, don't you? Did that go over big with the girls in France?"

"Until you came along I never smiled."

She was about to reply when the waiter came over to take away our plates and see what else we'd have. She ordered brandy and coffee; I just ordered cognac. We had dined as well as I could remember ever having done. We'd started with a crab cocktail and moved to a salad and then a steak with sautéed mushrooms and scalloped potatoes. We'd drunk a good château Bordeaux that I had picked out, conscious of the price on the wine list, but determined to have it.

We had also danced. There was a wonderful small orchestra and we had toured the floor several times before eating. The band had played "Oh, Lady Be Good," just as the one in Galveston had. It amazed me to have come away from that first fragile meeting and for it to have continued. I had gotten chills when we were dancing.

The country club was even more elegant than I had expected. There was a good crowd out for dinner and some of the men were wearing tuxedos. Fortunately for me, there were other men scattered here and there who were dressed as I was. Of course, country clubs were pretty scarce down along the border, so I was not exactly an authority on such places, and neither was Dennis. I had always been under the impression they were mostly used for golf. The orchestra was playing a song I knew and liked. I said, "Shall we dance some more, or are you about ready to go? I'm not used to being out with women who go under assumed names, so I don't know what is appropriate."

"What assumed name?" She leaned back in her chair, and it put her breasts, especially her nipples, on prominent display.

I tried not to be caught staring. "Smith. Or did you decide on Jones?"

"Smith is my real name—my maiden name, which I have reverted to."

"You're not kidding?"

She shook her head slowly from side to side. "No. Why should I kid about that? Besides, I thought you were the kidder."

"You didn't answer my question."

She waved her hand in the air. "The cigar smoke is getting a little thick in here. Why must men light cigars when they finish eating? No, let's go. We can go to my house and talk." She reached behind her for the sequined wrap that went with her gown, and adjusted it around her bare shoulders. She started to get up.

I said, "Wait a minute." I looked around for the waiter. "I've got to pay the check."

She gave me a curious look. "You really are the country bumpkin. This is a country club. You don't pay cash in here. You sign the chit and then they send you a bill at the end of the month."

"You mean I can just sign for this?"

She gave me the same look. "Of course you can't. You're not a member, are you?"

"No."

"Then how could you sign?"

I frowned slowly. "Somebody has got to sign."

"I already have."

"I see," I said. I could feel a mixture of embarrassment and anger rising slowly through my central core. "In other words, you paid for this evening."

"Not really. I haven't personally paid the check. No."

I tapped the tabletop with my forefinger. I said, "You picked this place knowing I wouldn't be able to pay the bill. You want to explain that to me?"

She shrugged. "I never thought about it. Besides, what difference does it make? Your face is getting red for no reason."

I probably flushed even more. I said, "When I take a lady out I expect to pay for the evening. Call me old-fashioned, but that's just the way I am. I damn well don't appreciate you setting me up like this."

"You're being silly." She stood up. "Let's go."

I rose also because I didn't have much choice. I said, "This makes me mad as hell."

"Why are you getting so exercised? What's the point?"

"The man pays."

She laughed. "A man is paying. This membership is still in Douglas's name. He bought us dinner. Satisfied?"

I stood there looking at her, steadily. I was angry, but I didn't know how angry I wanted to be. She struck me as the kind of lady who might get her back up and take a position and stick to that position. And I didn't have the time to outwait her if such a situation should occur. I said, calmly, "You don't really suppose that is going to make me feel different, do you, knowing your ex-husband paid?"

She tossed her head. "Oh, stop being so stiff-necked. What difference does it make who paid? You're not good-looking enough or rich enough or smart enough to have so much pride. People are starting to stare at us. Let's get out of here. We can argue about it at my house."

"Douglas's, you mean," I said. I never could resist twisting the knife, even when it was in my own back.

•　　•　　•

We had coffee. Or rather, she had coffee, which she'd fixed herself rather than rout out her maid. I made do with brandy and soda. We ended up sitting across from each other before a big window that faced on her street. There was a small, round table between us that was higher than the coffee table. I'd had enough to drink that my hand tremor was under control.

Even though it wasn't all that late—I reckoned it to be not quite eleven o'clock—I felt strange sitting in that house alone with that beautiful, desirable woman who had a streak of something in her I couldn't place. I said, "So why did you do that to me? You must have known I would resent it."

She cocked her head in that way she had. The lights were down low, but I could see the furrows in her brow. She said, "I didn't think you had very much money. It seemed the easiest way. If we'd gone somewhere else you would have insisted on paying. I thought you'd take it as a joke that Douglas was buying."

"Some joke. Yeah, I loved that." I took a bitter swig of my brandy.

"How was I supposed to know you'd get all silly and be jealous? You certainly have no reason. Even if I had given you permission, which I don't. And certainly he can afford to buy us dinner a thousand times over."

"Genevieve, that ain't the point and you know it. And what caused you to decide I didn't have much money? You met me in an elegant hotel, I bought expensive champagne, and I'm wearing new clothes."

She gave a little helpless motion. "I don't know. You're different. You act like you don't care much about anything. And when I met you you weren't wearing new clothes. You were dressed like you were going flying. You looked like Eddie Rickenbacker. But mainly it's this way you have about you, like you really don't give a damn and you are not wearing any price tags. I've never met anyone like you before, but I bet he wouldn't have much money if I did."

I sat back in my chair and looked out the window. It was a moonlit night and the trees along the street cast interesting shadows. We had the lights down in the sitting room so you could see out very well. I couldn't figure this woman out. But then, that was no trick for me. I doubted I'd ever figured any woman out. The truth was, I didn't know much about women. Outside of relations there'd been just two kinds in my life: those I had courted as a young man in high school and college, and those I had slept with, usually whores. But whoever they were, I had never been involved with them. I had never cared much nor thought about them, nor included them in my thinking when I thought about myself. But now had come along this Genevieve, a woman I'd met when she'd been sitting by herself in a nightclub. Hell, nice girls didn't do that. At least, they hadn't before I'd gone to war; but then, so much had changed.

And she was certainly a change; bought me dinner and then analyzed my finances. And here I was about to go off to west Texas. I said, "I've come to the conclusion you are crazy."

"Why would you say that?"

"It's the only way I can explain some of the things you say and do."

She got up and took her cup into the kitchen. I could hear her clattering around even though it was a big house and the kitchen was several rooms from the parlor. But the house was quiet. I had no idea where the maid was. Maybe it was her night off or maybe she wasn't a sleep-in maid. I called out, "You didn't answer me. I called you crazy and you didn't say anything."

She still didn't say anything but the clattering had stopped. I stood up and faced the direction of the kitchen. "I'll be leaving in a few days and all these things have to get said. I might be gone a considerable stretch of time. Are you listening to me?"

She suddenly materialized in the dim light of the dining room, coming toward me. Somehow she'd found time to shuck her sequined dress and put on a light, flimsy robe. She was carrying a cup of coffee in one hand and a bottle of brandy in the other.

"*You're* crazy to go to west Texas."

"We were talking about *you* being crazy. How did you have time to change clothes?"

She sat down on the sofa divan in front of the low coffee table. It was where she had sat the first time I'd visited her. Only this time she made room for me and patted the cushion beside her. "Bring your glass." She held up the brandy decanter. "I got the stuff right here."

I stepped away from my seat by the window and walked over to the little grouping around the coffee table. I sat down in the soft cushion of the sofa divan. It seemed to push me in her direction.

She turned toward me, the coffee cup at her lips, looking at me over the rim. Lord, in that light I could see that nature had just been extra good to her. If she'd have looked much better, I couldn't have stood it. She said, "Tell me you're not really going looking for oil in west Texas."

I got a little annoyed. I said, "Have I said anything since we first met to lead you to believe I *wasn't* going looking for oil in west Texas? Have I mentioned the Gulf Coast or the border or downtown Dallas? Where comes this confusion?"

She shrugged and took a sip of coffee and put her cup on the table. "I just thought maybe it was a whim. It's a perfectly stupid idea."

"You may think so, but that doesn't make it so. The way your mind jumps around, I'm surprised it ever lights on one subject long enough to pollinate."

She turned back toward me. We were sitting very close together. Her robe had parted just enough so that I could see the velvet whiteness of the inside of her thigh. It made my throat throb. She said, "When are you going to quit wondering what is on my mind and pay a little attention to what's on my body?"

I gave my head a decisive shake. I said, "I spend an *inordinate* amount of time thinking about your body. But until I figure out that jitterbug of a mind of yours I am not going to commit myself any further. I won't step off the bank until I know how deep the river is. I'm a newborn when it comes to high-toned babes like you. You could have me walking in circles and baying at the moon in about a minute and a half if I didn't watch myself. I have no intentions of allowing you to chew me up one day and spit me out the next."

She put her hand behind my head and looked me deep in the eyes. "You are so *serious*. Were you always this way?"

I didn't respond to her touch. "No, I've mostly been a devil-may-care kind of fellow. I'd take a dare and you didn't have to say it twice. But you scare me."

"What can I say to unscare you?"

"Say you'll come out to west Texas and take a look at our operation."

She took her hand away from my head and lounged back on the couch. "Now who is talking crazy? Come out to all that heat and dust and rocks and uncivilized living? There are people out there who have never seen a chair, much less a knife and fork. Good God, no!"

"We might hit a gusher."

She sat forward again. "Willis, give up this silly idea. There is no oil in west Texas. Not a drop. You are on a fool's errand."

"How do you know?"

"Douglas says so."

My face flamed. I gritted my teeth and got out one word. "What?"

"Well, don't look like that. I was only trying to help. I had to call him about something to do with the house and I brought up the subject of what you were going to do in west Texas." She put up her hand. "No names were mentioned. But he said there was no oil west of San Antonio. And certainly not where you are talking about. He said that was all hard rock and couldn't be drilled. He said if there was oil there, wouldn't the big companies like Texaco already be there? Of course, I didn't have any idea. But wouldn't they?"

I stood up. I had a little brandy left in the glass in my hand and I swirled it around and then finished it. I set the glass on the coffee table. "I'm going. You are one too many for me." I turned around and started for the front door.

"When will I see you again?"

I didn't turn around. "Obviously pretty damn soon, since I can't seem to stay away from you. Say hello to Douglas for me."

I spent the next couple of days looking at airplanes and listening to Dennis complain about the difficulty of getting men and equipment and supplies ready for a trip out west. If it had been me, I'd have done a lot more than complain. I'd have given the whole idea up and gone off and got drunk. But Dennis was one of those bulldoglike creatures who will not be beat by sin or situation and he was going to drill an oil well in west Texas if it harelipped the governor. I admire his perseverance, but doubted its real benefit. But then I remembered how he'd often worked all night to have my plane in the best possible shape for the next day's mission. I hadn't slighted his stubbornness then.

I finally decided on a JN-6H. Of course, it was a two-seater biplane as were all the other Jennies, but the 6H had an expanded wing span of forty-three feet seven inches. That picked up some 120 extra square feet of lift and extra surface in case you had to stretch a glide. They said the plane would cruise at ninety miles per hour, but what little I flew her caused me to doubt that figure. I figured the airplane was a little slower than that, but it was nimble enough and handled smooth as silk. It gave me a good solid dependable feeling. The only thing I really disliked about it was that the extra wing area made it squirrelly in crosswind landings. I had some trouble getting the outfit that owned the plane to let me fly it solo but when they saw that was the only way they were going to sell it to me, they finally caved in. After that I took the plane up and wrung it out a little. I stalled it and spun it and did some aeronautical maneuvers I hadn't done in a long time. It was as much a trial for me as it was for the airplane. I had forgotten how much I had missed flying and I had forgotten what a boost to my confidence it was. I felt like a different man as I taxied the airplane across the grass field toward the hanger. I could still do something few other men could do and I could do it damn well. I was not earthbound. I could go where others could only look. I could see clouds from the top and I could see a brighter sun. I got out of the plane and told the manager of the company that he'd just sold an airplane and to get in touch with Mr. Atlas's office. I'd have further instructions for him, but for the time being I wanted the airplane left alone.

They had asked for $2,500 for the plane only. I had agreed to $2,200 for the plane and a package of spare parts that I was sure to need. I drove away that day well-pleased. When I had been flying I had thought of my daddy. Maybe, as a man who could use guns better than most, that was how he had felt—that he could do something unusually well.

That night, Dennis reported that he had made some progress. He'd gotten a fireman hired and a floorman, and had given them fifty dollars each in advance to seal the bargain. But he said, "Willis, we got to get this show on the road. Them two will get liquored-up and next thing you know, I'll be out a hundred bucks and two hired hands."

I said, "What about your supplies?"

"I got HOMCO working on it. They ain't never helped rig up for a well where we're going, but they be trying to think of everything that could possibly happen. I'm taking extra drill stem in case we twist a bunch off in some hard rock, and I'm taking extra casing and I'm loading up on a new rook bit. Got rotary heads in it. Damndest thing."

"You figured out how to get water?"

He gave me a desperate look. "There's got to be a way. You say there are towns out there. They got to have water."

I nodded. "Yeah, but my land is ten miles from the nearest one. You going to run a pipeline?"

He scratched his head. "No, but I got me an idea. I'm looking at a hell of a big boiler. I might just be doing some hauling."

I hadn't told him what Genevieve's ex-husband had said. I didn't see the point. If he was going to drill a dry hole, it might as well be on my land. I said, "Don't forget, when you are arranging train space, to save room for my airplane. Or rather, I should say, Mr. Atlas's airplane." I told him the dimensions of the wings and the fuselage.

He said, "You want me to have a look-see when they take the wings off? Make sure they don't leave no parts missing. Hate to get out in that bad country and find out we are missing an aileron."

"I'll get you to take a look when they've got it disassembled and before they go to crating it. By the way, what is HOMCO?"

He gave me that despairing look he sometimes wore. "Boy, you really don't know nothing about the oil patch. HOMCO is the lifeblood of the business. They can get a part to you in the middle of a hurricane with a flood rising and get it there dry and on time. HOMCO is the Houston Oilfield Material Company. And don't forget it."

Dennis was a passionate man about some matters.

With time running out I called Genevieve and invited her to go for a flight. Her country club might be exclusive but I knew another club that was even more exclusive. I picked her up the next morning at a little after ten and drove to the airfield. I'd had the hotel make us up a picnic basket and I was going to fly us to a spot I'd picked out and we could have lunch under the wing. I didn't know how that stacked up against golf and tennis and "no cash allowed," but I was at least going to show her my side of things.

The plane was ready and gassed and out of the hangar when we got there. We walked over to it. She was wearing what women called slacks, but they were just pants cut along a different line to make them look feminine. As a general rule I was against such crossing of the lines, but I had to admit they looked damn tasty on Genevieve. The slacks were a light tan and made out of linen. They followed, with a delicate accuracy, every mold of her body. She was wearing a crisp white blouse with a colorful scarf tied around her neck. I had warned her it would be windy and she accordingly had braided her hair and tied it with a ribbon. It was a warm day and we weren't going to be flying very high, but I had put one of my old flight jackets in the cockpit she'd be occupying, just in case she got cold.

A crewman from the flight service came out from the hangar, but I waved him away. I wanted this to be my show. I walked her up to the front cockpit, just under the wing, and showed her how to put her foot on the reinforced area and to avoid the fabric and step up to the cockpit. She swung her leg over the side and then stepped in with no trouble. I raised myself up on the step and leaned in to get her settled. I showed her how to lock and unlock her safety belt and what all the controls and instruments were and what she was supposed to leave alone and what she might touch.

I looked at her. She smiled back. "You're not scared?"

She shook her head. "No. Of course not. I know you are an excellent pilot."

"I am," I said. "But you have no way of knowing that yet. Put on your goggles. I'll get the picnic basket and then we'll be on our way."

I transferred the picnic basket from the car to the rear cockpit, set the ignition switches, pulled the wheel chocks, and spun the propeller. It caught first time through and the plane began to edge forward. I raced under the wing and climbed quickly into the cockpit before the plane could begin moving very fast. I strapped myself in, put my own goggles on, and taxied toward the runway. As I came about with the nose into the wind, I rammed the throttle home and gave the plane enough flaps for a quick takeoff. We lifted free of the ground and the airplane became a living thing, a phenomenon that I never tired of. When we were a few hundred feet in the air I turned east and kept on climbing. Genevieve turned to look back at me. Her teeth were dazzling as she smiled at me. The wind was singing through the wing struts and whipping around our heads so talk was impossible even though she was no more than three feet from me. I nodded at her and smiled back and watched as she looked over the edge of the cockpit at the ground below. I noticed she moved with the airplane. If you bank left in a plane, most people will continue to sit bolt upright, not leaning with the motion of the airplane in the bank. People like that don't really like to fly. By trying to maintain their position in relation to the earth below, and not to the airplane, they show they are uncomfortable and afraid. I was very pleased to see how easily Genevieve adapted herself to the motion of the plane. For some reason I was not surprised.

I did not go directly to our destination. For a few moments I flew over downtown Houston and then turned the plane toward River Oaks so that Genevieve could see her house from the air. She got very excited, leaning far out of the cockpit and pointing downward emphatically, like I needed her to show it to me.

Finally I turned the plane toward my destination. I was taking us to the San Jacinto battleground which was some twenty miles northeast of downtown Houston. It was at that spot, on the banks of Buffalo

Bayou, that General Sam Houston and his ragged army had surprised General Antonio López de Santa Anna and his Mexican army, and won Texas's independence from Mexico in 1836. It had been turned into a park and a hallowed place in history and was more visited by tourists than Texans. I had scouted it out the last time I had flown the plane and it seemed a good place. They had some flat, grassy meadows and there was plenty of trees for shade. There was also the San Jacinto Monument, which was made out of granite and rose an impressive distance in the sky. I didn't figure to have any trouble finding a place to land. It was a weekday and I didn't expect much of a crowd of tourists cluttering up the place.

I followed the meandering Buffalo Bayou, flying at about twelve hundred feet. It was a beautiful day with almost no cloud cover, and just warm enough to feel comfortable.

As I turned toward the monument which had become visible against the sky, Genevieve turned and looked at me and pointed toward the park. I nodded and she clapped her hands in approval.

I made a one low pass over a flat meadow a little ways from the monument, to make sure it was clear, and then turned into the wind, killed power, and let the airplane find the ground. We went running across its even surface, with the grass making whispering sounds against the spokes of the wheels. I slowed the engine and taxied over to a little grove of oak trees. We were a half mile from the monument and had the place to ourselves. I killed the engine and jumped out. I was in time to help Genevieve down as she came climbing out of the cockpit. She stood there looking up at me, and there was something in her eyes I'd never seen before. She said, "oh my, that is so thrilling." She put her palm on my cheek. "I feel like I've never looked at you before."

It embarrassed me. I turned away. I said, "Let me get this basket out while you find us a spot to spread out."

The hotel kitchen had packed us cold chicken and a dish of boiled shrimp in a cocktail sauce, and potato salad and sliced tomatoes and pickles and olives and some bread and cake. They'd also added two bottles of wine, one white, one red, which I had been assured were first-class even though I'd never heard of either chateau.

Genevieve got the cloth spread and began setting out the dishes. I opened both bottles of wine and set them aside to breathe a bit. Then I lolled back on an elbow and looked at Genevieve. I couldn't find anything not to like about her.

She was on her knees, setting out the plates and the silverware. She took a moment to look around her and then to smile at me. "I must say," she said, "your country club has a great deal to recommend it. I especially like the transportation. Makes it seem rather exclusive."

I stretched my arms comfortably. "You haven't found out, yet, about 'exclusive.' "

I did not intend to talk seriously to Genevieve at that point. All I intended for the luncheon, was to make her more relaxed with me. And if she wanted to be impressed with me as a pilot, well, that was all right, too.

As it turned out, she wasn't very talkative either. Mostly we ate and drank and looked at each other. The food was good and so was the wine and the weather. From time to time little groups of people would start our way, attracted by the airplane, but I would frown them away. We were left to ourselves, which pleasantly suited us both. Finally, when we were drinking the last of the wine and looking at the remains of the lunch, Genevieve said, "I don't think you care much for me."

That astounded me. I said, "Like hell I don't. What would put an idea like that in your head?"

She circled her arms around her knees and hugged them to her breasts. "Well," she said, "you never ask me any questions about myself. You know nothing about my background beyond the fact that I was married. I know far more about you. For all you know, I could have been one of those ten-cents-a-dance girls."

I looked at her narrowly. I had the feeling I was being played with. I said, briefly, "Code of the West, ma'am. We never ask a stranger where he's from or how much he paid for his horse."

She threw a fork at me. "I'm serious. It hurts my feelings. If you cared at all about me, you'd at least be a little curious."

I stood up. "Let's get packed up. I want to take you somewhere you've never been. I belong to a very exclusive club and I might just get you in as a member."

"Really?" She scrambled up and began packing the picnic basket while I went over to get the plane ready. I thought the picnic had gone about as well as I could have hoped for.

She was surprised when I put her in the rear cockpit. I said, "We're going to ride double."

She said, "Are you going to teach me to fly?"

"Not the kind you think of. No, I'm going to introduce you to a very exclusive club. Even more exclusive than the country club."

She wanted to ask more questions, but I was busy setting the ignition switches and admonishing her not to touch anything. After that I pulled out the wheel chocks, pitched them in the front cockpit, and then pulled the propeller through. It caught as quickly as it had before, and I ducked under the wing and ran to the rear cockpit and climbed in beside Genevieve. I was forced, because of the tiny space, to sort of mash her up, but I got the plane pointed into the wind, rammed home the throttle, and felt the surge of power as the prop bit into the wind. In a second we were running across the meadow and the tail was lifting up and we were flying. Beside me I could feel Genevieve give a delicious little shiver and take hold of my arm—gently, in case I should suddenly need it.

I flew straight toward the San Jacinto Monument and then circled it so Genevieve could have a feeling of seeing the top up really close. She said, "Ooooh, it looks so big."

After that I pulled the plane around and headed west, back toward the Houston area, climbing all the time. I wanted to be somewhere around five thousand feet when we got in the general area of River Oaks, her house, country club, and all. As we flew I showed her how the stick worked and what the rudder pedals did, and the function of each instrument. I especially called her attention to the altimeter, the altitude register. It showed us to be at about fifteen hundred feet and climbing. Like a clock, one little hand pointed at a number while another, longer hand, circulated faster, clicking off the feet in hundreds.

I tapped the glass over the instrument. "Can you read that? Can you tell me how high we are above the ground?"

She studied it, frowning. Finally she said, "The short hand shows a thousand feet and the big hand shows six. I'd say we are sixteen hundred feet and going up."

"Very good. Do you know how many feet are in a mile?"

She gave me a pained expression. "I would have studied if I'd known there was going to be a test. Somewhere around five thousand."

"Five thousand two hundred and sixty."

"Why are we going so high?" She looked over the side of the cockpit, gazing at the ground below. "Wow. Everything is getting awfully small—or else we're a long way away. My gosh, I can see all of Houston. I think I can see River Oaks."

We were passing through three thousand feet, but we were already over Houston. It was a warm summer's day and airplanes didn't climb as well when it was hot. Something about the heat making the air too thin and the propeller not getting a good bite.

I put the plane into a left-hand climbing turn, intending to bring us out at five thousand feet, approximately over River Oaks. Genevieve said, her lips against my ear, "Why are we going so high? Are you going to throw me out?"

"No. We're going to my club."

"You've got a club in the clouds?"

I nodded solemnly. "Doesn't everyone?"

She put her lips back to my ear, which tickled but was the only sure way of being heard over the wind and the engine. "Were you hurt in the war? Something to do with your head?"

I gave her a quick smile. "You guessed my secret."

She looked over the side of the cockpit again and gave a little shiver. "Willis, you are scaring me. We're so high! Let's go down some. I've never been this high before."

Just then we hit a convection layer and the plane bounced around a bit. Genevieve's eyes got big and she threw her arms around my neck and squeezed me like a lemon. She said, "Oh, Willis, I'm scared. We're too high! What if we fall?"

She was getting in the mood I wanted her in. I said, "Not much more." I reached out and tapped the altimeter. We were at forty-six hundred feet and swinging around nicely to arrive over the River Oaks part of Houston right on schedule.

"What are you doing? *Brrrrr*. It's getting cold." She put the leather jacket I'd brought around her shoulders. "This is crazy. Willis, what is going on?"

I watched the altimeter hit five thousand feet and pass on through. Looking over the side, I could see River Oaks below. I took the stick between my knees, sliding down in the seat, and reached out my right arm and pulled her to me.

She came, but there was a little reluctance. "What is this? What are you doing?"

I pushed her to cross over my legs. I said, "Straddle me."

"Willis, this is crazy," she said, but she did as I asked. After a moment she was directly in front of me, her arms around my shoulders, her lovely face no more than a few inches from mine. I could feel the vibration of the engine throbbing through both of us. "What is going on?"

"I'm going to make you a member of a very exclusive club." I put my hand behind her head and pulled her lips to mine. I kissed her warmly and deeply, with growing passion on both our parts. The kiss had taken her off-guard, but once she was into it she had surrendered herself fully.

Finally she pulled back. "Wow. Good gosh. A kiss is different way up in the air. What is this exclusive club you are talking about?"

I directed her attention to the altimeter which was at around fifty-three hundred feet. I said, "You're now a member of the mile-high club." Then I paused. "Well, I should say you're an auxiliary member since you haven't met the full requirements for official membership."

"What does that take?" The wind had blown her hair loose and it was swirling around her head.

I said, grimly, "If you were wearing a dress instead of those slacks I could show you in five minutes."

It took her a moment to get it, but then she said, "It may take a contortionist in this little cockpit, but maybe I can get out of these pants."

It alarmed me. I wasn't ready. I said, "No. We don't know each other that well." To make my point I pushed the stick forward and kicked in the left rudder and went into a fairly steep circling dive. I could see Hobby Field off to the south. It wasn't that far away.

The dive got Genevieve's attention. She slid off my lap and snuggled down in the cockpit, holding on to my arm. She said, "Is this your revenge for the country club? If it is, I swear I'll never do it again. My God, you're going to kill us!"

We were in a dive but it was nowhere steep enough to alarm anyone. But I guessed Genevieve's conscience was hurting her. We were making one hundred fifty miles an hour, which was a little much for this plane. I gradually eased the stick back and shallowed out the dive. I said, having to speak loudly, "Well, as long as you are sorry and know you were wrong."

She was huddling against me with all her might. "I'm sorry, I'm sorry!" she said loudly.

" 'I was a snob.' "

"I was a snob! A terrible snob. I did you wrong. I'll never do it again!"

I was making a straight-in approach and the airport was no more than ten miles away. Our altitude was down to a thousand feet. I throttled back the engine.

"You are forgiven," I said, "on your solemn oath to never do anything like that again, and to admit that the mile-high club is a much more exclusive affair than any country club."

But she was sitting up and looking forward through the cockpit screen. She could see how close the landing field was and feel how the airplane had relaxed from the strained vibration caused by the excessive speed.

I said, "Do you swear?"

"You son of a bitch," she said. "You scared me on purpose. For what reason?—that's what I want to know."

I waited until we had touched down and the undercarriage was running smoothly over the grass landing strip. Then I turned, and looked at her wearing my big leather jacket, cuddled up in the corner. I said, "When are you going to quit feeding me what the horses won't eat? You think you are going to lead me around and I'm going to buy every one of your little skits?"

She tossed her head as I turned the plane back for the hangar. "I don't know what you are talking about."

"Like hell you don't. You were about as scared up there as I was. You couldn't keep the grin off your face. And, by the way, don't lean with the bank of the plane if you want to be thought of as terrified."

"Just where do you get your crystal ball?"

"With you I'm beginning to think I don't need one. You're an actress. Unpaid probably, or at least indirectly paid, but you get up these little scenes and you get me to play my part and you do yours. Of course, yours is much better. I don't know if you do this with everyone, but you damn sure do it with me."

"You're crazy, Willis. Do you know that? You're absolutely nuts. I never heard such nonsense."

"Everything is a drama with you," I said. "I didn't fully realize it until I got you up in the air where I see better. But every one of our encounters has been a little drama that you've played out for your own amusement or gratification or whatever it is you get out of it. But now we are going over to your house and we are going to have another little play, only I'm going to direct this one."

I cut the ignition and killed the engine. The line boys were coming out of the hangar to take charge of the plane. Genevieve had gotten very quiet. I jumped out of the cockpit and then held up my arms to help her down.

She hesitated. "I'm not sure I want to come."

"Oh, but you have to. It's my turn. And you want to be fair, don't you? Of course you do."

She came over the side and I eased her to the ground. As she straightened up she breathed, "You son of a bitch," in my ear.

"Thank you," I said. "But you damn me with faint praise."

She gave me a look. "Why couldn't you have been the hick I thought you were? Hell, you're nothing but a kid."

I shook my head. "Not after fighting a war."

"What are we going to talk about that is so important?"

"All in good time," I said. I walked her toward the car.

Driving, she said, "Do you realize you never did ask me anything about myself?"

I turned the corner out of Hobby Field and said, "Then tell me. People usually do when they are ready."

She tossed her head. "You don't really want to know. You think I am what you see. You think I grew up some rich, privileged little girl who had her own way all the time."

I glanced at her, watching her hair in the breeze as she unwound the scarf from it. She was looking straight ahead. "Well, weren't you?"

She gave her head a firm shake. "No, I wasn't. I grew up in severe circumstances in east Texas."

That brought a small smile to my face as I thought of my uncle Warner and my aunt Laura. "East Texas, huh? Ever heard of the little town of Overton?"

"I certainly have. My father was the pastor of the First Baptist Church there."

I laughed out loud. I couldn't help myself. "*Your* daddy was a Baptist preacher?" I laughed again. "Boy, that is a good one. You will pardon me but you seem about as much the churchgoing kind as I am."

She turned fierce eyes on me. "How dare you say that. I had a strict upbringing. And then I went to Mary Hardin Baylor College for Women, which is the Baptist equivalent of a nunnery. So don't think I came to this play girl image so easily."

The heat of her words slowed me down a little. I did not know how long ago my uncle had located his horse ranch in east Texas, but it should have been somewhere in her time. I said, "All right, if you are from Overton then you would know Warner Grayson and his wife Laura."

She frowned. "They sound familiar."

I gave her a sly smile. "They should. My uncle is damn near famous as a racehorse breeder. People come from all over the world to see his horses. So . . . if you are from Overton as you say you are . . ."

"*Was.* Not 'are.' " She glared at me. "What did you say his name was?"

"Warner Grayson."

She nodded. "Yes, now I remember. Something to do with horses."

"Oh, sure, now that I've told you."

She was not happy with me. "Are you calling me a liar?"

I shook my head. "No, just a good actress. What, if I may ask, got you out of that east Texas paradise?"

She sighed and looked away. "The first time on my own. I came to Houston to get a job, any kind of job. But I was spoiled and didn't do well. So I went home."

"And?"

"And they discovered oil in Kilgore, just ten miles down the road. Everything changed after that."

I looked over at her. "Is that where Douglas found you?"

She nodded quickly.

I said, a little edge in my voice, "I guess that is one way out of a bad situation—marry your way out."

She looked at me and there was a kind of appeal in her eyes. "Willis, I was desperate, being shut down in that small village, then Mary Hardin Baylor, which was even worse, then failing on my own." She stopped, and said in a calmer voice, "It didn't seem like such a bad choice at the time."

"But what did he want with you? You called me a hick. Or you said you thought I was a hick. What the hell were you?"

She gave me a firm look. "A damn good-looking young woman from a good background who knew how to act in civilized company."

"And a damn fine scene arranger."

CHAPTER
8

⟨～～～～⟩ WE SAT at the table by the window, across from each other. We were drinking brandy. The maid had brought in the bottle and two glasses, but Genevieve, sensing the talk might get delicate, had sent her off to find work in distant parts of the house.

Genevieve said, "What is this 'actress' nonsense? You know I'm not an actress."

I smiled slowly. I said, "I can see the cunning lying behind your eyes as you set up another scene to be played your way."

"I resent that."

"You might resent it but it don't make it any less true."

"Then you tell me what you're talking about, Mr. Smarty Pants."

I took a sip of brandy and then sat back and looked at her. "It appears to me that you like to arrange the people in your life to suit certain characters they ought to play. I think you've got me down as the smitten young swain who would run to eat cake crumbs from your dainty fingers, but who, unfortunately, is still suffering from battle shock from the war and could use some nursing and mothering."

That got a rise out of her. "Oh yeah?"

"Yeah. Why else the country club? Because you didn't think I had much money. That's make-believe. You've already said you don't know much about me. No, the country club made our social positions clear. Or it was supposed to."

"Willis, you are talking rot."

"Well, it doesn't matter. I don't care if you want to play pretend or not. With one exception. And that is me and you."

"There's no you and me." She tossed her hair and frowned and looked out the window.

"Oh, stop that," I said. "There's no crowd, Sarah Bernhardt. You know damn good and well there is a you and me. You know it and so do I."

"You are a marvelous pilot," she said. "I will grant you that. I can't remember if I asked you before—were you an ace?"

"Cut it out. Genevieve, are you coming to west Texas with me?"

She slowly swiveled her head from the window to give me her full attention. "Are you mad? Do you seriously think I would willingly go to such a place? I've got a perfectly lovely life here. Why would I want to run off and play the pioneer woman?"

"If there was sufficient inducement."

"And that would be?"

"I'll give you just one guess."

"You?" She pointed at me and then gave a low chuckle. "You would be inducement enough? Willis, you are a wonderfully handsome and charming young man, but, please. You called me Sarah Bernhardt, but I hardly think you are the Sheikh of Araby, though you'll need to be with all that sand out there."

I took a sip of brandy. I wasn't expecting it to be easy work. I said, "It's the best offer you've got. You bore damn easy, Genevieve, and there's nothing around here to keep you excited. You won't have anyone like me to do your little playlets with. You'll end up with another boring businessman and that will just mean another divorce."

She cocked her head. "I find it damn condescending of you to think you've got me all figured out. And what about you? I don't know a thing about you except you're a dancer and can fly a plane."

I spread my hands. "What else is there?"

"Be serious."

"There's nothing to tell. My mother comes from solid Baptist Virginia stock. She met my father through her sister and lost her head. I've already told you my daddy was a bank robber until he got pardoned. After than he ran a casino and a saloon in Del Rio. They tell me he was a famous gunman. I never discussed it with him. His name is Wilson Young. He and my mother are deep in Mexico. Probably had to do with an attempted robbery of a quarter of a million in gold bullion some five years ago. My daddy had something to do with the affair."

She looked thoughtful for a second. "It seems like I remember something about that. Didn't he prevent the robbery?"

I smiled slowly. "That's the story I heard. I'd want to hear it from those who really know."

"Didn't he get shot?"

I nodded. "So the newspapers said." I stretched my arms over my head and yawned. "Sometime I'll see him and get the straight of it."

"You are really not close. That's a shame."

"Yeah, in one way I guess it is. You think I don't have any money. I could have a lot of money if I cared to ask my daddy. He's as rich as pork fat. But I don't happen to be in an 'asking daddy' mood."

"That's terrible you have so little in common with your father. He is your father."

I got an annoyed look on my face. "Me and my daddy has nothing to do with you and me. But you're right about having nothing in common. And that includes my mother. She believes in Jesus and my daddy believes in taking other people's money away from them. I don't care for either end of the taffy pull."

"You are not a Christian?"

Now I was irritated. "No, but not for lack of my mother's trying. Look here, are you coming to west Texas with me or not?"

She put her hand to her breast. "Is this a proposal of marriage, Mr. Young?"

Twilight was lighting the trees with an afterglow. I said, "Why not?

I doubt I can do any better than you. I want you to come with me because I don't want to leave you here. If it takes a wedding, all right."

"Just out of curiosity, is there a town there?"

I frowned. "Not directly. Pecos is the biggest town, though it ain't much. It's mainly a six-grade school and a couple of saloons. It's right on the railroad and also the closest to my land. But there's some other little settlements around. As long as there is water in the Pecos riverbed there'll be people trying to raise cattle. I'd say, from where we'll be, it's no more than ten miles to another human face and an unpainted building."

"I suppose it's hot."

"Boiling in the summer. Cold as hell in the winter."

"So there is a chance that people go crazy from the heat."

I nodded slowly, not sure where she was going. "I suppose so. Why?"

She suddenly stood up. "Because we should be having this entire conversation out there. It's insane."

I said, in a reasonable voice, "I don't know why you'd say that. Men and women have been going places together for a good number of years. That's all I'm proposing. You were the one mentioned marriage."

"Willis! You are not proposing a weekend in Galveston or a quick week in New Orleans. You are seriously asking me to accompany you to one of the hellholes of the world, and stand around while you drill an oil well in the ground. Are you nuts?"

I shook my head. "No. You got that part wrong. I'm not going to have anything to do with the drilling of the well. That is all up to Dennis. I will have a lot of time to be with you."

She crossed her arms across her breasts and walked to the center of the room and then looked back at me. "What, if you can tell me, makes you think I would even consider doing such a thing without a gun to my head?"

I raised my eyebrows and shrugged. "I've got to admit it is asking a fair amount."

"Why would you even want me to go? Willis, as I've said before, we don't know each other that well."

"No, it was me who said that. Only we weren't talking about going to west Texas. We were heading for bed."

"All right, forget that. Why would you want me to go?"

I looked down at my hands. It was getting dim in the room. I said, simply, "Because I can already tell I will miss you if I go and you stay."

She let her hands drop to the side and stared at me. "Willis, hell! That's no reason for such a step. Just because you think you might miss someone. People go off every day and leave people behind they are fond of. Missing happens. It's just something that happens."

I shook my head. "I know that. And I know sometimes it is unavoidable. But when you can do something about it then it's foolish to put yourself through such pain for no good reason. If you'll come with me I won't have to miss you and you won't have to miss me."

She half smiled. "That is beautiful, simplistic reasoning. But it's a little too simple. Willis, I'm not going to drop my life and follow you out to west Texas, no matter what you're going to be doing out there."

I studied her for a moment. "Is that your final word?"

"Of course it is. I'm very fond of you and you are a very attractive man, but I'm not exactly a camp follower."

"How much fonder of me would you have to get in order to go?"

"A whole lot."

"Can you do it in two or three days?"

"Of course not."

"So that is it. The discussion is closed?"

"As far as the grandiose and distant plans go, yes. Unless you have any other ideas."

I stood up and pushed away from the wall and started walking toward the front door. "I reckon not." I paused and turned her way. "I'll try and see you again before we go."

"Willis . . ." She started toward me. "Please don't be hurt. This is not directed at you personally. I wouldn't do this with anyone."

"Then I'll be bidding you good night."

"No kiss?"

I glanced back as I opened the door. "Not for me. Too painful."

She stood there. "I hate for you to leave like this."

"So do I," I said. But I went on through the door, closing it behind me, and went out to the car and started it and drove to the hotel.

CHAPTER 9

WE WERE riding the chair cars. We had Pullman berths but we wouldn't make use of them until the train was nearly to Austin, and that was still a far piece down the line. This particular line we were on was the Southern Pacific and it was one of them big operations like the Union Pacific or the Erie or one of the others up in the North. Besides sleeping cars, this one had a dining car and a club car where you could get a drink or smoke a cigar, and I had heard they had a barber on board who'd cut your hair or give you a shave. I looked out the window at the passing landscape and rubbed my jaw, feeling the two days' growth of whiskers. I hadn't shaved because there hadn't seemed much point. I hadn't gone back over to see Genevieve or met her anyplace so what did the whiskers matter? I didn't know why I hadn't tried to contact her again before we left. Genevieve had struck me as a pretty strong-willed woman, and once she'd given her say on a matter she wasn't likely to change her mind. And even though I cared for her a great deal I knew that I couldn't go off to the wilderness of western Texas for maybe six months and expect to come back to Houston and find her just as she'd been when I left. So it was either her coming with me or me forgetting her.

Except she was pretty hard to forget. She was a job of work to forget. A man wanted to bring himself a sack lunch if he went on a job of forgetting her because he'd be there a long time before he got it done.

I didn't have a sack lunch but I stared out the window and worked at it. Somehow the miles that kept clicking off on the rails didn't make it any easier; harder, if anything.

Dennis and I were riding in the big double seats that faced each other at the end of the car. Dennis was riding backward and I was riding so I could see ahead when the train went around a curve. The train had pulled out of Union Station a little after two o'clock in the afternoon. We'd been going another two hours and weren't due in Austin until after nightfall, sometime near seven o'clock. We could eat dinner in the dining car whenever Dennis wanted. I didn't care. I wasn't hungry.

Dennis was riding with a bottle of whiskey on the seat next to him. I wasn't drinking, but he was having a nip every once in a while. He was about half satisfied with the shape of matters, and fifty-percent worried. He'd managed to hire three supposedly experienced drilling hands. One was a derrickman, one was a fireman, and one worked the floor and the mudpit. I had a hazy idea about what all that meant, but not much more. They were riding in the car immediately behind us. Dennis had placed them there because he didn't believe in the hired hands mixing in with management. He'd said, "Now, I know it don't seem democratic to you, my lad, but you can't have all this mixing-around out on an oil well in the middle of nowhere. Breaks down discipline. We had discipline over in France during the war. Had to. Didn't see no common enlisted men mixing in with the officers like you, no sir!"

That had caused me to laugh since Dennis and I had drunk many a bottle of cognac together.

But he'd been adamant on the subject. "You're going to work men under the conditions we going to face out yonder, and you got to make them look up to you and trust you and follow orders. Yes sir!"

It all sounded a little silly to me and I said so. I said, "Fine, those boys back in the car behind us are working stiffs. And you tell me you are management. Well, what am I? I'm certainly not management. What am I doing up here with you? Hell, I ought to be back there where I belong."

But he'd just pushed against his seat back and pulled down at his undershorts, which were starting to ride up on him, and said, "Naw, you're capital. You're ownership. Hell, you are more high-toned than me, and I'm the drilling superintendent."

It all made me laugh. Me and hired hands in the rear coach may have been the only ones not kidding ourselves. Me, because I had nothing to lose and was giving away nothing, and the hired hands because they were drawing wages. We would all come to the same level once Dennis and Teddy Atlas got a look at the country we were heading for. I had only been half kidding when I'd told them that water sold for more than whiskey.

I put my forehead up against the glass and stared out at the countryside. We were still in the soft country, gently rolling hills covered with green grass and dairy cattle and gentle oaks and cottonwoods. We were coming into the little German settlement of Brenham. We'd stop long enough to unload goods from Houston and take on cattle feed and milk cans for the dairy up the track and then be on our way. The station was right in the middle of the town and every soul in sight had stopped dead and was staring at the train like they'd never seen one before. I felt like opening the window and yelling something smart like, *Hey, rube, how are the ham trees growing this year?*

But who was the rube and who wasn't? They were staying in their comfortable homes with the ones they cared about, and I was the idiot leaving a woman who fascinated me.

Dennis spoke. "Gonna be a long trip."

That was true. We'd be three days and three nights just getting to Pecos. That seemed like a long time on the train, I wondered what it must have been like when they went in wagons and on horseback.

But the trip wouldn't be over once we got to Pecos. That was when the hard times were really going to begin. I had no idea how we were going to get all the heavy equipment Dennis had brought, out to a site on my land. And I sure as hell didn't know where we were going to get water in abundance, or any other kind of supplies. Dennis was planning to pick up three or four local men to roustabout on the rig but I doubted he was going to have much luck. The kind of men he was going to run into didn't work unless they could do it from the back of a horse. But he felt he was bringing his skilled labor along in the men he'd persuaded to come. He reckoned he could get by with any kind of strong back and no brain for the rest of the crew. "We ain't going to be working three towers," he'd said. He'd had to explain to me that a "tower" was a work shift, usually eight hours. He'd said, "We'll just drill for ten or twelve hours and then rest up the balance of the day."

The balance we'd be working was at the height of the summer's heat. I wondered if he had any idea how hot it could get.

A man named Joe Cairo was our fireman. He was a middle-aged, peaceable-looking man who'd been around oil wells for twenty years. If there was one man that could be called the foreman, after Dennis, it was him. He was short and square-built, with hard hands and big hairy forearms. Dennis said he'd seen the man work three days and three nights without a break. "We're lucky to get him," Dennis had said, "even at the price he's asking."

We were paying a premium for the men, mainly because of the location where we were to drill. There were plenty of men looking for work, experienced men, but very few who wanted to go where we were going. Those who had prior knowledge of the country couldn't be hired for any amount. Those that didn't, were afraid of the unknown. Then there was the matter of the bonus. It was the custom, so I understood, to give a bonus to the crew when the well was brought in. Of course, if the well was being drilled by a big company in a proven field, there was no bonus. But if it was a big wildcat gusher, I'd heard the bonus could run to hundreds, even thousands of dollars per man. For that reason most roughnecks wanted to work on rigs where there was a chance for that kind of bonus. Nobody gave us a chance of finding any oil in western Texas—not unless, as one man said, we took it with us.

Charlie Haas was the young man who'd be in the top of the derrick. It was the most dangerous job on the drilling rig and, even with big companies, the derrickman drew down a quarter more an hour than the rest of the crew. I figured Charlie was costing Dennis plenty—probably for an hour what I'd been making for a day's work.

A man that I only knew by the name of Joel was Dennis's main floorman. What that meant, I didn't know, but Dennis said the floor crew was the backbone of a drilling operation, and you had to have at least one man in that crew who knew what he was doing and could hold the operation together. Well, that was Joel, but it didn't tell me a hell of a lot. He was a strongly-built man of about thirty who didn't appear to know how to talk. At least, I'd never heard him say much more than a grunt and a nod. But Dennis said he could work the tongs or the chocks and blocks, and wouldn't drop the last stem back in the hole. That was good enough for me so I was glad to have old Joel along, though I was starting to wonder about myself and what I was doing there because I didn't know the tongs from the chocks, much less the blocks. But my big value, according to Dennis, was that I knew the country and I'd be instrumental in getting all the equipment transferred to the drilling site and setting up the supply lines.

Dennis didn't seem to realize I hadn't been in the Pecos country for almost ten years and didn't, as near as I could remember, know a soul in the whole area. But Dennis didn't want to hear any of that kind of talk. Dennis was an optimist; I couldn't remember if he'd been that way when he was seeing me off on missions against the German flying corps, but he'd certainly been one since we'd become reacquainted. "You got to believe it, son," he'd said. "You got to know that that oil is down there and just waiting for you to find it. Every time I see the drill bit cut into the dirt and start down, I know I'm going to strike oil. Besides, I know the Lord is on my side—our side. He wants us to find oil for His greater glory."

That was another thing I couldn't remember about Dennis when he'd been my mechanic. I couldn't remember if he'd been a Holy Joe then or not. It didn't seem like he had. But it made sense that if anyone was going to believe in a deity that could control your destiny, wartime would be ideal and fertile ground for religion. I had started to ask him why the Lord should give a hoot whether we struck oil or not, or how it came to be for His greater glory, but I decided to let it ride. Dennis was quick enough to start thumping the Bible without any encouragement from me. I'd never come to ask how he'd got started off on that particular path. That was his business and I wanted to leave it like that. I myself had never felt the tug that Dennis assured me I would one day feel. The whole business, I figured, was for women and the weak of mind. My mother was still determined in my case, but she was a long ways away.

We went on through Austin and headed for San Antonio, arriving there late that night. We had a layover but it wouldn't be long enough to make it worth our while to get a bed in a hotel. In an effort to get to know the crew, I started in by asking Joe Cairo if he knew his last name was the same as that of a town in Egypt.

He studied me for a long moment, slitting his eyes in his weather-treated face. Finally he spit on the platform outside the depot where we were standing and said, with a little bit of a menace in his voice, that he knew his last name was that of a town in the state of Illinois, but he wouldn't be knowing anything about such places as I had mentioned. He kept giving me that hard look the whole time it took him to say it, and I got the distinct feeling he felt I'd tried to pass some kind of insult on him.

They say education is a wonderful thing—at least that was what our professors up at the University in Austin had tried to impress upon us—but right then I had the feeling that sometimes it wasn't very smart to know more and different material than your immediate colleagues. Besides, Joe Cairo was a valuable man. He could fire a boiler and run a rig. I couldn't.

Dennis said to me, as we left San Antonio and got lined out for the run west, "Do I take it you don't care whether we bring in a big gusher or not?"

I said, "Well, of course I hope you have good luck, for you and the rest of the crew. Of course I do."

"Uh-huh, but you don't care nothing about yourself? I mean, you don't want no big bunch of money for yourself?"

"We've had this conversation before, Dennis. Of course, I realize you got to have enough to live on, but money for money's sake don't mean much to me. I got everything I want or need."

"What about that girl, that lady? You think she's going to follow you around while you hire out as day help? You think she's going a week without a bath? Hah!"

My face burned a little at his words. I had plans—if Genevieve had been interested in me—a way to have raised my station in the world. I could have accommodated her and seen that she had a bath often enough. But I'd be damned if I was going to tell my plans to Dennis. Besides, they weren't plans anymore, just daydreams.

I said, "Hell, Dennis, I thought you were so all-fired fixed on doing good. How does money get in there? Ain't there something about a rich man and a camel in the Bible?"

"I wouldn't be calling the Bible into this, was I you."

We'd gotten to where we bit at each other every now and again. I think there was a kind of pressure on both of us, but for different reasons.

I could understand the pressure on Dennis. Hell, half the train was hauling his gear. There was his drilling equipment, including the rotary table and the pipe and the casing and the boilers, and all the paraphernalia that went with it. But we were also hauling a big Ford stakebody truck and some big tents and living furniture, as well as my airplane. The cost of freighting all that stuff the six or seven hundred miles we were going was enough to carry a dozen families through some lean years.

It was midmorning when we pulled into Hondo, a little town southwest of San Antonio. We all got out and stood on the platform. I reckoned we were all hungry, but the train wasn't going to be in the station long enough for us to hike to a nearby cafe and get something.

Joel came up to me. He stood there, looking square and solid. He said, "Be you a floorman?"

I shook my head. "No."

He stared at me and I could see him running over the other possibilities: fireman, no; driller, no—Dennis was the driller—derrickman, no. There wasn't anything left. He said, with a kind of snobbery I'd never encountered before, "Hell, you ain't nothing but a roustabout."

It stung me. I was surprised I replied, but I did. I said, "No. I'm the pilot. The *only* pilot. There are several floormen."

He gave me an unkind look and turned around and walked back to the others. I could see him talking to Charlie and Joe Cairo and pointing back at me. I was surprised I had felt called upon to give myself an identity, a status. It wasn't my style, especially with a blockhead like Joel.

Charlie called over to me, in a good-natured voice, "A pilot? What kind of pilot be you? A sky pilot? You a preacher man?" They all laughed.

Dennis came out of the depot where he'd been talking to the traffic agent. He'd heard the last of it. He stopped and stared at his hired men. "I won't have that, Charlie. That's damn near blaspheming, and I won't have it. You three get back on the train and keep your mouths shut."

Well, that hadn't made me look good. It had appeared that I'd needed Dennis to protect me. The job was going to be rough enough without getting off to a bad start with the crew. I said, back to Charlie, "Do I look like that kind of pilot? You take me for a preacher?"

Joe Cairo answered, and he did it in a hard voice. He said, "You look like a jellybean to me."

It was clear the crew had taken a disliking to me, and I didn't even know why. Likely it was because I didn't mix with them or speak their language. I was a non–oil field person on a drilling operation and I dressed different and hung around with the boss. Yeah, it was one more factor to be happy about.

Dennis called out, "God damn it, I told you boys to get back on the train. You are drawing wages so do as you are told. Get back on the damn train and mind your mouths about matters ain't none of your business."

I said, low and hard, "Shut up, Dennis. Ain't you got brains enough to see that just sets them against me?"

It startled him a little. He didn't speak for a second and then he shrugged, looking a little ashamed. "Aw, shit, they'll come around once they get to know you. I don't like people throwing preachers around, that's all."

I said, so he'd understand me, "You look after the preachers and I'll look after me."

"Little association with preachers wouldn't hurt you none."

"Why? Have they got a direct telephone wire to God?"

He gave me a look—what kind I wasn't sure of—but didn't say anything.

We got back on the train and it pulled out of Hondo and we continued our journey. I would be content should the train run on forever. I had no desire to dismount in the Pecos River country. I knew we were a hell of a lot more comfortable on the train.

Out the grimy window of the chair car I could see a knot of men gathered around the little wooden depot that announced itself as the cattle town of Pecos. They even had a sign hanging off one end of the depot to make sure you didn't get the place confused with, say, Dallas or San Antonio.

I didn't know if the crowd of men was there as a regular thing to meet the train, or if they were there as a result of Dennis's barrage of telegrams to the sheriff. We had a lot of equipment on that train and we needed to get it unloaded fast, and just Dennis and I and the three men we'd brought with us weren't going to get the job done. Some of our cargo was big and it was heavy and we needed some strong backs and willing muscle to get it off the train. Dennis had wanted to wire the mayor to ask him to employ as many men as he could, but I'd succeeded in convincing him that, likely, Pecos wouldn't have a mayor—or a city council or aldermen or any other civic worthies. I'd said that the sheriff would be his best bet. I knew they would have a sheriff because every county in Texas was required to have one.

And a sheriff was a hell of a lot more likely to know who was looking for work and who needed a payday.

Dennis had wired the sheriff, saying he'd pay three dollars a day for common laborers and would take all he could get. Three dollars a day was high wages in a place where there weren't no wages of any kind to be had, and I figured we'd be popular as long as we looked like big-city suckers come to town.

We stepped down carrying our personal luggage and the clump of men immediately moved our way since we were the only passengers getting off the train. Cries of, "Who doin' the hirin'?" and, "I'm ready to work!" suddenly filled the air. I shied away from Dennis so as not to get caught up in the swirl. It was hot. My God, it was hot. It was as hot as that country can get in the summertime. I headed for the shade of the depot, leaving Dennis and his crew to handle the applicants.

I stood in the comparative coolness of the station house and watched the three-ring circus going on outside. Dennis had a limited amount of time to get all his cargo off the train so he was hiring anybody that applied who looked like they could stay upright in the heat. The three roughnecks were acting as straw bosses and the whole bunch swarmed over the freight cars like so many ants at a picnic. All Dennis wanted at that stage was to get his equipment off the train. There'd be time enough later to figure out how to haul it to the drilling site. Meanwhile, hands that were a good deal more used to bridle reins, were hurrying to unload heavy drill stem and pipe and other parts of the drilling operation. When they got to my airplane, I intended to go out to do a little supervising of my own.

"You with that bunch out there?"

I turned around. I may have missed him in the dimness of the shack, or he might have come out from the ticket agent's booth, but there was a man standing there. He was wearing a dusty hat and a black suit of clothes, complete with collar and tie and a gold chain across his vest. I said, "What?"

He was smoking a big, thick cigar and he pointed it toward the platform where all the activity was going on. He said, "Is this that bunch I been hearing about was coming out here to drill for oil?"

He had a certain authority about him. I judged his age to be in his mid-fifties, but only because of the gray in his ample mustache and what hair I could see.

I said, "Yes, that's the drilling crew."

He gave a snort. "Ain't no oil out here. Only a damn fool would come to the Pecos country to seek oil."

I gave him a look. "How do you know I ain't the damn fool?"

"Because you're in here. If you had a small fortune sunk in a venture like this one, you'd be out there looking to the details."

I couldn't argue with that logic, so I kept my mouth shut.

He said, "My name is Crater, John Crater. I'm the local magistrate around here."

"You mean you are the justice of the peace. We don't have magistrates in Texas."

He gave me a hard look. "You mean, you are from Texas and you were willing to come on this fool's errand? I thought the whole crowd would be from out-of-state."

I said, "You sound like you are kicking about this. We're bringing jobs and some fresh money. You ought to be glad."

His face kind of soured. He said, "This is wild country and we got some folks around here don't take much to set them off. I'm glad for the money you are bringing, but I can warn you right now that you had better not be bringing me any trouble. And you can pass the word along about that. This place don't get many strangers, and the locals don't always know how to treat them."

I said, "If there is any trouble, we won't start it. And my name is Willis Young and it is my land we'll be drilling on. And while word is being passed, you might send it around that I don't like trespassers."

He studied me for a second. "Young . . . Young. You wouldn't be any kin to Wilson Young?"

"You mean the bank robber?"

He shrugged slightly. "He never robbed any banks around here. But I did hear he owned some land. Is it yours now?"

"Yeah."

"You ain't said if you was any kin to him."

"No, I haven't, have I?"

"But you got his land and you got the same last name. You an outlaw too?"

I swung around and gave him a look, but didn't say anything.

"Because if that be the kind of outfit you've brought into this quiet town, me and you is gonna tangle."

I turned back to him, ignoring the flurry outside. I said, "Judge, we are a peaceable group of hardworking businessmen. Any trouble will start with the townfolk. You understand?"

We were quiet for a moment while he sucked on his cigar and I anxiously watched the progress of the train being unloaded. My plane was in sections inside a boxcar and I couldn't tell if they'd worked their way that far back.

Judge Crater said, "It appears you sent a blizzard of telegrams to the sheriff. That was a waste of time. I'm the authority around here."

"Judge, we didn't know you existed. Ain't a lot of information about Pecos in the Houston Public Library. But I knew there'd be a sheriff."

"Well, your crowd seem to have a bad case of the wants. You want all the big wagons we got, all the draft animals, and all the big trucks we have."

"We've got to get this equipment to the well site. And it's heavy."

"You got some nerve, young man. This town ain't but about seven hundred inhabitants. What transportation equipment we have is already being put to good use."

I gave him a long, thoughtful look. I said, "Yeah, but I somehow get the feeling you could be a real help in getting such equipment lined up. After all, you are the power around here."

He pulled his chin, "Maybe when I meet the head man some sort of deal can be struck."

I gave him a thin smile. "Would that deal involve money?"

"All deals involve money, sonny boy. Time you learned that."

"And I thought you'd want to give us a warm welcome."

He gave me a direct look. "You forget one thing, sonny boy. Your outfit is here. You have arrived. We don't have to lure you out here. You're on the spot, and with all your equipment. I reckon without the help of the town you'll be in a hard way."

All I could do was shake my head. He was a prime example of the type of old nestor I had warned Dennis we'd run across. Low and cunning and only interested in what was in it for him. And this one had to turn out to be a judge.

I was about to walk out of the depot to warn Dennis what was coming, when I happened to glance out a window facing the street. There, in face and embodiment, was a woman who stopped me cold in my tracks. She was standing by a buggy, watching the unloading. She was close enough so I could see that her pale pink lips were slightly parted. She had on a poke bonnet, but it was pushed back far enough that I could see the full glory of her sunshine-colored hair. It was one of the most magnificent sights I'd ever seen, like a beautiful sunset that catches you unawares and causes you to draw in your breath.

Her face was lightly tanned, as you would have expected in that country, but it was beautiful. I don't know why it was beautiful, but all its parts seemed to go together in a harmony that produced beauty.

I could see she was not from wealthy people, not unless they were eccentric, because her gown was of the plainest gingham and was colored gray. She wore no facial makeup and no jewelry. I was dumbstruck staring at her. I had the strangest feeling that I could feel a power emanating from her. It was a feeling of goodness, of happiness, as if all was right with the world and all in it.

She couldn't have been more than twenty years old, and lived in one of the worst hellholes in Texas. And yet I was feeling drawn to her as I never had been before in my life.

And then she turned and looked directly at me through the window. Her eyes were innocent and deep blue, and her gaze seemed to say she knew I had been watching her. Almost involuntarily I took a step backward. Her eyes seemed to come straight through the window and infuse the inside of the depot with her presence.

The judge was looking at me strangely. "What the hell is the matter with you? You look like somebody hit you in the head with a wagon tongue."

It was about the way I was feeling, such had been the impression the girl had made on me. I didn't want to point because she was still looking through the window at me. I said, "Who is that? Who is that girl?"

The judge rolled his fat cigar around in his mouth and said, "What girl, boy? Who you talking about?"

I took my eyes away from her for the second it took me to face him. "Her." Again I didn't gesture. "Out the window there. Standing by a buggy. She's got golden hair. Wearing a gingham frock."

I thought he'd never look. Finally he glanced out the window. He looked for a second and then turned back to me. "Ain't no girl out there, boy. Heat getting you?"

I swiveled my eyes back to where they had been looking. Sure enough, she was gone. I strode quickly to the window, hoping to see where she might have went, but there was no sign of her. The buggy and the horse just stood there alone. It made me wrinkle my brow. Unless she had gone into the milling crowd unloading the train, she could not have vanished so fast. The depot was at least fifty yards from the dilapidated town and I would have seen her if she had walked there. In desperation I turned to the judge and began describing her.

He said, in that judge's voice of his, "What's this girl to you?"

I stumbled. I couldn't really explain. Finally I said, lamely, "I don't know. She looked like someone. She was a pretty girl. What else do you need to know?"

He took his cigar out of his mouth and gave me a stern look. "I'm gonna give you some advice for nothing. And you better take it. Might save you a whole lot of trouble. The boys around here don't like no outsiders messin' with their womenfolk. You can spend all the money you like and we'll take it, but the womenfolk ain't for sale. Near as I know, ain't a lady in this town over the age of fourteen ain't already been spoke for."

"It's not like that," I said. I was going from window to window, trying to catch sight of her. And it *wasn't* like that. I did not feel toward her as I had felt about Genevieve. In fact, I couldn't have said how I felt. All I knew was that I had to see her again, talk to her, touch her.

The judge was following after me. He said, "Boy, I don't know what you are up to, but you better not go charging around here looking for some girl that belongs to another man. Somebody liable to give you a bellyful of lead. You understand me, boy?"

The pull of the girl was still strong and the judge's voice was irritating. I whirled on him. I said, "You old fool, if you can't tell me her name, then shut your mouth. You're going to get your fair share of the money we're bringing into town. That is, if you do your job and do what you're told. But if you call me 'boy' again I'm liable to squash that cigar in your face."

It caused his mouth to drop open, and he took a step backward. "Why . . . why . . . why, I never in my life . . ."

But I wasn't paying him any more mind. I had spotted a man with a badge on his chest, standing on the platform, speaking with Dennis. If anyone knew who the girl was, it would have to be the sheriff rather than that stuffed shirt of a judge. I jerked the door open and stepped out on the platform. I was confident she wouldn't be hard to identify, and to find. No town the size of Pecos was going to contain two such angels, at least, such delicately beautiful women, anyway.

Outside, it appeared the train was nearly unloaded. I could hear the engine getting up steam. The train was moments from pulling out. I walked up directly to where Dennis and the sheriff were standing. I had no intention of standing on ceremony. I said, "Sheriff, my name is Willis Young. I've just seen a young lady and it is important that I know her name or how to find her."

The sheriff had been talking to Dennis, but he stopped and turned to look at me. He was a man of about Dennis's age, with a weathered face and strong, square shoulders. He was wearing a gun but I could see the hammer was tied down. I doubted he allowed much shooting in his town. He said, "What?"

I repeated myself. I said, "She's got golden hair and delicate features and she's wearing a gray gingham gown. I'd reckon her to be about twenty."

The sheriff looked at Dennis. "He with you?"

Dennis nodded, but he was giving me strange glances. "He's the land owner. Sort of my partner."

"Do you know what he's talking about? This golden-haired girl?"

"He didn't see her," I said quickly. "And I only seen her through the depot window."

Dennis said, "Willis, we are kind of busy here. This is going to be a close thing to get unloaded. This is Sheriff Lew Wallace. Maybe he can help you out a little later."

The sheriff nodded. He said, "I'm trying to get some big wagons up here so we can start loading up. We are having to make up some big teams to handle the pull."

I saw it wasn't going to do any good. They probably thought I was crazy, but I was determined to find that girl. I said, "Does the description I gave ring any bells with you?"

The sheriff rubbed his jaw. He said, "Well, you come at me so fast I ain't sure I caught the whole of it."

I started to describe her again, but Dennis all but pushed me aside. "Willis, we've got to get this equipment off the train. We can go into all this later. Why don't you take over and boss one of the crews? We're short on our men."

I didn't know much about men, and even less about unloading oil-field equipment. Besides, my mind was still on the girl. I turned toward the town.

Pecos wasn't much of a town. The commercial part of it was a staggered line of buildings, maybe some ten or twelve in number, fronting on a street that ran between the town and the railroad. There were two or three saloons, a cafe, a sort of a hotel that advertised weekly rates and running water, and several dry-goods establishments, all three of which appeared to double in the grocery trade. I saw a Baptist church, and what I took to be a Catholic mission. The residential area was scattered sort of haphazardly around, as if people had just stopped and said, *This looks like a pretty good place to build a house.* I certainly couldn't see any pattern to the place. There were no streets laid out or any seeming plan; about all the buildings of Pecos had in common was a weather-beaten look and a sort of tilt, as if the next gust of wind would blow them over. Maybe at one time some of them had seen paint, but wind and sand had scoured them all down to a sad grayness.

I stepped up on the near end of the boardwalk that ran along the business section. As I walked I glanced into what stores I could, hoping to catch sight of the girl. There weren't many women around, golden-haired or not. All I saw were a few in a mercantile, looking over cloth goods, and a waitress in the cafe.

I stopped when I got to the last building, which happened to be a bank. I glanced in through its curtained windows but there was no golden-haired illusion in there, though I thought that was where she should have been kept, considering her hair.

I stepped off the boardwalk and looked at the straggling houses. She had to be in one of those, but I sure as hell couldn't go knocking on doors. The crew already thought I was different.

But what I couldn't get onto was the fact that nobody seemed to know her. It was impossible to believe that the townspeople could be blind to such delicate beauty. Hell, maybe I was losing my mind. Maybe I'd dreamed the girl up. Maybe I'd been on the train too long, drunk too much whiskey, listened to Dennis about drilling for oil too long. Maybe my mind had slipped.

And then a thought hit me and the whole situation became clear. I had the answer, but it wasn't the one I wanted.

She had got off the train to stretch her legs or to look for a cafe to get a bite to eat. Likely, the conductor had informed the passengers that the stop in Pecos would be an extra-long one. It made perfect sense and explained why no one seemed to know such a striking girl. And when she'd disappeared so suddenly, it had been to reboard the train which was but a few steps from where she had been standing.

I was now all in a dither to get back on the train and have one more look at the girl, maybe ask her name and where she lived. But the engine was blowing steam and thinking about getting under way. There were four passenger cars and I took off on a dead run for the one nearest the engine. I ran into the conductor as I swung aboard.

He said, "Here, what are you doing back aboard? We are about to pull out. Unless you want to go to El Paso, you better get down."

I brushed past him and swung open the door to the first car. I said, over my shoulder, "Forgot something. Be right off."

She was not in the first car. I was not hurrying now, and I made sure of that. I walked carefully down the aisle, looking intently on both sides. The train was not so full that she would have been hard to find.

She wasn't on the second car. I was starting to get anxious. There had been a few young women in the car, but nothing like her. As I passed into the third car I heard the sound of the train whistle. It was the engineer's warning that anybody that didn't want to ride had better get off.

But I still wouldn't let myself hurry. If she was aboard, I was not going to overlook her. If I had to, I'd jump off the train at full speed.

The third car was a bust, and halfway down the fourth and last car I felt the jerk as the engine powered up and took up the slack in the couplings between the cars. In another moment we'd be rolling.

I finished the fourth car about the time the train reached the speed of a man walking. I let myself out into the vestibule, stepped down to the lowest step, and then hopped off onto the ground.

If she was on the train, she'd been well-hid. I walked back toward the depot with my head down, discouraged. I was aiming to step inside the depot again, but Dennis got in front of me and hailed me down. I didn't see the sheriff. Dennis said, "Where in hell you been, Willis?"

I shrugged. "Been trying to figure out where that girl went. Thought maybe she'd got back on the train."

He frowned at me. "What has come over you? I expected to find you mooning around about that Genevieve back in Houston, but you ain't gave her a second's thought. What are you, fickle? You're not here a half an hour until you got you some blonde spotted."

I said—wearily, because I was tired and confused—"I told you it was not like that, Dennis. There was something strange about the girl."

He said, "Huh! I would guess so. If she was the peach you claim she is, she ain't got no business in a wallow like this place."

I flashed at him a little. "I tell you, it's nothing like that. Forget she's a girl. She was different. You could feel a kind of power coming off her, a sort of pull, you might say." Then I realized how strange that must have sounded, so I shook my head and said, "Forget it. How we coming on the equipment?"

Dennis pushed his hat back and looked around. Now that the train was gone, it was easy to appreciate the vast amount of equipment and materials we had stockpiled. He said, "We are having trouble getting enough big wagons with teams. This is going to take longer than I thought. What I been figuring is that the first thing we ought to do is put the airplane back together and fly over the terrain and see what we're faced with."

I said, "That makes sense." It would give me a feeling of freedom to have the plane ready to fly.

Dennis said, "Look here, I'm gonna be involved around here for a time. Why don't you go on over to that place that calls itself a hotel and get us lined up with some rooms? There is five of us."

Which I already knew, but I guessed that Dennis figured I was off my rocker and needed reminding. So I just nodded and started walking across the open ground toward the commercial center of the municipality of Pecos.

Halfway across, I stopped and took a look around. Just off to my left, across the railroad tracks, I could see the cut line of the Pecos River, the only dependable water for two hundred miles in any direction. Of course, I couldn't actually see the river, but I could follow its course by the salt cedar and mesquite trees lining its banks. If I remembered correctly, you had to be mighty thirsty to take a drink out of the Pecos. In the years it overflowed its banks, it would leave behind big patches of snow-white alkali when it receded. I had heard that at one time oak and sycamore and cottonwood trees had grown alongside its waters, but as the river water had soured, the good trees had died, leaving only the salt cedar which didn't seem to care what it drank.

But I was interested to see that farmers from the town had dug irrigation canals and were raising crops. Up near town it appeared that most of the fields were taken up with truck, garden vegetables and melons and whatnot. But farther out, I could see some fair-sized fields of corn. I could even see some gentle hills that appeared to be covered with grass. Of course, there were milk cows up in town, but I saw a goodly number of range cattle scattered about. It surprised me. Pecos must have been having one of its wet years—which meant at least one rainfall.

Still, it was hard, desolate country—"hell on women and horses," as the saying went. Another thing they said about the Pecos country was that it was thirty miles between towns, and a mile farther between trees. It was easy to believe.

I stepped up on the boardwalk and opened the door to the hotel. It and the bank were the only two-story structures in town. But, judging from the way the hotel seemed to be braced for the wind, I decided that I wanted to sleep on the first floor.

It made an attempt to look like a proper hotel. It had a lobby with several hard-backed chairs scattered around, and even a desk for the clerk who rented the rooms. I didn't see any sign of a dining room, but then, I hadn't expected to, any more than I expected to see a barbershop or an elegant bar like the Galvez featured.

The desk clerk was a stoop-shouldered old man. He asked me my business in town while I signed his register. He was a little disappointed when I only wanted two rooms. I guess he had expected we'd put up the whole gang we'd hired to help unload.

I took the two keys and my valise that I'd rescued from the depot, and walked down the front hall. They did not have electric lighting. They didn't even have gas. All they had were coal-oil lanterns spaced every so often down the dim hall. I looked in the first room and decided it would do fine for Charlie and Joel and Joe Cairo, as there were four beds in the room.

I went on down to the end of the hall to the corner room. It was a good deal brighter and cheerier, having windows on two sides. There were two beds and a good-sized table that Dennis could use for his work. I pitched my valise on the nearest bed, broke it open, and pulled out a bottle of whiskey. I'd been wanting a drink for some time. There was a pitcher of water and some glasses on a sideboard. I wasn't afraid of the water because I knew it hadn't come from the river. The town had a well. In fact, several of the houses around town would have wells. There was water under the ground, but it was shallow and not of much volume. You couldn't water your stock on what you could get out of a town well. Most of them were hand-dug and went dry from time to time. Water was a mighty iffy article around the Pecos country.

I mixed me a drink of about half-and-half and took a good swig. It wasn't too bad, just a shade on the brackish side. I freshened it up with a little more whiskey and then went over and sat on the bed I'd slung my valise on. I could see in two directions, for all the good it did me; Pecos wasn't all that scenic. I just sat there drinking and trying not to think about the golden-haired girl.

After about an hour, the door opened and Dennis came in. He was nearly soaked-through with sweat. He headed for the whiskey. When he had a drink in his hand he said, "What this country needs is a damn good rain. And some real dirt instead of this god-awful sand, and some trees. And a whole bunch of stuff to make it fit to live in. I know you told me how bad this damn place was, but you didn't say it was *hell*. Hell on earth."

I shook my head. "It ain't *actual* hell." I paused. "But it is a good ways southwest of heaven."

CHAPTER

DENNIS SAID, "Well, you sure didn't exaggerate when you was telling me about this country. If anything, you didn't give it its just due. This has got to be the most sorry-assed place I've ever set foot on. And you didn't exaggerate about what we were likely to *not find* here. I'm mighty glad I brought damn near everything."

"How are you coming along on the transportation?"

Dennis leaned back in his chair and rubbed his chin. It made kind of a scratching noise. He said, "Well, it's as bad as you said it would be. They do have one big truck here, and that, along with the one we brought, should handle the boilers which is the heaviest items. The sheriff is trying to get together some big draft teams and some big wagons, but we got a world of drill stem and pipe and everything else. I'm anxious to see where we got to get to. They tell me we are standing in paradise, next to the outlying country."

I shrugged. "If it's still the same, that would be the truth."

"I'm anxious to get your airplane assembled and get up in the air and take a look at what we got to go through."

"Shouldn't take long. You did bring gas, didn't you?"

"Of course. Ain't airplane gas, but it will work all right. I don't guess they got a gas station in this town."

"I would doubt it. Before you put any gas in any airplane I'm going to fly, you be damn sure you strain it through a chamois skin at least."

He flicked me a mock salute. "Yes, my lieutenant!" Then he fixed me with a gimlet eye. "You have any luck finding your yaller-haired girl?"

"I didn't look for her," I said briefly. I stood up. "Let's go see if we can find anything to eat. I think this town has only one cafe. We better get there before they run out of everything."

As we walked down the shaky boardwalk toward the cafe, I asked Dennis how long he figured it would take to get the airplane rigged-up.

"I reckon it will take a little better than a day. I'll get Joe Cairo to help me. He's about as good a mechanic as I've run across. I don't guess he's ever worked on an airplane before, but machinery is machinery. I'll put Joel and Charlie to work helping the sheriff get the draft stock lined up."

"What can I do?"

He cut his eyes sideways at me. We both knew I was not much good at mechanical work. He said, "You want to fly an airplane *you've* worked on?"

"A good point."

"You might talk to the blacksmith. We got to get fixed-up with some kind of big tank we can haul water in. You've seen those trucks they carry gasoline in?"

"Milk, too. Same shape."

"You reckon you could draw something like that up? Show it to the blacksmith and see if he thinks he can make it? Has to be made out of light sheet iron or tin. Weigh a ton full of water."

I waited until we had got a table in the cafe and had ordered before I told him about Judge Crater.

He made a face as I described my talk with the justice of the peace. "Yeah, the sheriff already warned me about the son of a bitch. The onliest thing wrong is that he really does have all that authority. Sheriff

Wallace said everybody knows he's as crooked as a snake, but nobody can do nothing about it."

"What are you going to do?"

Dennis shrugged. "Pay the son of a bitch off, I reckon. Don't seem to have no choice. He can shut us down cold if he takes a mind to."

"On what basis? We're not breaking any laws. I'd tell the son of a bitch to go to hell if he comes around with his hand out."

"Willis, you know where we are the same as I do. The sheriff says he is the law and there's nothing to be done about it. Sheriff Wallace says the judge's territory takes in three counties. He may just be a justice of the peace, but he's a damn big one and he's backed by the state of Texas. The sheriff says the judge can call in state law, even the militia, if he's a mind to, and Wallace says he is just mean enough. We ain't back in Houston or Austin or somewhere there's legal help. This guy can charge us with pissing on a public street and there's nothing we can do except pay a fine or go to jail or both."

"I don't like it," I said. "In fact, it makes me angry as hell."

"Well, you got plenty of time to get glad in them same pants that you are wearing. I don't reckon the judge is losing a lot of sleep over your state of mind."

There wasn't much reply to that. Besides, it wasn't my money being used for a bribe. I did start to ask Dennis if going along with immoral and illegal acts was okay for a Christian, but a soft spot of kindness caused me to hold my tongue. Dennis looked like he'd had about all he could handle for one day. I didn't see no point in stretching him further.

Next morning I did more or less what Dennis had asked. I went around to the blacksmith's and drew him up a plan for a tank we could haul water in. He took it and studied it and turned it this way and that. What he didn't like were the rounded sides. He was a man used to working in straight lines, in squares and box shapes. Finally, he reluctantly said he'd give it a try. He had a welding machine that ran off a gasoline generator and he figured he could just about handle it. The biggest problem was that the lightest material he had was some quarter-inch-thick sheet iron that was usually used for roofing material. It was going to make the tank uncommonly heavy, even before it was filled with water. He said he could order some one-eighth-inch-thick sheet metal but it would take several days to get in. I figured we didn't have the time so I told him to go ahead with what he had. He wouldn't give me a price; said I'd have to wait until he could see how he was going to make out, bending that heavy iron the way we wanted it. If he saw he couldn't do it, it would cost us a fifty-dollar bill for his effort. I thought that was fair, and said so.

After that, I found myself wandering around town, looking into this establishment and then that one. Somehow I always seemed to work the conversation around to the golden-haired girl in the gingham dress.

For all the good it did me. Mostly what I got were blank looks and an occasional, "Who?"—but not much else. The most reliable source I asked, the few women I was able to talk with, said without question that no such young lady had ever lived around Pecos, or even visited, for that matter. One weathered woman, looking old beyond her years, asked me just how long I thought such delicate skin and bright hair would hold up come the first sandstorm or the first winter blizzard. She said, "You ain't going to find any of them flappers out here, mister. No rolled-down hose and turned-up hair. This country takes the paint off of buildings and the pretty off of women in mighty short order."

I went back to the hotel, shaking my head. I knew I'd seen that girl, could still see her in my mind's eye. The only explanation that worked was that the girl could not be from the town. I had asked enough people to be sure. A girl that looked like her just didn't go unnoticed. I had even wondered if she couldn't be off some ranch miles out in the country, but all my sources had shaken their heads and denied that possibility. "We know ever' ranching family within twenty-five miles, and ain't none of them got a female like you describe. And they got to come to town sooner or later. Ain't nobody can stay out in them badlands by theyselves."

I had a drink of whiskey and waited on Dennis. When he didn't show up I went and had a bite of lunch by myself. It turned out there was another cafe in town: a little place run by a Mexican family. They made a good *carne asada* and featured fresh fruit on their menu. That part surprised me, but it seemed that this little corner of hell grew some of the best melons and peaches and plums you were likely to find. They also had fresh vegetables, and I was content to lay off the potatoes and biscuits for a while and make do with the garden fixings and tortillas made out of fresh cornmeal. The little cafe was the first decent consideration I'd found in the damn country.

To kill time, I went around to the livery stable and rented a horse for the day. I didn't have anything particular in mind, just thought I would ride out and look the country over. The last time I'd been in the Pecos River country, I'd been with my dad and I'd been all of sixteen or seventeen years old. Naturally I'd viewed the country through his eyes. When you were around Wilson Young you tended to be influenced and swayed by his personality, which was a decidedly firm one. Now I wanted to look at the land with my own eyes, older eyes, eyes with some experiences that even Wilson Young couldn't claim. He may have been in fights for his life, but never, I reckoned, at fifteen thousand feet up, with enemies that could come at you from any direction.

I headed generally north out of town, aiming for where I remembered my land was. I had no intention of riding all the way to it, at least not that day. I just wanted to amble along. It had been some little time since I had been on a horse, but it's not something you forget easily. Besides, the old nag they'd given me at the livery stable was just as content to take it slowly in the afternoon heat.

Once I'd left the Pecos River valley, I could see the lay of the land, and it was not promising. The terrain was rolling plains, but it looked as dry as a Carry Nation saloon. There was greasewood and some mesquite, but most of the growth was cactus and brambles and rocks. Overhead, the sky was a brilliant blue with an unblinking sun as yellow as the girl's hair. You not only felt the heat from above, it even radiated up from the ground. I couldn't see how anyone could make a living

off such dirt, if it could be called that. Off in the far distance I could
see a cow or two, but they were about as scarce as the grass. I expected
that if my daddy could see me out inspecting my inheritance, it would
give him a good laugh. Not many men were able to give their sons a
gift that left them poorer than before the bequest. It just fitted in with
Wilson Young's sense of humor. Yet all I had to do was play the dutiful
son, tell him I was sorry for going against his will, and I could have
all the money I could spend.

I didn't need or want money that bad.

After an hour or so of wandering around, I turned back toward
town. You could examine the land from atop a horse, but an airplane
would give you a better view. As I rode I wondered how Dennis was
coming along putting my plane together. The faster we had wings, the
less confined we'd be.

Dennis came in little before six o'clock, looking tired and dirty and
disgusted. He said, "I swear, I never run across a bunch of people in
one patch so mean-spirited and cheap and suspicious and mistrustful
and downright coldhearted as this gang around here." He got the bottle
of whiskey and a glass and sank down on his bed.

I let him get a drink down before I asked him exactly what he
meant. "You got an example or are you just condemning the town
from border to border?"

He gave a little annoyed toss of his head. "This ain't something I
find very damn funny. I got a big job on my hands and, except for the
men I brought, I can't get no cooperation out of nobody without putting up money first. I'll give you an example. I needed a team of mules
this morning to move around some equipment and supplies. Make it
easier to load. Well, the man I am hiring to freight two wagons to the
drilling site—at a damn good price, I might add—wanted five bucks
for that team of mules for the day and wanted the money first before
he put on a foot of harness."

I had to admit that was bit narrow. But I said, "Does this man
know for certain he's got a freighting contract?"

Dennis almost came off the bed. "Hell, yes! I've already given him a hundred-dollar advance. Cash money. And he has a hissy fit over two mules. Hell!"

"Just that?"

"Hell, no. I had to work six men this morning, not counting the crew we brought. Well, they wanted lunch. So I went down to that cafe we ate at—Etie's, ain't it?—and made the arrangements to come back and pay after they'd ate. But no. They wanted some money up front. I give 'em twenty dollars, and when I went in for my own lunch at about two this afternoon they claimed I owed eight more dollars! I wanted them to show me how nine men could have eaten more than twenty dollars' worth, especially when their blue plate special is just six bits and a steak is a dollar. Turned out they had served sixteen who *claimed* to be working for me. At least that is what *they* claimed." He shook his head and lifted his glass to his lips. "This place beats all I've ever seen. I thought I'd seen cheap and crooked, but I hadn't seen nothing."

"Dennis, I hate to be an 'I told you so,' but I did. I told you you weren't heading for paradise."

"Yes, but you didn't say we were heading for Pinch-Penny City, neither."

"It's a poor place, Dennis."

"It ain't just the bunch of them being skinflints that gets me. It's how ungrateful they are, how stingy, how hateful."

That surprised me. " 'Hateful'?"

"Hell, yes. Here we are coming to this one-dog town and bringing more money than they've seen in a hunnert years. You'd think they could at least be pleasant about it. I don't expect them to be grateful, but I don't care much for being sneered at and disliked for giving them jobs and money. It don't make no damn sense, but they act like they hate you for giving them a chance to earn a little money or do a little business." He threw his head back and finished his drink. "What's the matter with these folks, Willis?"

I thought about it for a long moment. As he'd been talking I'd realized it had reminded me of my mother's work among the poor and needy on the Mexican side. Instead of being grateful to her they'd resented her even while they were eating the food she'd brought them. It hadn't bothered her; she'd just kept right on doing what good she could. She'd told me, "Don't blame them for being poor and don't blame them for hating you for pointing it out. And I point it out, me and the other ladies in the church, every time we bring them help."

I said, "Dennis, you want them to respect you and be grateful. Instead they envy you and wish you their same lot. Listen, this has always been poor country, as far back as you want to go. And the people who have lived here have lived hardscrabble lives. Nothing comes easy here. Nothing is pretty or soft or nice-smelling. It is hard and rocky and barren and poor and people who have lived here have grown accustomed to snatching for anything they can get their hands on, whether it belongs to their next-door neighbor or to you. The life has made them hard and cheap and crooked and mean-spirited and ungrateful. When they steal or swindle, in their minds they aren't committing a crime, they are surviving. After a while, you'll start to understand."

Dennis got up and came to the table and poured himself out another glass of whiskey. He shook his head. "I don't know. I swear I've never seen so many narrow-faced son of bitches with their eyes set so close together. I think some of them's mommas and daddies go to the same family reunion."

"I wouldn't doubt it," I said. "I would imagine there is a shortage of brides and grooms as a general thing. Some of them might have had to dip back into the family to make a marriage."

Dennis sighed and shook his head. "Hell, I don't care if they married their sisters, as long as they help me get this work done."

"What's the condition of the airplane?"

"Ought to be ready tomorrow." He made a grimace. "I wish to hell I could say the same about the rest of the work."

"Where are you hung up?"

"Where *ain't* I hung up? I can't get anything to stay done. As soon as I reckon a thing is set, like loading twenty stands of pipe on a wagon, I come back around and find the men who were supposed to have done it squabbling amongst themselves about who is supposed to do what. I wish you'd find that angel of yours. Maybe she could take the devil out of these folks and I could get some work done."

I frowned. "Exactly what angel are you talking about?"

He waved a hand. "Why, that golden-haired girl you claim you saw."

"I never called her a angel."

"Yes you did. You said you'd seen an angel."

I gave him a look. "I meant an angel like she was so damn beautiful. All perfect and golden. I didn't mean an *angel* angel. Hell!"

Dennis gave a snort. "I know that, sonny boy. For the right reasons. Ain't no more angels on earth. They all rose up with Christ."

I slid him a sly look. "You know, I'd think these folks around here would regard you as an angel. You appear out of nowhere, bringing miracles, jobs and money, when they had no reason to expect such."

"There's more truth in that than you mean. I know you are ragging me about them being so damn ungrateful."

"Maybe it's because you don't look much like an angel. Maybe if you lost about twenty pounds."

He looked stern. "You want to watch your mouth about such matters. You are comin' damn close to blaspheming."

"How come you say there ain't no angels now? Why not?"

He stood up. "I ought not to be talking to a heathen like you. You need to read the Bible and then you wouldn't have so many smart-aleck questions. Listen, there was angels all around in the Old Testament. Plenty of them. Talking and teaching and leading and doing God's work. Then you get over into the New Testament and they go to slacking off. That was because Jesus had showed up with a whole new deal and he was handling things on the spot, so to speak. 'Course, a few was still around while Christianity was getting shaped-up, but now if you got any questions, all you got to do is go to the Good Book."

I was lolling back in my chair, enjoying the slight riding I was giving him. "So you claim that the girl I saw couldn't have been an angel noway, nohow."

He snorted. "What would an angel want with you? Good heavens, don't make me laugh, I'm too hungry. C'mon, let's go get some grub."

There was no shortage of flat prairie to use as an airstrip. Dennis and his helpers had put the JN-6H together in an old warehouse and it was a simple matter to push back the big doors and roll the airplane out onto smooth ground. The Jenny had been built as a trainer so there were two seats, one in front for the student. The instructor usually flew in the rear seat since the visibility was actually better from the second seat.

I got in and buckled up my harness and Dennis pulled the prop through a couple of times while I had the ignition off. The engine was going to be a little stiff, and the carburetor needed priming.

Finally he nodded at me that he thought it was ready. I flipped the ignition switch. I called to him to let him know that the engine would be firing as he pulled the prop through: "Switch on. Watch your body."

It took three tries, but then the engine caught, coughed once or twice, and then settled into a smooth roar. Dennis hustled around to climb into the front cockpit.

The sound of the airplane's engine, so different from any sound they'd heard before, had acted as a clarion call to half the town. Before Dennis could get himself strapped in, there were fifty people surrounding the airplane—to the back, on both sides, and even in front. A few were dangerously near the whirling propeller, which, even though it was only idling, would take an arm off as neatly as a knife. I began motioning them back and Dennis even stood up in his cockpit to wave his arms and yell at the ones in front, especially those near the prop. Finally Joe Cairo and Charlie saw the problem and began pushing and pulling people out of the way so I could begin to taxi. I did so gingerly, for the crowd was moving along with me, gawking like idiots, and some of them rushing up to touch different parts of the airplane. I saw it was no use yelling or scolding. They simply had no idea how to act around an airplane.

But finally I got a break through the pressing throng and I eased the throttle forward, the engine beginning to whine faster and the wheels rolling us away from the gawkers. Finally I was clear and I taxied out onto a broad strip of prairie that I had examined the day before, both from horseback and afoot. There were some small rocks and low bushes, but it was straight and flat enough that I thought the airplane could handle it. I taxied downwind at a clip that soon left the townspeople behind. Dennis turned and gave me a thumbs-up as I swung the plane around into the wind. I was cramming in the throttle even as I turned the plane, so that by the time I was aimed into the wind we were really starting to roll. I was heading right back toward town, toward the warehouse and the crowd of people. Not a one of them moved backward. If anything, they sort of surged forward toward the plane. But it didn't matter. I had reached a speed where the tail of the airplane had come up and the control stick was feeling light and alive in my hands. I pulled back slightly on the stick and the airplane lifted smoothly, leaving behind the rough ground and riding a smooth layer of air. I looked over the side of the airplane as we passed over the crowd not thirty feet below. Hell, I was certain I could have come within a foot of their upturned faces and they wouldn't have moved, much less blinked. This was big doings. In their lives, seeing an airplane up close and watching it take off was the acme of excitement most would ever achieve. I doubted that more than a half dozen had even seen a plane, unless it was the mail plane to El Paso, and that would have been a speck—ten or twenty miles away. But it was their lives and they could live anyway they wanted. Wasn't none of my business.

I banked the airplane back around to the east and came in over the town. I was going to take my bearings from the center of town. Once over it, I turned due north and flew at about eight hundred feet above the ground. We wanted to be able to see some horizon but still be able to study the terrain. Dennis turned in his cockpit and motioned me lower. He would need to see what kind of ground his wagons and his trucks would have to go over. I dropped down a couple hundred feet and directed my attention straight ahead of the airplane. I was

looking for the plat marker. When Wilson Young had brought me with
him to look at the new land, he'd also brought along a surveyor to
make sure there was no question about whose land was where. When
he'd finished his survey, the surveyor had driven an iron rod deep into
the ground at the southeasternmost corner of the land. Four feet of
the pipe had stayed aboveground and the surveyor had painted it red.
I knew that red paint would be long gone, but I figured the rod was
still there. The surveyor had told my daddy that that marker was due
north of the center of Pecos at a distance of about ten miles. The pipe
would be hard to spot from the air, but I felt sure we'd come across it
with some diligent searching.

Then I saw it. Or rather, I saw its shadow, since the eastern sun
was up and blazing and making the shadow a bigger mark than the
rod itself. I motioned for Dennis to look so that he could see. The rod
was on top of a gentle little mound that had so much salt in the earth
it looked like it had snowed. I rolled the airplane on its side and threw
it into a hard left turn, descending as I did. It was no fence post
and it wasn't part of the natural growth of the land. For a second my
mind leaped back to that day so long past when I'd stood there with
my father, Wilson Young, and watched the planting of the boundary
marker. At that time I hadn't known the day was coming when I'd
inherit the land as a punishment.

I tapped Dennis on the shoulder, reaching forward. He looked
around and I motioned on toward the north. He nodded and I straightened up the plane and once more took up a northerly course. The plat
of land was almost square. I intended to fly around its borders and
then crisscross it a few times to give Dennis an idea of the terrain he'd
be working with.

As well as I remembered, the eastern line ran north about five
miles and then turned west for six or seven miles. After that, back to
the south for about five miles and then due east for six or seven more
miles and we should come back out around the boundary marker.

I took the airplane up to about fifteen hundred feet to cool us off
a bit. It was a little cooler, but not much. That was a powerful desert
below us, and an even stronger sun above.

I started crisscrossing the land, giving Dennis a god idea of where he might want to drill. To see the same amount of land on horseback would have taken him days. And he would have had to go on horseback since no truck could have gotten over some of the rough spots below.

Finally I flew back to the boundary marker and then banked the plane in a turn back to Pecos. When I figured myself about two miles from the town, I killed the engine. It grew quiet. All you could hear was the sound of the wind through the wire struts between the two wings. We were only at about five hundred feet, but that was plenty. The Jenny would glide like a seagull. I was hoping that if the townspeople didn't hear the sound of the plane returning, they wouldn't come swarming out and clutter up the ground I planned to land on.

It appeared to be working, for as I aimed at the old warehouse I was going to use as a hangar, I didn't see any suicidal throngs of gawkers crowding toward the plane. I was down to fifty feet, with the warehouse a quarter of a mile away. Now a few people were starting to materialize, but not in such numbers as to be a danger to us or to themselves.

Just before I touched down I pulled back slightly on the stick and flared out the little plane so that I made a three-point, full-stall landing. We weren't doing more than twenty miles per hour when we hit the ground. I never had to touch the brake as we slowed over the rough ground and came to a stop not ten feet from the big mouth of the warehouse. Dennis turned around in his seat and gave me a look with his eyebrows raised. I just yawned and showed my palms upward with a shrug as if it wasn't anything to be remarked.

Dennis and I jumped down, and Joe Cairo and Charlie came out to help us push the airplane into the warehouse. Dennis said, to both of them, "I want somebody watching this airplane all the time."

Charlie said, "Does it pay wages?"

Dennis gave him a sour look. "Of course it pays wages, Charlie. Everything that gets done in this damn town pays wages. Why should you be different? You been here long enough for the stingy to rub off on you."

As we walked toward the hotel he said, "That bunch crowding around like they did, made up my mind to something."

"What?"

He shook his head. "Never mind. You don't need to know right now. I'll tend to it tonight."

"You want some help?"

"No. I figure you will object. I want it done before you see it."

"You are making me curious."

"Good. Just remember how close those fools came to getting us and them killed, the way you were trying to get around them on take-off. If you hadn't been able to bring that plane in dead-stick there is no telling how many we'd've had across our landing path. I think I got a way to make them respect that plane a little more."

I couldn't get another word out of him, but at lunch he started talking about the difficulty of freighting his equipment across that barren plain. He said, "I like that mound your boundary pole is on. Looks like there is salt all around it. It could be another salt dome. As far as I can tell, it looks to be as good a place as any, judging from the rest of the land, to spud the first well in. At least, it is the closest place to town." He gazed across the cafe. "Wouldn't that be something—to find another salt dome out here like Spindletop? Boy howdy, wouldn't everybody have to eat their words then!"

"When are we going to start freighting the equipment and the supplies?"

He grimaced. "Start tomorrow. I don't know how many days it is going to take. I just hope we get it all out there before we kill every mule and oxen around this place."

"That water tank is not going to be ready any too quick."

The waiter brought our food and Dennis started cutting his tough steak. "We'll have to make do with what water we can carry in barrels. First thing is, we got a derrick to build, and boy am I glad I brought as much lumber as I did. Biggest piece of wood around here appears to be a toothpick."

"Obviously you've noticed all the trees around here."

After lunch I asked him again what he was going to do with the airplane that night, but once again he declined to answer. I said, "Look here, I got a right to know what you're going to do to a machine I'm flying."

"Ain't got nothing to do with your flying. Airplane will fly just the same."

He left me baffled and with orders to go and spur on the blacksmith to greater efforts in constructing the portable water tank. I shrugged it off. I hadn't figured the trip to Pecos was going to be a pleasure outing.

CHAPTER
11

⌒⟍_____⟍⟍ THE DIFFICULTY in freighting the materials and
equipment did not come from any lack of good-sized rolling stock. At
one time there had been a borax mine near Pecos, and a few of the big
sturdy wagons still remained. The problem was finding the teams to
pull such a load. It was going to take a team of at least six oxen, or
twelve mules and horses, to move such a burden, and there just weren't
that many draft animals to be had, not ones that could be matched up
in teams. Dennis had a teamster putting together what he could, but
when the first wagon rolled out the next morning at dawn, it was clear
that the job was going to be a strain on the animals. By the time the
sun was up good, it would be ninety degrees and would just get hotter.
The worst of it was the draft animals having to carry their own water,
which cut down on the size load they could haul. Water weighs around
seven pounds a gallon and every animal could drink and would need
at least twenty gallons daily.

The blacksmith was moving along with the big water tank, but we
were both worried about what it would weigh when it was filled with
water. He said, "I don't know, sonny, I ain't never built nothin' like
this afore, but it appears to me you goin' to have a hell of a time gettin'

it where you want it when it's all full of water. My guess is this thing is going to hold three or four hundred gallons. That's a passel."

I didn't know how much it was going to hold and I didn't figure he did, either. I'd had some geometry and trigonometry, but not enough that I could put it to use figuring out the capacity of the tank. I didn't figure the blacksmith had had any, either, nor algebra.

We had the two trucks: the one we'd brought out and the one Dennis was renting in town. They were both Ford stake-bodies, but I doubted they could haul the water tank. The wagons were actually stouter than the trucks, and had bigger beds. We had to carry all the drilling pipe that Dennis had brought on the wagons because the pipes were too long for the trucks. It would be horse and mule and oxen power that got us moved.

I saw the first two wagons off with Dennis along as a passenger and direction giver. He was the only one who'd seen where they were going. The rest of the men, except for the drivers, had procured horses somewhere and they were riding escort. There were about ten of them, including our three. They'd be needed at the destination to do the unloading.

After the wagons were gone I went to the Mexican cafe and had breakfast. I ate some chili and eggs and then wandered out into the street to see what was stirring. It was very quiet after all the hustle and bustle to get the wagons loaded and away. I could see the sheriff in his office and Judge Crater in a kind of saloon-cafe that Dennis and I never went in. I could see the judge distinctly through the dingy plate-glass window. He was sitting at a table by himself, drinking a cup of coffee. He had on a black suit just like he had worn the day I'd met him, except this time he was wearing a bow tie. It made me wonder what kind of a man, even if he was a justice of the peace, would wear a coat and tie in such a place and in such a climate. A sudden urge to know more about this man who was flagrantly robbing Dennis came over me, and I pushed through the door and went up to the bar and ordered a mug of beer. After I was served I turned around so I could see the rest of the room. There wasn't another soul in the place and the judge was staring at me fixedly. The place wasn't so big that I had to raise my voice. I said, "You think you'll recognize me next time?"

He put his coffee cup down so hard it made a thud. He said, "Are you passing a smart-aleck remark on me, young man?"

I said, "No, nothing intended. Just noticed you giving me a good looking-over."

He kind of sneered. "You bunch think you can come down here with all your money and have things your own way."

I leaned against the bar. The bartender had gone into the back. I said, "Don't get me mixed up with money. I'm poor as Job's turkey. It won't be worth your time to threaten me." I regretted the words almost the instant they were out of my mouth, but I had been smoldering toward Crater ever since Dennis had told me the judge was shaking him down.

His next remark was a few seconds in coming. I expected he was making sure he'd heard right. Then he said, in a grating voice, "Does the fact that you git to fly around up yonder in an air-e-o-plane make you think you be somethin' special? Does it make you kind of light-headed where you go to mouthin' off to the recognized law around here? You looking to spend some time over yonder in our jail?"

"No, Judge, I ain't. I—"

He cut me off. "Just what did you mean by them words of yours? About me threatening you. Something about it wouldn't be worth my time? Let's get your meanin' clear."

I kept the bar solid to my back. I shrugged. I said, "I just taken notice that you were charging this oil-drilling company some pretty heavy fees and I couldn't figure out what for. What does a justice of the peace have to do with a drilling operation?"

He studied me for a moment and then he stood up and took off his frock coat. He laid it carefully over the back of the chair he'd been sitting in and then he started toward me. He took measured steps with his eyes fixed on my face. I was somewhat surprised to see that he was wearing a gun. It was a revolver and he had it in a holster high on his belt. He was wearing orange galluses that glared against the white of his shirt.

He stopped right in front of me. I took a swig of beer from my mug while I looked him in the eyes. He was bigger than I'd thought. And uglier. He put out a forefinger and tapped me in the chest. "You are either mighty dumb or mighty scatterbrained. Either way will get you in trouble, you go to making remarks about me taking illegal money. You'd have to prove that."

I finished my beer without unlocking my gaze, and set the mug on the bar. "In your court, I would guess."

He gave me a thin smile. "Not much law out here. I got a lot of jurisdiction and several sheriffs answering to me. Let's hear another smart remark, sonny."

I pushed away from the bar and stepped to the side. I was getting a little tired of having him in my face. But I had amazed myself. I had no direct part in the enterprise, no ax to grind, no profit to be gained, no nothing except to kill some time and be with a friend. And the first thing I do is make an enemy out of the most powerful man in the county. That wasn't overly bright, even for me. If I wanted to antagonize someone, it looked like I'd usually picked an occasion where there was some possible profit in the endeavor. But I had chosen this man just because I didn't like him. My inflammatory remarks weren't going to save Dennis a nickel, and in fact might cost him something extra. It appeared that my best move would be to make as graceful an exit as I could. I put a quarter on the bar to pay for the beer, and turned to face the judge. I didn't know what I meant to say, but what came out was, " 'Judge not, lest you be judged.' " And I waggled my finger in his face as I said it. It was a biblical quotation I guess I'd heard my mother say. It was a hell of a time for me to suddenly start coming up with Bible quotations.

But it had the effect of stunning him so that he stood there with his mouth open. While he was quiescent I turned on my heel and marched out of the place.

I let the screen door bang shut, feeling like a damn fool for what I'd just done. Crater had taken off his coat to show me he meant business, and I had no doubt that he did. The day would come when he'd want payment of some kind from me, and I'd better have it or I'd

find out what the inside of a pissant jail looked like. Maybe ol' Wilson
Young had been right about me having as much judgment as a rocking
chair.

I went back to the room and killed time until lunch, then went
behind the hotel to the Mexican cafe and had a small steak with fresh
tomatoes and sliced onions, and a big glass of cold beer. As it was, I
didn't really want that much of it except the cold beer. It was just
about too hot to eat.

I wandered out of the place and down toward the old cotton warehouse we were using as a hangar. We had the big doors locked and
Dennis had hired a man to keep watch over the plane. We were afraid
some of the locals would get to fooling with it and do it damage. The
watchman wasn't around, which didn't surprise me. I unlocked the
big padlock and pushed one of the doors back and went inside.
The plane was sitting there looking whole and unmolested.

Except that something about it didn't look quite right. I pushed
the other door back to get more light on the subject, and walked farther
inside. The closer I got, the more something didn't look right. The
nose of the plane was facing me, and the big cowling and engine hid
most of what was behind. It was only as I got to the leading edge of
the wings that I saw it.

There was a Lewis machine gun mounted on the fuselage right in
front of the forward cockpit. It was a Lewis mchine gun identical to
the ones we'd mounted on French Spads and Mieuports. I had no
doubt that at one time that same machine gun had been mounted on
a plane I had been flying. I figured it had crossed the Atlantic in the
footlocker of one Sergeant Dennis Frank. But what it was doing on a
Jenny in deep west Texas, was more than I could figure.

I walked around the wing and came up to the fuselage and stepped
up and dropped into the front cockpit. The machine-gun grips were
right there, right where they should be. Beside the gun was an ammunition pan. I leaned forward and opened the lid. She was prime full
of belts filled with .30-caliber machine-gun cartridges. Two hundred
rounds. The ammunition didn't look at all old or decayed. The copper
heads of the cartridges gleamed dully even in the dim light. The gun

was synchronized with the cam shaft to fire through the propeller. All it took to make the gun operational, was to slip the first cartridge in the belt into the firing chamber and pull back the receiver.

I wondered what Dennis had in mind. Did he plan to shoot up the town if things didn't go his way? With this baby you could blow hell out of a town in a way my father had never imagined. Maybe it was Dennis's answer to Judge John Crater. Maybe the next time Crater put the bite on him, Dennis would have me fly him over the judge's house while he shot the roof off.

I climbed out of the cockpit, shaking my head. It was one too many for me. I walked on outside and gazed off to the northeast. The wagons and the trucks would have been on the road about four hours. I wondered how they were making out. Maybe they'd broken down and needed help. Maybe I'd find them near some flat, and I could land and ask Dennis were we expecting a war.

I went back to the cockpit and leaned in and switched on the ignition and gave the primer a couple of pumps. I wasn't going to bother pulling the prop through. The engine was loose now, and should start easily. I put the throttle on the lowest setting and then went around to the front of the plane and pulled the prop through a revolution. That was to get oil up in the cylinders. After that, I cocked one end of the prop high and pulled it down and through. The engine sputtered and coughed, and then caught. For a second it ran rough, then it got smoother and smoother. Ever so slightly the plane began to edge forward, pulled by the propeller. I rushed around the end of one wing and caught up to the fuselage just as the plane began to move at about the speed of a man walking. I stepped up on the wing and climbed into the front cockpit. I had caught the townspeople off-guard. They were just starting to show up as I poured the throttle to the instrument panel and felt the plane surge forward. In a second we were bumping and racing over the uneven ground, leaving the gawkers behind. In another second I eased back on the stick and let the airplane soar into the open air away from the ground. Within a few moments the altimeter showed I had reached fifteen hundred feet, which not only brought a better view, but also relief from the searing heat of the

ground. I banked toward the east and then, using the town as a nav-
igational aid, struck off north, looking for the caravan heading for the
drilling site—the white mound near my boundary marker that Dennis
thought might be another salt dome, the formation that had vaulted
us into the "machine age" by producing enough oil to make enough
gasoline to run the engines of the world.

Within a few moments I saw one of the trucks. It was either broke
down or stuck in the rough terrain. I circled them, coming lower and
lower with each pass. There were four or five men standing around
looking like they didn't know what to do. I could see that one man
was under the truck. When he came out, I recognized our lead floorman, Joel. He looked up at me but didn't wave or make any gesture.
While I watched, he put the men with him to pushing the truck while
he got in the driver's seat. After a moment or two the truck appeared
to move. I couldn't tell if that was under its own power, or because of
the men pushing it. I could tell it was loaded down with some heavy
cargo. It appeared to be parts of the boiler. Obviously, I could not give
them any help, so I turned northward again, searching for the rest of
Dennis's expedition.

I was not long in finding them. I estimated they were about eight
miles from town, with about another two or three miles to go to Dennis's selected site. I swooped in low to see how men and animals were
doing. The oxen hitched to one wagon looked pretty good, but the
horses pulling the other didn't look so hot. They had called a halt and
the animals were standing deathly still, with their heads hanging, looking like they would have sold their places for next to nothing. There
were two wagons and the other truck. Lumber to build the rig seemed
to be the main cargo.

I saw Dennis up at the front, standing beside the truck. He took
off his hat and waved it as I flew over. I made another pass and then
climbed back to an altitude of around a thousand feet and watched to
see them get going. You could tell the animals were reluctant, and they
were pulling relatively light loads. I didn't know how they'd bear up
under the rigors of hauling the pipe.

I watched as they went creaking away, the teamsters cracking their bullwhips with vigor. I was in that layer of air where the warm air rising from the ground below meets the cooler air from above. It's called a convection layer and it will bounce you and your plane around pretty good. I figured it would take the caravan another hour to reach the site, so I pulled up another five hundred feet and went cruising around to see what I could see. I banked the airplane and flew off toward the northwest. After I'd flown a few minutes, I noticed what seemed to be a small line of hills or outcroppings off in the distance. It was such a change from the otherwise featureless landscape that I decided to go investigate.

Within a few minutes of flying I could see that they were a definite feature on the desert floor. The outcroppings weren't exactly small mountains, but they weren't little humps or hills, either. As I got closer I was amazed to see what appeared to be a pretty fair-sized cabin at the foot of one of the bigger buttes. Out behind it was a barn and a few corrals and another small building. I could see several horses in one of the corrals and there even appeared to be a few milk cows eating baled hay in another catch pen. But then I was amazed to see, on the other side of the butte, a field of either wheat or hay or something. I pulled the airplane up and rolled it to the left to make another pass. I had seen what I took to be a corn field full of green stalks. But how could this be? Where were these people getting their water? Who were these people living fifteen or twenty miles from town who seemed to be thriving?

I lined up on the house and lost altitude, coming down to around eight hundred feet. The cabin seemed to be big enough for at least three or four rooms and it had a cook shack attached. It was built of stone, with a corrugated-tin roof. It had a fireplace on each end. As I passed the end of the property, something caught at the corner of my eye. Something had stepped out from under the front porch, but I had not been looking in that direction and had only a glimpse. I pulled the plane up and then rolled it over and cut the power and came gliding back toward the cabin with the engine just barely ticking over. At first I saw nothing, but I kept dropping lower and lower until I was down to no more than two hundred feet. There was still nothing as I approached the ranch house except the horses and cows out back. Nothing was stirring in the house. But I couldn't get that flash out of my mind's eye. It had been golden. A gold that I had seen only once before. I continued to drop lower and lower as I started to pass in front of the house.

And then I saw her. She was standing back underneath the porch, but I was low enough and far enough away from the front of the house that I could get a good look.

It was her. There was no question about it. She was slim and shapely and her hair was that startling color somewhere between the sun and twenty-four-karat gold. The only difference was that she was wearing a blue frock that I was willing to bet matched her blue eyes.

She made absolutely no sign as I flew by. You would have thought it was every day that an airplane flew right across the front of her house.

But all I could think of was that I had found her. Maybe she lived so far from town that the townspeople never saw her. Maybe they were blind. It didn't matter. I had located her.

But I had to break out of my astonishment because I was about to fly into the ground. I shoved the throttle home and pulled up, going for altitude so that I could look the place over for a clearing where I could set the airplane down. I went up to five hundred feet and began to circle over the ranch house, hoping she'd step out from the cover of the porch and look up. It seemed like such a usual thing to do that I couldn't figure it when the ground stayed bare of her presence. Hell, how many people, with an airplane circling overhead, *wouldn't* be curious enough to take a few steps off a porch for a better look? What kind of girl was this? She hadn't looked half-witted from the view I'd had of her at the depot. But here she was acting as shy as a ringtailed wampus kitty.

I had to bring my attention back to my flying. A couple of the buttes were almost up to the altitude I was cruising at. I winged over southward, getting away from the line of hills. I flew back and forth in front of the ranch house, looking in vain for a half-mile stretch, or even less than that, where I could put the plane down without tearing up the undercarriage. But it was the damndest thing; two miles from the little ranch, the ground was smooth and flat. But any nearer to where the girl lived, and the desert floor was rent with barrancas and crevices and washouts and gulleys. And when it wasn't going down, the ground was rising up sharply with little buttes studded with big rocks. I couldn't believe my bad luck. I had found the girl and now, with a meeting imminent, I couldn't find a place to land the damn airplane. Oh sure, I could have landed two or three miles away, but I wasn't about to try and walk that far under the afternoon sun. People died that way or went blind or crazy or both. Besides, I had a duty to Dennis, to see how his caravan was faring. To see the girl, I was going to have to find some other means of visiting her than by airplane. I reckoned the distance from town, gazing off in its direction, as closer to twenty miles than fifteen. I doubted I could rent a horse that could make that sort of trek alive. Perhaps someone in the town would have a light truck or automobile I could rent—I doubted it, but it was my only hope.

As I flew toward the site of my boundary marker I got to mulling over what I had seen at the ranch in the hills. Astounding as the field crops and the girl were, I had been most stunned by seeing what I took to be a group of black-and-white Swiss banded oxen. There must have been eight of them. I'd been so excited about seeing the girl that I hadn't made too close an examination, but such draft animals would be a godsend, especially considering the condition they were in. If any muscle power could pull our water tank, it would be draft stock like those oxen.

But I forgot all about that as I spotted Dennis and the wagons and truck dead ahead. They had stopped at the bottom of the little mound. Some of the men were unloading the derrick lumber and some of the teamsters were trying to get some water in the horses and oxen. I dropped down low, and several of the men waved their hats at me. There was good flat land all around so I flew on for about a mile, dropping down until I was just off the prairie, looking for rocks or any uneven ground. It looked smooth as asphalt. I pulled the plane up to about a hundred feet, did a left wingover and then lined up at the wagons, killing the power and letting the plane's momenteum carry it along. The wheels touched and I let it roll until it finally stopped not twenty yards from the lead truck. I saw Dennis break away from a group of men and come walking my way as I climbed out of the cockpit. Once I was still, the heat hit me like a physical force.

Dennis came up looking as dry as if he'd not lost a drop of sweat. He said, "Hot enough for you?"

"How come you ain't sweating?"

He shrugged. "I'm sweated out. Ain't got none left to give."

And then I could see the white lines of salt along his khaki shirt and pants. I could feel the sweat, unbidden, starting to run down my back. I said, "At least you made it. First time I flew over, I wasn't so sure."

He looked back at his caravan. "We're in trouble on the livestock. We simply can't carry cargo and enough water for the animals. And these animals are tough and used to the climate. We've got to get that water tank built and get some water up here at this end, else we're just going to be hauling water for the animals and we'll never get an oil rig put together."

I started to tell him about the golden-haired girl I'd seen again, but I checked myself in time. Instead I told him about the eight oxen I'd seen. He frowned at the news. "Hell, how are we going to get word to the rancher we want to hire his teams? You say you couldn't land. We could try and get there with a truck, but that would be mighty risky in this country. Have a breakdown or drop the front end off in a gulley and a man would be in a world of trouble."

"But those oxen could pull the water wagon. And it will take a wagon. The trucks are too short-bodied and I don't think they've got enough power."

We walked over to where his men were wearily unloading the equipment and materials. The animals looked completely worn-out even though they'd been given some water.

Dennis said, "We'll wait until after dark to start back. We've brought grain and we'll feed the livestock and give them the last of the water. It shouldn't be too hard a pull back home."

"No, but these animals will have to rest. You can't make another trip tomorrow."

"No," he said, "we can't." I had never seen Dennis look so beat-down. He said, with a little smile, "I guess I didn't listen too close when you were telling me about this country. Hell, I thought you were exaggerating. I didn't think anyplace outside of hell could be this bad."

"You thinking of giving up?"

He gave me a shocked look. "Boy, you better get in out of the sun. Something is wrong with your head."

"Speaking of that—when are you going to put up some shelter for the men?"

"I'll bring up those big tents next trip."

"Don't forget to peg them down good or they'll leave for Kansas. The wind can blow around here."

"I wish it would blow those oxen you were talking about, over closer to me."

I shrugged and turned away. There was nothing more to say. I would have liked to have talked about the golden-haired girl, but Dennis would have just made fun of me. I started toward the plane and was a half a dozen paces on my way when I realized I hadn't asked Dennis about the Lewis machine gun. My mind had been so full of the girl and the oxen that my main question had flown out of my head. I turned back. Dennis was leaning against the wagon that the men had finished unloading. There wasn't a sign of shade anywhere. I said, to his back, "Dennis, what the hell is that machine gun doing on my airplane?"

He turned around to face me. He was looking amused. He said, "So you taken notice of that, did you?"

"Are we planning on invading Mexico or what? I wouldn't mind shooting up that judge's house or chasing him down the street. I take it you didn't buy that in town."

He laughed. "Naw, tell you the truth, I been lugging that damn thing around ever since I liberated it before we come home from France. I got curious if I could get it to synchronize on that JN-6H. Works like a charm."

"You ain't had that ammunition since France."

"Naw, I run across that in one of them Army-Navy surplus stores. Bought three pans."

"Dennis, that's six hundred rounds. You reckon that's enough? I mean, hell, are you sure this is even legal? We got a warplane there, and we ain't even a country."

He shrugged. "It was just a lark. I'll take it off as soon as I can find some breathing space. Meanwhile, we have got to find some way to get that water tank out here. These damn draft animals can drink as much water as they can haul."

I made a futile gesture. "I'll get back to town and see if I can scare up anything else. But I think we've contracted for every bit of livestock that is loose in the whole county. Maybe there are some dogs would like to work."

He shook his head. "I can't say you didn't warn me. But wasn't the war worse than you'd expected?"

"Just the shooting part. The girls and the drinking were better than I'd hoped for."

I flew back to Pecos and managed to land and get the plane in the warehouse without killing any townspeople. The machine gun looked stranger than ever as I dismounted and got ready to shut the plane up. I thought of taking away the pan of ammunition but decided it didn't make any difference. I didn't reckon there was anyone around town who knew how to operate a Lewis gun.

I didn't bother to go by the livery stable or the livestock barn. I knew what they had left there, and it wasn't much. I went to the hotel and changed shirts and then lounged around town. I didn't see the judge but I did drop in on Sheriff Lew Wallace. He was sitting in his little office at the jail, fanning himself with part of a newspaper. He had his boots up on the table and looked as hot as anybody else. "Come in," he said. "Set down. Tell me what I can do for you."

You'd have called him a serious-minded man, but one who didn't work at it. I sat down in a straight-backed chair and told him that

Dennis had had a rough first trip of it. "He'll have to wait until tonight to make it back, and that with the livestock pulling empty wagons." The sheriff shook his head. "I told him we weren't set up for the job he had in mind."

After that final statement it didn't seem there was much to say. It was extra-hot in the sheriff's office and I didn't have anything to fan with. I said, "How serious do you reckon it is to ruffle the judge?"

He stopped fanning and shook his head. "Yeah, I heard you put the spurs to him. That ain't a practice I would encourage. He's got a lot of power and, between me and you and the bedpost, he's about half mean. For some reason he has taken a dislike to you folks coming in here. I think it's been damn good for the town—money, jobs. But Judge Crater likes the attention on him. He don't like playing second fiddle to nobody. I wouldn't cross him no more, was I you."

I stood up. "I'm not going to be here long enough to irritate him, Sheriff. I'm just along for the ride."

Then I went over to the blacksmith's shop and was pleasantly surprised to find that the water tank was finished. It was big, all right, just as the smith had said. It was ten feet long and four feet wide and three feet high. Empty, it looked heavy. I didn't want to think of it full of water.

The smith said, "You know, you be going to need another tank out yonder where y'all are headquartering. You can have it at the site and haul this one up and empty it into that one and then come back for another load of water."

I looked at our transport tank. The smith had it hoisted up on a block and tackle from a huge beam at the top of his shop. I said, "You better start building it."

"You better find a way to haul this sucker." He put his hand on the big tank that took up much of his shop.

"Yeah," I said. Though I hadn't the slightest idea of how.

I went ahead and ate supper at the Mexicans' by myself. I didn't look for Dennis back until sometime in the early-morning hours. As wore-down as those animals had looked, they were going to need a long rest and then a slow trip back to Pecos.

I ended the evening with a few drinks in my room and then turned in. I might have gone to the cafe and saloon but I wasn't anxious to run into the judge again. I was going to have to remind myself I was not a social reformer, and to keep my opinions to myself.

I was asleep by eleven o'clock and slept solidly until I heard Dennis come fumbling in at some early-morning hour. He lit the lamp and didn't make any attempt to hold the noise down. Finally he got his clothes and boots off and he blew the lamp out and I heard him fall heavily into the other bed. He sounded tired.

I was up and dressed by daylight. I tried to be quiet, for fear of disturbing, Dennis, though it looked like it would take a bomb to rouse him. I had a strong desire for some coffee and breakfast, and was just on the point of heading across to the Mexicans' when there came a light rapping at the door. I stepped swiftly across the room, glancing at Dennis. But I needn't have bothered; he was still about a foot deep in that bed.

I opened the door and a man was there who looked vaguely familiar, though I couldn't place him. I stepped out into the hall and shut the door behind me. "Got a man sleeping in there. He was up all night."

The man, who was slight and skinny and a little past middle age, said, "I come to see Mr. Frank. Got some news for him."

"That's him sleeping. He was up all night getting back from his haul. Didn't he turn the stock in with you? Ain't none of them dead, are they?"

He was chewing on a matchstick. "Naw, they be all right. I didn't see him when they come in. Stock is wore-out, though."

I figured that was what the man wanted. I recognized him now as the owner of the livestock barn. I said, "Well, you knew it was going to be a hard pull. We need some stouter draft animals."

He looked a little impatient. "That's what I come to tell Mr. Frank. Somebody done dropped off eight big oxen with orders to lease 'em out. I thought he'd be interested."

I stared at him for a second, startled. I said, "What did you say your name was?"

"Martin. Cloyce Martin. Been around here thirty year. Everybody will tell you I know my livestock."

I was still not sure I'd heard right. I said, "Mr. Martin, did I understand you to say you had *eight* oxen come in first thing this morning?" I was getting goose bumps.

"Yessir, that's a fact. An' it be a mystery to me when they come in. I was there before sunup and they was already there, standin' in a pen like they was right at home."

"Who . . . who brought them?"

He shook his head. "I ain't got the least idear. Left a note sayin' he'd take a dollar a day per head for regular draft work."

"You got no idea?"

He shook his head. "Far as I'm concerned, they might as well have dropped out of the sky. I ain't never seen no cattle looked like them."

I felt very odd. I said, "Do they have a kind of black band around the middle? Black-and-white-colored, but most of the black is around their middle?"

He gave me a suspicious look. "How come you know that? You know whose cattle they be?"

I shook my head. "No, no. I just thought I saw some like that when I was flying around."

"Is that you up there in that aeroplane?"

"Yeah. Listen, Mr. Martin, let me get Mr. Frank up. He is going to want to see these oxen."

I ducked back into the room and gave Dennis a good, rough shaking. He come up snorting and saying, "Who—Wha—What?"—and blinking his eyes like he'd never seen daylight before. I said, "Wake up, Dennis. Mr. Martin from the livestock barn is here. He said he's located some new oxen and we better get them tied down before somebody else does."

He blinked and screwed his face up. "Oxen? Did you say *oxen*? What happened to our oxen?"

It took a good deal of pulling and pushing but I finally got him out of bed and dressed and about half-conscious. I had not told him they were Swiss banded cattle because he wouldn't have known what I was talking about. But now, because of the shock that was running all through me, I did.

We were about to go out into the hall to join Mr. Martin. He fiddled with the doorknob and frowned. "What the hell is a Swiss banded oxen? Never heard of them."

I said, patiently, "I didn't, expect you had. That breed of cattle would be about as scarce as goodwill around here. I haven't got the slightest idea how they got in these parts." I waited a beat and then I said, "Those were the eight oxen I told you about flying over yesterday. At a ranch at least twenty miles from here."

He stared at me and then he blinked. He said; "Go on with you."

"It's the truth, Dennis. It's got the hair standing up on the back of my neck and I haven't told you the half of it."

The amazement was still on his face. "You must be wrong. It can't be the same cattle."

I shook my head. "No mistake. Ain't but one breed marked like the Swiss banded. It's the same oxen."

"Maybe somebody is trying to do us a good turn."

"How'd they get those cattle this far in such a short time?"

He frowned. Then he opened the door. "Let's go see. Might be a simple explanation."

"Yeah, sure," I said. I was thinking about the golden-haired girl.

We joined up with Martin and headed for the livestock barn. I had deliberately not told Dennis that Martin didn't know who owned the cattle or where they'd come from, other than the note as to what was to be charged for their use. It wasn't long before Dennis began asking Martin the same questions I had. When he got the answers, Dennis turned around and looked at me wide-eyed. I didn't change my expression.

And then we got to the livestock pens and Mr. Martin led us around to where the oxen were. Dennis stared. He said, "I never seen no cattle marked like that in my whole life."

"Yes you did," I said dryly. "When we were stationed at that airdrome near the Swiss border."

He turned from the fence and stared at me. "And how'd they get here?"

"I don't know," I said. "I wondered that when I flew over them. I also wonder how they made it across twenty miles of desert in the little time it took."

But Martin wasn't interested in either miracles or coincidences. He said, "But, say, look at the size of these brutes. Ever' one of 'em will go over two thousand pounds. Why, they could pull the earth if they could find someplace to stand."

Dennis rubbed his jaw. He said, "And that note was all that was left? Nobody's name? No farm or ranch name? Nothing?"

Mr. Martin shook his head. "One thing we ought to get straight— that dollar a day per head is what the owner wants. I got to see to their care and upkeep. That'll cost a pretty penny. This kind of stock can eat a barn. And I got to make a little profit."

I said to Dennis, "They are what we need to haul the water wagon."

He nodded, though he still looked startled. He asked Martin what it would cost to rent the whole team.

Mr. Martin appeared to study this, but I figured he already had his figure in mind. He said, "Well, sir, I'm gonna have to ask you twenty-four dollars a day for that team. I know that might seem a mite steep, but I'm gonna be put to considerable trouble just riggin' up the harness for these big brutes. And did I mention how these kind of cattle can eat? Lawdy!"

"You got a deal," Dennis said. Have them ready by noon." He looked at me. "You say that tank is ready?"

I nodded. "All we got to do is shove a wagon in there and lower it in place. Of course, we're going to have to secure it. And then fill it with water. I ain't got no idea how much it is going to weigh."

We were already walking away, heading for the blacksmith's shop across town. Dennis said, "Those are the biggest oxen I ever seen. If they can't pull it, it can't be pulled."

I walked along with him, searching for the right words, wondering if I even should tell him. Finally I stopped him in the middle of the back street, very near to the Mexican cafe. I said, "Dennis, I saw those oxen when I flew over that ranch."

"I know. You told me."

I still hesitated. Finally I came out with it. I said, "I also saw the golden-haired girl. She was watching me from underneath the porch roof. I flew back and forth in front of the ranch house but she never would step out."

He cleared his throat. "Same girl?"

I nodded.

"On the same ranch where those oxen came from?"

"Yes."

"No mistake?"

I shook my head. "No."

"Let's see. . . . Now this is the same girl that nobody else but you knows about. People lived here for years and never heard of anybody like her. First time you see her, she vanishes the next second. *This* time she won't come out from under the porch roof to see an airplane flying by. Is that the same girl we are talking about?"

I said, evenly, "Yes."

CHAPTER
12

DENNIS SAID, "Bullshit."

I didn't get angry. I knew how thin it sounded. I said, "I seen her the same as I seen the oxen." I pointed toward the livestock barn. "You believe in the oxen, don't you? You've seen them."

"Oh," he said. "The oxen. You reckon it was your golden-haired girl brought 'em to town for us?"

I was starting to heat up a little. I said, "Just forget it, Dennis. Let it go. I didn't expect you to understand. If it don't run on gasoline, it ain't real."

He put up his hands, mocking me. "No, no. I believe you. It all makes sense now—how them oxen come all that distance. Your golden-haired angel just picked 'em up one at a time and flew them to town."

"Shut up, Dennis."

But he was off and running. "Why, no wonder she didn't come out from under the porch to see an airplane. Being an angel, flying wasn't nothing to her. Listen, next time you see her I want you to tell her how much I appreciate her help. I know she's doing it on account of you, but I still appreciate it."

I had my fists balled at my sides. "You're the one believes in angels. I just saw a girl. I didn't see any wings. You tell me someday how those oxen got to town. But you say another word about the girl and you are liable to be hunting around on the ground for your teeth." I turned on my heel and started for the blacksmith shop, leaving a surprised Dennis Frank in my wake.

He called after me. "Willis! Hey, Willis! Now c'mon, don't get angry. I was just funning you. We got to get a crew together and get a big wagon over to the blacksmith's shop."

I crossed the street away from the blacksmith's and kept walking. I *was* angry. I couldn't say why, but I definitely did not like to be chaffed about that girl. Maybe it was because I wasn't sure I was seeing her myself. There was something very strange about the whole business, and Dennis, instead of helping me make sense of it, just wanted to hit me on my sore toe. Whatever was going on with that girl was greatly beyond anything I had ever experienced. In the first place, the very sight of her made my heart light up, and in the second, all sorts of strange things happened. Either she disappeared into thin air, or eight huge oxen moved themselves over twenty miles of rough country and left a note. Not to mention her seeming to live on a ranch where they could grow wheat and corn and other crops when nobody else in the whole country could grow anything but hard times.

So I didn't need some joker making fun of her, or of me seeing her. I had wanted to help Dennis, but if he was going to turn into a smart aleck, I wanted no part of him or his so-called oil well.

I veered over to the right, went into the Mexican cafe, and sat down at a table and had a couple of beers. By the time I was finished, I'd cooled off considerably. It wasn't Dennis's fault he was the way he was, any more than it was my fault I was like I was. We all want each other to be this or that, and that is seldom the case. Wilson Young had not wanted me to go off and fight what he considered was someone else's war, but I'd done it just the same. That was me being me. And it was him being him when he'd turned me out of the herd and cut me off with nothing but two hundred thousand acres of hell. If Dennis had told me about seeing some golden-haired girl, I'd have probably given him the horse laugh just like he'd done me.

I got up and wandered over to the blacksmith's shop. I wasn't feeling roughed-up at Dennis anymore, but I wasn't going to let him find that out the easy way.

When I got to the blacksmith's I was surprised to see that Dennis and a crew had already brought a wagon down from the livestock barn and the big water tank had been lowered into it and was in the process of being secured. The tank had looked big hanging in the air, but it looked even bigger in the wagon, even if the wagon was one of the big, heavy-duty borax-mine conveyances. They'd brought the wagon down pulled by two mules, but it wouldn't be any mules pulling it once it was full of water. Joe Cairo, who as fireman and chief water-tender would know better than anyone, estimated the tank was going to hold somewhere between eight hundred and a thousand gallons. That was a good deal more than either me or the blacksmith had estimated.

The tank had a six-inch hole at the top so that it could be filled up. The hole had a hinged lid that closed watertight. There was a railroad water tank just past the depot, and I figured that was where we could fill it. The blacksmith had put a one-inch tap at the end of the tank so water could be drained out. He had already finished one of the vats we'd be taking up to the site to hold water. It wasn't much, just a tub about six feet in diameter and about three feet deep. But it would hold enough water to keep the teams watered as we made the many trips it was going to take to get materials and equipment to the site.

I was kind of standing over in the corner, staying out of the way and not saying much. Dennis gave orders for Joe Cairo and Joel and Charlie to take the wagon down to the livestock barn and see about getting the oxen hitched up. As the wagon pulled out, he came over to me. His eyes searched my face. He said, "Look here, Willis, I didn't mean no harm. I know that you are a sensitive fellow and I ought to watch my mouth. But you know me—I forget myself. I'm sorry I made you mad, and I don't want you scattering my teeth all over the country."

I was still cool. I said, "You got it right about speaking before you think. You are big on religion and churches. What if I was to wade in and go to saying you just imagined all that stuff preachers talk about. What if I was to make light of that? How would you feel then?"

He blushed and looked down. "I wouldn't care for it," he said slowly. "But it ain't quite the same, Willis, as you's talking about a girl you can't seem to nail down."

I put up my hands. "There you go again. You can't help yourself, can you?"

"All right, all right," he said. "I'm sorry again. Let's just forget all about it, what say? It's nearly lunchtime. Let's go get a bite to eat."

Dennis took a caravan out that evening, headed for the site. The eight oxen seemed to have no trouble pulling the big wagon loaded with at least eight hundred gallons of water. Joe Cairo claimed it was closer to a thousand, but, whichever, it was mighty heavy. I figured the least it could have weighed was three or four tons. But the oxen seemed to pay it no mind. They just went along placidly and patiently, lowering their big shoulders when they hit an uphill pull, but otherwise seemingly unconcerned about the job ahead. The blacksmith had finished the two big troughs and one was loaded into each of the two trucks. Dennis took along what other equipment he could cram into the beds of the stake-body Fords, but he didn't add any to the burden of the oxen. He figured they'd make the trip in about four hours, rest and sleep and eat for another six hours, and then start back the next morning. He'd rest the oxen all that day and then repeat the trip the next evening, only this time he'd be taking two other wagons pulled by mules and horses, and the oxen we already had. They'd be carrying the important parts of the drilling rig. Now that they had water and feed on the other end, they could do heavier work. As Dennis had said, it was time to get started doing what we'd come to do. We didn't mention the girl again, or how the oxen had arrived in town, or who they belonged to. I saw them off that evening. Dennis's crew had finally shaken itself out to about another half-dozen men in addition to the ones we had brought. He said a few of them might even make decent hands. He also said we had a long ways to go before we'd see much of a hole in the ground. It was becoming more and more clear that this business of drilling an oil well was a good deal more complicated than it had first seemed.

I went to bed early that night, mainly because there wasn't anything else to do. I intended on getting up early and flying over to the site to see if Dennis and his crews were on schedule and not having any trouble.

Our bedroom faced the only main street in town. Once I'd put the light out, I could lie there and look out through the window and into the darkness. The only building on the far side of the street was the railroad depot, and it was just a dim light in the distance. A freight train out of El Paso came through every night about two A.M., but that was a long time off. I liked to hear its lonesome whistle but I figured on being asleep long before that.

I still had my eyes open, staring out the window, but they were beginning to flicker closed every second or two. In another two or three minutes I was going to be asleep.

I just caught a glimpse. It was a figure going down the boardwalk right outside my window. My eyes had been half-closed and, for a half a second, I thought I was dreaming. Then I sat bolt upright in bed. I had seen a flash of a gray gingham gown and a poke bonnet that did not quite hide the sunshine curls that looked radiant even at the time of night, and without a light showing. In a terrible state of excitement I jumped out of bed and ran to the window. The pane was up but a screen prevented me from looking up the street in the direction the figure had been hurrying. I jumped for my jeans and tugged them on as fast as I could. Without bothering about footwear or shirt, I ran out of my room and through the lobby to the front door. A sleepy desk clerk looked up, but I paid him no mind. I hurried through the door and onto the boardwalk and looked anxiously up the street. It was deserted. There wasn't even a drunk weaving his way home. The street, on both sides, was as empty as my hopes.

I stood there, shrunk down. I could have run to the corner and then the next, and then looked over at the next street. But I knew it was pointless. She wouldn't be there. She was never going to be there. The only place she existed was in my head. I had made her up. Why, I didn't know; and why she looked the way she did, I had no answer for. I had never been partial to blondes even though I had been exposed to a good many of them. I did not understand what was happening with my mind; I did not understand why I should be seeing visions; I did not understand why I would put a cream-skinned blonde girl in a place of overheated dust and blowing sand. It appeared that my imagination didn't have much sense. All I knew was that I was going to dismiss the girl from my susceptible brain and never think of her again.

I went slowly back into the hotel and down to my room. Before I got into bed I pulled the shade on my side of the room so as not to be tempted to see any more visions. I had a quick drink and then crawled into bed. I lay there for a while and then I got up and had another drink. If I couldn't get to sleep, I'd drink whiskey until I passed out. But I wasn't going to think about that golden-haired vision.

I woke up late. My watch said it was half past seven, and my head said I'd had more than a little help from the whiskey in getting to sleep and getting such things as imaginary visions out of my mind. But—what the hell—I was young and healthy, and a hangover every now and then wasn't going to kill me any more than being late for breakfast.

I went down to the hall to the bathroom and had a shave and saw to my teeth and had a wash. After that I got dressed and went to the Mexican cafe for breakfast. They had fresh cantaloupe so I had some of that, along with some fresh peaches and a glass of orange juice. I finished it off with three eggs and some tortillas, and pronounced my hangover cured.

It was about nine o'clock and I figured Dennis should be well-started back to town unless he'd had some trouble. To me, the main function of the airplane, with or without the machine gun, was to give the caravans a quick method of communication with the town and its resources. I figured I was running a little late on surveying Dennis and his party. I started for the old warehouse at the northwest end of town. As I neared it I saw a man standing in the middle of what people in Pecos liked to call their "Second Street." To me the only way you could tell it from the desert was by the occasional wagon tracks.

As I got closer I could see that the man was wearing a black suit and was holding on to his coat lapels, one in either hand. It was Judge Crater. He did not give me a chance to speak first. When I was about ten yards away he said, in his gravelly voice, "Where are you bound, young man?"

The sight of him was enough to irritate me, and I was about to make a sarcastic reply when I reminded myself there was no use looking for trouble. I didn't, however, care to be addressed as "young man" in such official tones and have my where-tos questioned. I told him, in as civil tone as I could muster, that I was on my way to my airplane.

He said, "And do you plan to rise that aeroplane off the ground?"

That did make me smile. I said, "Yes, I plan to 'rise' that plane off the ground—rise it off a good long ways."

He let go of his right lapel to point a finger at me. "After taking counsel with some of the leading citizens of the town, we have decided that the constant taking-off and landing of that contraption is an unnatural act and is subject to a tax for civic disturbance."

I didn't know what he was talking about, and said so. "Civic disturbance? The only one of those I know about is when the civilians get in my way when I'm trying to take off and land."

He raised his voice like he was pronouncing sentence. "That infernal contraption is causing an unnatural commotion. It is frightening the women and scaring the horses and causing the milk cows to go dry. From here on in, it will cost you, or the company that contraption belongs to, three dollars every time you rise it off the ground, and another three dollars when you set it back down again."

I stared at him like I was looking at the village idiot. "Why, you are crazy! You can't tax a man for flying his airplane. Planes fly all the time, everywhere, and they don't get taxed. There's a mail plane comes over here every afternoon on the way to El Paso. You going to tax him?"

He had both his lapels again, and a mighty satisfied look on his face. "He don't rise up and set down here. You do."

"Well, you can go to the dance by yourself if you think I'm going to hand over six bucks to you every time I take my plane up."

He shook his head. "Oh, I won't be collecting the money. Not my job. I just decide the tax, I don't collect it."

"Well, then, your court clerk or whoever it is, can go to hell."

"Won't be my clerk. Collecting is the sheriff's job."

I realized then why the sheriff hadn't wanted me to get on Crater's bad side. He didn't want to have to do the dirty work I would cause. I said, to the judge, "You are trying this because you think I was not respectful enough to you."

He said, in that pompous voice, "Ain't me, young man, it's the office."

"All right, the office. But this is not even legal. You can't collect a tax just on your whim. Why don't you tax us for hauling water out into the desert? It would make about as much sense. That's an unnatural act, taking water to the desert."

He gave me a flat smile. "Maybe you've got something there, young man. I hadn't thought of it. Your boss, Mr. Frank, is an easier man to deal with than you seem to be. He understands matters of commerce."

I spit on the ground. "Stealing, you mean. You won't collect a dime from me. And neither will the sheriff."

He gave me that peculiar smile again. "Then we'll just have to impound your flying machine."

That took me up a notch or two. Perhaps it was a thing he could do. But I said, boldly, "You have no right to confiscate people's property. Where the hell you think we are—Germany? I've already fought that war. You come near my airplane and there is liable to be another war."

He said, sounding well-satisfied with himself, "Oh, won't be me doing the dirty work. That's Sheriff Lew Wallace's job. You just take that aeroplane and rise it up in the sky and set it back down here again and try and not pay up six dollars and we'll see what happens." He nodded his head toward me as if to make it clear who it was going to happen to.

He was crowding me with the sheriff. Sheriff Wallace had been cooperative and helpful to our expedition and I didn't want to drag him into the middle of the dogfight we were having with Crater. I knew Dennis would feel the same way. But the judge was insane if he thought we were going to pay that kind of blackmail to "rise" a plane up in the air and land it. "Listen, that airplane doesn't even belong to us. Belongs to a man in Houston."

The judge was still looking satisfied. He said, "You be the one driving it, so I reckon you be the one paying."

I couldn't help it, I was getting angry as hell. I said, "If you're going to rob folks, why don't you get a gun and do it proper?"

He said, "Oh, I've got a gun. But I don't need it."

Then I remembered he'd been wearing a sidearm at the depot. I said—and I was about to boil over—"Well, I got a gun too. Let's just see which one is the biggest."

"You threatening me, young man?"

I knew I had to get away from him before I got in bad trouble. I stepped away from his presence and deliberately turned my back, walking toward the old warehouse.

His voice followed me. "You threatening me with a gun, young man?"

I yelled over my shoulder without pausing, "You're a damned old crook and you are going to get caught. I'm going to get in that airplane and fly to Austin and see whoever is in charge of crooks like you, and get you some time in the penetentiary up at Huntsville."

Behind me I heard a deep chuckle. "You do that, young man."

I opened the warehouse doors and rolled the airplane out. It caught the first turn and I ran around, with the engine ticking over, and climbed into the front cockpit. Normally I would have gotten into the rear one, but something was seething inside me. For a few seconds

I sat there, the propeller idling, the airplane gradually creeping forward, while my mind played with a thought. I knew it was goofy thinking, knew that it would be a mistake, but I was dying to open that pan of ammunition and stick that belt end into the firing chamber and rack back the receiver so that I had a live gun at my fingertips. Then I wanted to climb over the town and dive down on Judge Crater and stitch a line of bullet holes just off the tips of his boots.

But I knew I couldn't do it. Dennis hadn't realized he was arming a madman with an automatic weapon when he'd installed the Lewis. No, the best thing I could do was fly to wherever Dennis was and talk it over with him. But it was a sure thing that we couldn't hangar the plane in Pecos, not at six dollars a round-trip. Hell, I doubted if they got that kind of landing fees at the big airports in New York or wherever.

I took off and turned east, staying low, flying at about five hundred feet. The warm air was doing nothing to cool me off, but then, it would have taken more than some air to calm me down where Judge Crater was concerned. I kept the plane straight and steady and on a route that would intersect Dennis and his caravan.

I saw the line of trucks and wagons after about five minutes. I went into a shallow dive and flew over the lead truck, waggling my wings. As I rolled over and turned back I could see Dennis leaning out of the passenger window of the lead truck, waving both arms. I dipped down and flew right over the top of him and then turned south and picked out a landing place in the flat country. About two miles ahead of the caravan I rolled into a turn that would have me landing to the south, into the wind, toward the oncoming trucks and wagons. I had been able to see, even from the air, that the livestock looked much better than before. Having plenty of water and those eight big oxen to do the heavy work, had seemed to perk the whole string up.

I landed easily, avoiding the rocks and cactus, and then taxied out of the line of march of the caravan. I switched off the engine and then sat there in the heat for a moment while I watched the caravan approach through shimmering heat waves. Finally, when it was only about a hundred yards away, I vaulted out of the cockpit and sought what shelter I could from the sun by kneeling down below the lower wing. As the caravan came abreast I saw Dennis jump from the cab, keeping the truck rolling. He waved the whole combination to keep headed for Pecos. They had only about five miles to go, by my calculations.

He came up, dusty and worn-looking but with a cheerful expression on his face. He rubbed his hands together. "Kid, for the first time since we got here I feel we are making some progress. We've nearly got a camp up. We've got plenty of water and hay at the well site for the livestock and we are starting to move in the equipment to build a drilling well. I got to tell you, I despaired for a little while, but now I am beginning to see light."

I hated to give him bad news while he was feeling so good, but he was going to find out sooner or later. I said, "We got some trouble with Judge Crater."

The joy went out of his eye. He said, warily, "Now what?"

I told him and his shoulders slumped and he groaned. "Oh, that son of a bitch. Is he going to think of every way there is to rob us?"

"I don't know about that, but I do know he wants six dollars when I land back in Pecos. I was thinking we could keep the plane out here."

He shook his head. "We ain't quite set up for that. But soon. Meanwhile, we'll have to do what that greedy bastard says. I'll fly back with you and handle the financial end." He paused. "And listen . . . I want you staying as far away from that man as you can. You may not mean to, but I think you antagonize him."

"I'd like to antagonize him on a permanent basis. You don't know how close I came to putting that Lewis machine gun to work on the judge."

"I'm taking that son of a bitch off," he said firmly.

I shook my head. "No. And not because I'm a hothead. There's a bunch I don't care for around here. I think we need to keep us an ace in our hand."

He looked at me for a moment. "Well, all right. But don't you be doing nothing rash."

"I'm not going to do anything rash but we've got to find some way to get that vulture off our backs."

Dennis grimaced. "I know. And now you are starting to understand how he's had me over a barrel." He waved his hand. "Hop in and I'll prop you. It's too damn hot to be standing around here."

I grabbed him by the arm. "Dennis, we got to do something about this. Get it settled. And not just the airplane, though six bucks ain't nothing to sneeze at."

"Look, we'll go ahead and let him blackmail us for a couple more days. By then I can get it fixed up to keep the plane at the well site. We'll rig up some way to protect it from the wind and sand. But for the time being, let's just go along. He's got the cards."

I let go of him, reluctantly. "All right. For your sake. But we have got to put a stop to this. He's just going to want more and more."

We took off and I found that I was not flying directly back to Pecos but instead was wandering up to the northwest. It was there I had seen the ranch house with the oxen. And also, the figment of my imagination, the golden-haired girl. Obviously I was not going to tell Dennis that I thought I'd seen her on the boardwalk outside our room window. In fact, I wasn't going to tell anyone, including myself. She was forgotten. I was just flying up toward the area of the ranch to see if that, too, had been a delusion of my mind.

After about ten minutes Dennis turned around in the forward cockpit and looked back at me in a questioning manner. He wanted to know where we were going. I made a circular motion in the air with my finger to indicate I was having a look around, reconnoitering. He shrugged and turned back to the front. I saw him take hold of the handle of the Lewis machine gun and sight down the barrel. He probably would have liked to shoot up Judge Crater as much as I did.

I saw the buttes rearing up from the desert floor. They were to the north and about five miles away. I was flying at fifteen hundred feet to get the cool air. I began to let down slowly so that as I passed over the craggy hills I'd be able to have a good look for the ranch house.

The line of buttes had seemed to be about five miles long and I had not noted any landmarks to guide me to the ranch house. The fields of wheat and hay and corn should have been easy to see, but I may have imagined them, too. Once you get good at imagining golden-haired girls, a wheat field ain't nothing to conjure up.

I veered over and started down the line of craggy humps, looking for anything familiar. Dennis turned around and made a questioning gesture. I pointed emphatically toward the ground and he hung his head over the side of the cockpit and peered down.

Then I saw it. The ranch house was partially hidden by one of the highest buttes, and you could only glimpse it when you were right over it. But there was no mistaking it as I passed by. I banked quickly around to my left and came buzzing back toward it head-on. Dennis was looking at me again and I pointed downward again. Now the fields were plainly evident. Surely Dennis couldn't miss those. Except they looked different. The corn was no longer green and the hay and the wheat were laying over like they'd wilted.

I throttled down and passed over the house at no more than a hundred feet. It looked deserted. Worse, it looked as if it had been deserted for a long time. There was no more livestock around; no horses, no steers, no milk cows. Certainly no oxen.

I was getting too low. I crammed in the throttle and climbed for altitude. At five hundred feet I rolled over in a hard bank and flew back over the ranch, coming from back to front. There was no sign of life of any kind.

It made me sick inside, but it was all the proof I needed. I was no longer looking for any illusions. I'd had my fill.

Dennis turned back to me and lifted his palms as if to ask what all that was about. I just shook my head and set a course for Pecos.

I landed and taxied up to the warehouse and then switched off the magnetos with the nose of the airplane close enough to the ware-house to be in the shade. I was looking around for the judge as I climbed out of the cockpit. Dennis got down about the same time I did and wanted to know what the sightseeing trip was all about. "How come you to fly over that deserted ranch house a couple of times? That supposed to be where the magic oxen came from?"

I looked at him straight-faced. "I was looking around for the next drilling site. You told me, high ground. That's the highest around here."

"Hell, Willis, I said high ground, not mountains."

"Those aren't mountains, Dennis." I had suddenly spotted the judge coming our way. I figured more peace would be attained if I wasn't around. I said, "Dennis, roll the airplane on in, will you? That's a good fellow."

I took off, making sure my route did not bring me in contact with Crater. I'd done my work in the judicial system for the day. The rest was up to Dennis.

The next day the outfit really got rolling. By now men and animals were used to the grind of moving heavy materials across a desert and they were finding ways to do it easier and faster. Dennis even claimed that some of the horses and mules were gaining weight on the diet of feed and work. Nobody bothered to dispute him.

On my part, I stayed out of Crater's way. One day I rode out to the site on the oxen wagon and then spent the night in the tent city we were erecting. The boilers were up and in place and ready to go. There was plenty of water for steam but there was nothing to burn to make the steam. Dennis had finally figured out that I hadn't been kidding when I'd told him there was nothing to burn on the desert. He ended up by ordering a car load of coal. It was an expense and a trouble he hadn't counted on, but it couldn't be helped.

They were starting to build the drilling platform floor and were about to start up with the derrick. I went back to town before they could get going good. The men had sorted themselves out now. Our three had begun to act as foremen of a sort, overseeing the work of the men from town who knew nothing about oil wells. Dennis estimated he'd be able to get three drilling-platform hands out of the townfolk, and another two or three for roustabouts and men of general work. The jobs had come to be prized once they saw that Dennis was paying off in real money and that the job had a chance to last for a time. Every day there were more men who tried to get hired or, more likely, rehired. But we were reaching the point where Dennis just about had his crew together.

It was boring in town for me, especially since I wasn't taking the airplane out. I spent my time trying not to think of the golden-haired girl, and dividing my time between the Mexicans' place and the railroad depot. I stayed out of the cafe saloon because that was where Crater held forth, and I had no wish to find myself inside any sort of jail. Occasionally I thought about Genevieve and once went so far as to write her a letter. The doing of it had surprised me since I'd considered my feelings much too hurt by her to want any further communication. But I'd comprimised my lack of principal by making the letter as formal and noncommittal as possible, holding myself to details about the countryside and the progress of the oil-drilling venture. I was a good deal less than accurate about both the harshness of the land and our progress on the well. From my letter you'd have thought Pecos occupied a valley in Eden and that we were only about a foot from an oil bonanza. I didn't feel a damn bit guilty about the lies. Genevieve was a hell of a woman, but she didn't want to make any sacrifices for a man.

The load of coal arrived and was duly loaded into two wagons and shipped to the well site. A day later Dennis arrived with the return caravan and announced that we were through with town and ready to go to work. He said, "Gather up your gear in the next day or so and fly the plane out to the well. I've got you a nice landing strip cleared off and marked with barrels. It ain't graded, but all the big rocks and cactus are cleared off. Crater shouldn't interfere with you leaving. He'll be looking to collect when you return. Only you ain't going to be returning except in an emergency."

I said, "How soon you expect to start drilling?"

"Hell, we're drilling now. Spudded the bit in yesterday morning."

I was amazed. I said, "You mean the derrick is built?"

"Derrick is built, boilers are firing, pipe is stacked in the rack. Boy, we're a going concern."

"We are going to actually do this? Really drill for oil?"

"Hell, yes. What did you think we came out here for?"

I shrugged. I'd never really given it any thought. I said, "Find new ways to spend Teddy Atlas's money?"

"I hope you get out of here without Judge Crater putting you in jail, but I ain't betting on it, that mouth of yours."

"Don't forget you are on my land before you get so uppity."

"Don't forget, I got a lease."

"Don't forget I got an airplane with a Lewis machine gun mounted on it and plenty of ammunition."

CHAPTER
13

 THE DERRICK rose up out of the desert floor like some tall, skinny, wooden butte. It was so high it seemed I'd spotted it almost as soon as I'd taken off from Pecos. As I neared the site I was amazed at the progress that had been made. What had once been a tangled, jumbled mass of materials and equipment had somehow been transformed into a neat and orderly camp and a functioning and busy seeker-after-oil. There were four big tents that could each easily have accommodated ten men or served as a mess hall. I figured one or two were barracks for the men, and the others, storehouses for goods and equipment. There were a few smaller tents and rope corrals for horses and oxen. The trucks were parked in place and I could see the boilers throwing off steam.

As I got nearer I could make out the figures of the men working the rig. The derrick was built of crisscrossed timbers so that you could see right through it. The first man I saw was Charlie, right up in the very top of that derrick. Hell, he seemed to be about as high up in the air as I was. It scared me to look at him. And Dennis had wondered if I'd like to be a derrickman. No thank you. Anytime I was more than six feet off the ground I wanted a set of wings holding me up.

I flew over the camp, looking down at all the faces looking up at me. It appeared that Dennis was sitting amid some machinery on what I took to be the drilling floor. It was raised on blocks about some four feet off the desert. I saw him pull on one lever and then another. There were several other men on the floor with him and they were concerned with a pipe that was running through the middle of the floor and on down into the desert. I could see that the pipe was spinning and seemed to be biting its way into the ground below the drilling platform. I circled the derrick and waved at Charlie. He didn't wave back. He was standing on a little board and reaching out to pull a stand of pipe out of a bunch and swing it over so it would hang down toward the middle of the drilling platform. I had an idea that it would be lowered somehow and then connected to the pipe that was slowly going into the ground. I didn't know anything about it, but that seemed a likely explanation of how they made a deep hole.

I came around again, dropping a little lower so that I was almost below the top of the derrick. I had seen the barrels outlining the landing strip that Dennis had talked about, but I wanted to be sure that was where he wanted me to set down. As I circled I saw him give me a quick wave and then he pushed all the levers in front of him forward. It seemed to shut the operation down, because the three men on the drilling floor stepped back from where the pipe was going down and sort of sagged off and relaxed. Dennis ran down the steps from the platform and headed over toward the landing strip, waving at me to come on. I circled wide so as to come into the wind and pointed the airplane toward the camp. I touched down and was rolling to a stop by the time Dennis arrived. There were two men behind him, carrying a big tarp and some stakes and rope and a big maul. I climbed down and Dennis said he was amazed I had made it out of Pecos alive and was not in jail. We didn't do more than shake hands. He turned away to direct the men in the securing of the airplane. He had them roll it in among two of the big tents. The first thing they did was tie a tarpaulin around the engine. After that they covered the Lewis machine gun. I saw them giving it very curious looks and I wondered what tall tales Dennis had made up to account for the gun's presence. Finally, they drove stakes and tied the plane down fore and aft and at each wing tip. It was going to take a mighty big wind to shake the plane loose. But as I watched the men, working under Dennis's supervision, I began glancing around. As neat as the site had looked from the air, this was still, after all, just a bunch of tents in the desert. And I was watching my only means of departure rapidly being immobilized. I didn't want to be on the site of a drilling well. And I damn sure didn't want to camp out in the badlands for however long it took to either find oil or give up. I suddenly realized that what had begun in the splendor of a Galveston luxury hotel was ending up amid rock and sand and bitter water and probably a cook who specialized in opening cans of beans.

Dennis clapped me on the shoulder once the plane was tended to. "Well, you're finally here. Come on up with me to the drilling floor and I'll show you how one of these babies operates."

I said, sarcastically, "I can't contain my enthusiasm."

"Naw, come on. We'll put you to work. Hell, I bet you learn to like it."

"We can get some money down on that," I said. But I allowed myself to be dragged and prodded in the general direction of the rig.

It wasn't at all as complicated as I'd thought or as Dennis had made it sound. The whole idea was to spin a string of pipe down in a hole with a bit on the end and keep adding pipe the deeper you went. The pipe was spun by a mechanism called the rotary table which was fixed in the middle of the drilling-platform floor. This rotary table had jaws, which the roughnecks called "chocks," which gripped the pipe. When the steam power was laid on the rotary table spun and made the pipe spin and cut its way deeper and deeper into the earth. As soon as one stand of pipe was down in the hole, another stand was swung over by the derrickman and then that stand was screwed onto the stand already in the hole. It was all about the same principle as using a brace and bit to drill holes in wood.

Dennis, as the driller, sat over behind a big chunk of machinery. He could, when he wanted to, drill, or he could pull the pipe out of the hole by a big cable on a drum. He called that a "draw-works." They had all kinds of unfamiliar names for things, but it still came down to the fact that they were sticking a damn big straw in the ground and hoping to suck up some oil.

I was a tad weak on that point. I understood the oil was down deep in the earth in pools, but I couldn't quite figure out what would make it come rushing up the pipe if they were to hit one of these pools.

But I was impressed by the rig; it was big and it was powerful and I figured it was dangerous. Dennis said we pumped enough steam to drive a railroad locomotive, and you could be on the drilling platform and just feel all that power making things shake. It made you think that, if Dennis pushed or pulled the wrong lever, the whole damn thing might get loose and a steam line could break away and cook everybody at hand. But in addition, everything that was used, from the tongs that you used to grab the pipe, to the blocks that you used to collar it, was big and heavy and made out of steel. And on top of that there were any number of steel cables flying all over the place. I figured the rough-necks earned every dollar they got paid.

Taken all in all, it was about as undesirable a spot as a man could think up. There was not even any comfort in the food. As I had suspected, most everything came out of a sack or a can. A man could have all the beans and rice and potatoes he wanted. Anything that would keep, we had in abundance. Anything fresh didn't have a chance in that climate. Dennis had hired the cook out of the cafe in the town and I had asked him how come he hadn't brought out a slaughter steer from town or perhaps a pig or so. He'd just shook his head. "Mister, it would be the waste of a good beef. Even with the dozen men we got around here, the meat would spoil in this heat before you could get two meals out of it. You'd have to butcher that steer by halves and I don't think they can stand it."

So there was no fresh vegetables, no fresh fruit, and no fresh meat. Other than that, the menu was fine. But what the hell difference did it make to me? By my own admission I didn't care much about anything. So what did I care where I was or what I had to eat? I'd met Genevieve and, for a brief while I'd thought there was something worthwhile to be had. But then, she hadn't cared about me, so I was back where I'd started. And then the golden-haired girl had come along, but she didn't exist, so you can't care about an illusion. So where I was and what I was doing shouldn't have made me the slightest difference. And I reckon they didn't. Still, all in all, I would have preferred to not have cared in a more comfortable place.

We did have one luxury. Some forward thinker had brought out a bunch of laying hens, and we had a chicken coop and a fenced-in chicken yard. Not only did that keep us in fresh eggs, but the clucking and squawking of the chickens gave an oddly comforting sound to the place. It made it seem a little less like a desperate venture by crazy men in a badlands desert.

Dennis had his home and his office in one of the big tents. He had two cots and one of them was for me. First night, Dennis turned the lantern down to about half, and we had a drink of whiskey. I was a little bit curious about the lantern but he explained you could see silhouettes through the canvas and he didn't want any of the men seeing us with a bottle. "I've gave orders there is not to be any drinkin'. Any man I catch drinkin' is fired on the spot."

I stared at him in disbelief. "You can't keep this rough a bunch from taking a drink. Why, hell, you couldn't fire Joel or Charlie or Cairo, for certain."

He nodded and turned the lantern back up now that we had full glasses and the bottle was put away. "I know that. But this way it kind of holds it down. It is mainly for these new hands we've hired out here. They ain't used to this kind of work and being out away from home. You let the drinking get started in an oil camp and it can blow you up faster than a well-head fire. I'm hoping to get a few of these boys trained up so we can go to working two shifts. It costs money to be out here so you might as well be drilling every minute you can."

I settled in as well as a man could settle in such a spot. I had no work so I idled my time by loafing around the rig and the cook shack and talking to anyone who had just been in town. Naturally, we had to keep bringing in water. The town was our only source. That meant a lot of work for the eight Swiss banded oxen, but Dennis took it extra easy on them. We both didn't know what we'd've done without the mysterious cattle. The water tank was simply too heavy for any other team we had. They made a trip about every three days, and rested and ate and tanked-up on water in between. Dennis had turned back to the cattle and livestock barn all the other oxen and mules and horses. He had the two trucks, and with the banded oxen for heavy work, we were pretty well set.

And meanwhile the drilling went on. One day, after I'd been in camp about a week, Dennis announced they had reached a hundred feet. I asked if that was good, considering the time they'd been drilling. "Damn right," he said. "We've gotten through a shelf of hard country rock. Stuff's as hard as granite. The rig proved it could take the pounding that kind of drilling lays on it. And we made four round-trips, which gives the crew considerable training."

A round-trip, I had learned, was when they pulled all the drill stem out of the hole, changed the bit, which would have all the teeth wore off it, and then put the string back in the hole. It was hard work for all concerned, and Dennis was trying to train one of the townsmen into being a derrickman so he could spell Charlie from time to time. So far, the man hadn't worked solo, so Charlie hadn't gotten much rest.

Dennis had a desk in the tent, a little lightweight affair, where he kept what he called his "well log." It was just a line marked off in feet and showing certain significant events in the life of the well. Mostly they were "tailings" that came floating out of the top of the casing head. Whatever the bit was drilling through down at the bottom of the hole would come up to the top of the hole and Dennis would collect the samples and smell them and taste them and make pronouncements. "Schist," he might say. "Hope to hell we don't have much of that. Hard as hell, and tricky. Stuff can grab your drill stem and twist it in a knot." Or: "Sand, damn it. Might look like clay to you, but it's sand, and that, my boy, is where the oil lies."

Every twenty or thirty feet of depth, Dennis would be deviled with pockets of salt water. It would suddenly come spurting up the pipe, drenching everybody on the drilling floor, and then would flow for about twenty or thirty minutes, causing everything to almost come to a standstill. "Damn salt water!" Dennis would swear.

I wondered where it came from.

"Aw, hell, I think half the world underground is made up of salt water. Never drilled a well yet, didn't almost drown in the damn stuff."

But even though Dennis cussed the salt water, it was still useful. Not all the water we hauled went to use for man or beast. It seems you've got to water the hole you're drilling. We had a small gasoline-powered pump that drew water out of one of the small tanks the blacksmith had made and conveyed it by hose to the top of the well casing, where it could run down the hole and cool the bit and cause crumbly dirt to turn to mud so it wouldn't be collapsing around the pipe. Still, getting doused with salt water wasn't a sought-after condition, and Dennis particularly hated it. Said it chafed him under the arms and in the crotch. And, of course, we didn't have enough fresh water for many baths by the crew. There was not enough water to get them all clean so Dennis decreed they'd have to go dirty or pay two dollars for a bath. Naturally, there were no takers on that proposition, with the exception of Joe Cairo and Joel—and Dennis and myself, of course.

I didn't go up on the drilling platform very often. It scared me. When Dennis would throw the lever and kick in that steam engine and the rotary table would start spinning, turning all that pipe, the whole damn rig shook. I didn't know how Charlie stood it as high up as he was. And then there was always some piece of iron hitting another one and making a hell of a racket. It may not have been dangerous but it sure as hell *sounded* like it.

We had been on the site about three weeks. At least the crew had. I'd been tardy. But by now, word was leaking back to town that there was real activity right out in the middle of the desert. Machinery was running and men were working and oil was being searched for earnestly. I guess the teamsters who drove the trucks in for supplies, or the men who handled the oxen, were spreading the word. It wasn't long before we began to get visitors. Oh, they didn't come in hordes, but an occasional Model T, or some other runabout that could handle the desert, would motor out, loaded to the gills with gawkers, to see what opportunity might present itself. Eventually, men started bringing their families out in buckboards. They helped themselves to our water while they had a look around and then had a picnic or even spread a wagon cloth and spent the night. Dennis was half-suspicious that some of the women weren't family at all, but ladies of the night who might corrupt the crew. Dennis was almighty scared of having the crew corrupted by either evil women or by drink.

But they weren't much of a bother, even though most of the men who came out were looking for work. Mostly they just stood around looking wise and nodding and acting like they knew what they were looking at.

In three weeks of drilling we had reached one hundred sixty feet. It was hard going all of a sudden because we'd struck granite and it was wearing out bits faster than we could jerk them up and replace them. Dennis got worried we might run short so he sent word to the telegraph office to send in an order for a dozen more.

To my delight Judge Crater hadn't put in an appearance. I had been halfway expecting—since his landing-fee scheme had gone sour— to have him show up and put some new tax on us, like for drilling for salt water and polluting the land. But so far, he hadn't shown up.

I was bored. A couple of weeks in a tent is plenty. You add to that the desert and lousy food, and company that might be a shade more stimulating than talking to a cow, and you did not have a situation that made a man leap out of bed every morning with a glad cry, eager to meet the new day.

I had a return letter from Genevieve, but it didn't have much to say. She did take me to task for sounding so cold and distant in my letter but that didn't bother me any. She said the social scene in Houston was in a mad whirl and I ought to come back and squire her around. I figured she was just kidding, because she knew my opinion of the merry social scene. She said she'd bought a new eight-cylinder Packard runabout with a golf-bag compartment. In my reply I said that we had leased eight oxen and that they could spot her Packard eight-cylinder and have plenty left over to pull down a building in downtown Houston.

But I made it a brief, noncommittal letter. I wrote it the night before the water wagon was going back to town so they could take it. It was sad being connected to town at an oxen's pace, but it was better than getting in trouble with the judge.

The numbers of our visitors were picking up. Some days there would be as many as ten or twenty standing around gawking. I had no earthly idea what they thought they were seeing. Some few still came a-horseback, but the balance overloaded old Model T pickups and jalopies. I wondered how they figured it was worth the gas and the wear and tear on their vehicles for such a trip. There were no jobs to be had. When Dennis had been begging for hired hands, only a few fore-sighted men had taken the relatively high-paying jobs and they weren't about to relinquish them now.

Our crew had leveled out at an even fourteen, counting the two teamsters who kept the oxen plodding back and forth to Pecos. In skill they ran from Joe Cairo, who could do anything on an oil rig, to a huge, burly man who had to be shown which side of the pipe wrench to use. But he was as strong as any two men there, and for that reason he had value.

I took the plane up every few days just to keep my hand in and to get away from the boredom of the camp. When he could, Dennis came along with me, scouting for his next location. The way it was looking to me, there wasn't going to be any need for another drilling site. It appeared to me that the Llano Estacado—or Staked Plain as it was called in English, which was what these high plains were called— was made out of solid rock. I figured Dennis was going to spend all his money on drilling bits before we struck anything.

Then one day, when we were drilling at around two hundred feet, I was standing near the rig and I began to feel the earth shake slightly beneath my feet and heard a distant rumble like far-off thunder. I looked up at the rig. Dennis had stopped drilling and was listening intently. Joel had stepped back from the rotary table and was looking very alert. The other two men on the platform floor looked confused and uncertain. They were boll weevils, rookies, new men to the job. Joel waved them back from the rotary table. Our audience, who had been standing a respectful ten or twelve yards back, now began to press forward like they had good sense. I guessed that they were following the principle of, *If something is going to happen and you don't understand it, get as close as you can.*

I wasn't but a few feet from the rig. I stepped over and put my hand on one of the timbers of the frame. It was trembling, and not from the power of the drilling. Dennis had shut his engines down. As I stood there, I saw the casing began to vibrate, and then Dennis stood up and tilted his head back so he could see up into the derrick. "Charlie!" he yelled. Without pause the derrickman grabbed his safety rope and slid the forty feet to the ground. Then Dennis came hustling around his draw-works, waving his hand at Joel and the other two roughnecks. "Let's go!" he said. "Something is gonna blow."

They clambered down the steps of the drilling platform and then raced off twenty or thirty yards. I went trotting after them. I said, to Dennis, "What the hell is going on?"

He was breathing hard and staring intently at the rig. "I think we hit it, Sunny Jim. Sounds like gas pressure. In a minute it is going to blow out."

"Oil?"

He gave me a blank look. "Oil? Hell, yes, oil! Nothing else makes that sound, and I've heard it a dozen times. That's gas pressure shoving the oil to the surface." He smacked me on the back. "Son, we've hit it! Hot damn!"

I was watching the crowd of gawkers. If anything, they had pressed closer, now that the rig was deserted. "What about them?" I said. I motioned toward our visitors.

"They'll just get a little oily," Dennis said. He was almost jumping up and down.

I said, "I've heard these things can catch on fire."

Dennis gave me a full-faced sour look. "Now you've done it. You had to say that, didn't you? You could have gone all day without saying that. Damn it!" He walked toward the gawkers, bawling at them and waving them back. Slowly, reluctantly, they moved back to a position of safety.

I stood there, waiting for something wondrous to happen—what, I didn't know. All I knew was that there was noise and commotion and Dennis's assurances that we had "hit it." Strangely, I was wishing that Genevieve was there to witness whatever was going to happen. I understood that my request that she come with me had been unreasonable. She would have died of boredom in Pecos and certainly an oil camp was no place for a lady, but I felt she would have been thrilled by this underground commotion. Sort of like going big-game hunting. I did not know why it was Genevieve who jumped into my mind as someone whose company I wanted on this auspicious occasion, but she had. It sort of disturbed me, as if I were carrying a torch that I didn't know was lit.

Dennis came back, having dispersed the sightseers. He and the rest of the crew were staring intently at the well. The faint roaring noise began to grow louder and louder.

"Here she comes!" Dennis said excitedly. "HERE SHE COMES!"

Even I was getting excited. I had seen photographs of oil gushers where the stream of black oil had come rushing up the casing and soared over the top of the derrick. Sometimes it carried the pipe along and flung it into the air like so many broomsticks.

The noise grew louder and louder. Behind me I heard Joe Cairo say to someone, "That don't sound right."

But I didn't care. I was swept up in the excitement of the moment.

The roar grew to a rumble and then came bursting out of the casing, up through the rotary table, halfway up the derrick.

It was a moment before I realized it was water. But it was water that was different than when we'd hit the pools of salt water. There'd been no force behind the salt water, and it had been gray in color. This water was crystal-clear and coming out of the ground with great force.

Behind me I heard Dennis say, "Aw, shit!" His tone was full of disgust. I couldn't understand it. We'd hit water before and he hadn't sounded so discouraged. I turned around. I said, "What's the matter? What's happened?"

It was Joe Cairo who answered me. He looked as discouraged and down in the mouth as Dennis did. They all did. He said, "Artesian well. Underground spring."

"So?" To me it didn't seem any different than the saltwater pools. "What difference does it make what kind of water it is?"

Dennis started toward the rig. The rest of the crew followed. The crowd of onlookers had already began to crowd around. Some of them were standing in the stream of water that was straying out from the side of the rig. More than a few had their faces upturned to the falling drops. I saw a man catch some in his cupped hands and bring it to his mouth and drink. In an astonished voice he called out, "Why, it's sweet water!"

And then more tasted it and some of the men and one or two of the women began to dance around in the falling geyser like they were in a shower bath. They were whooping and hollering and carrying-on like a bunch of kids in a candy store.

I said to Dennis, as we walked toward the rig, "Look here, isn't this a good thing? It will solve our water problems. I don't know what it tastes like, but it's got to be better than that poison we bring in from town."

"Willis," he said, "we're drilling for oil, not water—no matter how good the water."

We were mounting the steps to the platform floor. He looked over at Joe Cairo. "You reckon it's already twisted the pipe?"

I became aware of the terrible clanging and banging coming from the well casing.

Cairo shook his head. "Ain't got enough pressure. That just sounds like the drill stem rattling around in the casing. But we need to do something 'fore we get flooded out here."

I got hold of Dennis's sleeve. I didn't understand all I was seeing. "What's happening? What are you going to do?"

He paused to give me an answer. "There's two things we can do. We can try and drill down through this artesian spring and go on about our business. If we can do that, we can bust the pressure of the spring and keep it from fighting us. In fact, it can even help us because some of the force will be turned downward."

"What's the other thing?"

He made a face. "It ain't good. We'll have to pull the pipe out of the hole and move the whole kit and caboodle a ways off. That'll mean taking down the derrick and dismantling the boilers. All the work to be done again."

I was anxious. The idea of all this sweet, pure water in the middle of the desert was exciting. "Why can't you just keep drilling and pay the water no mind?"

He looked at me like I'd been held back several grades. "Hell, Willis, go stick your hand in that stream gushing out of the hole. Feel the pressure. It is hard enough drilling in this formation without a young river flowing upstream against you."

Everyone in the crew was standing around the platform, getting wet but not minding at all in the heat, and looking around and talking it over among themselves. Finally, Joe Cairo said, "Dennis, why don't we give this thing a day or two before we go to start drilling again? The pressure might back off. I've seen these springs blow in like a woman caught her husband in the wrong bed and then peter out in a week until they were just handy in keeping the bit wet."

Dennis nodded. "That's what I was thinking. I don't want to risk the drill stem against this pressure. Hell, it can't blow like this too long."

But you couldn't have told it from the way our visitors were acting. They were jumping all over and dancing and sliding back and forth in the mud that was forming. You'd have thought we'd dug this well just for the purpose of giving them a shower.

I said to Dennis, "What happens if you move the rig?"

"A lot of work." He shrugged. "We pull up the pipe and stack it and move it all to a place we think is away from the artesian spring."

"What happens when you pull up the pipe? Does the fresh water keep flowing up through the hole?"

He shook his head. "Of course not. When we take out the pipe and the casing, there is nothing to support the hole. It collapses on itself and the water gets shut off."

"Just like that?"

"Just like that."

I looked at the crowd around the rig. Somehow their number seemed to have grown. I said, "I got an idea some of these folks around here wouldn't take kindly to that idea."

Dennis gave the crowd a bare glance. "What folks? Who you talking about?"

I said, "The folks who live here. The ones rooted in this worthless soil. The ones who are jumping up and down in that springwater like it was gold."

CHAPTER
14

DENNIS SAID, "Hell, them yahoos are trespassing." He waved at the townsfolk. I noticed that some few of them had jumped in their jalopies and were hightailing it back to town—to spread the word, I figured. This was probably as big an occurrence as when the borax mine had shut down.

Dennis said, "They be standing on ground that ain't theirs and drinking water that ain't theirs. And when I shut it off, there won't be nothing for them to trespass about."

By now we were in the midst of the spray near the well. It was twenty degrees cooler than where we'd been standing. Charlie said, "Boy, I could stand some of this cold water up in the top of that rig. I could work a double shift in this stuff."

And the water was much cooler. In fact, it was cold. Dennis said that was the way of underground springs. They were always cold. I got a little deeper into the mist, just enjoying it.

Dennis said, disgust in his voice, "Of all the damn luck. This one is going to be a son of a bitch to cap if it don't fizzle out."

Joe Cairo said, "Dennis, seems to me we ought to git some good outten this water while we got it."

"How you figure?"

"Well, we been drinkin' that poison we been truckin' from town. Now we got this good, sweet water. Be a shame to let it go to waste. We ought to empty that rotgut out of our water tanks and fill them up with this here water."

Joel said, "And the water tank ain't left for town yet. We could fill it up and save them oxen a trip."

Dennis nodded up and down, slowly. "I reckon we can do that." He turned around. "Joel, why don't you and your floor crew get a big hose and rig it to the top of the casing? Then use it to clean out them tanks and fill up everything you can."

I said, "Be damn nice to have food cooked in real water. That other stuff makes everything taste like soap."

He turned around on me. "Don't get too used to it. We come out here to drill for oil. Remember?"

"Still, the water's nice."

He turned back to Joel. "Listen. I don't want this water making a mudhole out of the camp. I'm going to let it run for three or four days, see what it does. But after you get everything filled up, I want you to run that hose out in the desert. Run it downhill if you can." He looked around, at the tents and the other equipment. It was all getting pretty wet. He said, "Joel, you better get high behind on that hose business before the camp floats away."

I turned, with my back to the rig, and looked out over the terrain. We were drilling on a hump or a high point, but what was interesting was the way the ground lay. Due west of us, the ground dropped away like somebody had scraped it down with a shovel. It formed an almost perfect basin about a mile and a half long, by about a half mile wide. One could almost imagine it had been the bed of some ancient river, long since gone the way of all old rivers.

But it occurred to me that if enough water could be put in the basin, you'd have one hell of a fine lake for watering cattle or irrigating crops. A big lake in just such a place could make the surrounding desert bloom like a rose garden. I thought it was too bad that we were

drilling for oil and not water. The water well we had would go a long
ways toward filling the basin up.

Unless it fizzled out. Which Dennis was counting on.

That night the wind got around to coming out of the northeast so that
it blew the geyser of water over toward the tents. It was odd and
somehow very comforting to be lying there on your bed in the desert
and hear the spatter of drops of water on the top of your tent like it
was raining. It wasn't constant, like a steady rain, because sometimes
the geyser would blow in one direction and the wind in another. Still,
there was enough of it to give you a nice illusion of being in a rain-
storm. Especially the temperature. The fine spray coming off the geyser
had soaked the air in the area, and it was so cool a man might have
wanted a blanket for his bed.

Dennis was working at his log and I sat up on my bed and swung
my legs around. I had a tin cup and a bottle of whiskey under my cot.
I got the whiskey out and poured myself about a third of a good drink
and then sat there sipping it. I said, "Dennis, don't you think that water
might be as valuable as oil in this part of the country?"

He was at his "desk," with a lantern turned down low. Now he
trimmed the wick and turned it up so he could see back to the corner
where I was. He said, "What are you talking about—water worth as
much as oil?"

"Well, I've heard if you can irrigate a desert you can grow just
about anything. We could make a hell of a big lake here and raise
cattle."

He found his own whiskey and poured himself out a little. "You
have gone plumb loco. Mr. Atlas didn't contract with us to go into the
truck-farming business. He wants oil. And so do I. I want to open up
a field, Willis. Can you understand that? You got any idea how the
man that developed Spindletop felt? Pretty damn important. Well, I
want a little of that."

I hesitated, not quite sure how to say what I wanted to. I said,

"Did you notice those people here today? Coming out of nowhere? Damn near out of their minds with that water."

"Yeah, reminded me of a bunch of drunks at a church social."

I hesitated again. I said, slowly, "Maybe they won't let you shut that spring off. Maybe they are going to demand that water."

He looked up and his face was hard and set. He said, "I'd like to see somebody come on land I've got legally leased and tell me where I can drill and what I can drill for."

"You never know what that maniac Crater is liable to do. Depends if he thinks he can make money out of it."

"Crater or no Crater, he can't interfere with this operation. This would have to go to law, and I'd reckon Teddy Atlas could have a passel of lawyers down here make this judge stop and think."

"I'm glad you're not worried." I tipped my cup up and finished the little bit of whiskey. I hadn't really wanted it; it just seemed to go with the rainlike sound on the tent.

Dennis gave me the fish-eye. "Maybe I'm looking in the wrong direction. Maybe it be you that is interested in that water. After all, we are on your land. Maybe you'd like to make yourself a nice little lake and set up for a cattleman. Or maybe charge your neighbors for watering their cattle."

I laughed. "This is open range country, Dennis. You can't keep your neighbors' cattle away from water. Water and grass are for everybody. And I couldn't charge them."

"Then what would you want to do it for?"

I laughed again. "I don't want to do it, Dennis. You were the one said I did."

He turned back to his desk and his work. "Likely this is all just watermelon talk. I wouldn't be surprised if that spring runs down within twenty-four hours. I hope so, because I'd sure like to get back to drilling. These last tailings I was looking at before that water blew everything to hell, looked pretty damn promising."

•　　•　　•

Two days later the spring was blowing just as hard as ever. The hose that Dennis had caused to be connected to the casing and then run down the hill, was in place and pouring the water down toward the basin. It was a big hose, about four inches in diameter. It looked like a firehose, and enough water had passed through it that you could see where it was making an impression even though the thirsty soil sucked it up about as fast as it come out of the hose.

Dennis was growing more and more impatient, and his temper wasn't helped any by the number of gawkers coming out from town. Their number seemed to grow by the hour and some of them had had the temerity to inquire as to what Dennis was going to do with the water. He didn't get asked but a few times before it became clear to the rest of the crowd that he wasn't in a mood to discuss the question.

Some of the visitors had even brought small barrels and other containers in their trucks and their wagons and were busy filling them up from the end of the hose. I could imagine that the fresh springwater, after a lifetime diet of shallow-well water and the undrinkable Pecos River water, must have seemed like champagne after mud. I knew the food around the camp had certainly improved in flavor and it had to be because of the springwater.

But all of the water wasn't running off down the hose. There was a very loose connection at the well casing, and a good deal of water flooded over into the camp. It didn't take long for our visitors to turn it into gritty mud and go to tracking it everywhere. Dennis was outraged. He said, "Son of a bitch, all these people come out here trespassing, and—if that wasn't enough—they go barging into private areas like the tents the men sleep in, even the cook tent! Next they'll be coming here into my office. I'll be taking a shotgun after 'em, they're not careful."

Of course, he didn't mean it, any more than he meant to swear at the gawkers. But the geyser of water had done considerable damage to his plans and was making him impatient and irritable.

He was standing in the opening of our tent, staring at the well. A fine mist of water floated into the tent where he made an opening by parting the flaps. It was immediately refreshing. But Dennis said, "I swear, may I never take another step on this good earth if that damn spout of water ain't pumping harder. I can see the casing head and it's sprung a bigger leak from that hose and is throwing out a spout of water bigger than it was in the first place."

"Is the pipe looking like it will hold?"

"Yeah, so far. Though it wouldn't surprise me none if it come floating up any minute now. I—*Hey, you! Get outta that tent! This ain't a damn public park!*" He turned back into the tent, dropping the flap and cutting off the draft of cool moisture. "I swear, I may have to shut this camp down to visitors. I'd hate to do it, but I might just not have a choice, this keeps up." He sat down on his cot. "And meanwhile I'm paying better than a dozen men to sit around and do nothing but sleep and eat. Hell!"

I said, "Why don't you try to drill? It can't hurt to try, can it?"

Since we'd come to the campsite he'd taken to chewing tobacco. I guess he figured such a nasty habit was all right out in the field. But, truth be told, he got absentminded every now and again and would spit just wherever he was. It had got so I didn't make a practice of walking around the tent in my bare feet. He spit out the front of the tent, throwing back the flap, and said, "Yeah, yeah it can hurt." He shook his head balefully. "You could cut into another underground spring and they'd combine and you'd be a blowed-up sucker. You could have pipe scattered all over this prairie."

"Well, we can't just sit on this thing. You going to move the rig?" I was hoping, if he did, that there'd be some way to keep the spring flowing. Maybe he could leave his downhole pipe in place so the hole wouldn't collapse.

He sat back down on his cot and grimaced. He could barely sit still, he was so agitated. "Willis, I'm damned if I do and damned if I don't. See, we're a-settin' on what you call an anticline. That's geologist talk, but what it means is the earth kind of rises up and makes a fold way down deep. I thought it was at first, but I got damn sure when that artesian spring blew in. See, the same conditions that make for underground water with that kind of force are the very same conditions where you are likely to find oil. I hate like hell to move from this spot."

"I thought you said this was a salt dome."

"It is. A anticline and a salt dome are one and the same."

"Then how come this is sweet water and not salt?"

"The one ain't got nothin' to do with the other. We hit enough salt water, if you'll recollect. This here artesian spring is being driven by the same kind of force that causes oil to come bursting to the surface."

I said, "Well, you've got to decide something sooner or later. Teddy Atlas could show up any day. And what would you tell him?"

Dennis looked stricken. He said, "You could have gone all day without mentioning that."

"What are you going to do? Drill or move the rig?"

He shook his head. "I hope I may never get off this cot if I know the right answer. What I'm going to do is wait another twenty-four hours and hope something happens."

We left it at that and went over to the cook tent for a bite to eat. There was a crowd of about twenty or so gawkers standing around watching our every move. I couldn't figure out what the attraction was. I could have seen some point to their curiosity if we had been drilling or doing some other activity around the well. But nothing was going on except a spray of water was soaking everything in its path and a hose was pouring water into the sand of a shallow basin. Other than that, a lot of bored and restless oil-field workers were lying or sitting around, either napping or talking or whittling or doing other very unremarkable things.

But our audience showed up every day. They came out in their Ford and Chevrolet touring cars and pickups and in their mule-drawn wagons. It was an easy trip now for draft animals because there was certain water at the end of the line. Even the autos, which tended to overheat, could be cooled off with the springwater that was freely abundant. In effect, our water well had made it an easy trip out from town. No longer was a man setting out into the great unknown where he had to pack for his own survival. Coming out from town a man knew if he could make it ten miles he'd find help.

I finally figured it out that, since most of the gawkers didn't have jobs or work anyway, it made them feel less useless to come out and watch us rather than hanging around town. And now that *we* wern't working, they could come out and feel equal, if not superior, to us. But the shutdown was taking its toll.

The crew was growing more and more restless and Dennis was close to popping his cork. I was beginning to chafe, myself. I hadn't heard from Genevieve in quite a time and she was much in my thoughts. It had been some two weeks since I had written her last, but no reply had come. Perhaps she had forgotten me, perhaps some other man had come into her life. All I knew was that I was growing restless in the big middle of nowhere and if we weren't at least going to drill an oil well I felt like getting in the airplane and heading for civilization. I figured I could fly along the railroad track and drop down every so often for gasoline. It wasn't good using car gas in an aircraft engine, but a little wouldn't hurt. Eventually I'd begin coming to towns that had airports, and would be able to gas up properly.

But strangely enough, the one thing that bothered me the most was the lean, hungry, weather-beaten faces of our crowd of gawkers. They just stood there, motionless and silent, watching with eyes that had grown dull staring out over the desolate prairie and waiting for something good to happen in their lives. Most of them had been waiting a long, long time. The sheriff had told me that the reason there weren't more drunks in the town was that nobody had money for liquor. He'd said, "Hell, you can't blame them. Not a damn thing to hope for. Ain't no use hoping for a good crop because it ain't going to rain. No use hoping for the borax mines to start back up because the borax played out and they know it. In fact, ain't no use hoping for a damn thing because it's not going to happen. Why don't they leave? What for? They'd still be as ignorant and helpless someplace else. Besides, most of them don't have the money. This is all they know. This is what their daddy knew and their grandfather. And it is what their kids will know. You cut one of these folks and they'll bleed that brown Pecos River water. I came here ten years ago as a temporary constable when the mine was working and there was trouble from time to time. I stayed on . . . well, I guess I stayed on because I ain't got no more sense than the rest of these folks. The town needed a sheriff, and Lord knows, it's an easy enough job. But don't think too hard of them. This country will wear you down. And if the country wasn't enough, there's always Judge John Crater to make their lives miserable."

Dennis waited two more days and then he finally started drilling. He went back to work because it was obvious the spring wasn't going to diminish—in fact, Dennis was about halfway convinced that it was gaining in volume—and because it was too much trouble to move the rig. He hated to battle that surge of springwater, but he'd said that if he could just get down through it fifteen or twenty feet he might well drill around the main stream and have easier going.

The scary part was when he hooked the pipe string back up and let the whole shebang down in the hole and started up the rotary table. It was clear it was a battle, and you could see how nervous the rough-necks on the drilling platform were. The pipe was rattling around aboveground, and it was difficult for them to make up the connection as a new stand was swung into place. Up in the derrick I could see that Charlie had added another safety rope to the one tied around his waist. I didn't know if that was so wise. If that pipe came flying out of the hole, he might not want to be encumbered.

If the rig had been noisy before, it was even more so now. I could actually hear the pipe rattling against the casing as it reacted to the strong current of uprushing water. Dennis sat behind his engines and his spool of steel cable with a concerned look on his face. He would only set the rotary table to spinning in short bursts, shoving forward a lever quickly whenever he thought he might be overtaxing the string of pipe. Joe Cairo had told me that a good driller—and Dennis was one—could tell by the feel of his control handles what was going on down in the bottom of the hole, even if it was a thousand feet deep.

I watched for a while, watched Dennis worrying and the crew working with half their mind on the job and the other half on what could happen at any second. And, of course, all of this was being done in a rush of water that shot halfway up into the derrick and flooded all of the rig and everything for fifty yards around. Even our rubberneckers had had to move back out of the way of the spray. When he'd restarted the drilling, Dennis had released the artesian well from any constraints and it was blowing full-steam. I had to agree with Dennis that the spring was, indeed, going stronger. But, oh, how pleasant the cold water was in the hot dry air. I could even see one or two of the roughnecks, who were, of course, soaked to the skin, give a slight shiver every now and again.

It seemed odd to think of a word such as *delicate* to describe what Dennis was trying to do on the giant rig with the heavy machinery and tools, but that was what it appeared to me as. He would spin the pipe with his rotary table for a few moments at slow speed and then, when he saw or imagined some slight break in the water's force, would pour on the steam and force as much progress as he could. There had been about ten feet of the last stand of pipe sticking out of the hole. In four hours of drilling he had cut it to five. It was not much to show, but it was progress.

He quit two hours later, claiming the roughnecks were taking too much of a beating, but I think it was to rest his nerves. He's gained about seven feet on the artesian spring.

I went into our tent where he'd disappeared. He was sitting with a glass of whiskey in his hand looking wet and nervous. He said, "I hope to never rest in a bed again if that ain't shaky work. I tell you, that whole rig is shaking. I look up at Charlie and I can see him nearly getting shook off his perch. And I ain't certain from one second to the next what is going to come out of that hole."

Dennis had drilled down to the platform level so that the roustabouts could reattach the hose to the mouth of the last stand of pipe. Now the water was no longer drenching the area but running back down into the basin.

I said, "You going to keep on?"

He shrugged and took a drink. "I got to because I don't know what else to do. But don't get the idea I'm happy about it. It is scary as hell listening to that pipe rattle around and feeling the downhole pressure suddenly let up. But, hell, if I can just get through that spring I'll be all right. Once I can get a stand of pipe clear through it, it has got to go around. There'll still be water in the hole, but that spring will have to find a new channel rather than coming up our pipe. Let it stay underground where God meant it to."

"Aaah," I said, "now you are interpreting. I thought you let the Bible and the preachers do that."

"Willis . . ." he said, with a kind of pained look on his face. I guess he wasn't in the mood for any of my joshing about his religion.

Dennis seemed to have new confidence the next day. He had the crew up early and on the job after a quick breakfast. He even seemed to have renewed confidence in his drilling. "I ain't letting no damn gout of water interfere with my business," he said.

But he still seemed to take it cautiously, winding up the steam engine to full force only every so often. Nevertheless, he got another stick of pipe screwed into the collar of the one in the hole and gradually seemed to be gaining on the artesian well.

Our visitors were right on time. About two hours after sunup they started showing up in their autos followed by the ones a-horseback or riding a buckboard. They had learned to keep a respectful distance back from the rig. The cook tent was set off from the others and mostly they tended to cluster around the down-sun side of it. According to individual taste they squatted or hunkered down or stood around with their arms folded, their eyes squinting into the glare as they watched every move on the rig. You would have thought they held stock in the company, so close was their scrutiny.

About midmorning I went into the cook tent and got a tin cup of coffee and came out and stood in the sun drinking it. The sun could get so hot that even hot coffee fresh from the pot tasted cool. As I stood there one of the gawkers detached himself and came awkwardly up to me. He stood there, just to my side, until I lowered the coffee cup and acknowledged his presence. "Yes?" I said. "What can I do for you?"

He was a little dried-up shrimp of a man, with black, gnarly whiskers shading part of his face until he could afford a shave. He had on a khaki shirt with permanent sweat stains under the arms and thread-bare elbows looking like they were going to poke through at any minute. He said, hesitantly, "Say, cap'n, I an' the rest of the boys was kin' of wonderin' 'bout that water. That springwater. Be he going to turn it loose again pretty soon? Let it run outten that hose?"

I shook my head. "He's trying to drill through it." I was very conscious of the need in the man standing next to me. It was so palpable I could feel it. It said, *I need a job, I need a way to make some money to support my family, I need a break in this life to feel like a man, I need help because I am so tired of being broke and whipped down and stepped on, and life has got to be better than this. I need to be able to stand up and be counted and I don't mind working for it so long as my children and my wife can be proud of me.*

I could hear every bit of that, though all he did was stand there trying to look humble and in his place and not be a bother to the big oil man. He said, hesitantly, "I don't reckon I unnerstand you, cap'n. What's it mean, him trying to drill through it? Drill through what?"

I could feel the eyes of all the spectators on me. Except for different body shapes they were very much like the little man who had summoned the nerve to accost me. None of them ran to fat and very few had shaven in the last several days. All of their clothes looked thread-bare and nearing the end of the line. Mostly, though, it was the eyes that got me. They were glued on me like I was holding a bag of cash and was only waiting to decide who to give it to. I said, in answer to the question, "I told you. If he gets a length of pipe down through the artesian spring, the water will not have an opening to come to the surface. So it will go around the pipe and go on about its business. You understand?"

He licked his parched lips, still with that needy look on his face, and said, "But that won't have nar'en to do with the water comin' up, will it, cap'n?"

I was starting to feel uncomfortable, and not just a little guilty. I even felt guilty about the cup of coffee I was holding in my hand while the other men had none. I quickly poured it out. I said, patiently, "No, if he gets through the stream the water will be shut off."

He didn't look shocked or hurt at the news. Not even sad. He didn't even blink. I think he had been resigned to hearing that sort of news all his life, and one more stick in the eye didn't matter. He turned around to the others and said, matter-of-factly, "They be gonna shut the water off."

It was enough to bring the crowd to me, something I would as soon not have had happen. A tall, skinny man wearing a sweat-soaked felt fedora said, "How come you wanna do that? This here is the most water we ever seen. And we never knowed there was that kind of water anywhere 'bout these parts. Cold and sweet. We never got no water like that in our wells."

I said, "That's because it is down deep. You don't have the equipment to drill that deep. This well is down over two hundred and fifty feet."

That brought a whistle from somebody and they looked around at each other. Finally the tall man said, "Well, how come he don't let that water flow? We can use that water."

That made it easy for me. Now I could talk in terms they could understand. I said, "Because we're here to drill for oil and that artesian well is getting in the way. But if we bring in an oil well, you'd be amazed at the prosperity and good business it will bring to this area. Pretty soon other oil companies, big companies, will come here and they will spend plenty of money. There will be lots of jobs, jobs for every man."

They just stared back at me. They knew about water; they didn't know about oil. Water meant crops and healthy livestock. Water meant a way to combat the hazards of the desert. They could drink water, they didn't know what you could do with oil. Besides, the water was right there in front of them. They could see it. Already, little pools of it were gathering in places in the basin. A man could water his horse at one of those little pools. But oil? That was just some more talk, something all of them had heard plenty of in their lives. They stood there, staring at me.

"Damn it," I said, "It's not my fault! I haven't got any say! Hell, I'm not on the payroll." I was suddenly angry. I hated their accusing eyes, like I was the root cause for their miserable lives and the lives of their families. I said, still angry, "Why the hell do you stay here in this godforsaken place? Why don't you move to somewhere you can get a job or farm. Hell!"

Slowly, as if I was throwing them out and they were leaving with dignity, they turned, one by one, and made their way back to the far end of the cook tent and started watching the rig again.

I let out a short, blunt oath and hurried across the muddy ground to the tent Dennis and I occupied. Only when I was inside, with the flaps closed and sitting on my cot did I feel halfway comfortable again. Damn it, I thought, they had no right to blame me or anyone else in the drilling crew for cutting off their water. *Their* water! And what right did they have to even be standing on the land? It was my land, land given to me by my father. If anybody had a right to the water it was me, and I damn sure didn't want it. I resolved right then and there that I was getting out of the place just as quick as I could. I hadn't even been as sick of the war as I was sick of Pecos and its inhabitants.

After I'd sat and stewed for a while, I got up and slipped out the end of our tent and then climbed the slippery steps and went up on the drilling platform. A lot of mud was oozing out around the pipe in the hole and the roughnecks were having a hard time keeping their footing. I went over to where Dennis was sitting at his controls. The rig seemed to be vibrating and shaking even harder than it had been the day before. Dennis nodded at the mud and said, "I—I—I'-mmm du-du-drilling thro-through sand." The vibration was making his voice quiver and stammer.

I said, "Is that good?"

"It means I'm in the middle of the artesian well. Stands to reason a underground stream would be flowing through sand. It sure as hell can't flow through rock."

"How much progress have you made?"

He throttled back on the rotary table so that things felt almost stable. "We've got another stand of pipe in her. If I don't break through tomorrow, I don't know what I'm going to do."

"Well, you're giving this part of the desert a damn good sprinkling." I nodded off toward where our visitors were still gathered. "You've got a mighty interested audience over there."

"They got a ways to wait before they see or taste any oil."

"I don't think it is oil they are interested in."

"Then they are nuts as well as being backwards and dumb enough to elect that crook Crater. Justices of the peace are elected, ain't they? I'd hate to find out he's appointed by the governor."

"I don't know how JPs get their commissions, but I do know your crowd is not a damn bit interested in you getting through that stream and cutting it off."

"Hell, don't they understand I got a ways to go before I can hope to hit oil? This ain't going to be no shallow field. I can already tell by the samplings I'm getting up. I—"

He stopped as a yell came from over at the boilers. He glanced over at Joe Cairo's wave, gestured back, and then began pulling levers to bring the power of the rig to a standstill. He took off his rough leather gloves. "Guess Joe is letting the pressure get too high. But it is taking all the power we got to keep this operation headed down and not up."

"Dennis, that crowd that is standing there day after day didn't come out to see us drill for oil. They come out first looking for any jobs might have been overlooked when they discovered you were paying real money for workers. Then the water come in and they came back for that."

"What is the matter with them? An oil field would mean all kinds of jobs and prosperity. This water ain't shucks to an oil field."

"Like you say, Dennis, they ain't exactly forward thinkers. They can see the water and know what it can do. Oil, that's another duck. I would bet you nine out of ten don't know the gasoline they run in their vehicles comes from crude oil. Water, they understand. You can water a horse or a cow with water. And if you'll look right close you'll see more buckboards and saddle horses among that bunch than you will roadsters."

"I see a few pickups. And I rented a stake-body truck, don't forget. They is enough vehicles in that town they ought to know about oil."

"Dennis, this is a mighty poor locale. Most of those vehicles are old and nearly wore-out. Except for Crater's coupe. It's the only car in town anywhere near new. Point is, water could save this place. Couldn't you leave the pipe you got in the hole there, and move the rig? You got enough pipe for a new hole."

He gave me an amazed look. "Have you gone off your rocker? You get ahold of some bad whiskey or what? You are talking like a man with a paper asshole."

I leaned up against his cable spool, even if it was greasy. I said, "Oh, Dennis, what the hell difference does it make? Ain't no oil out here, and you know it as well as I do. If there was any prospects the big oil companies would have had rigs all over the place."

I shouldn't have said it. It hurt him. I could see him flinch when I said that part about him knowing there wasn't any oil in the area. He spoke and his voice was cool. "You could have gone all day without saying that, Willis."

"Aw, hell, Dennis, it come out wrong. You know I don't know anything about drilling for oil."

" 'Way you talk I must not, either. Which makes me a confidence trickster. Getting Teddy Atlas to finance an operation I knew was doomed to hell. I should have told him, if I'm an honest man, that I was drilling for water."

I hung my head. "Damn it, stop that, Dennis. You are the only reason I am out here in this hellhole, and if you get down on me . . . Look, those townspeople been getting to me. They look so damn pathetic. I got to thinking about filling up that basin with fresh water—what it would do for them."

He gave me a square look. "I'm in the oil business, Willis. I leave the charity work to the Red Cross."

"All right, all right. Forget I said it, will you? Just as a favor to me, consider the words never left my mouth. Okay?"

Joe Cairo was signaling him from the boilers. He gave a wave and turned back to his engines and levers. Just before he threw the power in gear he said, to me, "Okay. The hell with it. No offense taken."

"None intended."

But my words were lost in the noise of the machinery coming to life. I carefully made my way across the slippery floor and went down the steps to the stability of the ground.

That evening, I was glad to see that things were back to normal between Dennis and me. He was a good man, a kind man, and I had spoken thoughtlessly about his livelihood, the thing he could do that he was proud of. It was the same as if someone had criticized my flying. But Dennis had forgiven me, chalking it up, I expect, to my comparative youth and bad judgment. We ate in the cook tent and then retired to the tent—him to work on his logs and his reports, and me to read a Zane Grey book I'd gotten off Joe Cairo. It was pretty heavy going, but it was better than staring at the canvas ceiling. Finally I put it aside and said, to Dennis's back, "When you think Teddy Atlas will show up?"

He turned on his camp stool to face me. "Don't even speculate on that. That is the last man I want to see."

"I thought that would be Judge Crater."

"Well, him too," Dennis admitted. "But I'm less ready to face Mr. Atlas. I don't want him to come way over here and find me bogged down in an artesian well."

"Will you seriously pull that downhole pipe if you can't get through the water and have to move the rig?"

He laughed without much humor. "Hell yes, Willis. What would you think? I got a bunch of pipe down that hole. That stuff costs money. Why, you want to pay for it and let the townspeople or whoever these folks are, have their well? Cost you a lot of money and would cost me a lot of time replacing it."

"Of course not," I said. I sat up on my cot and swung my legs around. "But I was thinking the town might want to raise the money. You know I haven't got enough money to buy a straw, let alone a stand of pipe. But they might get together and pool what they got. Maybe they could get enough together."

He shook his head slowly at me. "Willis, they don't have that much money in the whole damn town. This place don't even have a bank. Besides—" He pointed a thick forefinger at me. "Besides, I intend on getting through this mess."

"It was just a thought." I tried to say it casual.

He cocked his head at me. "I thought you didn't believe in the Bible, Willis."

"What are you talking about?"

"Sounds a lot like you are aiming to be your brother's keeper."

I gave him a sour expression and changed the subject. "Listen, I been thinking. There's a butcher shop in Pecos that has got a cold locker. That means they always got fresh meat. What if I was to fly into Pecos tomorrow and get thirty or forty steaks? Get 'em packed in ice and they ought to last through two suppers. Bet the men would like to have some meat that hasn't come out of a can."

Dennis scratched his head. "I don't know," he said hesitantly. "I'd hate for you to have another run-in with Judge Crater. He's spoiling to lock you up. And as soon as you land he's going to be on your ass to collect his landing fee."

"Give him six dollars," I said. "I know it is robbery but I think the meat is worth it."

"Yes, but I don't want to find you in jail."

"I won't sass him, even though he needs sassing more than any man I've ever known."

"Let me think on it. If you do go, for Pete's sake, don't bring him back with you."

"I thought it was Teddy Atlas you didn't want to see."

"Him too, but Crater is closer."

Two days later he was a lot closer. Charlie, up in the top of the derrick, was the first to spot him. He yelled out, "Look yonder! Ain't that the judge's car?"

Our whole crew was well-acquainted with the judge and held him in some apprehension. They had all heard about my run-ins with the man as well as the open secret that he was milking Dennis and saddling him with back-pocket taxes for damn near everything we did.

I jumped up on the platform floor to have a look, and Dennis shut down the power to stand up and shade his eyes and look in the direction Charlie had pointed. He was still a far piece off but there was no mistaking the color of the Judge's green Reo coupe. I said, in disgust, "Oh hell, not that son of a bitch!"

Dennis sighed and sat back down at his seat behind the equipment. The rig was quiet enough for me to hear him say, "Now, I wonder what that vulture wants. Be certain he is coming with an empty sack and expects to go home with it filled."

I walked over to him. "This can't go on, Dennis. Besides, we are standing on land I own. There is nothing going on here that he can levy a tax on."

But I had to rush my words and scramble off the platform to keep from getting soaked. As soon as Dennis stopped drilling, the water from the sping would come surging up around the pipe and go shooting up toward the top of the derrick. As I hurried away I heard Dennis call out to Joe Cairo to bank his boilers as we were more than likely going to have to shut down for a time. It was still midmorning, the coolest part of the day, and I knew it was going to irritate Dennis to lose the drilling time. But it could be more costly to irritate Crater by ignoring him. The bastard was a spherical son of a bitch—a son of a bitch any way you looked at him.

Charlie called down, "He got him a passenger. I think it be the sh'urff."

I could hear Dennis grumble. But he did say, "Let's hope it is the sheriff. He may be our only protection."

Judge John Crater stepped out of his auto and stood for a moment looking around. A faint haze of dust had followed him in, and for a second that obscured the starkness of his outline. But it soon cleared. The judge was wearing his usual dark suit with a vest and tie, only this time it was a bow tie. As a concession to the confines of his auto, he was not wearing a hat and the gray in his hair was clearly visible. It made him look no less lethal. He stood there, standing quite still,

and slowly looked the site over like some well-satisfied owner surveying his holdings. At least that was the way it looked to me. It was my
thought that he looked like a man holding a biscuit and trying to decide
where to take the first bite. I had no doubt that he considered the site
and the equipment and all of us as his private resources to be utilized
at his whim.

Sheriff Lew Wallace got out of the passenger side. He didn't look
at the judge but instead started walking toward the drilling platform.
As he went, looking for Dennis, I assumed, he spoke to first one and
then another of our gawkers, calling them by name and greeting them
in a friendly manner. I felt like Dennis did; I was glad the sheriff had
come to maybe hold down Judge Crater.

Dennis had come down off the rig. I went toward him just as he
and Sheriff Wallace shook hands. The sheriff glanced up at the rig. "I
hope our coming didn't cause you to knock off work." He cut his eyes
back toward where Crater was still standing, glowering.

Dennis made a face. "Not really. We need to get the fireboxes on
the boilers cleaned out. Getting too much ash in there. Can't get as hot
a fire."

The sheriff glanced up at the spout of water shooting up the derrick. He said, "I've heard all about your water well. That's all anybody
in town has been talking about. They're scared you're going to shut it
down. Water is a big item around here."

Dennis had a cud of rough cut in his jaw. He spit in the mud and
rubbed it around with the toe of his boot. "Sheriff, I can appreciate
how these folks think about a deep well. But I got a contract with a
backer to drill four oil wells. The contract doesn't say anything about
a water well. As a matter of fact, this artesian well I've struck is playing
hell with my schedule. It was going to be close enough on the money
to get those four wells drilled without this mess, and a mess is exactly
what it is."

The sheriff looked over to where the gawkers were standing
around, mostly inspecting Judge Crater uncertainly and, it seemed to
me, with a little apprehension. The sheriff said, "Yeah, but to folks in
this part of the country that spout of water is liquid salvation. I've

tasted some that got brought back to town, and it has been a long, long time since I tasted anything that good and it was water."

Dennis made a little groan. "Lew, don't you start on me. I've had it from all sides." He jabbed at me with his thumb. "Even from the ace of the skies here. You got to understand that I got a contract. The man advanced me money to do one thing, drill for and find oil. Develop a field. He could have me in court and maybe in jail for fraud if I didn't do my damnedest to fullfil that contract."

"I understand," the sheriff said. He glanced toward where the judge was still standing. "But I'd be on my guard. Trouble might come from any direction."

Like it was his cue and he'd been waiting in the wings, the judge suddenly started walking toward us. He paid the crowd of gawkers not the slightest bit of attention and they sort of involuntarily shrank back as he passed by. He was clearly walking straight for Dennis and, when he was about ten yards off, he said, in that gravelly voice of his, "Mr. Frank, I want to talk to you."

Dennis waited, flanked by me and the sheriff, until Crater got closer, and then he said, "Talk away, Judge, I'm all ears."

Crater halted and looked over toward the well. We were a good forty yards away but a fine mist was blowing over from the spout of water. Crater let the coolness wash over him before he turned back to Dennis. He said, "Quite a little town you've got here, Mr. Frank."

Dennis, even though he knew better, said, "Oh, is this your first visit out? We get so many. . . ." He let his voice trail off.

You could see that it got to Crater. If he'd come out before, he damn well would have been noticed. His voice was even less friendly when he said, "I want to talk to you. In private."

Dennis looked around. Our tent was about fifteen yards away. He shrugged and said, "Well, my office is in that tent yonder. Will that be private enough for you?"

Crater had never so much as glanced at me. Now he said, "If it's the best you got, it will have to do. Lead the way."

They marched off, Dennis taking it careful through the mud and the judge lifting his shoes with distaste as if he were walking in some-

thing worse than mud. Me and the sheriff and the rest of the rubberneckers watched their progress until Dennis parted the flaps of the tent
and let the judge in.

I looked at Lew Wallace. "What does he want?"

He shook his head. "He didn't tell me, but you can bet he didn't
come out here to wish you good luck. My guess it's got something to
do with the water. That's been causing a hell of a stir in town."

"What business is it of his? As far as that goes, he's trespassing.
This is my land."

We heard a voice, raised slightly, and then another one answered
it back. The sheriff and I both turned at the same time to look toward
the tent. The flaps were parted and we could see some dim movement
within. I glanced over. The yard birds had good hearing also. They
had inched forward toward the tent and were standing at the alert.

Now I heard a voice, distinctly louder. I recognized it as Dennis.
I seemed to hear something like, "I'll see you in hell first!"

And then there was a sharp rejoinder in a low, gravelly voice. I
knew who that was. The sheriff and I looked at each other. Lew Wallace said, "Don't sound like they are getting on their best."

"You think we ought to go in there? Dennis has got an Irish temper.
And if the judge is trying to squeeze him . . . well, I don't know what
might happen."

But before we could move, Dennis suddenly appeared through the
tent flaps. He motioned at me and the sheriff. He said, "I wish you two
would come here. Sheriff, I think you are an honest man and I want
you to hear what this tinhorn jackleg is trying to hold me up for in
the name of the law."

A little startled, we started that way, but before we had taken many
steps, Judge Crater came busting through the flaps. He said, "Sheriff!
I want you to shut this operation down right now. *Right now!* Right
this very minute. And if anybody interferes with you in the perfor-
mance of your duties, I want you to arrest them." Then he turned
sideways and pointed at Dennis. "And I want you to arrest this man
for contempt of court right now!"

Dennis said, grimly, "The hell you say. Anybody needs arresting here, Judge, it be you."

The judge drew himself up and pointed at Dennis again. "Sheriff, I demand you arrest this man right now. Put the handcuffs on him."

It was a little warm where we were standing. The wind had shifted and was blowing the spray away from us. Lew Wallace wiped his long sleeve across his brow. "Did you say for contempt of court?"

"Yes! Damn it! Have you gone hard of hearing? Arrest him!"

Dennis stepped in front of the judge. He said, "Just a Billy hell minute. Any arresting gets done, we gonna start with this crooked son of a bitch." He whirled around to face Crater. "Tell them what you asked me for. Say it in a loud voice and tell everybody. I dare you!"

But Crater just kept insisting that the sheriff arrest Dennis for contempt of court. The sheriff said, "Judge, we're not in your court. As a matter of fact, this is private property belonging to a third party. We ain't actual got any right to be here."

Dennis stepped forward and jabbed his finger at Crater. "Sheriff, this son of a bitch asked me for two thousand dollars if I wanted to go on drilling. Said he's shut me down if I didn't fork over the money. Ain't that bribery?—or something else? What do you call it? Forcing somebody to—Willis, what is that?"

"Extortion," I said.

"Yeah," Dennis said, "the son of a bitch tried to extort me."

Crater was livid. He looked like he was going to bust. He said, "You better watch your language to a officer of the court."

"And you better watch your language to a man that is drilling for oil. Don't you get it in your mind that you can interfere with me. You've already robbed this outfit of about twice what you made last year. Don't push me, Crater."

The judge leaned in toward Dennis's face and said, with venom in his voice, "Let me tell you something, Mr. Big-shot Oilman, the state controls all the water. You are into state water. We'll see about getting you shut down."

Dennis's neck was swelled up and his face was nearly purple. He said, in a loud voice, getting right in the judge's face, "I just want you to tell everybody within earshot what you asked me for in there in that tent! I dare you to tell them that you said if I'd give you two thousand dollars we could go on as we had been. I demand you tell these people that you extorted me, you son of a bitch!"

Crater was a heavy-built man. His face was heavy and his eyelids were heavy, so that his eyes were just slits in his heavy face. He had a vicious, menacing look about him that quickly assured you he was not concerned with your best interests. He said, sweeping his arm around to include our gawkers, "I call on these citizens to witness what I am saying now and what I said earlier to Mr. Frank. This is state water and belongs to the people of the state of Texas." He pointed a finger at the motley crew that had edged forward. "And that is you. This is *your* water, not some Yankee carpetbagger's come down to steal it from you."

A sort of ragged cheer went up from our yard birds. I didn't think that half of them knew what the judge was saying, but his statement had been delivered in such a way that they felt called upon to applaud and let out a few whoops and hollers.

But it made Dennis even madder. He said, "Why, you suck-egg dog, don't you call me no Yankee! And you and I both know what was said in there. All right, if this is the state's water, *they* can drill for it. I'm going to pull my pipe out and the hole will collapse and there'll be no water for nobody. It'll be two hundred fifty feet underground. See how much good you can get out of it then!"

The judge swept his arm and pointed at Dennis. He said, to the sheriff, "Sheriff Wallace, arrest that man. You heard him threaten to destroy government property, property of the state of Texas."

Sheriff Wallace pushed up his hat brim with his thumb. He said, "Well, Judge, I don't see how we can do that. There's a question of jurisdiction."

"You're within your jurisdiction. Carry out the order."

The sheriff nodded. "Yeah, I'm the sheriff of Pecos County and we are in Pecos County. But I don't know what your magistrate's district is. I ain't ever seen it up close. As far as I know, we might not be in it, and I don't want to go to arresting a citizen on false authority. That would be false arrest and he maybe could law me over the matter. Take me to a court of law and win damages. No, sir, I reckon the best thing we can do is get on out of here. Bunch of rough-looking ol' boys watching us pretty close."

Crater was clearly furious. I couldn't tell if he was more angry at Dennis, or at the sheriff who was showing him up. But he said, in a cold voice, to Dennis, "You can rest assured that this matter is not closed. If this lily-livered sheriff won't act on my orders I'll find someone who will. This water belongs to the state and you are going to get shut down. I'm going back into town and get off a telephone call to the attorney general's office in Austin and we'll see just how much longer you go on defying the law."

Dennis said, through clenched teeth, "Don't forget the part about you asking me for two thousand dollars."

The judge leaned toward him. "I'll have the state militia called out! See if you can defy them!" Then, without another word, he turned and started for his car. Over his shoulder he called, "Staying with these lawbreakers, Sheriff, or are you riding back with me?"

The sheriff gave us a regretful look. "Maybe I can calm him down." He turned to hurry after the judge, catching up him as the judge climbed behind the wheel of his auto.

We stood stupefied, watching, as the judge started his green Reo and roared away in a cloud of dust. We saw the little wave the sheriff gave us, but it was small comfort. Dennis turned to me, a worried look on his face. "Can he do that, Willie? Can he call out the state militia to shut us down?"

I shook my head slowly. Law training had not been part of my curriculum at the university. I said, "I don't know, Dennis. Why did you have to make him so damn angry?"

"Forget that. He made me mad as hell the way he was trying to dig around in my hip pocket. And it's not my money. It belongs to Teddy Atlas. But *is* water a state resource?"

I shook my head again. "I don't know. But I do know he is determined to cause you as much trouble as he can, even if he has to lie and cheat to do it."

"You think he can shut the rig down?"

I nodded. "I think he has that in mind, and he doesn't much care how he gets it done. Right now I am thinking we should not have let him leave here. The sheriff won't help him, but if he gets to calling back and forth between Austin, no telling who or what will be getting off that train. Dennis, he is an official of the court. We shouldn't have let him leave until we got him sweetened up somehow."

Dennis said, "That bastard has shook me down for the last dime. Just so much I can take."

Our crew had slowly gathered around and now there was a babble of voices expressing views of a surprising variety. Dennis cut his hand through the air. "Everybody shut up. Go back about your business. I got to think."

I didn't. I knew we could not let the man get near a telegraph or a telephone wire, or we were through. We might be proven right in the end, but that would take too long. Dennis had put too much into this effort in deep west Texas to have it ruined by a self-important crook. I was going to stop him.

Dennis turned to me with a bleak face. He said, "You were right about him all along, Willis. You said that judge was going to be trouble. I should have listened to you. I just never thought we'd get in this much trouble. As sure as I'm standing here, that man is going to find a way to ruin me."

"No he's not," I said. I turned on my heel and started toward the airplane. "Come help me get the canvas off the plane." I started walking toward it.

Dennis was coming along at my heel. "You going after him, Willis? Listen, tell him we can work out a deal, tell him I was hasty. Just keep him from getting the state government involved."

He was still talking as he pulled the canvas cover off the engine cowling and off the upper wing. I pulled off the canvas that protected both cockpits and threw it on the ground. Then I climbed in the forward cockpit. The machine gun was in place and the ammunition pan was at the ready. I opened the top of the pan to be sure the belts of 30-caliber bullets were still there.

Dennis came around to the side of the plane as I set up the mixture for rich and turned on the ignition and switches. I said to Dennis, "Wheel the nose around and then pull it through. The prop."

"What are you going to do, land near him and talk him out of wiring Austin? You're good at that, Willis. You know how to talk high-falutin."

I said, "*Will* you swing this plane around and then pull that prop through so I can get off the ground? Every second you waste puts them that much closer to Pecos."

That moved him. In a moment he had wheeled the Jenny around so that I was lined up for takeoff. Then Dennis pulled the prop through while I had the ignition off. That was to get gas in the carburator.

Now he said, "Switch on?"

"Switch on."

With a practiced rocking motion he gave the prop a spin and the motor roared into life. Within two minutes I was racing down our "runway" and a minute later, was pulling the plane into the air. Almost immediately I banked south and began looking for the road we had created with all the traffic back and forth to town. I climbed to five hundred feet and walked my eyes up the path in the desert, looking for a green Reo coupe.

CHAPTER

15

IT DID not take me long to pick them out. As
soon as I reached altitude I singled out the small auto trailing the plume
of dust. Because of the rough terrain Crater wasn't able to drive more
than five or ten miles an hour. Consequently, it looked like they'd
covered no more than three miles from the oil camp by the time I had
them spotted. I was flying off to their right and I put the plane into a
shallow left-hand bank and turned to do a flyover past them. I glanced
down at my altimeter and, at two hundred feet, leveled off. Then I
immediately made a sharp right turn to put me on a path parallel to
the automobile's. I glanced over. I could see Crater with his head out
the window staring at me. But I ignored him. I was watching his car's
progress, trying to judge its steadiness of speed. I was wishing that
Crater would come to a stop, but I had no time to wait. I didn't want
them getting any farther from the oil camp than they already were.

By now, even flying as slow as I was, I was a mile ahead of the
auto. I leaned forward, opened the pan of ammunition and fed the
first cartridge of the belt into the firing chamber of the Lewis machine
gun. I was not at all nervous. Though it had been some time since I'd
done such, I found my hands moving mechanically. When the car-

tridge was securely home, I pulled back on the bolt and the Lewis was armed. A touch on the trigger would send a steady stream of lead toward whatever I pointed the plane at. Once the gun was ready I turned right and flew across the path of the auto, losing altitude down to a hundred feet. I flew on for about a mile and then made a one hundred eighty–degree turn and started back toward Crater's coupe. It was bumping slowly along the desert path. I could just barely make out the form of the sheriff sitting in the passenger seat. As I neared, I saw him glance out toward me. I hated that the sheriff was in the car but it was too late to do anything about that.

I wanted the car to stop, but it was unlikely that it would do so on its own. When I judged that I was about five hundred yards from the car, I put the stick forward and started my run. I wanted to be as low as possible but still have the nose down. Of course, I didn't want to be so low there would be any danger, but I wanted to be low enough for the most accurate shooting.

Now I was flying by one hand, my left, on the stick, and my eye glued to the sight on top of the Lewis machine gun. My right hand was on the machine gun's trigger mechanism. Between the bouncing of the car and the slight up-and-down movement of the airplane in the hot air, aiming was more difficult than I wanted. But I had no choice. The distance narrowed, the car suddenly swelled in size, and I could see Lew Wallace's startled face, as it must have looked like I was going to fly right into them. I fed in the slightest bit of right rudder so that my gunsight focused just in front of the car. When I felt I could wait no longer, I fired. It was a medium burst, and I had just a glimpse, as I swooped over and past the car, of a line of puffs of sand stitching the desert some ten yards in front of the car.

The clatter of the Lewis was still echoing in my head as I pulled back on the stick and then kicked the Jenny into a hard right-hand Immelmann. The Jenny was no Spad, and it was not the maneuver to be pulling that close to the ground. I quickly fed in more power as I felt the bird shudder, wanting to fall off on one wing. A spin would follow if the airplane didn't quickly regain airspeed. I pushed the nose over and kicked in left rudder to bring the plane to level flight. It responded slowly, but it did respond. When the airplane was under control again I glanced to my right at the auto. I had had the impression, as I flew over, that it had stopped. But it wasn't stopped now. The judge had it going as fast as it could, and it was bouncing and jouncing around as if it, too, wanted to fly.

It made me angry. He should have stopped. Did he think he could outrun an airplane? Next, he would take out his big revolver and try to outgun my Lewis. I made a diving right-hand turn and immediately lined up my sights just in front of the coupe. Obviously I was going to have to shoot closer to get Crater's attention.

I was low and the plane was bouncing around in the hot, rising air, and the car was jumping around too. I decided to fire from a greater distance than before, and draw my fire back to the auto. I squeezed the trigger and was amazed to see a line of sand puffs heading straight for the front of the car. With the Lewis still clattering I heeled the plane slightly to the left, just in time to miss the body of the auto. I saw metallic strikes hit the bumper and the hood and, it seemed to me, make a few holes in the left front tire. I stopped firing when I was nearly on top of the auto, pulling the plane up into a shallow climbing turn. My altimeter was not too accurate at such low altitudes, but it said I was still doing aerobatics at fifty feet off the ground.

I went out a little farther from the car and made a gentle, gliding left-hand turn, wondering what the occupants of the Reo were thinking after my second pass. It had scared *me*. The plane had bumped at the wrong time as I'd squeezed the trigger and I'd damn near shot the inhabitants. Fortunately, I'd been far enough back that it had allowed me time to correct.

As I finished my turn, I could see that the coupe had stopped. The sheriff had gotten out on his side and was shading his eyes, staring at me. I wondered about the judge. I was still about a half a mile away, and I waggled my wings to reassure Lew Wallace, though I doubted he knew much about air-to-ground signals. I still hadn't seen the judge. Lew had walked away from the coupe, heading to the rear. I think he was reading my mind, though I hated to fire another burst to get the judge out of the auto.

But as I neared I saw him get out on the driver's side. He left the door open and began half running, half walking, in the general direction of town. I dipped the nose and slipped the airplane to the left to get a good lead on him. He glanced up at me just as I fired. The metallic chatter of the Lewis was followed almost immediately by a line of sand-bursts some twenty yards in front of Crater. It stunned him, from all appearances. He suddenly stopped and threw both hands around his head and stumbled backward as if shoved by a mighty hand. I guessed that aerial attacks were a little unusual in Pecos County.

I watched him over my shoulder as I crossed the road and started to make another one hundred eighty–degree turn. I didn't know how many bursts it was going to take to get him walking back toward the oil camp, but I had plenty of ammunition. One thing I knew for certain; he wasn't going near a telephone.

He was still standing there as I turned back for another run. He dropped his hands from his head, but he hadn't gone in the direction I wanted him to. I could see Lew Wallace yelling at him and beckoning. He wasn't paying any attention. Then he became aware that I was coming at him again. He turned to face me. His face had gone white and his eyes were big and round and his mouth was open. I pressed the trigger and started walking a line of bullets in his general direction. I never got close. Almost at the sound of the first shot he suddenly whirled and went, in a peculiar gait, running and walking back toward the sheriff. Lew Wallace looked up at me and pointed north, toward the camp. I waggled my wings. The sheriff caught Crater as he came stumbling up, and together, they began the long walk back toward the drilling site.

I flew spirals around them until they had gotten a good half mile from the auto. When I felt sure the judge couldn't change his mind and run back to his car, I climbed for altitude and set a course for the oil camp. I did not intend for them to walk the whole distance. Once I had landed I was going to send our truck back for them.

When I got over the camp I circled at altitude to make sure the two little black dots in the distance were still heading in the right direction. I knew the oil camp was just about the last place John Crater wanted to be, but I felt sure that Lew had explained to him that it was either that or bake to death in the desert. When I felt sure they were still coming, I pushed the stick forward and went down for a landing. Once on the ground I taxied toward the camp. I could see Dennis running toward me. He walked along by the wing for the last ten yards. And then, when I cut the ignition, he was up on the plane before the prop could finish turning, groping his hand out toward the Lewis to see if it was hot. I took off my shoulder harness and stood up, pushing him aside as I jumped down. I said, "Yes, it's been fired."

He turned to look at me and his eyes were as big as the judge's had been. He said, "I knew it. I knew it. I told Joe Cairo that was machine-gun fire. I hadn't heard it since France but it ain't something you forget. I said it was a Lewis machine gun. My God, did you kill 'em?"

I walked over and picked up the canvas that went over the engine and the cowling. I said, "No, I didn't kill anyone. I may have killed the judge's car, though. The damn fool didn't leave me no selection. He wouldn't stop."

Dennis stood and stared. "Lord love a frog! You actually *shot* at 'em? You *strafed* 'em? Land o' goshen!" He stood there staring at me. "A judge and a sheriff?"

I was cinching, the canvas tight. "They won't be sending any telegrams," I said, grimly. "And if you don't want them to die from sunstroke—at least, the sheriff—you had better send a truck out after them. They're walking this way. Right about now I'd reckon Judge Crater would give you all his money and a free day in court just to come play in your artesian geyser and cool off."

"Great bullfrogs and billy goats!" Dennis started off at a run toward the tents, yelling for help. "Joe! Charlie! Joel! Quick, damn it!"

But before I could get canvas over the cockpits and the machine gun, he was back, tearing the tarpaulin out of my hands. "That Lewis!" he yelled. I didn't reckon I'd ever seen Dennis so excited. He jumped past me and stood on the step on the lower wing and went to working on the wing nuts that mounted the machine gun to the airplane. "I can't believe you actual fired this gun at them. *Strafed* a judge!"

"What in hell are you doing, Dennis?"

"I got to hide this damn Lewis gun. I got to hide the evidence. You don't know nothing about a machine gun."

I said, "Dennis, they got holes in the judge's car. They saw me."

He came down from the plane, carrying the Lewis cradled in his arms like a baby. He said, tight-lipped, "They dreamed it. They had too much sun. They imagined it. They got overexcited."

"They imagined three strafing runs?"

He jerked his head. "Get that pan of ammunition and follow me. We got to get busy. I already sent out the truck, so we ain't got much time."

We took the gun and the ammunition and hid it in our tent in a big packing crate that some delicate equipment had come in. Dennis put the lid back on the crate and hammered home a few nails that were sticking up, with a pipe wrench that was easy to hand. Then he looked at me, "Do you realize what you've done?"

"I don't know what you think I've done. The airplane was in my care. I just took it out for a spin."

"And shot up a judge and a sheriff whilst you was at it." He said it bitterly but there was a thin edge of humor lurking around the border. "I just hope you didn't hit Lew Wallace."

"With what? Hit him with what?"

He stared at me. "Your position is that you didn't shoot at their car, that coupe of the judge's?"

"With what? I don't carry a gun and you don't see one on the airplane."

He stood there, thinking. After a moment he said, softly, "It just might work."

"You said yourself there was no telling what they might have imagined. Sunstroke, all that heat. Maybe drinking a little."

He tapped on top of the crate. "But everybody would have heard that Lewis. Sound carries in this dry air like angel wings."

"How many of these people have ever heard an aerial machine gun?"

"Not very damn many," he said. "Let's go wise up the crew before the judge gets back."

"What about the rubberneckers?"

"The hell with them."

"Might feed them a meal."

He paused. "You're either getting softer, or smarter. Good idea."

Once outside, we drew the gaze of the whole crowd. They had been looking in the direction they'd seen the truck leave, but now they turned around and stared at us, me especially. Dennis called for members of the crew to join him over at the rig and whispered to me to speak to the cook. I slid into the big cook tent and told the cook I wanted him to fix a lunch for the twenty or twenty-five townspeople hanging around outside. His mouth fell open and he looked atonished. He said, "Say what?"

I told him it was Dennis's orders. He looked grim. "Well, it won't be nothin' but beans and bread. We ain't set up to serve vittles to that kind o' crowd."

"Give them some coffee also," I said. Then I went outside and announced the news to the threadbare crowd. A ragged but surprised cheer went up. They immediately began crowding the entrance to the cook tent. I could hear the cook swearing and telling them to get back until he was ready to serve.

I got there just as Dennis was talking to the crew. He looked hard at the men we'd hired from the town and said, "Now, I want you all to remember you got good jobs here, and you wouldn't want to do nothing to put them in hock."

Charlie said, "What's this, Dennis, you fixing to cut wages?"

Dennis jerked his hand for him to be quiet, but it was Joe Cairo who said, "Lie low, Charlie. This ain't about wages."

Dennis gave him a grateful look. He said, "Now, some of ya'll may have heard that blowhard judge threatening to shut us down. I hear his auto broke down on the way to town. I sent one of our teamsters out to fetch him and the sheriff back in the truck. But I got to warn you, he is liable to come back here with some mighty wild stories."

Charlie laughed. He said, "About being shot at by a aeroplane?"

Again Joe Cairo did the work. All the smart hands knew they didn't want to be unemployed in the middle of nowhere. He said, "Wise up, Charlie, and shut your yap. Just tell us what the deal is, Dennis. I'll see that everybody understands." He glanced around. "Especially the new men."

Dennis raised both hands in the air. He said, "The deal is, we don't know nothin' from nothin'." He nodded his head. "That plane has never left the ground this entire day and you don't know nothing about any machine guns. I don't even know if there is such a thing."

I said, with my tongue in my cheek, "No, but there are Mexican bandits roaming around, this close to the border."

"Yeah," Dennis said. "Yeah, Mexican bandits. Any shooting got done, it was by Mexican bandits. And Willis Young ain't been out of this camp for a minute."

They all turned and looked at me and I gave them a little wave. I had no idea what they thought of me. I did no work, other than to fly the airplane, and I was on close terms with their boss. They may have thought I was one of the money backers.

Joel, standing there solid and silent, said, jerking his head toward the cook tent, "What about that bunch? They got eyes and ears."

Joe Cairo said, pointedly, "Joel, why don't you and Charlie go over there and explain it to them? You do the talking. Don't promise nothing, but make it clear that them as sees things our way might come into some luck."

Joel and Charlie left and the rest of the crew drifted off, and Dennis and I stood there in front of our tent waiting for the truck to return. The geyser was putting up a good stream and the mist was very cooling.

Dennis said, tensely, "I hope to hell we know what we're doing, shooting at a state magistrate and flouting the law. Hell, might be more than an oil well at stake here."

"I'm the one did the shooting, Dennis. Any trouble, it is mine."

He rubbed the stubble on his chin. "How you reckon the sheriff will jump?"

I shrugged. "I don't see where he has much choice except to say what he saw. He don't like the judge, but he's an honest man. He's got to do his duty."

We didn't have long to wait. Within five minutes after the meeting broke up, the truck came grinding into camp and stopped about thirty yards from us in the area where we kept all the moving stock. The vehicle had no more than come to a stop when out hopped Judge Crater, looking madder than a wet settin' hen. We were the first things his eyes lit on, and he came scurrying over to us in that peculiar half-walk, half-run I'd noticed before. His face, even beneath a deep tan, was bloodred, and I could see the cords standing out in his neck. He wanted blood, preferably mine.

He came straight toward us, the sheriff trailing behind, shaking a big, sausagelike forefinger. He kept on shaking it until he had it in Dennis's face. He said, his voice almost choking with rage, "Now I got you! Now I got the both of you sons a bitches! I'm gonna have the pair of you up yonder at the state prison in Huntsville, an' you ain't never gonna get out!"

Dennis looked annoyed. He slapped the judge's hand away. He said, "Don't be shaking that finger in my face. It's got a nail in it."

Dennis tickled me, taking it as cool as he was. It even put smiles on the faces of a few of the men who could hear what was being said. I said, "what is the matter with you, Crater? What is your problem?"

He swung on me and began shaking that finger again. He was so angry he could barely speak. "You!" he sputtered. "You—You—You—" He gulped air and finally got something out. "You made an attack on us from the skies in that aeroplane! An would have kilt us both if I hadn't been so nimble. I'll see that you get a ride on Old Sparky."

I yawned. Dennis wasn't the only one who could be cool. "Listen, Crater, you better not be threatening me with the electric chair. I think you been out in the sun too long. You say you got attacked from the skies? Well, that was the sun. That, and your criminal nature. You tried to extort money from Mr. Frank here and the consequences caught up with you. It's God's way. He struck you down. That was your attack from the skies."

He stretched himself up until he was nearly standing on his toes.

I didn't recall ever having seen another human being that mad. He said, his voice quavering, "Don't you talk *God* to me, you heathen. Don't you blaspheme to me, you scoundrel!"

I said, "Better watch that talk about God. They say He knows where every sparrow falls. And I would reckon a bunch have fallen at your feet."

He had caught sight of the plane over Dennis's shoulder. The rig did not quite hide it. He pointed, shaking his finger. "There! There it is! There is the engine of destruction. I see it plain as day, plain as when it was attacking us from the sky over our heads. Sheriff Wallace!"

Lew Wallace had been standing in the background, both thumbs hooked in his wide belt. He was standing kind of slouched down on his hips. He said, "Yeah? What do you want, Crater?"

The judge stepped back until he could point at both Dennis and me in a sweeping gesture. "Arrest these two men! And confiscate that aeroplane. It's evidence."

Lew Wallace scratched the back of his head. He said, "What do you want me to arrest them for, Judge?"

Crater Whirled on him with an astonished look on his face. He was truly surprised, as I reckoned he had a right to be. "For what?! For what? Why, hell, you was right there with me under that hail of death. What do you mean, 'what for'?" He reached over and tapped me in the chest. "This pup here tried to kill the both of us. And he ruined my automobile."

The sheriff looked at me and then at Dennis and just the hint of a grin tugged at the corner of his mouth. He said, "I don't remember nothing like that, Judge. Maybe you did get too much sun."

Dennis said, "Look how hot and bothered you are, Judge. Get out in that desert under all that sun, a man can go off his head."

Crater stared at us and then around at the sheriff. "Off my head? Let's just go take a look at my coupe, at the bullet holes in the hood. Maybe my auto went off its head and imagined them bullet holes."

Dennis said, "Maybe you got attacked by Mexican bandits. I heard there is a right smart bunch of them around here."

There were murmurs of assent from the crowd. The judge stared in astonishment. "Bandits, hell! You were trying to keep me from reaching a telegraph office or a telephone instrument. So this young fool came at us with his aeroplane."

I said, nonchalantly, "That airplane is good for sightseeing and giving people rides, but it don't shoot bullets." I jerked my head. "Go on, have a look for yourself."

Crater said, rising up on his boot toes again, "I ain't got to take a look at nothing. Sheriff, arrest these two men. Put them in that truck and we'll go back to town and you can jail them."

Lew Wallace stood there looking at the judge for about a half a minute. He spit on the ground and then he said, "You know, Crater, you are a state-appointed magistrate. I'm a sheriff elected by the people of Pecos County. Now, the way I see it, this here oil-well operation came into town and throwed some jobs and some money in the way of the people of this county. Done 'em some good. But ever since this oil bunch got here you have been seeing how much money you could get out of them. You—"

Crater said, in a loud voice, "You better watch your mouth there, Sheriff. I may just decide to cause you a little trouble."

Wallace's voice got silky. He said, "Let's see who can cause who the most trouble. I know you have been sticking Mr. Frank up with every kind of levy and tax and license you could think of. And I got no doubt you tried to extort two thousand dollars from him or else you'd shut him down. Well, it happens I don't want him shut down. I wish he felt different about this wonderful water well he's drilled here, but it belongs to him. And he says he's here to drill for oil, so that settles that. You ain't going to interfere with him no more and that includes your so-called attacks from the skies. If you'd've stopped like I was trying to get you to, I doubt that there would have been a bullet fired." He stopped and grinned big. "And that includes them Mexican bandits."

The judge was still sputtering. "I *order* you to arrest them."

The humor left Lew Wallace's face. He said, "Goddammit, Crater, you ain't the boss of me. The people of this county are. Your job is to magistrate the crimes I bring to your court's attention. Right now the only crime I see is you, and if you're not careful I'll throw your ass in jail. Then see how easy it will be to get through to the state capital. I been getting more and more tired of the way you treat the people of this county. They got a hard-enough life without you making it harder."

I thought Crater had swelled up as much as he could, but, at the sheriff's words, he managed to expand another inch or two and get even redder in the face. Civilian or military, I didn't believe I'd ever seen a more self-important or pompous individual. Now he pointed his finger at the sheriff and his voice was fairly shaking. He said, "Do you mean to tell me, *sir*, that you intend to side with this band of scofflaws in the face of orders from the duly constituted law of this country? Do you? By God, I'll have *you* arrested!"

The sheriff said, with disgust plain in his voice, "Oh, shut up, Crater. For some years I've watched you walk around here swelling an' blowing and generally making a nuisance out of yourself. I let it go because it was mostly small stuff that didn't make a hill of beans in this little out-of-the-way place that is fast disappearing. But now it looks like these people might have a chance, what with this new activity around here. So you are to leave them alone. And I mean that, Crater. You don't and you'll find yourself in a world of trouble. I got a record of some of your misdeeds and I got witnesses. You go ahead and telegraph the state capital and get some state militia down here. But I know the law, and I know I'm the chief law enforcement officer down here, and I'll decide who gets locked up. Savvy?"

The judge just stared at him, his jaw working but not a sound emerging. Dennis cleared his throat. He said, "Now that that little misunderstanding is cleared up, we can all get to work."

The sheriff said, "Dennis, I'm going to go get me a good drink from that spring that's spurting up and then cool off in the spray. After that, I ought to be getting back to town. You reckon you could figure me a way?"

Dennis said, "Sure. I can send the truck in. You'll have to ride with the judge, though. I don't want the son of a bitch around here any longer than need be."

I said, "Sheriff, I'll fly you in. How'd you like that, an airplane ride?"

He looked very uncertain. "Why . . . why, I'd never thought about getting that high up in the air. Looks kind of fearful to me."

Dennis said, "The lieutenant is about the best aviator around. You couldn't be safer in your own bed."

Lew Wallace glanced over at my plane. He said, "Let me get me that water and think on it. This is all brand-new to me."

The judge said, loudly, "Damn if I'd go up in an aeroplane with the young bandit. Scoundrel. Scalawag."

I turned on him with some heat. "Listen, you fat frog, I resent you saying I was shooting at you. If I'd been shooting at you, you'd be in about six pieces right now. Don't you ever go about publishing the idea that I ever fired at you. You're a damn liar."

Dennis said, "Besides, I want the judge riding in the truck." He grinned big in his broad face. "That is going to be the most expensive truck ride he ever took. I expect to get back every cent he cheated me out of."

It was a good deal later and all the parades and circuses and rodeos were over. I had flown the sheriff into town although he'd been scared stiff. Once on the ground he'd expressed a desire for another such experience but I doubted he meant it. As we'd flown over the judge's auto, he'd looked down and then turned around and gave me a long look followed by a wink. I felt very friendly toward him. He had turned out to be an unexpected and valuable ally.

Dennis had sent the judge in via the truck. In spite of his threats Dennis hadn't charged the judge for the ride, though he'd said, grumbling, "I damn sure ought to have."

Now it was after supper and good and dark and we were sitting in the tent having a last drink of whiskey before retiring for the night. I said, "Dennis, were you surprised when Lew Wallace took the stand he did?—in opposition to the judge."

Dennis shook his head. "Naw, I knowed all the way that Lew was a good man."

I laughed. "Oh, bullshit. You didn't know any such of a thing. You especially didn't know that Lew didn't have to take orders from Crater."

"Well, it worked out, didn't it? Baron von Richtoff. Or whatever his name was."

"Richthofen. The question is, what do you think is going to happen now? I ain't so sure this is all over with. Crater don't strike me as a man with a bad memory. I think about the time he gets the upper hand, all of this humiliation is going to come back to him. You think he can really get the state militia out here?"

Dennis shrugged. "Do I bear some resemblence to a lawyer or a court official? I don't know. All I know to do is keep drilling this well and let the rest of the bullshit straighten itself out. I ain't a complicated man, Willis. I'm having enough trouble with this well without worrying about anything else."

"So, what do you think we ought to do about matters?"

He drained his glass and set it down with a clump on the little table and said, "I don't know about you, but I'm going to turn in. I've had about all the lawyering I can take for one day. I'm going to get a night's sleep and eat breakfast like I was a normal man and then get on about my work."

I grimaced. "You're lucky to have work to get matters off your mind, keep you occupied."

He was sitting on the side of the bed in his underwear. He said, "Huh! Seems to me I heard something about you going back to practicing your old trade. Must have been pretty good shooting in that desert heat with the plane jumping all over hell. Sheriff told me on the quiet that you just stitched a line right across that hood. Said you never come close to hitting nobody."

I said, with a little heat, "I fired warning bursts across the road in front of him. If the judge had had any sense he would have stopped and I wouldn't have had to have shot his damned car."

Dennis yawned. "Well, however it come out, you done some damn good work today. I don't know what would have happened if the judge had got to town, the mood he was in. I think you made things work out for the best and I'm much obliged. But now I got to sleep."

Nothing happened for the next several days. Dennis drilled and fought and cursed the strong artesian spring without making much headway. In three days he gained half a stand of pine. And then they discovered that some of the downhole pipe was starting to bend. If it bent, it would break, and if it broke, it would come flying out of the hole. Dennis's answer was to sink more casing pipe down around the drill stem to strengthen the whole works. He was doing everything he could do but it was clear he was worried. At the present rate, he was going to tear up the rig before he beat the force of the spring.

The sheriff came out for a visit. He said wasn't much going on in town. For some reason the luster had worn off our natural spring and our rubbernecker population had all but disappeared. The sheriff said it was because the wives had realized the husbands wern't going to get jobs and they preferred them loafing closer to home.

But some use was being made of the springwater. A few enterprising individuals had taken several barrels back to town and were said to be selling it at a nickel a glass. The sheriff said they were doing a right brisk trade.

Dennis said, "I'm glad somebody is getting some good out of that confounded spring. It's going to ruin me."

The sheriff had brought the mail out. It didn't amount to much, mostly bills, but there was a telegram addressed to Dennis in among the pile. I'd been hoping for word from Genevieve but it was not to be. I had written a letter since my last one, inquiring as to the reason for her silence, but it, too, apparently was going to go unanswered. I handed the telegram to Dennis and he took it as if I were offering him a live snake. He said, "Oh, Lawdy, what is this? I never got a telegram in my life that was good news. The only reason the telegraph company stays in business is to send out bad news." He turned it over and over in his hand and then looked at me. "I'll bet you a ham sandwich," he said, "that this is from some government official threatening to throw us under the jail or take the rig if we don't do what that goddamn judge says."

The sheriff said, "Hell, Dennis, open it. Knowing is not worse than imagining. Besides, I don't care who they send down here. I can hold them off long enough for you to get to Mexico."

Dennis got a kind of sick grin on his face, but he finally unfolded the brown envelope and took out the message. It didn't take him but a moment to read it and then his face went chalk-white. He said, "It's worse than I thought."

He passed the message over to me and I understood his shock. It was from Teddy Atlas and it said simply, ARRIVING AFTERNOON TRAIN IN PECOS ON 18TH THIS MONTH STOP ARRANGE TRANSPORTATION TO WELL SITE.

Dennis said, "Oh my God!" He put his hands to his face and went to rocking back and forth like a women comforting a child. "Oh, for crying out loud! Why now? Why now?"

The sheriff was mystified. "What's all this about? What's wrong?"

I said, briefly, "The backer is coming. The man who put up the money."

"What's wrong with that?"

"He ain't going to be real pleased at our progress. In fact, he's gonna be downright upset about us being hung up by an artesian spring that has got us stopped and is about to tear up some equipment. He's gonna want to know why we ain't drilling for oil."

Dennis took his hands down from his face long enough to inquire when the eighteenth was. I hated to give him the news. "Two days from now. About this time of day in forty-eight hours."

"Oh hell!" Dennis said. "I can't get a break. Damn, damn, damn!" He disappeared through the flaps of our tent and I knew what he was after. I wanted to get to him before he got too much of it. Fortunately, the sheriff was finished with his visit. I thanked him for the mail and watched him drive off in his rusty old Model T pickup. Then I turned for the tent. Sure enough, Dennis had the bottle in hand and was commencing to do some serious drinking.

I sat down on my cot. "Oh hell, Dennis, put that bottle down and quit acting like the floodwaters are rising. So Atlas comes out here and finds you fighting an artesian spring. So what? Can't be the first time it happened."

He gave me a sour look. "No, but it damn sure is the first time any logheaded driller wasted so damn much time and equipment and supplies on one." He raised his chin. "And I about halfway blame you for that. 'Way you were going around whining about these poor people and how bad off they were. What this water meant to them. Damn! I believe I'd've pulled out of that hole a week ago if it hadn't been for your mollycoddle talk."

"Atlas isn't going to know when you hit that spring. Tip the word to the boys to keep their mouths shut. He won't have to know. You can start moving the rig tomorrow."

He stared at me like I was a dunce. He pointed in the general direction of west, toward the big, wide basin. He said, "Have you taken a look at where that water has been running off to the low place in the prairie? Maybe you ain't noticed that pool down at the bottom of it. If we had the fish, we could stock it and make a good living as fishmongers. Not notice! Ha ha." He circled his hand over his head. "This whole damn area is so saturated your boots stay muddy. How am I supposed to explain that?"

"Then tell him the truth. Tell him you thought it would be easier to drill through the spring than move the rig."

He fell back on his cot, shaking his head. "Hell, Willis, you don't know nothing."

"Well, what's he going to know?"

He got himself up on one elbow and stared at me. "He's going to know I fouled up. He's going to know I've spent all this time and I ain't down but three hundred feet. He's *for sure* going to know I've spent a hell of a lot of money. He's going to know I've paid out bribes. He's going to know I had a judge's auto machine-gunned. He's going to know I ain't no closer to oil than I was when we were talking about it back in Galveston."

"So what? So what if he finds out the absolute worst? What's he going to do? You got a contract. He's got to live up to that. Maybe he won't let you keep on drilling but I know for a fact you got the money to drill two wells if you don't produce nothing but sand."

He sat all the way up and stared at the floor. "Willis, I wish I was in your position. Listen, let me explain it to you so you'll understand. In the oil business a man ain't got but one thing he can pledge against money, and that's his reputation. His *reputation*, Willis." He hit himself in the chest with the flat of his hand. "*My* reputation. It's all I've got. And once Atlas gets here and sees the mess I've made, it will be gone. Teddy Atlas knows enough folks in the oil business to start the ball rolling. From there it is downhill. In a month my name will be mud. I'll be known as the guy who wasted two weeks trying to drill through solid rock and an artesian spring. All the contracts in the world can't cover that up, because it is the truth."

We were quiet for a moment. Dennis kept staring at the floor while I tried to think of something to say to make him feel better. I was handicapped by my ignorance of the oil-drilling business.

I said, "But what could he expect, Dennis? This was virgin territory, unproven. A long shot. Hell, the man makes his living off of long shots. Any man that deals in the fight game has got to have seen some bad days."

Dennis looked up. "Willis, that ain't the point. I should have known to have pulled out soon as I hit that spring. I'm the one wasted all the time and money—not the water, not the rock."

"You just tell him we had some bad luck. It can happen to anyone."

Dennis laughed without humor. "Yeah, Willis, that's easy for you to say. You can get in the airplane and fly away."

Of course, I couldn't, and he knew it. The airplane belonged to Teddy Atlas just like the say about the drilling. I was caught on Atlas's hook just as much as Dennis was. I said, "Oh, the hell with it." I got the bottle of whiskey and poured myself a tumblerful. I said, "I think I told you a couple of months ago, or maybe it was a couple of years, that I didn't give a damn about anything. Well—" I threw the whiskey down my throat and said, "Aaaahhh," as it burned its way down. Then I belched. "I told you I didn't give a damn about anything. Well, I spoke too soon. I do care about something. I don't exactly have a name

for it yet, but I feel the first faint stirrings within my lifeless breast of
the harbingers of involved compassion."

Dennis gave me an odd look. He said, "You know, it kind of gives
me the chilly damps when you talk like that. I know I don't understand
what you're saying and I'm hoping you don't, either."

I reached for the whiskey bottle. "We got a day and a half left
before we have to face Mr. Atlas. Let's get drunk and say the hell
with it."

Dennis reached out and took the bottle out of my hand. "Ain't
nobody going to get drunk. I need you sober. You're smarter than
anybody around here and if anybody is going to think of anything, it
will be you. And I've got to get that rig going and keep it going. I'll be
drilling from now until you land with Mr. Atlas in the passenger's
cockpit."

I surrendered willingly. I really hadn't wanted to get drunk. I was
only offering because I thought it would console Dennis, but he'd taken
the responsible view. If I didn't already admire him, I would have
admired him for that. But I said, "Did you get that Lewis remounted
on the airplane? I'd like to have it in place when I go into town to get
Atlas."

He looked up at me, startled. Then he saw that I was joshing him
and gave me a disgusted wave of the hand. "Very funny, very funny.
Were you going to have another try at the judge, or maybe shoot up
the train in hopes of getting Atlas?"

I shrugged. "You remember our orders in France. If your primary
target is unavailable you go for the first target of opportunity."

CHAPTER

THE WESTBOUND train arrived in Pecos around four in the afternoon. There was just the one passenger train that stopped in either direction. There were a couple more express trains between San Antonio and El Paso but they just whizzed right on through the Pecos depot as if it wasn't there. Which it really wasn't, from a commerce standpoint. There were barely enough, freight and passengers for the two trains that did stop. The town stayed in a perpetual state of fright that the railroad company was going to cut them out of the route and just proceed as if they really weren't there. If there was ever a town that needed a shot in the arm, it was the hamlet of Pecos.

But I wasn't concerned about that on the day Teddy Atlas was to arrive. My instructions, as I prepared to leave, were frantic and contradictory and damn near physically impossible. Dennis vacillated between having me getting us lost in the desert, to telling Atlas the whole story so he wouldn't be badly surprised when he got to the drilling spot. I finally stopped his fulminating by suggesting I unfasten Atlas's shoulder harness and then turn the airplane upside down at altitude.

"Other than it being murder, it sounds like the solution to your problems, Dennis."

He'd grimaced. "Aw, go on with you. You better get in there. Don't be late. Tell him whatever you feel like. Hell, you got a stake in this."

"No I don't, Dennis. Not the same one as you."

He sighed. "Just hurry up and go get him. Quicker he sees the mess I've made, the quicker he'll get over it."

I made an early start. I wanted to get in well before train time, even in spite of the possibility of trouble with Judge Crater, though I really doubted such would happen. Without the sheriff to back him up he was just a mean old man.

But I wanted to get in early just in case we were wrong about the train arrival time. I didn't figure it would do Mr. Atlas's temper any good if he he were left twiddling his thumbs in the waiting room of the depot. Also I wanted to get in early enough to have a leisurely meal at the Mexicans' and drink three or four cold beers. It seemed like a year since I'd had a cold beer. We hadn't been on site in the desert all that long by the calendar, but the conditions kind of made time slow down. And I wanted to have a visit with Lew Wallace and see what Crater had been up to as regarded the state attorney's office. Crater didn't strike me as a man who let a grudge go unpaid.

Then there was the mail. I had a letter to Genevieve to mail and I wanted to get that off. She still hadn't written in answer to any of my previous letters, just that one initial offering from her, like the sort of note that got passed around in polite society between folks who visited each other. But out of loftiness I had kept her apprised of our trials and tribulations, even trying to explain the engineering and technological problems as best I could. I had nothing from her but she had an accurate history of our attempt to drill an oil well in Pecos County. The only item of any interest that I had left out had been my sightings of the golden-haired girl. I had not mentioned her not out of any regard for Genevieve's feelings, as much as the certainty on my part that I had been touched by the sun a few times too many.

I wasn't worried about the plane or about the landing fee. If the judge decided to lay claim, I intended to put the matter into Mr. Atlas's hands and let him deal with it.

I landed a little after noon and taxied up to the old warehouse and pushed the plane inside. We still had a lease on the building so I pulled the big door shut and locked it with the padlock.

Lew Wallace's office was empty and I figured I'd catch him later. Most likely he was home for lunch. I walked on up to the Mexican place, drawing my fair share of stares as I went along, and turned into the cool interior and sat down at a table. The proprietor greeted me and I ordered a steak with some fresh *ensalada* and a beer. He brought me the beer and then left to see about my order. I was just taking a drag on the mug of cold beer when an unpleasant voice disturbed my peace and quiet. The interior of the cafe was a little on the dim side, so I had trouble recognizing the judge as he stood framed in the doorway with the sunshine behind him. He leveled that god-awful finger at me and said, "I heared the sound of your aeroplane machine and I figured I'd find you here. Dark as you are and the way you seem to prefer this place, might be you got a little greaser blood in you."

I sighed. I said, "Crater, I ain't hit an old man all day, but I'm willing to make an exception in your case."

All of a sudden he pulled out that big Colt revolver I had seen him carrying. He didn't point it at me but I was damn well aware of it. The little cafe got very quiet. No one moved. Crater said, "Why don't you come on and try, sonny boy? Scairt? Ain't as much fun when you be on the other end of the gun, is it? Me and you know the truth of what you done to me with your aeroplane, and if that lily-livered sheriff would back me up I'd have you hung."

I put my hands in my lap, being very still. I didn't know what the old fool was capable of, but I had no intention of sitting there and being shot. I got the weight on the balls of my feet, ready to spring to either side. I said, quietly, "Crater, don't point that revolver at me. I'm not armed and I'm not wanted for anything. You shoot me, even shoot *at* me, and it will be you going to Huntsville."

He didn't immediately put the pistol back in its holster, but he did let it waver away from my general direction. He said, still in that mean, gravelly voice, "You got trouble, boy. You got plenty of trouble. You think you are riding high on the hog because of what you think you got away with. Well, you ain't got away with nothin'. I'll be coming for you soon enough."

Then he did put the pistol away, did an about-face, and marched away. I didn't realize how tense I'd been holding myself until he was gone, and I let out a breath and collapsed into myself. As far as I was concerned, John Crater was not a threat to be taken lightly. I had kept my voice calm and quiet when I'd told him to point his revolver elsewhere, but inside, I was shaking I was so scared. For all I knew, the old bastard was just enough of a tyrant to shoot me and claim it was a state execution. He'd been the big frog in a little mud puddle for way too long.

The effect was to spoil the pleasant meal I looked forward to. Oh, I ate the steak and the fresh garden vegetables and drank several beers, but the bloom was off the rose. The proprietor, a polite little man, must have felt it also. When I paid he said, "I am very sorry, *señor.* I wish thees bad thing does not happen here."

I said, "Mr. Morales, if I'd known it was, I'd've never come in. Sorry for the trouble."

I walked over to the main street, where the post office was. It was located in the back of the general mercantile so you could buy a stamp when you bought a shirt, or vice versa.

I went up to the counter and called for all the mail for our outfit. They had a list of our names and bundled it together. I got it and then went and sat down in a chair by the front window to go through and sort it. Of course, I was hoping for a letter from Genevieve, but I soon saw that I was going to be disappointed. It made me get half a mind to go back up to the counter and get the letter back that I'd written her, but then I decided the hell with it.

And then I got a big surprise. I had a letter from my aunt Laura, my mother's sister, who was married to Warner Grayson, the horse breeder and trainer. They had a place up in east Texas where Uncle Warner raised and trained a mixed bag of quarter horses and thoroughbred racing stock. I had heard it said many a time that he was the best in the Southwest at his trade. I didn't know because I didn't know horses that well. But I did know that my daddy, before they were related by marriage, had bought every one of his getaway horses from Uncle Warner. Of course, that was back in his outlaw days. It was only after the governor pardoned him that he met my mother through Warner and his wife Laura.

I tore open the letter with great eagerness. It was an unexpected bonus. Some two weeks past, more out of boredom than anything else, I'd written them, telling of my latest endeavor and more or less bringing them up-to-date. We had never stayed in close contact, but, outside of my parents, they were the only blood kin I had and I was fond of them. Aunt Laura was a good deal like my mother except she was somewhat looser and would take a drink from time to time and didn't, I believed, know the Bible by heart. Uncle Warner was a man of dry wit and good advice. According to stories I had heard from my father before the differences had pushed us apart, Warner Grayson was not a man to be taken lightly, either with guns or fists.

But there was a letter from them, or rather from Aunt Laura, as Uncle Warner wasn't much of a hand for correspondence. The letter was—by necessity, because we hadn't seen each other in some time—a little vague and wandering. But I read about Uncle Warner's latest trades and how my aunt was getting on, and then I was shocked to read that my parents had come back from Mexico and were at Del Rio, picking up their old life. My mother had telephoned and my aunt had phoned her back and they had corresponded and were nearly caught up. My Aunt ended the letter with a stern admonition for me to write my parents, especially my father, and to let family be family again. She wrote,

> *The differences between you and your father were silly in the first place. You are both too headstrong for your own good. Now, make it up with him and get home and get out of that awful country you are in and that awful business. You will ruin your clothes if you get that petroleum oil on them.*

I put the letter down and stared out the dusty window of the store, looking a long distance away. I knew I wasn't ready to write my father the kind of letter my aunt had in mind. As far as I was concerned he was the one in the wrong, and I knew he wasn't going to take the first step, just as I wasn't.

I had enough troubles without thinking about my father and his attitude toward a son he didn't approve of. I had no intention of walking around with a mind full of such matters. A lot of water had passed under the bridge between me and the ex–bank robber for us to just take up standard relations on the advice of an aunt—and a sort of eccentric aunt, at that. I looked up at the clock. It wasn't even three o'clock yet. For lack of something better to do, I got some paper and an envelope and a pencil from the postmistress, and sat down and composed a quick reply to my aunt's letter. I expressed the thought that I was very glad my mother was back in the home she liked and hoped she hadn't suffered too much on their long stay in Mexico. I deliberately avoided the subject of my father but I did assure her I was not long for the far west Texas country. I wrote,

> Through a series of unfortunate accidents I fear we are going to lose the drilling contract. Our backer is due at any time and when he sees how stymied we are by that artesian well I reckon he will withdraw his support and money. Apparently we are a lot better at drilling for water than oil, so you don't have to worry about me ruining my clothes.

I kept it light and appreciative for the information she'd conveyed and closed with the hope that I'd be seeing them sometime in the near future. The letter had buoyed me up. It had been the taste and remembrance of another time and place when things were pleasant and fun and badlands like the Pecos country didn't exist. I stepped out of the store with a gladdened heart and made my way down to the sheriff's office. He was sitting with his boots up on his desk and his hat pushed back on his head. He gave me a greeting and bade me take a chair. I sat down and he said, "Hear you been stirring up our judge again."

It made me a little warm to hear it put like that. I said, "Listen, that son of a bitch drew a gun on me. Not only that, but he the same as said he was going to find some kind of way to railroad me into prison. And all this time I'm sitting there trying to drink a beer."

The sheriff brought his feet to the floor with a clump. He said, "Yeah, he kind of give me the picture. Of course, he didn't tell it exactly like you did. But I wouldn't worry overmuch about that pistol of his. He couldn't hit a cow if he was riding it."

I was still angered. "Next time I may feed it to him."

He scratched his jaw. "Willis, that man is still an officer of the court and he could cause you trouble. He may be a sorry son of a bitch, but I'd try to stay out of his way, or at least try not to get crosswise with him." He put one boot back up on his desk. "Anyway, what brings you to town, besides the beer down at the Mex place?"

I told him, as briefly and as safely as I could, making it sound like a routine visit from our backer, with everything all hunky-dory and apple-pie smooth. I didn't mention Dennis and I were quaking in our boots and fearful of our continued presence in the oil-drilling business.

The sheriff got out his watch and looked at it. He said, "Well, you ain't got long to wait. Train ought to be in the depot in the next fifteen minutes, be blowing for the river crossing in less than ten." He heaved himself to his feet. "I reckon I'll just go along with you. Likely the judge will be there and I'll kind of keep him herded to one side. I don't think it would be good if your important visitor got mixed up in one of Crater's little pranks."

I was grateful and I said so. We set out to walk to the depot, a distance of a little less than a hundred yards. Before we were halfway there I could hear the far-off moan of the steam whistle as the train announced its coming.

The sheriff said, "Going to be a little early, maybe. Depends on who the engineer is."

We got to the depot and, sure enough, I saw Crater hurrying up the street in our direction. The sheriff saw him also. He touched the brim of his hat to me and said, "I reckon I'll go stop a train wreck before it happens. The judge has got that make-trouble gleam in his eye. If he figures out you are meeting someone important to your outfit, he'll turn cartwheels."

I said, "I'm much obliged, Lew. It might be awkward if he came up at the wrong time waving that revolver around and threatening to arrest me. Might give our visitor the wrong idea."

I thanked him as he walked off and then looked up the track for the train. It seemed like forever that I had seen Teddy Atlas in his perfectly tailored clothes with his perfectly muscled prizefighters. I didn't plan to say much to him. My job was to transport him to the drilling site. After that it was up to Dennis to do the talking.

But as I looked up the track, seeing the thin plume of smoke in the distance, I couldn't help thinking of my mother and father being back in Texas. It sort of gave me a pang in the chest and a tug at my heartstrings. There had been some plenty good times when I was growing up. The stand-off had come only at the very last. My father had wanted me to stay at the university and I hadn't. And when you disagree with Wilson Young, be prepared to disagree all the way. There is no back-up in him.

Actually, as the crow flew, or a JN-6H, Del Rio was only about two hundred and fifty miles. If our business got straightened out with Atlas, I could take a couple of days and fly up there. I badly wanted to see my mother and assure her I was all in one piece and hadn't gone to the devil. And I wanted to see my father. He could have mellowed, though I doubted it. Anyway, I suddenly realized how much I missed the both of them.

But then the train was coming in, thundering and blowing steam and making the ground shake. When it stopped, Teddy Atlas came down the steps, looking natty and cool in a white lawn suit with an open-collared blue shirt. Behind him came a tall, muscled specimen carrying four bags, one under each arm and one in each hand. He had the face of a man who had spent some time in the prize ring and I had no doubt he was one of Mr. Atlas's former fighters, now converted to valise attendant. Atlas recognized me with a casual wave of his hand. "Oh, you're the pilot. Good."

I said, since it might become important to remember later, "And the landowner. Or the lease holder, as Mr. Frank likes to say."

The muscled chap got off the train and stood at the ready, obviously awaiting orders. Mr. Atlas included him with another wave of his hand. "Oh, this is Leon. He watches out for me."

Leon didn't nod so I didn't neither. He did not look to me to be a man of pleasant temper. I resolved to keep our relations on a formal basis.

"You have an automobile?"

I shook my head. "That's something that is in mighty short supply in this town." I pointed down the back street that ran in front of the Mexican cafe and ended at our hangar/warehouse. "But the airplane is right at the end of that street. About a hundred and fifty yards. Maybe a little more."

Mr. Atlas grimaced. "But it's so dusty."

I said, "You'll pretty well have to make up your mind that you are about a mile outside of civilization. But once in the airplane I can get you to the well fairly comfortably."

"Is it always this hot?"

I cleared my throat. It was about like discussing getting shot. If you never had been, you couldn't understand those that had. I just said, "Yeah. When we get a north breeze."

We started walking, with Leon carrying the four suitcases. Two of them were of a pretty good size and two were more like valises. I doubted if half of them were for Leon since he was dressed in denim workpants and a khaki shirt. Which made me wonder how long Mr. Atlas had come to stay. Or maybe he just changed clothes a lot. I thought of offering to help Leon carry the bags, but since Mr. Atlas hadn't seen fit to do so, I figured it was an internal matter and kept my mouth shut.

As we walked, Teddy Atlas commented on Pecos and none of it was favorable. I hated the damn place myself, but it galled me to have this dandy making fun of the efforts of people who mostly lived and died in misery. But I kept my mouth shut as Dennis had instructed me.

And then the corner of the warehouse came in sight and my heart sank. There, wearing his black suit and looking grim, stood Judge John Crater. Apparently Teddy Atlas was going to hear about the water well from our ill-tempered magistrate.

But then, I couldn't believe that. Of the townspeople, only Lew Wallace had known who was due to arrive and I couldn't believe that Lew would betray us by telling Crater. I was just going to see what it was all about. Knowing the judge, it wasn't going to be good.

He stood there, as we neared, with his arms crossed on his chest. When we were close enough, he flung out his hand, pointing at me, "You, there! You, sir! I have knocked the illegal lock off your structure here and your aeroplane is con-fis-cated! And it will cost you a pretty penny to get it out of lockup. I warned you about payin' your landing taxes."

Mr. Atlas looked at him curiously and then at me. "Who the hell is this?"

I shrugged. "He's the local justice of the peace. He's been trying to charge us a fee for the landing and taking off of the airplane. He's nuts."

"More of your lip!" The judge drew himself up. "All that will accomplish will be to make me more intractable."

"As far as I'm concerned you are about as intractable as folks get. Now get out of the way, we've got business."

But Crater flung out his arms and barred my way. "No sir!" he said. "I've struck off your lock and put on one of my own device. And unless you pay what you owe, this aeroplane is confiscated."

Atlas was looking around. He said, "Are you kidding? You charge a landing fee for this?" He pointed out toward the desert. "Hell, that's a pasture and a damn poor one at that. You haven't got a landing strip to charge for."

Crater said, grimly, "Nevertheless. And there are a few other infractions that have to be settled. Until then that plane doesn't move."

I was about to heat up when Atlas reached in the pocket of his lawn-suit trousers and pulled out a healthy roll of money. He peeled off a fifty and held it out to Crater. "Will that do it?"

Crater stared greedily at the bill. I was just about to tell Atlas not to give him any money, when Crater reached out a bony hand and snatched it away. He said, "Well, all right, but this don't cover some of them other infractions." He gave me a hard look when he said "infractions," drawing it out about four syllables.

Atlas said, "Look, I don't know your business with young Mr. Willis, or whatever it is. But it's got nothing to do with me and I'd like to be on my way."

Crater gave a grunt and turned and inserted a key in the new padlock he'd put on the big door. I could see the one that had been there before lying on the ground. It looked like it had been pried off with a crowbar.

The judge left, still grumbling, and I pushed the door back. Leon helped me to roll the plane out at Mr. Atlas's order. As we pushed, I could see the muscles moving and working under Leon's shirt. He did not appear to be a man you wanted to tangle with, unless you were drunk or bigger than him.

I got the plane positioned but then I looked doubtful. I said, "I'm not worrying about the weight, but I don't know how you and Leon are going to fit in that front cockpit."

"I expected he would ride in the cockpit with you."

I shook my head with vigor. "No, sir. I don't want anything interfering with my use of the controls, and there is too much of Leon to get in the way."

Atlas sighed. He sounded like a man who is forced to endure one hardship after another. He said, shrugging, "If it has to be, it has to be. Please let it be a short time to the oil camp."

I wanted to say that all the oil we had was in barrels and was used to grease the machinery, but I kept my peace. I said, "It's a short flight there. Once airborne I should have you on the ground in fifteen minutes at the outside."

"Oh, well, I suppose I can stand even that for fifteen minutes. Leon, you get in first and get as much of yourself on the floor and out of the way as you can." He turned to me. "But we will have to put my luggage in with you."

"Some of it," I said. "What I can take."

But with this and that settled we finally got away. I took us up to fifteen hundred feet so Atlas could get a good look at the country and also to be in some cooler air. It was clear that Leon was no lover of aviation. He was skootched down in one corner of the cockpit, with his head down and his eyes shut. I'd seen him take one terrified look over the side as we'd climbed for altitude. After that he wanted no part of the scenic view.

Halfway there Atlas turned in his seat and shouted back to me that I should tell him what I was in trouble with the local magistrate for.

I just gave him a nod.

He yelled, "It's not good politics to get in bad with the local authorities. They can cause you trouble. Probably I can straighten it all out with another one of those ladies I just gave him."

I wanted to laugh but I didn't. He thought Crater was some petty crook that could be satisfied with a hundred dollars. Well, he would live and learn.

I waggled my wings as I lined up on my own personal little strip. I thought Dennis would want to be there to meet us. I figured he'd want to start making a good impression as soon as he could.

I taxied to my usual place, leaned the mixture until the engine quit, and then switched off the ignition. As best I could, I climbed out of the cockpit without disturbing the suitcases that had been my own personal passengers. I was going to leave their transfer to Leon.

Dennis was there, waiting. I walked over to him while Atlas and Leon were untangling themselves from the forward cockpit. Dennis had a worried look on his face. "What'd he say? What kind of mood is he in? Did he say anything about where I spudded in, placed the well? Who's that with him? Another moneyman? Did he talk to anyone in town?"

I had no intention of answering any of the steady stream of questions, but I didn't have to. Teddy Atlas came strolling casually up and shook hands with Dennis.

Dennis said, "Well, I hope you had a good trip. I mean on the train."

Atlas was looking toward the rig. He said, "A little slow. Well, I see you are up and running." He half turned. "This is Leon. I see you are living in tents. Will you tell him which one is mine? He can sleep in with your crew, however you have them arranged."

Dennis got busy snapping out orders and rushing around in a nervous attempt to make Atlas so welcome and comfortable that he wouldn't notice the well was pumping springwater. Dennis had not considered that Mr. Atlas was going to require a tent to himself so, in order to find the room, he was forced to turn Joe Cairo and Joel in with the common hands. They vacated reluctantly. I don't know what he was promising them, for I stayed at the airplane with Atlas and Leon. I was very apprehensive. I couldn't see a good outcome to the situation. Once Atlas was apprised of how his money was being used, he was not going to be happy. And Atlas did not strike me as a man content to be unhappy alone.

The official confrontation was not long in coming. Since they weren't drilling, the spout of water was rising high in the derrick and drifting over to where our camp was located. Mr. Atlas and Leon had gone off to get the moneyman settled, and me and Dennis were standing around. Atlas had not asked why we wern't drilling with light still up in the western sky, and we hadn't offered any explanation. I looked at Dennis. "I wish you would quit acting so damn nervous. Ain't nothing happened that is your fault."

He pulled at his collar. "I'm in charge, Willis."

He made me angry. "Well, quit sniveling. Damn it, you're jumping around here like some schoolboy caught with his hand in the cookie jar. Stand up to the son of a bitch. You are embarrassing yourself, and me in the bargain as your friend."

He gave me a shocked look. "You ought not to say things like that. Hell!"

"Then get some backbone."

• • •

Mr. Atlas put his hand up into the drifting mist of spray and then touched it to his lips as if he were confirming it wasn't wine or milk or some other liquid. He did it delicately, with a puzzled look on his face. We were all standing between our tents and the well. Dennis and Teddy Atlas were facing each other. I was standing by Dennis's side and Leon, likewise, was near Teddy Atlas. Our backer wrinkled his brow and put his hand to his mouth again. He said, sounding a little disbelieving, "Frank, this isn't salt water. What the hell have you gotten into here?"

I could almost hear Dennis swallow. He said, "Well, Mr. Atlas, the thing is, we got into a situation we couldn't control right off. But I'm gaining on it and expect to have the problem in hand right soon."

Teddy Atlas turned and looked off toward the west, at the big basin. Several sizable pools of water had managed to collect, even in the thirsty sand. He said, "Frank, unless there has been one hell of a rainfall, it would appear, judging from all that water, that you've had this little 'problem,' as you call it, for some time."

Dennis cleared his throat. "Well, Mr. Atlas, it was this way. See, we got into this little layer of water and it appears to be located in some base rock and that has made the drilling go a little slower than I'd expected. But, like I say, I think we got a leg up on it."

I didn't know how Teddy Atlas could look shaved and showered and cleaned and pressed out in the middle of a hot, dry desert, but he looked as cool as if he'd just stepped out of the barber's chair. But there was nothing cool about the frown on his face. He said, "Exactly how many feet have you made, Frank? You've been at this well over a month. How deep is your hole? What are you doing hitting water of any kind if you've been drilling steady?"

Dennis made a little motion with his hand. He and I were both conscious of the crew and a small contingent of rubberneckers standing around listening to what was being said. Dennis said, "Look here, Mr. Atlas, why don't we step over into my tent where I got my office? I got my daily logs there and I can answer all your questions."

Atlas's voice had gone flat. He said, "You don't need your logs to know how deep you are. Now, do you know at what depth you have drilled to? It's a simple question for a drilling contractor. You are a drilling contractor, are you not, Mr. Frank? That was what you represented yourself to me as."

I could see Dennis beginning to wilt under Atlas's brittle tone. I stepped in, trying to give Dennis a little time, "The fact is, Mr. Atlas, we—"

He froze me with a look. "When I want to know something about flying, I'll ask you. Right now we are talking about the oil business. But more important, we are talking about where my money has gone."

I said, with a little steel in my voice, "But you don't want to play it in front of the cheap seats, do you?" Atlas glanced at me and I jerked my head toward the crowd the conversation had drawn.

Dennis said, in a kind of pleading voice that I hated to bear, "Let's go in my office, Mr. Atlas. I got some drilling samples showing what we been having to go through and you can see our day-to-day progress writ down in black-and-white."

There had been some more persuading, but Teddy Atlas at last allowed himself to be led off by Dennis to our tent, which was out of the sight of the crowd. It seemed to me that Atlas was acting awfully unbusinesslike. He seemed less interested in gaining a true picture of the progress of the well than he was in embarrassing Dennis. From the moment he had arrived, he hadn't seemed at all interested in doing more than finding fault with Dennis. I didn't know, but maybe there was some clause in their contract that Atlas was playing to.

I stayed where I was. I didn't like seeing Dennis in the position he was being put in. I knew he already felt guilty and I had a feeling that Atlas wasn't going to do anything to help his feelings.

Leon went along but he was told to stay outside. He was some piece of meat. I figured he was three or four inches over six feet and well over two hundred pounds. And none of it was fat. It was his balding head that gave away the reason he wasn't still fighting in the ring. I figured him to be close enough to forty to be on speaking terms, but that didn't make him look any less formidable. To take him on,

I'd want a mule on my side and would hope he didn't knock the mule out before the mule could get in a few kicks.

I could just faintly hear Dennis and Atlas talking. Occasionally, however, Atlas would raise his voice and snatches of his words would carry plainly. "A damn fool would have gotten out of that strata long ago. Instead, you keep on trying to drill through an artesian stream running through granite. I guess if I hadn't come out here you'd have kept on drilling until all the money was gone."

It made me wince but I couldn't see how Dennis could defend himself.

Atlas's voice came again. "I'm looking forward to having my accountant look over your books. I see a lot of money missing."

Finally Dennis raised his own voice. "Well, damn it, Mr. Atlas, you wouldn't believe how they charge you here. They got a judge will pick you clean if you turn your back. He'll have the fillings out of your mouth."

Atlas said, in brittle tones, "I've met him. I had no trouble."

I stared at the tent, waiting for him to go ahead and finish by telling Dennis he'd bought him off with a little more than the going price. But he neglected that information. Instead, he said, "Now listen, Frank, we've got a contract. And you are not living up to it. I'm going to give you . . ."

Whatever it was he was going to give Dennis, I didn't hear, because Atlas lowered his voice. I had an idea, though, that it was not going to be a round of applause.

After a time they both emerged from the tent. They stopped a few paces from the flaps and Atlas turned to face Dennis. Dennis was standing with his back to the derrick. Leon was in the gap between them, on Atlas's right. I walked slowly in their direction. As I got there Atlas was saying, "Now, I want this mess set right and I want it done in record time. If I want, I can haul you into court for breaching this contract."

I was close by then and it made me furious. I said, "Hell, why don't you take the artesian spring to court? It's the real troublemaker."

He gave me a cold look. He said, "I told you to stick to flying the plane, sonny boy."

Before I could reply he had turned back to Dennis. This time his voice was harsh. He put out a forefinger and began jabbing Dennis in the chest. He said, "The last man who tried to cheat me didn't enjoy it very much. Especially while he was in the hospital."

It was too much for me. I stepped forward and knocked his arm downward to get the offending forefinger out of Dennis's face. I said, "Hey, who the hell you think you are talking to? This is an honest man." I stepped between him and Dennis and gave him a little shove backward. "Just who the hell you think—"

That was as far as I got. It felt like some giant hammer had suddenly propelled me sideways and backward. Then there was a flash of light, an intense pain in my head, and everything went black. For all I knew the end of the world had come.

I came to consciousness slowly and by degrees which was good since every move toward the surface was accompanied by blinding pain. Finally I opened my eyes and blinked rapidly. It was dark out but there was a lantern burning and I could see I was in the right tent and on my bunk. I could see a figure at Dennis's desk. I guessed it was him. I became aware that my head was damp and I put up a hand, wincing as I did so, for fear it would be blood. But it was only a damp cloth that someone—Dennis, I felt sure—had laid across my forehead. I was also lying on a thickness of cool, damp cloth. I made a little sound in my throat and immediately regretted it. My head was throbbing like a steam engine and the slightest movement was agony.

The figure at the end of the tent got up and turned my way. It was Dennis. He came to my side and leaned down to look in my eyes. "You awake, Willis?"

"Ooooh," I said. "Hell."

"I reckon you be hurtin'."

I worked my mouth around even though it made the top of my head hurt. I said, whispering, "Wha' happened?"

He looked grim. Then he glanced off as if he was considering his answer. He said, slowly, "I reckon I got us mixed up with the wrong people."

"Boy howdy, yes," I said, still whispering. If anything, my head was hurting worse.

Dennis said, "You think you could get a little whiskey down? It might help. I would reckon your head is hurting some."

I started to nod but thought better of it. I said, "Yeah. Let me try a taste."

He went off to the front of the tent and I lay there blankly, trying to remember what had happened. One minute I had been involved with getting Teddy Atlas off Dennis's back; the next instant I had come to in the tent in considerably more damaged a condition than I'd remembered starting out in. But strain as I might, I couldn't come up with a single detail of what happened to me. As unlikely as it seemed, I thought that perhaps one of the lengths of pipe racked up in the derrick had somehow fallen and landed on top of me. That was the way I felt, though I knew the pipe wasn't long enough to have reached from the derrick over to where we had been standing. But something powerful had got hold of me.

Dennis came back with a brimming tumbler of whiskey. He sat down beside me. He said, "Now you are going to have to try and sit up for this. If I pour it in your mouth I'm afraid you might choke."

He got his arm under my shoulders, though it hurt to have him do so and I made an effort to sit up. "Damn!" I said, amazed at how one of my shoulders hurt. "What the hell!"

But Dennis was holding the glass and I got my face down and sucked at the edge, pulling in the whiskey. Dennis tilted the glass as I made progress and kept on tilting until I'd knocked it all off.

He let me lie back, and I said, "Aaaaah." The whiskey had been hard to take but it was loosening me up like motor oil. Since I was already mostly up, I figured to go ahead and finish the job. Moving slowly, and with Dennis's help, I swung my legs around and put my feet on the floor. I discovered I didn't hurt all over, just in a couple of places. My left shoulder in particular was sore. I put up my right hand

and massaged it and flinched away from the pain. I said, "What happened?" My head was still throbbing like the worst hangover in the history of the world.

Dennis had poured the tumbler full again. He held it up to my mouth, but I took it out of his hand with my right and had a few sips before I asked again what had happened.

"It was Leon."

"What do you mean, it was Leon?"

"It was Leon what hit you."

I looked up at him in disbelief. "Leon hit me? What with?" I couldn't remember seeing Leon move, much less hit me. The last I'd seen of him he'd been on the other side of Teddy Atlas.

"With his fists."

I felt my shoulder again. "You telling me he darn near broke my shoulder with his fist?"

"Yeah. He hit you with his left on your shoulder to straighten you around and then he hit you over the head with his right. He meant to hit you in the face, but you ducked down after that lick on the shoulder. Well, not 'ducked down.' More like you was falling. So that big fist of his caught you on the top of the head. Knocked you about six feet and you was out cold before you ever hit the ground. He would have kept on but I went to screaming and the crew gathered around and Atlas called him off."

"Why, that son of a bitch," I said, slowly. I took in some more of the whiskey. "I don't think I'm going to take that off him. In fact, I don't take that kind of whipping off nobody."

Dennis shook his head. "I think you better not tangle with that Leon. Prizefighters, Willis—it ain't like a fight in the street. They know how to do it and they are trained. You're a good strong young man, but you ain't a match for such as Leon."

I was still hurting, but now I was angry. I reached down and got the wet clump of cloth Dennis had pillowed my head on and put it on the top of my head. It was no longer cool, and not particularly damp, but it was something to do. "How long was I out?"

"Couple of hours. Maybe a little longer."

"I just want to get it straight on what I owe that son of a bitch."

I could see his face clearly in the lamplight. He said, "Now, Willis, you are to leave that man alone. Next time he might kill you."

"Next time," I said, "I'll have a way to make the match a little more even. Maybe even tilt it in my favor."

"Willis, please leave Leon alone. I got all I can handle with Atlas."

I took some more whiskey. "How did that turn out?"

He sighed. "Not good. I'm supposed to start in moving the rig right away."

"What about the waterspout?"

"Oh, we're going to have to pull the pipe up. That's the first thing on the agenda. Of course, once that pipe is up, the hole will collapse and—good-bye spring."

"Is that the final word?"

He shrugged. "It was this afternoon when we went into the tent. We was supposed to go on talking but you kind of interrupted that. I been in here with you ever since we laid you out on your bunk. We thought the son of a bitch had killed you, and I think it scared Atlas. Joe Cairo loaded his pistol and went walking around with it in his belt."

"They done that for me?"

"No. They don't like Atlas. They heard him say he was going to bring in another drilling contractor. That pissed them off, especially Joe Cairo." Then he hastened to add, "Of course, they don't approve of what that Leon done to you."

"Can't you stall Atlas? Try to talk him into letting you keep on drilling for a little longer?"

Dennis looked at his work-scarred hands. "I reckon I could. Try and show a little progress. Ain't much to lose, and he's going to spend a pile of money moving this rig. We are supposed to talk some more tonight. In his tent. When you come around. He said to tell you he was sorry but you should have knowed better than to have laid hands on him in front of Leon."

I would have laughed, but I knew how my head would have reacted. "Damn kind of Mr. Atlas," I said. "About like carrying a rattlesnake around with you and then blaming the fellow that gets bit because you had the rattlesnake."

He said, "Well, if you reckon you are going to live, I will go call on Mr. Atlas before it gets too late. Have another try at getting him to let me try and drill through that spring."

"You think he'd really bring in another drilling contractor?"

Dennis lifted his palms up. "Who knows what that rich bastard is liable to do? But we do have a contract. Though, if he doesn't give me any more money, I'm as good as out of business. Things have cost three times what I'd thought they would."

"Didn't I hear him say you had breached the contract?"

"Oh, yes. But that don't make it so and it would be damn hard to prove in a court. We hit unexpected hard times and he knows it. Just because you are a spoiled brat doesn't mean you always get your way."

"That seems to be his intention." I leaned forward and put my head in both hands. Even my neck hurt. I was willing to bet that Leon had hit me so hard he'd knocked me down a couple of inches.

Dennis put on his hat. "Will you be all right while I step over and see if Atlas won't show some sense?"

"Is it after supper?"

"Yeah. You missed it. You hungry now?"

"I could eat." I wasn't really hungry, but I didn't think it would be too smart to keep drinking whiskey on an empty stomach. And the way my body felt, I was going to need more than another drink to dull down the ache and the throbbing.

Dennis said, from the door of the tent, "I'll tell the cook to fix you a plate and bring it over. You stay put."

"I can't wait," I said. "Is it beans and rice or rice and beans?"

"Both." He paused before he went out. He said, "Don't be lying there plotting how you are going to get back at Leon. This is one game where the cards are stacked against you. I don't expect you to pay me any attention tonight, but I'm going to remind you in the morning and keep on reminding you. You can't win. You are giving away too much muscle and all you'll do if you try, is make more trouble for both of us."

I had no doubt what he said was true. I had no chance against Leon in a straight-up fistfight, but there were other ways. I sat there not thinking about much of anything until the cook brought my food and then I ate, took another drink, and lay back down. My body wanted rest to knit itself back together.

Dennis won a little extra drilling time from Atlas to make a last try at getting through the water. At what personal cost to himself and his self-esteem, Dennis didn't say. It was a day-to-day affair. Atlas walked around looking like he might suddenly throw his hand in the air at any second and holler, "Stop!"

For my part, I stayed out of the way, keeping clear of Atlas and Leon. I didn't need it, but Dennis was there to remind me any second I looked like I might have forgotten. No one came forward to apologize. Leon seemed oblivious to my existence, and Atlas only occasionally favored me with glances of vague recognition.

I stayed in the tent a lot of the time. I still hurt. Dennis was drilling with a worried look on his face. After one day of his reprieve he came into the tent claiming he was making real progress against the elements. He said, "I got Mr. Atlas up on the drilling platform and showed him some of the rock samples that were coming up the pipe from the bit. Hell, he has to see we're making good progress considering the rock we're drilling through, never mind the force of the artesian water."

He sounded like he was trying to convince himself. I asked him what Atlas had said.

"Well, he didn't actually pass no comment on the matter, but anyone could see we been making good progress being down nearly three hundred feet against such conditions."

"But if he could have his way of having you move the rig and drill through something where you could go twice as fast, wouldn't he rather do that?"

"Yeah. I suppose so. But, hell, Willis, for all either of us knows, they is a great shelf of granite down there at two hundred feet all across

Pecos County. We don't know how thick it is. I might pop that bit out any second and be home free. Good-bye rock, good-bye water."

I figured we ought to start packing for home, but I didn't say anything. What I wanted was a lawyer to look at the contract. As the lease holder I wanted to see if I couldn't forbid Atlas from drilling on my land with any other contractor besides Dennis. Dennis had given it as his opinion that I couldn't, that I had made my contract with the company that Atlas controlled, rather than a contract between myself and Dennis as the driller.

I feared he was right, if for no other reason than the way Teddy Atlas treated me. I was no more important to him than any other tool or apparatus around the camp. If I had some control over his future fortune I believe he would have acted different. He probably would have let Leon beat me to death except for being unsure what the other men of the crew might have done if he had. He didn't know that they didn't have a very high opinion of me.

I had been thinking as hard as I could about some solution for Dennis—and me—out of the mess we were in, but nothing seemed to come to mind. What we needed was money and I didn't have any and neither did Dennis. I could not remember what Dennis had said Atlas had put up so far, but I had it in my mind that it was going to take about $125,000 to remove Atlas from the scene. That is if he wanted to sell. But I couldn't see any reason that he wouldn't. I didn't see any fortune to be made in that desert, but then, you never knew. Without the money it didn't matter.

Two days after Leon had tried to use me as a tent stake I was down fooling around with the airplane, checking the oil and making sure all the pitocks were clear of sand. Pitocks picked up the outside air and operated most of the instruments on the airplane. I was in the process of running a wire through one when it suddenly occurred to me that there was a telephone exchange in Pecos. I could call my uncle Warner or my aunt Laura.

I gave it not another second's thought, but immediately pulled the covers off the engine cowling, got the engine started and, less than five minutes after I'd had the thought, I was lifting the plane off the ground and climbing for altitude. I never looked back at the camp as I turned toward Pecos.

I made no attempt to sneak into my landing strip in the town. I set the airplane down and taxied up to the old warehouse and killed the engine. If there was any trouble with the judge I was just going to refer him to Teddy Atlas. I walked into town and hunted up the telephone exchange. It was on Main Street, in a little store. I went in. There were two women on duty. One was sitting in front of what I knew to be a switchboard with all the wires and holes. The other was leaning up against a counter. Over in the corner was a telephone sitting on a shelf with a chair in front of it. There was a kind of partition sticking out from the wall to give the caller some privacy. I really hadn't made all that many long-distance calls. I'd heard there was a way you could call and it would be charged to the person you were calling. That was the only way I was going to be able to make a long-distance call because I didn't have any money—maybe a dollar or two—and I'd heard those trunk calls were kind of expensive. I went up to the lady at the counter and discussed the problem with her. At least I knew a little about calling from an exchange since most of my long-distance calling had been done in that fashion.

"Oh yes," she said, "we do that even though it is a different telephone company that would be in the place where you are calling. But it is easily done. Provided, you understand, that the other party accepts the charges. We call it reversing the charges. If you'll give me the name of the party you are calling and where he or she lives, we'll be able to locate them through what we call Information."

I thanked her and gave her my Uncle Warner's name and my aunt Laura's. I'd speak with whoever answered the phone and they would accept the charges. The nice lady wrote all of this down on a piece of notepaper and bade me go sit by the phone in the partition. She said, "If we get either one of your parties on the phone, that phone on the wall will ring. You pick it up and start talking, Mr. Young."

It was clear the phone lady had been shipped in to work for this

local office since she was definitely a cut above the average resident of
the town. But I wasn't concerned about that so much as I was what I
was going to say if I got anyone on the phone. It didn't matter who I
got; my aunt and uncle were about equal partners when it came to
money and to business. I'd never asked them for anything that I could
remember. There never had been a need—not when you are Wilson
Young's son. So I reckoned that getting them over their initial surprise
was going to be the first order of business. I guess I was hoping Uncle
Warner would answer the telephone. I'd always thought he was easier
to talk to than my aunt about delicate matters. She tended to bore
straight in and make you explain yourself rather than letting you just
sort of slide the idea across.

I had little time to think. The phone jangled right in front of me
and the lady at the counter was signaling me to pick it up. Hell, I
hadn't had the idea an hour and now I had to put it into words. I
picked up the part they called the earpiece, or the receiver, and put it
to my ear. I got my mouth down close to the cone-shaped part you
talked over. I heard the operator's voice in my ear. She said, "I have
your party, Mr. Young, and they have accepted the charges. Go ahead."

I cleared my throat and said, a little louder than I needed to,
"Hello, hello? This is Willis."

I wasn't lucky. Aunt Laura's voice came over the wire. She said,
"Willis, honey, I'll swan. What in the world are you doing, calling up?
Don't tell me there's been illness or worse."

"No, no, no," I said, suddenly realizing that there probably wasn't
a woman alive who got a telephone call long-distance and didn't expect
it meant some catastrophe. "No, I'm fine."

But her voice was still strained. "Your mother, your father?"

I said, "Well, I reckon you've communicated with them since I
have. I'd guess they are fine." I hesitated and took a deep breath. I
said, "Aunt Laura, this is business. It is about money. I would sure
appreciate to talk to Uncle Warner if he is there."

She said, in that bright voice of hers that didn't stand for any
nonsense, "Well, it's all the same. He'd just have to talk it over with
me. But he's right here if you want. I'll put him on the telephone."

"Never mind," I said, resignedly. What she said was true. It would have to go through her one way or the other. I said, "Have ya'll got my last letter? The one where I am talking about the trouble we are having with the oil-well drilling?"

"My, yes, honey. Your Uncle Warner said if a horse was giving him the same amount of trouble, that he'd get shut of the beast before it killed him."

I said, kind of helplessly, "But what if that oil well was right in your backyard, right there in Overton? And what if it involved a friend who might have saved your life more than once? And what if you could stop a bad man from doing something real bad? Wouldn't it be worth the effort?"

She said, "Honey, just a minute. That is one big bunch of 'what if's.' Let me turn around here and talk to Warner."

Of course, while she was gone I realized I had not written her about Teddy Atlas. It was going to be hard to explain.

Then a masculine voice came on the line. My uncle Warner. I was very relieved. There was going to be a lot of explaining to do, and my uncle was a good listener. My aunt was, too, but in her own fashion. She interrupted and asked questions as you were going along. Made a difficult topic that much more difficult.

After we'd got the preliminaries out of the way I got down to the crux of the business. Some of it he already knew, the rest I filled in. I ended up by saying, "So what it comes down to is that I need somewhere around one hundred twenty-five thousand, maybe a little more, to get this Teddy Atlas out of the picture and have the control of the business in my own hands."

You'd have thought we were talking, about the price of hay the calm way he handled the request. He said, "And once you're in charge what do you plan to do?"

I said, into the telephone instrument, "Well, I'm going to make a lake right there on my land, that big basin. I'm going to turn that water well loose and let it flow. Then I'm going to have Dennis Frank dig another well on the edge of that basin not too far away. If he hits the water again, I'm going to let that flow into the lake. I figure two artesian wells pumping like they are ought to make a lake a mile long and a half a mile across and thirty feet deep. I figure it will make that desert bloom. I figure people will be able to graze cattle because some grass will grow and there'll be plenty of water for their stock. And then I figure we can scout out some sort of irrigation scheme for their crops. I figure it will change the place entirely."

"What about your friend? He doesn't want to drill for water."

"There should be plenty of money left so he can drill anywhere he wants."

"How would you pay back such a loan?"

I said, knowing that was my weak point, "By selling off acreage around the lake to those who wanted it. And I think there would be a big demand. Only thing is, these people ain't got much money. They would be a pretty slow pay."

"All right. I understand you. Now wait on the line while I talk to your aunt."

I wanted to yell at him not to talk to my aunt. I wanted to tell him I preferred he make the decision. But he was gone too quick and I was left with an earpiece that was as empty as a dry cow. I could hear the very faint murmur of their voices but I couldn't make out any of the words.

I waited.

"Willis?"

It had seemed like an eternity but I knew it had been no more than a couple of minutes. I said, speaking into the mouthpiece, "Yes, sir. I'm on the line."

"Willis," he said, and I could hear him as clearly as if he were in the room, "I have talked with your aunt and she agrees with me."

"Yes, sir?"

"I could help you and I want to help you. And I would help you if I wouldn't be standing in another man's boots."

My heart sank. I had been afraid this would be his answer. "Yes, sir," I said.

"You know that by rights you should be calling your daddy. As to the differences between the two of you, we have nothing to say. But if

I was to send you this sum of money, Wilson Young would not like me getting in between him and his son, and I wouldn't blame him. Even if he wasn't my close, close friend for a number of years, I still wouldn't do it on principle."

"Yes, sir," I said without much enthusiasm.

"Now, you know your business better than I do. But if I was making long-distance phone calls, I would be making one to Del Rio."

"I can't do that, Uncle Warner. I wish I could, but I can't. I tried to make the first move several times, but he wouldn't have it halfway."

"All right. Here, your aunt wants to talk to you."

I didn't want to talk to her, but I had no choice. She had plenty to say, most of it directed at what I was doing to my dear mother. I felt bad about that myself, so I didn't give her much argument on that score. She said, "Willis, I think you are trying to do a wonderful thing here, but you are going at it all wrong. Call your parents, son. It seems to me you don't have much time. You had better take advantage of the chance you have now. I know that country, and a lake would be wonderful. That part of the world, by the way, is where I met your uncle Warner."

I didn't want to listen to her tell that story again so I just said, "Well, we had better break off, Aunt Laura. I thank ya'll for listening."

"Call your daddy even if he is a hardheaded son of a bitch."

"I can't," I said and, after another moment, we rang off. I got up and thanked the lady at the counter and went out the door and stood in the middle of the street for a moment. I didn't know what to do. I'd played the only ace I had and it hadn't won the pot. I was out of ideas.

I started walking back toward my plane, my mind whirling. I'd been a fool to call. My aunt and uncle couldn't help me because of the circumstances between me and the retired bank robber and gunfighter. They weren't going to get in the middle of that and I'd been a fool to think they would. It was just that I was so desperate. I had never felt so helpless in my entire life. Maybe money did have its advantages. But then, so did not caring about anything or wanting anything or feeling much of anything. Once you let yourself get involved you were just asking to be hit with a stick.

The judge was waiting for me in the middle of the street halfway to my airplane. He said, "There are taxes to be levied."

I stopped in front of him and gave him a good looking-up and -down. "Atlas," I said. "That's the man you want. He owns the plane and the drilling rig and the whole shebang. Atlas, Teddy Atlas. And he's rich. Richer than anything you ever saw. Hell, you tried to hold Dennis Frank up for a lousy two thousand dollars. My lands! That ain't shucks to Mr. Atlas. You ought to come out to the well site and really gig him. No, wait. Wait until he comes back to town. You can nail him for all sorts of money."

Then, with him standing there with his mouth open, I stepped around his bulk and got the airplane and flew back to the rig.

I could see from the air as I came in for my approach that Dennis was still drilling. That was a good sign, or at least as good a sign as we could have hoped for. But whether he was making any progress against the rock and water, I couldn't tell.

I got the plane tied down and covered up and was sauntering toward the cook shack when I found my line of march interrupted by Teddy Atlas. Behind him was Leon, looking at me no different than he ever had. I was glad he bore me no ill will for stopping his fist with my head.

Atlas said, "Where you been in that airplane?"

I looked at him for a second and then decided against the first answer that came to mind. Instead I said, "I went to town."

"What for?"

"It was personal."

Atlas's eyes were kind of a cold blue, even on such a hot day. He said, "That is not your personal airplane. Don't ever touch it again without my permission."

I nodded slowly. "Sure. If you think you can fly it enough to keep it in rig."

His eyes narrowed as he studied my face. He said, "You know I'm not a pilot. What do you mean, 'keep it in rig'?"

"Well, Mr. Atlas, an airplane is like a living human being. It changes. The rudder changes, the ailerons change, the vertical stabilizer. They got to be adjusted so your airplane will fly in trim. If you don't . . ." I shrugged and stretched out my hands.

"So you were flying the airplane to keep it in, in rig?"

"Airplane has to be flown," I said evasively. I was not a bit ashamed of the lie I was telling. Of course, it was not a complete lie, but an airplane didn't go out of rig that fast.

"You just chose to go to town?"

"Something like that," I said. "But look here—if you don't want me fooling around with your airplane I certainly won't. Why don't you get another pilot? You could go into town and wire Houston and Dallas and San Antonio. I'm sure you might be able to find an experienced pilot who would be willing to come out here in this desert to fly an underpowered Jenny in hostile country where everybody in town, including the local law, is just waiting for you to crash so they can pick the gold out of your teeth. I could even give you some names. 'Course, you'd have to pay them." I paused significantly. "I was about ready to drag up anyway."

He put up a hand but the cold in the blue of his eyes didn't change. I figured it was a permanent condition. He said, "Wait a minute, don't start that kind of talk. You're not getting paid?"

I shook my head. "Not as a pilot. What I've done, I've done for the love of the skies." I looked at him quick to see how he'd taken the last remark but he didn't flinch. If he'd swallow that kind of talk he'd swallow an elephant. "But that old horse is about wore-out."

He eyed me again for about a half a minute and then slowly pulled out that roll of money he kept in his pocket. He peeled off a fifty and handed it to me. "Here."

I took it and looked at it. "So I get paid the same as the judge. Only thing is, I been on the job longer."

He made a sour face and handed me another fifty. As I took it he said, "All right, but just remember you work for me now."

"In the airplane," I said. "Only in the airplane." I started around the pair of them but stopped and pointed at Leon. "One other little thing. Your Indian here, Chief Big Fists? He ever hits me again you can figure on your airplane sitting in this desert and rusting. You'll pay hell getting another pilot out here. And that plane cost twenty-two hundred dollars. Ask yourself if old Leon is worth that."

Leon made a little start toward me, but Atlas put out his hand. He said, "Leon is only here to make sure no harm comes to me. What happened on that other occasion was a misunderstanding, a mistake. Leon misunderstood your intentions, that's all."

" 'That's all'? Hell, he damn near drove my neck down about three inches. Fighting is his profession, flying is mine. Suppose you make him go up with me. Just by himself. Let him see how it feels to not be able to do a damn thing about what is being done to you."

He gave me that blue-eyed stare again. "Let's let it go. Forget about it. Leon won't bother you again. Leon is here to look after my person. He misunderstood your intentions in using your hands on me."

Leon was giving me his full attention. I wasn't real sure if Teddy Atlas had trained him to heel or not so I figured I'd better let matters lie. I folded the two bills and put them in my pocket. But I couldn't resist getting in one last jab. I said, "Don't forget, you are standing on my land."

Atlas came back damn quickly. He said, "Which is under my lease."

I said, "Minerals only."

"Which includes right-of-way."

I patted my hip pocket. "Just so Leon understands, I carry a Derringer. It's small but it carrys one hell of a wallop. And I'll be on my land."

Atlas narrowed his eyes at me, but he didn't speak. After a moment he turned and walked away and Leon followed him.

That night I showed Dennis the two fifty-dollar bills and said, "Buddy, I think we've got them on the run." I told him the story of my encounter with Atlas and Leon. "At least the son of a bitch thinks I'm carrying a gun even if I'm not. Maybe he won't be so quick to hit. And, also, I sicced the judge on him while I was in town."

It didn't do much to cheer up Dennis. He just shook his head tiredly. "I don't know, Willis. I don't think anything can help."

"You didn't make much progress today?"

He shook his head again and sighed. "Not so you'd notice. And I about halfway believe that rock shelf runs all over this country. I bet if we were to move the rig a mile and a half in any direction we'd still hit that granite. And maybe that damn water."

"Well, given enough time you can get through it, can't you?"

He made a face. "I don't know. We are wearing out drill bits at a hell of a rate. When Atlas sees the way things are, he ain't going to put another nickel into the deal. And he's got my string of tools as part of his security."

That was the first time I'd heard that. "The hell you say! Dennis, that equipment is all you got in the world. Why would you risk that on a venture like this?"

He shrugged. "It was the only way I could get him to make the deal. The man with the money calls the tune. The rest of us dance to whatever it is the fiddler plays."

"How come you didn't tell me you put yourself in hock?" It gave me a bad feeling. I'd just been sailing along, not particularly caring one way or another. I'd figured Atlas would be the only loser.

"What good would it have done?" He glanced up at me. "No use you worrying, too. It wouldn't change anything."

I looked at the hundred dollars in my hand. It could be the last we'd ever see from Teddy Atlas.

CHAPTER
17

DENNIS WAS more right about Teddy Atlas's patience than either of us wanted to believe. A day and a half after I'd pronounced him "on the run," he told Dennis to start taking down the rig. He said he was tired of the "No progress" reports and he wasn't going to see his money wasted without giving matters a fair chance in some other location. Of course, the news spread immediately to our rubberneckers and there were loud groans and protestations. They knew the end of the rig meant the end of the water, and their hopes had been growing day by day as the little pools in the bottom of the basin collected and joined each other and began to look like serious water.

But it would be a little time before the springwater was lost. It took longer to take down a wooden rig than it did to put one up. Every piece had to be carefully taken loose and marked so it could go back in the same place when a new derrick was erected. And meanwhile all drilling stopped, the boiler went out, and the spring was free to shoot water as high up the derrick as it could. To speed the work Atlas hired some of the gawkers to help, but they proved to be more of a hindrance than a help. It gave me some measure of satisfaction to hear Atlas yelling at one of the new men who'd just made a blunder that would cost an hour's work all around to undo. Of course, Dennis was supposed to have the charge of taking down the rig, but he didn't spend much time at it. And our skilled labor, Joel and Charlie and Joe Cairo, were above such work so it was left to an almost wholly Pecos crew to do the work. Some of the new men, it seemed to me, quickly got on to the fact that the slower and sloppier they worked, the longer the job would last. It was very pleasant to watch Teddy Atlas lose his studied nonchalance and get furious as nothing seemed to get done.

And then, as the dismantling entered its second day, I got what was very nearly the shock of my life. A young man rode into our camp on a mule, calling out my name. He was bareback, with a rope bridle for steering, and he pulled up at the cookhouse and began yelling, "Mistuh Young! Mistuh Willy Young."

I heard him and somebody pointed me out to him. I hurried his way with the hope of putting an end to the "Willy" business before it could catch on. He sullenly looked down at me from the deck of his ill-tempered charger and inquired if I was "Mistuh Willy Young."

"Yes," I said, to quiet him.

He thrust out an envelope that had once been clean before it had undergone passage from town in his grubby hands. My name was written gracefully across the front of the stylish envelope. There was no other information to be gained from the outside. The mule rider said, "Lady give me that in town to fetch out to you."

"What'd the lady look like?"

He looked disinterested. "Jes' a nice-lookin' lady. 'Cept she din't gimme but a dollar to fetch this out so fer."

"Fine," I said. "Maybe she didn't know it was so 'fer.'" I reached in my pocket and handed him another dollar and then turned, staring intently at the envelope, barely daring to hope, and walked to my tent. I got inside and sat down on the end of my cot where the light was best. The handwriting on the envelope was definitely feminine and I didn't think it could be my aunt Laura's, I opened the envelope carefully. There was a single sheet of paper inside, carefully folded. I opened it up and held it up to the light. It said simply,

"You invite me out here and then you are not there to meet me. Meanwhile I suffer in this miserable dungeon of a hotel. Have you forgotten me so soon? I am paying one of the local stalwarts five dollars to mount his trusty steed and ride off into the desert and find you. I hope you receive this in time to save me from becoming permanently blinded by my gay surroundings."

It was signed, simply, *Genevieve.*

I let my breath out slowly and stared into space for a long moment or two. It was one of those dreams that came true even without you dreaming them because they seem too improbable.

I was not inert very long. I jumped to my feet, shucking my clothes as fast as I could. I grabbed a bar of soap and my razor and walked out into the spray from the well. Standing in the steady downpour I bathed and shaved all at the same time. As I rushed to complete the chore I calculated that she would have had to have come in the day before. Today's train wouldn't have arrived yet, so that meant she'd already had about twenty hours of Pecos. I was surprised she was still in the area.

I finished my washing and shaving in record time and then went back and started getting dressed. What clothes I'd had, had suffered from the traveling-around we'd done, but I got on my officer's boots and a pair of riding pants and a white shirt and declared myself looking as good as possible. I needed a haircut, but I ran a comb through it and then headed for the airplane.

I took a northerly course for the first few minutes so it wouldn't be readily apparent that I was heading for town. When I had gone far enough and high enough I began working my way back to the west and finally, with the camp a long way away, turned southeast toward Pecos. I was very excited at the idea of seeing Genevieve again. I simply couldn't believe she was in Pecos.

I landed and taxied up to the old warehouse. I didn't bother putting the plane inside. The judge would just try and impound it. But I wasn't worried about John Crater. I had plenty of Teddy Atlas's money in my pocket to buy him off. But it didn't matter. He was nowhere in sight. I hoofed it for the hotel as fast as I could. But as I was passing the sheriff's office a thought struck me. I couldn't leave her in that flea trap of a hotel. Surely there would be some nice, genteel lady I could board her with. And the sheriff was the ideal man to know who to apply to.

I found him in his office and laid out my plight with as few details as possible. I didn't tell him she was my sister, but I came damn near. He straightened up in his chair and said, "Well, happens I can help you out, young feller. My wife has been taking in boarders of the right sort for some little time and the last one just moved out. If your young lady don't mind plain but clean and wholesome living, I'm right sure my wife will be glad to have her." But he fixed me with an eye. "But don't you get it into your head that it's a place that you can flit around and visit your lady friend at any hour. The Missus has some strict rules."

I said, with all the sincerity I could raise, "There'll be none of that, Sheriff. She ain't that kind of lady. I would call her the kind you hoped to marry."

He got up. "Then I'll go and tell my old lady that she's got a guest. You say your friend is at the hotel? I believe I saw a very elegant young lady get off the train yesterday afternoon. Best you get her out of that hole as fast as possible. You got any idea how long she'll be staying, Willis?"

I flung out my arms. "I didn't even know she was coming, Lew. I hope she's going to stay a good while."

He gave me a knowing look. "Maybe she's got some ideas of her own."

"She's strong-willed, but I don't think she's that strong-willed."

"Well, you know where I live. You run along and fetch her. Never mind about her baggage, I'll send somebody for it. You just get hold of her."

She was sitting in the lobby of the hotel on one of those round settees that all hotels seem to feature. The one in this hotel had long since given up any pretense of being anything more than a shabby place to sit. Its red velvet was worn and tattered and the central post, the backing, was even tilting. But there she sat with her handbag in her lap, dressed very demurely in a gray day gown of ankle length that was clutched at the throat with a bunch of lace. She looked as pretty as she ever had, maybe prettier, considering her surroundings. But she wasn't just pretty. She had something in her face that I had never been able to define. She'd had it when she was playing the gadabout in short chiffon dresses and silk scarfs and jeweled high-heeled shoes. Now she had it in plain traveling clothes, in a place that was far from flattering. I decided it was character, even though that didn't completely cover it. There was an assurance there and a kind of knowledge that came from knowing she was always going to be on the side of good. That was it, I decided. She was good. She was a playgirl who knew all the latest dances and could drink half the night away but she was still good.

I pushed through the big glassed door and was almost in front of her before she saw me. "Oh!" she said. She put her hand up to her mouth in surprise but then almost immediately she stood up. I folded her into a hug and kissed her on the cheek. I said, "I thought you weren't coming to far west Texas. Got to missing me, didn't you?"

She said, breathlessly, "I've been sitting here scared to death. I think every man in this town has come by to ogle me through the windows. I was worried sick you wouldn't get my message. I would have hated to have gone back without seeing you."

I stepped back from her so as to have a full view. "You look like the wife of a Baptist preacher."

"Don't forget, my daddy *is* a Baptist preacher."

"What happened to the skirts that quit at the knee?"

"I considered where I was going and decided to pack accordingly."

I just looked at her face. I couldn't believe she was there. I said, "You are going to tell me sooner or later what got you on that train. Why not make it sooner?"

She said, "My, my, sir. Have you forgotten your fatal charm? What else could it be?"

I reached out and took her hand in mine. I said, "I would really like to believe it was the sight of my handsome face brought you all this way, but I got a sneaking feeling it was something else. Though what else it could be, I haven't the faintest idea. Hell, you didn't even answer my letters."

"Now, that is not fair. I answered one or two, but I am the worst correspondent in the world. I don't mean to be, but I can never get around to answering letters. I would have telephoned you if there'd been a way."

I said, "Well, come along. I don't want you staying in this hotel another minute. I've got you a room with the sheriff and his wife. That ought to be respectable enough even for a Baptist preacher's daughter."

She said, as I led her toward the door, "But my luggage."

I opened the door. "The sheriff will send somebody over for it. Is it still packed?"

"Yes. I didn't want the maid prying."

"A maid in this hotel? Don't make me laugh."

We walked out the door and, on the way over to the sheriff's house, I searched for some tactful way to ask her what she was doing in Pecos. Finally I gave up. I said, "Genevieve, you just up and coming this far for the hell of it doesn't make any sense. It ain't like you."

"Oh. You mean I'm too cold and calculating to act on a whim or a caprice?"

I was holding her hand as we walked. She had on a pair of fine leather gloves. The sheriff lived in a little residential section that was behind the town to the west. I said, "Now, don't try your feminine wiles on me. Just answer straight up to the question. What are you doing here?"

She smiled up at me with her white, glistening teeth. "You asked me. Or don't you remember?"

"That was two or three months ago. Maybe longer. To quote you, you 'didn't want any part of this horrible country.' And I can't say that I disagree with you. So why did you change your mind and show up?"

"You wrote nice letters."

"Goddammit, Genevieve, now cut that out and tell me what is going on."

But instead of answering she asked me a question. "Is Mr. Atlas still here?"

I stopped and swung around so that we were facing each other. "Did I write you about Teddy Atlas?"

"Yes, but you told me, back in Houston, that you were afraid he'd take advantage of Dennis. Has he?"

I gave her a perplexed look. "Say, how long have you been here?"

"Just since yesterday afternoon. The train was a little late or I'd have sent you a note yesterday, but it got dark and I couldn't get anyone to go. Why?"

"Because you seem to know a whole lot about these affairs around here."

Now she stopped. "Willis Young, you wrote me long, detailed letters. And I read them over and over. So there."

"Well, you still haven't said you've come on account of me. Are you going to say that?"

She gave me a coy smile and cocked her head. "Do I really have to answer that?"

"Come on," I said. I pulled her along behind me as we climbed up on the porch of the sheriff's big, two-story white house. It must have been the coolest place in town.

I was about to knock on the door when it suddenly opened and a lady that I knew as the sheriff's wife swung it wide. I knew that her first name was Sarah and that she was well thought-of by nearly everyone. She was one of those comely ladies who, flirting with forty, still looked nice in their dress and their hairdo and a slight touch of makeup. She welcomed us in with a lot of gushing and "my, mys," and said the sheriff would be along shortly with the young lady's luggage and meanwhile I should go in the parlor and rest myself while she showed Miss Genevieve her room.

It was about an hour later, when the sheriff and a helper had brought Genevieve's two suitcases and Mrs. Wallace had got her settled and unpacked, that Genevieve finally came down the stairs and joined me on the settee with the double doors closed.

Before I could speak she said, in a kind of pouty voice, that I hadn't even kissed her hello yet. Well, it seemed so unfair and out of the order of matters that I was flabbergasted. I said, "Well, yeah, and you ain't told me what you're doing out here."

"Don't say 'ain't,' Willis. It's so common. You never said 'ain't' before."

"I certainly did." Seeing that the conversation wasn't exactly going my way, I put my hand on the back of her head and pulled her face to mine and kissed her on the lips. I kissed her lightly at first and then with growing fervor as I felt her arms go around my neck. When we finally pulled apart she gave a little gasp and said, "Well. I think I have been kissed. And thoroughly, at that."

She still had that droll, mysterious way about her so that you never quite knew where you stood or even where you were supposed to be standing.

I said, in a kind of husky voice, "I am mighty glad to see you, Genevieve, for whatever reason brings you my way."

She reached up and pushed the hair out of my face. "The reason is you. Don't you have sense enough to know that?" She patted me on the forearm. I couldn't tell if she'd missed me more than she'd expected or if it was a delayed reaction to my previous charm.

"So you've just come to see me. Judging from the amount of luggage, you're going to stay a spell."

"I'm here to help you. Now. Tell me how things stand currently between Mr. Atlas and Dennis."

I couldn't get over the fact that I was sitting with this flowering blossom of young womanhood in a house in Pecos. It was like I'd gone to sleep and dreamed and woke up and found the dream was real. Every time I looked at her she seemed to get better-looking. She'd been wearing some kind of ridiculous hat when I'd found her in the hotel lobby, but now she'd brushed her hair down to its proper length and her face was just radiant. I said, "What?"

She laughed. "Tell me how things stand between Dennis and Mr. Atlas. As of your last moment with them."

"Uh, well, matters are not good. Dennis has been trying to drill through a granite shelf and an artesian well all at the same time. Teddy Atlas don't think much of the idea. He has just ordered him to move the rig."

"What! But won't that shut off the water?"

I nodded. "Yeah."

"Then we've got to act fast."

I stared at her, a little puzzled. " 'We'? What have 'we' got to do with it?"

"I was married to an oilman, Willis. You know that."

"Yes, but I don't want to be reminded of it."

Before I could say anything else, Mrs. Wallace came in and announced that dinner would be served shortly and that I—because of the special circumstances—was invited.

Of course, that put an end to any personal talk. Neither the sheriff nor his wife seemed inclined to ask after our history: how we'd met, how serious we were about each other. But even with the outside talk I was conscious of a tension that existed between Genevieve and myself. It was a tension mostly caused by the curiosity between us. Me about her, and her about me and what I'd been doing. We both had a lot of questions.

When dinner was finally, excruciatingly, over, I sat in the parlor with Lew while Genevieve went upstairs to unpack. Lew gave me a cigar for which I was very grateful since it gave me something to do with my hands. The sheriff said, mildly, "Willis, you been up to something? You seem as nervous as a man with a spider in his boot."

I laughed. It sounded hollow even to me. "No, just kind of more alert than usual. The big moneyman is out at the rig."

"So I've heard."

Genevieve and Mrs. Wallace came back downstairs and settled down in the parlor. That wasn't going to work, so I suggested to Genevieve that I show her a real west Texas sky so she could see how bright the stars were.

The sheriff said, "Willis, the stars won't be out yet, I—"

But he cut it short after a hard look from his wife.

Genevieve and I sat on the front-porch steps, sitting very close to each other. I put my arm around her and she huddled closer. The heat of the day was fading into a chilly evening. I said, "Have you come out here to marry me?"

She laughed lightly. "From a casual dance in a hotel in Galveston to a proposal of marriage on the porch steps of the sheriff's house. Now, that is moving around."

Lew had been wrong; the stars were starting to come out.

I said, "Probably you like this place, and I've got land here, but I wouldn't think you'd want to live here. Not a very active social life."

She said, "Do you have any idea how much money Atlas has advanced Dennis so far?"

I drew my head back in surprise and stared at her. "What?"

"Atlas has got a drilling contract with Dennis, but it is customary practice to dole out the money as progress is made. How deep is Atlas in for?"

I was still stunned. One minute I'd been talking marriage and the next, she was off on the oil business. I said, "How do you know about that?" Then I stopped myself and raised a hand before she could speak. "Never mind. You were married to an oilman. Hell, he must have talked business all the time."

"He did. That's what I'm doing here."

I stared at her so intently and for so long that she finally said, reaching out to pick at my shirtfront, "I swear, Willis, you look like you've lost weight. Is it just hard work or have you not been eating right?"

I said, "Are you crazy? Do you have any idea how much money you are talking about here? And, listen, trust me, Teddy Atlas is not the kind of man you can flutter your eyelashes at and he'll say, 'Why, here, sugar, just name your price.' I swear, what has gotten into your head?"

She made her eyes big and fluttered her hands like a flapper dancing the Charleston, "Oh, listen to the big businessman. What is it you think I'm up to?"

I grimaced. "From your questions I'd say that you are planning some fool quixotic attempt to buy out Teddy Atlas. For what reason, I don't know. But it won't work."

"Why not?"

I got up and stretched and turned to face her where she was sitting on the steps. "Because he's got *a lot* of money invested and he's going to want to get it back, probably with a profit."

"How much *do* you think Atlas has advanced Dennis?"

I shrugged. "I don't know. I know Dennis was angling for a hundred twenty-five thousand, but I know he didn't get that. And Atlas pinched him on the expenses. Dennis said he'd never have taken the deal if he hadn't needed the work so bad."

She looked off into the distance. "You said the contract was to drill four test wells. I'd be greatly surprised if Atlas advanced him more than fifty thousand dollars, maybe a little more. And now that he's seen how badly things are going, he's wanting out."

I was overwhelmed. She had swept in like a west wind, blowing sand, swirling dust. I didn't know which way was up. This sweet girl I'd left in Houston had turned into a businesswoman. I said, slowly, "let's say it is just fifty thousand. What the hell, that's just change. But you got to throw in the airplane for me and that's another three thousand." I leaned down toward her. "Where, exactly, do you plan to get that kind of money? I know you are dying to be a ministering angel but the price comes kind of high these days."

She lifted her head so that her fine, slim neck showed itself to good advantage. From somewhere she produced a cigarette in a long holder and lit it with a gold lighter. She blew out a cloud of white smoke and said, "My unfortunate divorce, happily, left me with certain financial rewards."

I threw my arms wide and gritted my teeth. "You are crazy. At least, you are acting crazy. I don't know how much money you got. I'm sure you were worth every dollar your ex-husband gave you. But there are better ways to spend it! Look around you. This country don't look poor by accident, it's the way God intended. There ain't no oil around here. I've only been in the oil business a few months but I know there ain't no oil under this sand and rocks. You could drill to China and not find enough oil to grease a gate hinge."

She blew smoke up into the air. "No," she said quietly, "but there is water. Artesian well water, according to your letters. You said you could make the desert bloom like a garden with one or two more water wells. Atlas is too stupid to know what he has. So is your friend Dennis. But I told you I had been to this country before. I understand it."

She had me baffled. I plainly did not understand this woman. I knew she was older than I was, but by how much, I couldn't have said. But, judging from her plans, not much. I sat down by her on the porch steps. I said, "Genevieve, there are plenty of better ways to waste your money than sinking it into this poor, rocky land. You could be talking seventy-five thousand dollars here, and that is a hell of a lot of money—I don't care how fast you say it."

She took my face in both her hands and gave me a gentle kiss. Then she said, "Honey, I want you to do two things: Go back to your oil camp and tell Teddy Atlas there is a lady in town who wants to talk some business with him, and ask Dennis how much money Atlas is out. Now, you can do that?"

I was kind of hurt. I had thought she had come to see me because of missing me and wanting to see me. Instead she had a head full of business. She wasn't interested in me as much as she was in a drill bit. I said, with a trace of bite in my voice, "Hell, can't you see it's dark? I can't land out there in the middle of the desert. There are no landing lights or any recognition lights of any kind."

She still had my face in her hands. I think she could feel my bitterness. She said, "The faster we get the business project out of the way, the faster we can go on to other things. Willis, I know you could fly an airplane in a hailstorm if you had to. Now, be a good boy and go on back tonight. You've got a good moon to see by to land."

I sighed. She was right about the moon. I said, gruffly, "Who the hell am I supposed to tell Atlas you are?"

She smiled prettily. "You'll think of something. I *wouldn't* let him understand we knew each other before. I have some names in the oil business I can impress him with."

I left Pecos that night a torn man. I could easily recollect my delight and happiness as I'd flown to see her. I'd thought then that she'd changed her mind and was coming to see me. But now it seemed there were other motives. It made me shake my head with the pain of the matter. It never failed; as soon as you started to care, the bulldog of misfortune would jump up and bite you in the ass.

Of course, I had no trouble landing. There was twice as much moonlight as I needed. I flared the airplane out near the ground, let it settle, feeling for the ground, felt it, and then let it glide along to where I usually parked it.

I got out stiffly, not tired so much as just kind of stove-up mentally. I was putting on the engine cover when I saw a light headed my way. It was Dennis carrying a lantern. He said, worriedly, "Boy, do you know what time it is?"

"Naw. I don't carry a watch."

"Well, you better start. It be after ten o'clock. Mr. Atlas is going to be almighty curious what you are doing out half the night in his airplane."

"Got lost and had to make an emergency landing." I tied the last canvas in place. "Let's get inside, we got some talking to do. I got news."

"Good?"

I shrugged. "Depends who you are and how you look at it."

We sat down and Dennis asked me if I'd really had to make an emergency landing in the desert at night. I gave him a look. "The story is for Mr. Teddy Atlas, dimwit. Listen, something big has happened and I don't quite know how to tell you about it. I want to put it in the proper light so you'll see the potential."

He was all eager, leaning forward off the camp chair he was sitting on. He said, "Well, tell me. Just come out with it."

"Do you remember that young lady I met in Galveston, and then later kind of courted while we were in Houston?"

"Sure. Real pretty, and a real lady. You took her flying. Now, what was her name? You said she'd been divorced from an oilman worked for one of the big majors. Don't tell me, it's coming."

"Genevieve," I said.

He snapped his fingers. "Yeah, Genevieve. It was right on the tip of my tongue. What about her?"

"She's in town, in Pecos."

He slapped his knee. "Well, good for you. No wonder you took out of here today like a bobcat with his tail on fire. That's quite something, her coming all this way to see you."

I said, a little bitterly, "She didn't just come to see me."

"Of course she did. You don't take a chance staying gone in Mr. Atlas's airplane for any other reason. Which, by the way, you are going to have to explain to him in the morning. The 'emergency landing' is good. So what about Genevieve?"

"I think a white knight has arrived to save us from the dragon named Teddy Atlas, except she's a woman."

"What are you talking about?"

"Genevieve. She's making noises like she plans to buy Atlas out."

He pulled his head a long way back and looked at me like I was telling bedtime stories. Finally he said, "We talking about the same woman?"

"Yeah, yeah, and yeah." I gave him a quick background about her interest in the area, most of which I was making up. I did not tell him that she was more interested in water than oil. Dennis was a crude man—oil, that is—and he wouldn't feel like he was being rescued if the idea was to pump water and make a lake.

He got out a whiskey bottle, late as it was, and poured himself a stiff one. I declined. He spent about half the glass thinking matters over. Finally he slapped his thigh. He said, "Willis, I don't figure this lady for a businesswoman out to make a buck. She's got some money out of her ex-husband and she figures to spend it on her new honey. You."

"Thanks for the flattering description. I don't think she is spending it on me. Listen to me, Dennis. I think this woman knows what she is doing. For instance, she wants me to find out exactly how much money Atlas has advanced you."

"The hell you say!"

"Yeah, and when she talks about the rock formations out here she sounds like she knows what she's talking about. She's made a guess about how much your contract calls for and how much you'd get on completion of a test well. Hell, I never heard the term, 'test well.' What does it mean?"

Dennis rubbed his chin. "It means she ain't no boll weevil. No greenhorn. She knows what she's talking about. How does she plan on going about this?"

"I'm supposed to tell Teddy Atlas that there is a businessperson in town who wants to talk to him."

"How did you get the word?"

"There was a note sent to the camp. I misinterpreted it and thought it was for me. So I flew in, only to find this person wanted to see Mr. Atlas."

"You ain't going to tell him she's a girlfriend of yours?"

"You better lay off that cheap whiskey, Dennis. Makes you ask stupid questions."

He stood up and put his empty glass down. "So, what are you going to do?"

"What is there to do? I'll tell Atlas in the morning that a business-person wants to talk business with him. Then I'll fly him in."

"If he'll go."

"Genevieve said she bet Atlas was dying to get out of this deal. She said she figured he'd sell at a sacrifice."

Dennis rubbed the bristles on his chin. He looked older standing there in his droopy underwear. "Well, I don't care one way or the other.

All I want to do is drill holes in the ground and try and find oil. It's what I do. Like you're a pilot. So I don't care who the moneyman, or -woman, in this case, is. What'd she guess Atlas was in for?"

"Fifty thousand."

Dennis nodded. "She is pretty good. That would have been an accurate guess if we weren't way the hell out here in nowhere. Atlas is on the hook for seventy thousand. The whole contract, as you know, is a hundred and a quarter, but I never had no hope of seeing the rest. If she can buy him out, that means I get to keep my string of tools."

"That's right."

He shook his head. "This is too much for me in the middle of the night with a derrick to tear down tomorrow. Tell me when things clear up. I'm going to bed. G'night."

"Good night," I said. I sat down on my bunk but I made no move to get undressed and get in bed. I was not at all sure how I felt about Genevieve's mission of mercy. I was adult enough not to be hurt that I wasn't the only reason for her visit, but I wouldn't have minded if she'd've been a little more interested in my company. And now I was going to have to pimp for her with Teddy Atlas. That could be dangerous. If he were to get it into his head that I was in some kind of league with her and was helping her with information or something, he might turn Leon loose on me to unsteady my head from my shoulders. I thought back on our conversations, brief as they had been, it seemed, to make sure that she would act like we had never met before. Atlas seemed to have a natural air of suspicion about him. He was always looking into matters and asking questions and poking his nose here and there. You can get away with that sort of progress if you've got someone like Leon around to take care of you. The thought of Leon irritated me. It wasn't right for a prizefighter, even if he was retired, to hang one on you when you weren't looking and had no expectation of being hit. It wouldn't have been a fair fight straight-up and facing each other with a timer and a referee unless I'd had a gun, much less the son of a bitch going to the unnecessary expedient of sucker-punching me. I got into bed, thinking about Leon and Atlas and Genevieve and Dennis. It seemed to me that life was getting uncommonly complicated. I wondered, as I lay down and adjusted my head to my makeshift pillow, what my daddy would have done in such circumstances. Pulled out a gun and changed a few attitudes, no doubt. But those days were over. Private wars were a thing of the past. Now you needed the government behind you if you wanted to have a war. Then it was fine; you could kill as many on the other side as you liked.

CHAPTER
18

TEDDY ATLAS looked at me in that suspicious way he had, and said, "What? What are you talking about?"

"Well, sir," I said, "like I was telling you, a message came out from town yesterday, asking for someone to come in and meet this businessperson. Wasn't no more details than that. So me being free, I thought I'd just fly into town and see what was up."

He gave me a sour glance. "In my airplane. Without asking."

I said, not letting any humor into my voice, "You was going to use it? I didn't know. No, sir, I should have never taken it if I'd known you'd be taking her up."

"Oh, shut up, Young," he said irritably. "We know you're the only pilot. But why didn't you speak to me about it?"

"You looked pretty busy, Mr. Atlas. I believe you were explaining to those roughnecks how to take down an oil derrick. I didn't want to interrupt. They all looked like they were learning so much from your instructions."

He turned around and looked at Leon and then he looked at me. He said, "Are you getting smart with me, Young?"

I shook my head. "Heavens, no. *I* don't know nothing about dismantling oil derricks. So I can claim ignorance of being smart."

I didn't want to keep on talking about taking down the derrick. Something very important was on the verge of getting decided, without Mr. Atlas being aware of it. There were about thirty stands of pipe down in the hole, not counting the outside casing pipe. Once you tore down the derrick you couldn't pull that pipe up. You needed a derrick with a crown block in the top and a cable that would attach to the stand of the pipe, run over the crown block and then down to the draw works on the drilling platform floor. Tear down the derrick and that artesian well would be gushing from here on out. That morning Dennis had proclaimed his intentions of leaving the pipe in the hole if Atlas persisted in moving the rig. Dennis had said, "Hell, I know I'm an oil driller, and that's a lot of pipe to leave in the ground for just water, but the way things are looking, Teddy Atlas is going to own that pipe shortly. I'd like to think I produced something for this long trip even if it is just water." He'd growled, "Ought to make you and them other groundhogs out there happy. I just hope your little angel can pull off a miracle. Meanwhile I'll stall moving the rig all I can."

Atlas was still not convinced I wasn't being uppity with him, but he said, irritation in his voice, "Well, who is this businessman? What the hell is it all about? Why should I go into town to see him? If he wants to talk business he can damn well come to where I am."

I didn't exactly relish telling him who was awaiting him in town, mainly because I didn't want Genevieve within a hundred miles of such as the likes of Teddy Atlas. But I finally came out with it. I said, "It's not a man, Mr. Atlas. It's a woman. A woman in the oil business. I guess she figured you'd understand her not wanting to come out to an oil camp, rough as it is."

He was surprised, but was not one to let it show. He said, "A woman? Out here on this frontier? She must be a lunatic. Fly right back into town and tell her I got no time for such foolishness. A woman. Hell!"

"She's not exactly a woman, Mr. Atlas. More like a lady."

"I'll just bet. What she knows about the oil business you could put in a pipe and smoke it."

I said, slowly, "Maybe so, I don't know. But she mentioned that her ex-husband was a high-up official with the Texaco company. Ain't that one of the big majors?"

He didn't answer, just frowned.

I said, "She give me to understand she got some money and knowledge about the oil business from her ex-husband.

He gave me a quick look. "Think she's got money?"

"I guess. I questioned her pretty closely, being like you, a little suspicious if she wasn't off her rocker. But I found out pretty quick that she knows more about the oil business than I do."

"That doesn't mean anything," he said. He stared off into the distance for a moment, thinking. He said, "What does she look like?"

It was not a question I wanted to answer. I hesitated, and finally said, "She's presentable."

"Young . . . old?"

I swallowed. "Youngish side."

"And you think she's got money?"

"Well, she didn't shy away from the subject. She talks in the thousands, if that is what you mean. But, shoot, she seen right off I was just a messenger boy. She tried to bleed me, but she found out right quick that the only thing I had to give was ignorance."

Atlas looked up at the sky, as if it changed from one day to the next, or month to month, for that matter. Then he looked around at Leon as if there were some answer there in the ex-prizefighter's face. It looked empty to me. Atlas heaved a great sigh. "Well, we might as well go in right now. Maybe we can make it in and back before lunch."

"We could have lunch in town. Beats this place."

Atlas brightened. "Yeah. That's a good idea. Go in and have a steak and a cold beer. There'll be nothing to this woman businessman, but it won't matter. I'll be glad to get out of here for a few hours." We were standing in the front of the town of tents. He had a clear view of the desolate desert. He said, "Tell you what, I'll go and have a shave and a wash-up. Might even change clothes." He gave me a wink. "You never know what business me and that lady might get up to."

I gritted my teeth but didn't say anything other than that we had plenty of time since it was still the morning hours.

Atlas turned to Leon. He said, "I want you to stay here and see how they get on with tearing down that derrick. Don't let these people bamboozle you. Remember, you speak for me. Keep them at work. No nonsense."

"Yes sir," Leon said. He put his hands behind his back and looked down at the ground.

I said, "Maybe I'll just have a wash, too, Mr. Atlas. I'll see you at the airplane."

I was already cleaned-up and dressed as well as I could be from the day before, but I ran a razor over my face even if it didn't need it. I was light-haired and light-complected and I didn't have to shave as often as blackbeards like Dennis.

I came out of my tent and started down toward the airplane. The route would take me by the boilers and then by the rig before I reached the airplane. There was a stack of scrap wood left over from building the derrick, that was mounded up near the boilers. On the other side of it, staring out at the desert and apparently taking a piss, stood Leon, looking as if he hadn't a care in the world. I quickly cut behind the mound of scrap wood, coming up behind Leon. Joe Cairo, tending his boilers, was in sight but he wasn't looking my way. No one was. Leon was still looking out in the desert, shaking his member as a man would shake the dew off a lily. I spotted a piece of lumber, a four-foot length of two-by-four pine that reminded me somewhat of a bat. I picked it up swiftly. Any second, Leon was going to turn around. I took two, three, four soft steps in his direction, drawing back my billet as I did, and then, when I was in reach to strike, I swung that piece of wood as hard as I could. I caught him just at the base of the skull at the back of his head. He never made a sound, but that wood meeting the back of his head made a very satisfying *thunk*. Leon never looked back, up, or sideways. Without a sound he just pitched forward on his face in the desert sand. I glanced around. There was no one watching except

Joe Cairo. He was standing in front of his boiler, grinning. He lifted a thumb to me and nodded. I gave him a thumbs-up in return and then turned and quickly made my way toward the airplane. I thought it would be a few minutes before Leon would be getting up. I knew for certain that Joe Cairo wasn't going to help him.

I had the canvas covering off the airplane and had her checked out by the time Teddy Atlas arrived. I'd watched him as he'd come walking up the path from the tents. He'd glanced over at the rig to see how work was going. I already knew. Dennis had a full crew busying themselves around the structure but not a lick of work was being done. Atlas had just sent a little frown toward the derrick, and kept on to the airplane. He was dressed pretty much as I was: white shirt, whip-cord jodhpurs, and riding boots. But there the comparison stopped. His had cost ten times as much as mine and were ten times newer.

He came up to the plane and looked around. "Are you ready?"

I gave him a little salute. He liked that sort of stuff. "Ready to go, sir."

He looked around again. "I wonder where Leon is?"

"I thought I heard you tell him to look after things here."

"So I did, so I did. But I at least thought he'd come down to see me off."

"Well, it's just a short trip, sir. Likely he's occupied." I wasn't doing all this ass-kissing for no good reason. I had a plan.

He started climbing in the front cockpit. "Likely so," he said. "Likely so. Well, let's go get this business over with. Money business most likely."

I reached into the cockpit and set the ignition and contact and then went around and spun the prop. It wasn't a job Mr. Atlas would lower himself to. When the engine was running smoothly I went around the wing and climbed in the rear cockpit. Looking back I could see Dennis standing on the drilling-platform floor, staring our way. I said, raising my voice a little to talk over the engine, "Did you tell Dennis where we were going and what for?"

He turned around and gave me a look. "Of course not. What business is it of his?"

I shrugged. "None, I guess." Then I glanced back over my shoulder as I let the airplane begin to roll forward. I didn't know how long Leon would be out, but I had no interest in seeing him any too soon. I pushed the throttle forward and went hurtling over the desert until the plane lifted off. I turned back to my right instead of left as I usually did, and flew over the camp. I saw the pile of wood, and a figure lying on the ground. It had to be Leon. He wasn't moving. I could see Joe Cairo going about his business. He didn't seem concerned. As I climbed for altitude I wondered if I'd killed Leon. I really hoped that I hadn't, though not out of fear of earthly punishment. I just didn't like the idea of killing a man in such an underhanded way. It seemed like something that Teddy Atlas would do.

I took up my residence in the Mex cafe to await Mr. Atlas's completion of his business. Once I'd given him her name and where she could be found, he'd made it clear that I wouldn't be wanted until we started for home. He didn't believe I could perform any useful function in the introductions since, according to my own testimony, I was viewed by the "woman of business" as just an errand boy. He'd enlist the sheriff's help to show him to his house and provide his bona fides.

It suited me. I had no desire to see him around Genevieve; I had no desire to see any man around Genevieve, but especially a man of his stripe. I found myself wishing it had been Atlas I'd hit instead of Leon.

It was too early for lunch, and I'd already had breakfast, so there was nothing to do but sit around and drink beer. Every five minutes I'd wonder what they were talking about and why it was taking so long. By rights he should have told her straight off he had nothing for sale and hustled on back. The longer he was at the sheriff's house, the wilder my imagination got. His kind of sleek, suave, turtlenecked rich-boy good looks probably appealed to women. Women didn't want an honest man, in spite of what they might say; they wanted a flash in the pan who could give them things. Things, that was all women wanted. I said it in my head the way I'd heard the deep-west-Texas men talk. *Thangs.*

But Genevieve wasn't after "thangs" or things or anything else that most women coveted. She was different. I'd known that from the very first. But exactly in what way she was different, I wasn't sure. Was she different enough to want a mess like myself? That remained to be seen. As near as I could figure, her visit was strictly business, though how it had come about, I figured to go to my grave trying to understand.

Finally the sheriff showed up. He stood in the door a moment until he could see me through the dim, and then made his way over to my table. He said, "Well, you resting easy?"

I shoved a chair out for him with my boot. "Sit down, Sheriff, and tell me what in hell is going on."

He let himself down, taking off his hat as he dropped. "Well, I don't know what they are up to, but they are giving it a good talking-over. I didn't hear 'em directly, but they was each sparring for a point."

I said, with a little quiver in my breast, "Did you get a look at them?"

He shook his head slightly. "Not directly, but I got a glance through the window as I was going down the front steps."

I asked him, too vigorously, "Were they sitting next to each other? Were they close?"

He gave me a strange look. "No. They was clean on opposite sides of the room from one another. What's the matter with you, Willis? I thought one of them was your moneyman and the lady was, uh, well, more friendly."

I ducked my head. "Yeah. Yeah. I don't know why I asked such a question."

The sheriff looked uncomfortable. He said, "Well, ain't none of my business what is going on here." He pushed himself up from his chair. "I reckon I better get on over to my office. Folks might be looking for me."

He left and then I waited. Finally, around two P.M., the lord and master himself showed up. He'd eaten lunch at the sheriff's (with my girl) so he wasn't hungry, but he did want a beer. I sat and listened, burning inside, while he described what had transpired.

He gave a good, deft laugh after he'd sat down. Then he had a swig of beer and wiped his mouth. He said, "She hadn't an idea, laddie, not an idea. Ha, ha, ha."

He laughed like he expected me to join him. He laughed like we were on the same team. It was all I could do to keep him thinking that. "Yeah, what'd she say?"

He took another drink and laughed again. He said, "It was what she didn't say, my boy. She knows no more about the oil business than you do. And God knows, that's not much. I'm halfway tempted to sell her my whole interest for a half. That puts me in the play for fifty percent and all my money back. What do you think?"

I thought I would like to hit him across the face with my beer mug, but I just ducked my head and said, "That's nice."

He said, "Oh, by the way . . . She wants a word with you. Something about flying her over the lease so she can get an idea of the extent of the thing. If you're finished here, why don't you run along and speak to her? About one more beer and I'll be ready to go back to the camp. Had an awfully good lunch at the sheriff's. Hope you made out as well."

I strolled out of the cafe and then I walked as rapidly as I could to the sheriff's house, about three hundred yards away. I didn't bother to knock or twist the doorbell. I wanted to see Genevieve and I wanted to see her fast. As I was pushing the door open, she was on the other side pulling it. When she had me in view she said, "Willis Young, have you finally taken leave of your senses?"

Standing there in the front hallway I said, "No, but I'd sure as hell like to know what you been talking to that blond-haired son of a bitch for four hours about!"

She put her hand on my forehead. "No, you don't have a fever. I guess you *are* nuts."

"Listen—" I said. She glanced over her shoulder to see that we were still alone. We were still in the entrance hall. She said, "Don't make a bigger idiot out of yourself than you already are. I hope to hell you didn't let this boyish anger spill over on Atlas."

"Listen," I said, "who the hell you think I am? Of course I didn't—"

But she put her hand across my mouth. "Yes, darling, I know you didn't. But we only have so much time here. Even your ignorant Mr. Atlas might catch on. Now, listen to me."

"What?" I sounded to myself like an ignorant messenger boy.

"I have told him that there are laws governing unexplored areas in the state of Texas that pertain to oil. I told him there were certain duties and levies pertaining to those areas where no drilling within a wide radius had occurred before. I told him I had consulted a lawyer."

"Did you?"

She gave me a despairing look. "Oh, for God's sake, Willis, you told me you had some influence with the justice of the peace here. Put this bug in his ear and have him start paying visits out to the drilling rig. Tell him the levy is twenty-five cents a barrel and the drilling permit is a thousand dollars."

"Will he believe it?—not the justice of the peace; he'll believe anything. But Atlas?"

She wrapped her arms around my neck and kissed me. She said, "Go, dearest, go. He's coming along but I've got a few more surprises in store for him. Tell him you have to come back tomorrow to take me over the lease. Now fly. Go, go, go."

The next thing I knew, I was standing outside, wondering what had just happened. I shouted back at the door, "Am I supposed to wise up the JP today or tomorrow?"

She said, cracking the door, "Tomorrow, of course. When you come in for me."

I left, not knowing what to think.

When we were in the airplane and the engine was idling, prior to me opening the throttle and leaving Pecos, Teddy Atlas made several statements that came as near as not to ending his life. He turned around in the forward cockpit and looked back at me. He said, "She wasn't bad, did you think? Sort of a drape shape, but I could see a body in there and it looked pretty good."

I gripped the stick and didn't say anything.

He said, "Actually, she looks younger than you told me. Takes the discerning eye, I guess. I might flavor this deal with a little Humpty-Dumpty, if you know what I mean."

I shoved home the throttle and the airplane responded so that it jerked his head back. I would have liked to have jerked it off. But, for the time being, I would hold my peace and let events take their course.

Dennis asked me that night what was going on but, for the life of me, I couldn't tell him anything constructive.

He looked mournful. He said, "We got some drilling done while Atlas was in town but I didn't make no progress except to wear out another drill bit. Say!" He suddenly snapped his fingers out in front of him. "Listen, did you know, while y'all was gone, that somebody whacked that big Leon with a piece of lumber right in the back of the head. Bastard was goofy as ol' Shorty McGinnis on a drunk for a couple of hours. We finally put him to bed and he slept it off. But somebody— and I imagine you wish it was you—coldcocked the hell out of old Leon. Found him lying over there by that pile of odds and ends we didn't use on the derrick. Found the very plank he was hit with. Was a *dent* in it. Imagine that."

I said, casually, "Didn't Joe Cairo know who done it?"

"Naw. Besides, you know Joe. He ain't much of a talker, especially about another man's business."

"Yeah," I said, "That's good."

"Nobody liked Leon. But he sure wasn't in no shape to come around checking on us. You sure ain't no more you can tell me about what happened in Pecos today?"

I shook my head. "Not now. Maybe I'll know more tomorrow, but I doubt it." I told him what Genevieve had told me to tell Judge Crater.

His mouth fell open. "Well, hell, why would she do that to us? I done paid that old turkey every cent he is going to get."

"No, no, no," I said. "She is not siccing him on you, but on Teddy Atlas. She wants to make the lease look less valuable. Of course, there are no such fines and levies, but Atlas won't know and the judge don't care. She wants him to come after Atlas like shearing sheep."

I flew into town early enough the next day so that I could have lunch at the sheriff's house. Genevieve looked a treat in a white organdy gown, but I felt a little stiffish around her. She asked me what was the matter and I said I felt like she was putting a little too much personality in her dealings with Teddy Atlas.

"Oh, Lord," she said, "how can you be jealous of that lounge lizard? If he was much more of a phony snob, I wouldn't be able to go through with this. Now, you just stop talking like that. This business is hard enough without stopping every five minutes to hold your hand. Have you been to see the judge yet, like I told you?"

"Well, no, not exactly. I thought I'd come up here and have a word with you and see when lunch was going to be."

"Lunch isn't for an hour. You prance on along and see the judge, now. Don't make it too obvious. I just want you to plant the seed. I'm trying to put pressure on Atlas. He is still far too proud of that drilling contract. He's an idiot, and that is the toughest kind to deal with."

I went on down past the sheriff's office and was lucky enough to find Judge Crater in. He was sitting tilted back in his chair with his black town hat on the back of his head. He brought his chair down smartly enough when he saw me. He said, his voice rumbling, "I see you are back with that aeroplane. I reckon you are forgetting a small matter."

I had six dollars out and ready to hand to him. He took it when I put it within his reach. I said, "I'm mighty sorry about that, Judge. Fact is, this new financier of all of our business was supposed to be handling such matters, and I found out he was letting them go."

Crater said, "No way to run a company. No, sir. Business is business and debts get taken care of on time."

I had surprised him by docilely coming in and paying my landing fees. It was the first time I'd ever done so. I said, "Well, sorry about that. I sure hope he knows about the dues and levies on unproven oil property. We could lose our lease if he let that slip."

He looked up sharply. "What's that? What's that you say? What levies? What dues, what taxes?"

I shrugged and leaned up against the wall. I said, "I'm surprised you wasn't on top of this. Oil drilling took off so fast in Texas that the first bunch never paid a dime in taxes to the local authorities. Oh, the state and federal boys got them later on at the pipeline and the refinery, but the local taxing district never seen a nickel. So with the drilling spreading, the local authorities have the right to levy a duty of about a quarter for every foot drilled. Or a flat twenty-five hundred dollars, whichever is greater."

He spit tobacco in a stained spittoon and eyed me with great interest. "Who the local authorities supposed to collect this fee offen? Would he have a name or a title?"

I said, sounding innocent, "Well, it is the man putting up the money, the backer. Ain't no use going after the drilling contractor because he hasn't got any money. And as it happens, our backer has just come into town about a week ago. You met him; he was the one give you the fifty-dollar bill."

"Oh, yeah," the judge said, rocking his head back and forth. A shifty gleam was coming into his eyes. "What was that gentleman's name?"

"Atlas, Teddy Atlas. He owns everything."

"An' you say they is a flat fee of twenty-five hunnert dollars?"

I nodded. "Exactly that. And I think this district ought to get it."

"When's he coming back into town?"

I shook my head and looked disapproving. "You don't want to hit him up here. Not the first time. You want to go out to the well so you can see the work in progress and challenge him right there. Later on, if you have trouble, you can nail him here in town."

He thought that over for a moment and then looked up at me. He said, "How is it you come to have this information? Is it reliable?"

"Oh, yes," I said, nodding. "I had occasion to make a long distance telephone call up to east Texas. That's where the big action is right now. Spoke with an expert. Oh, yes, this information is right on the money."

He got up and marched across the floor of his small office and patted me on the shoulder. "My boy, you ain't got no idea how proud this makes me, seein' you doin' your duty. I started out thinkin' you was gonna be a troublemaker, but I see you come around to the right way of thinking."

I said, trying to look modest, "I'm glad to help however I can, Judge. Was I you, though, I wouldn't put this off. Our moneyman could leave town any day and that would just leave poor old Dennis Frank, who hasn't got a nickel to his name."

The judge patted me again. "You are thinking right, son, thinking right. And I tell you what I'm going to do." He still had the six dollars crumpled in his hand. He said, and I could see the debate raging on his face, "I'm—Well, I'm going to give you a dollar back. And, by golly, the next two landings is free. What do you think of that?"

I had to admit I was overwhelmed. And I was. For the judge to part with so much as a dollar was a monumental change in fundamental character. "What can I say, Judge? You're the law, and the law is to be admired and obeyed. And respected."

"You're thinking right, son, thinking right."

I got back to the sheriff's house in time to finally sit down to a civilized lunch. We had fried pork chops that had been rolled in seasoned cornmeal, and fresh vegetables, and iced tea to drink. It was as well as I'd eaten since I'd come west. Sitting there, eating that good food and looking at Genevieve, the place didn't seem so bad—especially looking at Genevieve. It was odd to think back to a frame of mind that said I could take her or leave her. I must have been awfully scared to protect myself like that. But I wasn't scared anymore. I might not win, but I was going to put up one hell of a fight.

They let us have the parlor to ourselves after lunch. The sheriff went on back to his office and his wife said pointedly that she would be busy upstairs for some little time.

But with all that freedom, Genevieve didn't have much to say. She listened to my report and what I'd told the judge, and approved. She said it sounded hopeful. She had unbuttoned the top buttons of her dress so that some creamy skin that looked like it had been lightly toasted was revealed. It made me get a copper taste in my mouth and become uncomfortably aware of my manhood.

She wouldn't talk about how her negotiations with Atlas had gone except to remark that he now knew she was for real and a serious buyer. "But," she said, "it's going to slow matters down while he learns that I didn't come out here to be suckered by him."

I still couldn't get it straight in my head that she'd come all this way to bid on a worthless oil well. I asked her again to tell me where the negotiations were with Atlas—namely, price.

She sidestepped that. "We're not down to talking specifics. He needs to find out he's got a loser. We'll just have to wait and see."

"Wait and see." I had first heard that from my mother, and then from every other woman I was involved with. I was convinced they started saying it in the cradle. No matter what you wanted, it was always "Wait and see." I knew this woman was slightly older than me, but not enough to pull that "Wait and see" business.

I said, "Have you really got this kind of money?"

She raised her eyebrows. "I should hope so. Giving bad checks is against the law."

I sat down on the couch beside her and kissed her on that creamy patch of skin I could see. She immediately pushed me back. "You can't be the boyfriend right now, Willis. In fact, you've been here too long. We don't want people getting the wrong idea. It wouldn't take long for Mr. Atlas to smell a rat. Besides, you are supposed to fly me over the rig. Let me go change clothes and put on a linen duster and we'll go."

I stood there with a dissatisfied look on my face while she dashed upstairs. This was not going at all the way I'd planned. I stood there fuming until she came back down wearing a long gray cotton duster and a tight-fitting hat like a beret. I caught her at the front door. I said, "Damn it, Genevieve, what about us?"

She gave my hand a pat and said, "We'll see. But right now let's go look at that rig. I need to spot something to make Mr. Atlas see he's being a fool."

I followed her out the door mumbling to myself. She looked around. "What?"

I said, "I was wondering if Atlas wasn't the only one. Being a fool."

"Now, don't be silly. And hurry up. I am really looking forward to flying with you again."

We were walking down the street. I said, "That's not what I really want to be doing with you." And before she could open her mouth, I said, "And don't say 'We'll see.' "

Somehow I had lost my superior position of casual indifference to any commitment stronger than the next meeting, if there was to be one. I had, somehow—either through the loneliness of the desert or the desperation of my own soul—come to need this woman, and I knew, through intuition and personal experience, that neediness is not attractive. I would have to find a way to regain my old studied aloofness, my plainspoken elegance, my willingness to be sought but never to be the seeker.

When we flew over the rig I could see Dennis get up from his driller's seat and come to the edge of the platform and wave. Someone—Dennis, I figured—had persuaded Atlas that, with a prospective buyer looking them over they ought to look like a working oil well. Tearing down the derrick would sort of destroy the myth. At least, if nothing else, Genevieve was buying us a little more time to keep the water well flowing.

She turned in her seat and yelled something back at me. The engine noise and the wind tore her words away. I cut the throttle and then pulled the airplane up into a slight climb so that our speed dropped rapidly.

"What?" I yelled.

"That is a lot of water coming out of that well."

"I told you it was an artesian spring."

We didn't have but a half a moment. The plane was already wobbling into the edge of a stall. She said, "Atlas is a dope if he doesn't realize what he's got." Then she turned back around to the front and

I put the nose of the airplane over to gain some flying speed before we went into a spin.

When we landed back in Pecos I declined to walk back to the sheriff's house with her. She studied my face for a moment. "What's the matter with you? You act like you're pouting about something."

It was an opening I was not going to use. I said, slowly, shaking my head, "I don't know what I've got to pout about. You've come down here to save us. Last night Dennis referred to you as an angel and I don't think he was but halfway kidding."

She gave me one of her bright smiles. "But of course, you don't believe in angels."

"Not the heavenly kind, if that is what you mean."

"Just what do you believe in, Willis?"

I thought about it for a moment. "You don't really want an answer to that. You want to see if I can come up with some snappy answer like I believe in what I can see and feel and drink."

She nodded her head in the general direction of the rig. "That water—that water that is coming out of that well. That's just water to you, isn't it?"

"Well, it's wetter than a horseshoe or a saddle blanket. Yeah, it's water."

"Maybe it's more than just water. And maybe you were sent all the way out here so that it would be more than just water."

"You are not making much sense."

"I know you've been exposed to the Bible, because you told me so."

I shrugged. "I wasn't old enough to defend myself and my mother was determined. I went to Sunday school."

"Then you'll remember the story in John four when Jesus went to the well where the woman of ill repute was."

I groaned. I said, "Oh, don't you start, too. I get enough of this from Dennis."

She said, steadfastly, "If you drink from the water of Christ you will never thirst again."

"I'm not thirsty now," I said desperately. "It's just an artesian well,

Genevieve. Is that what has brought you into this thing? You think we are not turning out Christian water here?"

She smiled sweetly at me. "Someday Christ will take you in and you'll look back on these days and wonder how you got by without Him."

I said, "Listen, you never talked like this before. We danced and we drank and we had a laugh. What the hell is going on?"

"I still do those things," she said. "But I've been drinking the Lord's water a lot longer. You forget that I'm the daughter of an east Texas Baptist preacher." She said the last over her shoulder as she walked away, heading for the sheriff's house.

I said, "Wait a minute." A great unrest was churning inside me. "Are you an angel? I'm not kidding. Are you?"

She said, from ten yards away, "Bring Mr. Atlas in in the morning. We've got to get moving on this before the damn idiot orders the derrick torn down."

"Yeah, but are you an angel? You are scaring the hell out of me."

"Just have faith in Jesus and you'll never be scared."

"I don't know who Jesus is."

"But He knows who you are." She turned away again, but then stopped and called back again. "Don't worry about us. You and I. We'll be all right. Just get Atlas in here in the morning. He's going to ask you a lot of questions about what I said, but you don't know anything."

I watched as she walked on up the street, going past the Mexican cafe and toward the sheriff's house. Then I turned around, started the engine of the airplane, and flew back to the rig.

She had been right about Teddy Atlas questioning me. I hadn't no more than got the airplane tied down and covered up, than he was all over me. "What'd she say about the deal? She going to take my price?"

I just shrugged. "Mr. Atlas, I'm just the messenger boy to her. She asked me if I was a good pilot and she asked me how deep the well was. I told her yes to the first question and that I didn't know to the second. Oh, yeah, she wanted to know what we were drilling through. I'd heard somebody say something about limestone so I told her that. I also told her we had the water licked."

Teddy Atlas looked pleased. He clapped me on the shoulder and then dug in his pocket and handed me a ten-dollar bill. I didn't want it but I felt it would be out of character to refuse. I took it and pocketed it while Leon looked on wolfishly. He still looked like a man who'd had the hell knocked out of him.

Atlas said, "Good man. You keep on listening to every word she says and don't tell her anything about our business. What'd she think of the operation from the air?"

"She said she was glad to see the water still flowing because she knew that made the drilling easier."

"She said that?" Atlas put his hand to his mouth and laughed silently. He said, "This is almost going to be too easy."

That night Dennis and I sat talking in our tent. We were at the table and we both had a full tumbler of whiskey in front of us. Dennis said, anxiously, "You think she's going to buy the drilling contract?"

I shrugged. "I don't know. But I'll tell you this: She might be an angel. I mean, a real one."

He pulled his head back. "Go on with you!"

"I'm serious. We were having a prayer meeting right out there in the middle of the street. She recommended John four to me. Said I'd understand about Jesus from that."

He looked thoughtful. "John four. Doesn't come right to mind."

"It's about Jesus at a well with a woman, and they have a conversation about living water, or water where you won't thirst anymore. I'm telling you, she was talking like that right out in the big middle of everybody."

"Oh, sure," he said, nodding. " 'Twas the Samaritan woman." He frowned. "That's a passing strange passage to be quoting."

I thought it was about time he knew. Maybe he'd change his mind about what he wanted to do. "Dennis," I said, "you better keep what I'm going to tell you under your hat. But I believe she is more interested in water than oil."

He stopped with his glass halfway to his mouth. He looked distressed. He said, "Oh, surely not, Willis. You've misunderstood."

"I don't think so."

He looked upset for a moment but then he shrugged and took a jolt of whiskey. "I just want to keep on drilling. I got a pretty good hunch Mr. Atlas is going to shut me down and take my tools for nonperformance. I need that contract in kinder hands. And Miss Genevieve is surely that."

It was my turn to look distressed. I said, "Maybe, in some things. But she damn sure ain't laid a kind hand on me."

CHAPTER
19

WE WERE right in the middle of breakfast in the cook tent when the damnedest commotion I'd heard since the war, broke out outside. Dennis looked up from his tin plate of scrambled eggs. "What in hell?"

I got up. "Somebody ain't happy. And they are letting the world know it."

We broke for the door. It was late and only a few other men were in the tent. They joined us as we went outside. The first thing I saw was the judge's Reo coupe. It was parked right in the midst of the tents. Then I saw the judge. And Teddy Atlas and Leon, and the sheriff. The judge was shaking his finger in Teddy Atlas's face and threatening him with jail and prison and multiple fines and time on the chain gang if he did not immediately ante up the amount required. Teddy Atlas was holding a paper, trying to study it and looking more than a little confused. Leon was looking hard at the judge, especially when the judge's finger came dangerously close to hitting Atlas in the face, and Lew Wallace was watching Leon, with his hand resting lightly on the butt of his revolver.

I had told Dennis about what was to happen the night before, so he was not at all surprised. If anything, he was gleeful at the prospect of seeing someone else catch it from the judge. He turned to me and said, "Is he demanding twenty-five hundred? The price has gone up. Glad I ain't in this."

I had forgotten to tell Dennis that the judge was enforcing a new state law covering undeveloped oil land only. It was intended to protect the local taxing authority. I explained it briefly to him and he gave me a quizzical look. "I never heard of any such law. Undeveloped oil land? A tax? That's crazy as hell. Where did old Crater hear about it?"

I said, lowly, so none of the men around me could hear, "From me."

"Where'd you hear about it?"

"Made it up."

He glanced over at Crater plaguing Atlas and put his head back and laughed. "Boy howdy, that is a good one. Hoo boy! I like that law."

I could see a very harassed Teddy Atlas glance my way. He made waving motions toward the end of the camp. I knew what he wanted but I just stared back dumbly. In a moment Leon detached himself from the group and came running our way in a kind of lumbering trot. He pulled up in front of me and said, in his heavy voice, "Mistuh Atlas wants for you to get the aeroplane ready."

It was very strange. He had nearly knocked my head off and I had coldcocked him with a piece of lumber, but these were the first words he'd ever spoken to me. I said, leisurely, "It ain't that easy. Takes a little time to get the airplane ready. Tell Mr. Atlas, about fifteen minutes."

Beside me Dennis laughed. I watched Leon trot back and report to his boss. Atlas glanced my way and then suddenly ducked into his tent. Leon took up guard at the front flap but the judge was still preaching taxes and levies and money at the top of his voice.

Dennis said, "You better get the plane ready. If the deal with Miss Genevieve don't go through, we don't want to get on his bad side."

I said, "Has he got a good side?" Then I started off toward the airplane, not so much for Atlas's sake, but because Genevieve had told me to get him into town that morning.

Dennis came with me and it was but the work of a few minutes to get the plane untied from its moorings and get the canvas cover off. Dennis spun the propeller until the engine caught and I put on a little power and eased the airplane out into a takeoff position. I glanced over my shoulder and saw Atlas coming toward me at a pretty good clip. He was being pursued by the judge, who was somewhat handicapped by his bushy eyebrows and his ample girth and the fact that Leon kept getting into his way. The sheriff ambled along behind like he was enjoying the show.

Atlas arrived out-of-breath, and almost dove into the front cockpit. I taxied down my desert strip to get in position for the wind and slowly turned the airplane around. In the quiet of the idling engine I said, "What was that all about?"

Atlas swiveled around in his seat and gave me an outraged look. "I can't believe it, but that old outlaw wanted to collect fees and taxes from me for drilling in *unproven* territory! Have you ever heard of anything so ridiculous? I tried to explain that the government should make it easier to drill in unproven ground, but he wouldn't listen. He swears he is going to telephone the state capital and have the militia out here. He's crazy, isn't he?"

I gave it a moment's thought and then slowly shook my head. "I wouldn't bet on it. Some of these old JPs that been in office a long time have made some good friends up at the capital. It sounds like just the law they'd want passed. Way out here, it would be one of the few ways they'd have to pass the hat. They'd know the oil companies got to look at out-of-the-way places sooner or later. Be handy to have just such a law."

Atlas's face was furious. "That old fraud. He's not going to rob me and get away with it. Asked me for twenty-five hundred dollars. Can you imagine? Then raised it to three thousand dollars to drill on un-proved land!"

I had to fight to keep from smiling. It was just like the judge to add five hundred dollars to what he thought was a lawful fee. I glanced toward the camp. They were still coming our way. I said, "We better go. Do you have an appointment in town?"

"Yes," he said. "Get going."

Flying into town we ran into some bumpy air. I wasn't paying much attention to it until Teddy Atlas turned around to me and began making stabbing motions toward the ground. His face was pasty white and he looked like he was about to be sick. With a little bit of a shock I realized the man was about to be airsick. It shocked me because I couldn't imagine a man like Atlas allowing himself such a weakness.

But to keep from having the airplane messed up I put the nose down and headed for smoother air. By the time I lined up for the landing I could see that the color had returned to Atlas's face. By the time we landed I could see that he had also groomed and dressed himself for the meeting with Genevieve. I didn't know if lightweight flannel trousers and white silk shirts were the usual costume for business meetings, but that was what he was wearing. He also had on a gold wristwatch to make certain it was understood that he was a man not only of means, but of good taste as well. Before we left the plane he used a mirror he had with him to comb his hair and carefully put every strand in place. Then he added a blue ascot to the throat of his white silk shirt. If that was business attire, I was a truck driver.

He went off up the street and I went to the Mexicans' for the rest of my breakfast and some orange juice and coffee. I sat there, not in the best of humors. If selling the drilling contract to Genevieve meant her being in close contact with a snake like Atlas, I was not so sure I wanted to save the rig after all. What was the big deal about the water? And maybe Atlas wouldn't shut us down after all.

I took a drink of orange juice and thought, *Yeah, and I like Leon, too.* Still, I didn't like the situation. I had no doubt that I was, as Genevieve had said, pouting because I wasn't at the center of her attentions. But so what? I was supposed to be at the center of her attention if God was in his heaven and all was right with the world. She believed in God. At least she said she did. So did Dennis. But we were trying to do a very unfriendly thing to Teddy Atlas.

The sheriff came in, which interrupted my morbid meditations.

He sat down and ordered a cup of coffee and said the judge was really on the warpath and that Atlas might just find himself paying. "The last I saw of the judge he was headed for the train depot and the telegraph office. He is convinced his office is owed money." He cut his eyes over at me. "That is straight, ain't it? That law about a fine for drilling on unexplored land?"

I put my glass to my lips. "According to the people I heard it from."

"And they be reliable?"

"As reliable as they come."

He laughed and shook his head. As he was getting up he said, "Miss Genevieve wants you to come in the kitchen door. She's got something she wants to say to you."

"She wants me to wait in the kitchen?"

"Yeah, and she don't want a certain party seeing you, either. Say, what are y'all doing to that poor man? After the judge got through with him this morning I thought he'd be plumb wrung-out. Is Miss Genevieve the reliable party you got your information from about that fine?"

I didn't look up, just kept my attention on my plate. "Don't know what you're talking about, sheriff. Maybe you been in the law business too long. I've heard that makes you suspicious of everyone."

He gave me a little tap on the shoulder and laughed. "I'm going down to my office. You be careful of the screen door at the kitchen. It squeaks."

I left a little while after the sheriff and circled around his house until I could come up on the kitchen door from the back. I'd caught a glimpse of Atlas and Genevieve in the parlor and I thought he was sitting entirely too near her. When you are conducting business you can do it from across the room as easy as not.

I opened the screen door and let myself into the kitchen. Sure enough, it did squeak, but not so much to notice. The kitchen had a good smell: bread and apple pies and Irish stew and all those other smells you get in the kitchen of a woman who really cares about her house and her husband and family. It appeared to me that Genevieve would never have such a kitchen. She'd be too busy out making oil deals. It made me wonder why she'd ever divorced her first husband if she liked the game so well. Hell, they could have been partners.

I sat down at the kitchen table. It was a heavy, round affair and comfortable to sit at. There was the smell of fresh coffee about the place, but I didn't see a pot or a cup to drink it out of. I figured I'd better just sit still and wait for events to sort themselves out. The sheriff's wife might not care for me rummaging around in her kitchen.

Time dragged. I calculated I'd been waiting an hour with not a sign of anything happening. Occasionally I could hear the murmur of words, but nothing I could make out. I was just on the point of slipping out the back door and cutting around the house to have a peek in the parlor, when the kitchen door suddenly opened and Genevieve came rushing in. I said, "What in the hell have—"

But she cut me off. She said, "We don't have but a minute, and this might be hard for you to understand."

I said, grimly, "If it has got to do with you and Teddy Atlas, I won't have no trouble."

She sighed and rolled her eyes. "I'll overlook that insult. Look, you have to find a casual way to tell him something—ask him, really. Heavy crude is selling for about a dollar and a quarter a barrel. And that's at the front door of the refinery. We are six hundred miles from the nearest refinery down along the Gulf Coast at Houston or Baytown. Even Beaumont. Ask him if he knows what the shipping charges are by rail to get his oil, if he ever gets any, to a refinery."

"I take it it is high?"

She made a sweet little bow of her mouth. "I calculate he'd be losing thirty cents a barrel. Of course, he can always build a pipeline. That wouldn't cost more than a half a million dollars."

I frowned. I said, "You are making me out to be one hell of an authority about something I don't know anything about. Why didn't you tell him?"

She fluttered her eyelashes. "Because I'm playing the poor, innocent little 'thang' so the big bad oilman will take pity on me. Actually, he's trying to squeeze me like a sponge."

"You better not mean that literally."

"Oh, for heavens' sake, Willis. Grow up."

"Why can't I tell Dennis and have Dennis tell him?"

She gave me a look. "Oh, that would be smart. Dennis says, 'Mr. Atlas, I'm drilling you an oil well that will bankrupt you if we strike oil.' Don't be silly, Willis. I want you to just casually plant the idea in his head. I think that attack from the judge really shook him, though naturally he didn't mention it. I don't think it will take much more to make him accept my price and get out of here as fast as he can."

"Don't forget the airplane."

"He doesn't want the airplane. He thinks you'll leave and it will sit out here and rot."

"But I don't understand where I'm supposed to have got this information about the freight rates on oil-tank cars."

"Just say that while you were waiting you wandered over to the depot and got to talking to the freight agent. Tell him the agent was curious when you'd be needing tankers. And during the conversation he told you the price."

I gave her a slow smile. "You Christians play kind of rough."

She gave me a little push toward the door. "Go. Hurry up. He'll be looking for you. Listen, that water is needed, rough or not."

I said, "So you really are an angel."

"Get out of here before you ruin everything."

I stepped through the door and stood for a second on the steps. I said, "I don't believe in angels anyway."

"Go, go, go."

I found Atlas in the Mexican cafe, looking for me. He gave me an irritated look. "Where have you been?"

"Oh, over at the depot."

"Well, let's get moving. I want to get back; I've got some figuring to do."

I waited until we were nearly to the airplane before I said anything. He had been muttering about Genevieve and it hadn't been complimentary. I said, "Mr. Atlas, I was wondering, something the freight agent said. He wanted to know when we'd be ordering tanker cars for the oil. I never thought about it, but the railroad is the only way to get the oil to the refinery. I'm right, ain't I, that that's where you got to get it to? The crude oil?"

He looked at me with a little irritation. "When did you start making my oil your business?"

I said, defensively, "It's my land. I got a one-eighth override, so I'm interested in the profit. And I heard heavy crude is bringing a dollar and a quarter a barrel."

"Heavy crude? Now you know about the specific gravity of oil?"

"Dennis had got some books. Hell, I got a stake in this. I think we ought to find out about those freight charges."

He thought a moment and then he looked back over his shoulder toward town. We were standing by the wing of the airplane and I estimated the depot was something over a half a mile away. He said, "Can you land this thing beside the train station? I wouldn't want to be seen walking back there."

I said, "Get in. We'll go up and have a look."

He started to climb in the front cockpit and then he turned and looked at me. "You take it easy, you hear?" He stared hard at me. "I mean, something I ate this morning for breakfast. You take it easy. No cutting up."

"Of course not," I said. I spun the prop and got the engine running and climbed in behind the stick thinking, *Yeah, something he ate. What we got here, ladies and gentlemen, is a classic case of airsickness.*

I took off and circled back over the town, flying at about two hundred feet and looking down for an open space near the railroad depot. But something else caught my eye. For a second I almost didn't recognize her, and if she hadn't been wearing a yellow frock, I probably wouldn't have noticed. It was Genevieve. She had left the sheriff's house and was walking across the open ground toward the town. I let the airplane drift out toward the west as I watched her. It was with some astonishment that I saw her walk straight to the hotel and go inside. I could not, for the life of me, imagine what she would be doing in that fleabag hotel. I circled the town, flying slow, but there was no sign of her coming out.

Atlas was turned in his seat and hollering at me. Distracted, I brought my attention to him. He pointed down and I slowly shook my head. I said, aloud, though I knew he couldn't hear me, "No, we can't land. The ground is too rough."

I turned the plane for the oil camp. I was flying, but my mind was much occupied on the ground.

Right after lunch, Teddy Atlas wanted me to fly Leon into town so he could go see the freight agent, but I didn't feel like flying back into town and being near Genevieve when I wouldn't get to see her. I told Atlas the airplane needed some engine work, that it was malfunctioning.

That horrified him, the idea that he'd been flying in a malfunctioning plane, but he didn't press me on the matter. Instead he arranged with Dennis for Leon to be taken in the truck we were using.

That afternoon, late, after he'd finished drilling, I told Dennis what had happened. At first he didn't get it. His focus was all on the freight rate. He said, "My heavens: I never thought of that. Of course, I figured if we hit a discovery well, all the big companies would be out here and there would be pipelines aplenty. But if we just make a small well, it will have to be shipped, and I'd bet we'd lose money getting the crude to market."

"The hell with that, Dennis. What about me seeing her going into the hotel? What business has she got, going in there? Huh?"

He looked pained and waved a hand at me. "Willis, if you want something to worry about, worry about her getting a good look at you and coming to her senses. Hell, you idiot—she went back to get one of her valises they forgot to take over to the sheriff's house. She went back to pick up a dress one of the maids was cleaning for her. She left her favorite mirror in the place. Quit trying to make something out of nothing."

Looked at like that, my suspicions did see damn silly. There was nothing sinister about her going to a hotel she'd spent the night in. I said, "Yeah, you're right. I've been out in this desert too long. But she is so good-looking! I figure every man that sees her wants her."

"But she don't want every man. You think she was going to the hotel to meet a man? What man in this town could possibly take her eye? You have gone loco."

I had to agree. I got up. I said, "It's about time for supper. Let's go eat."

Dennis said, "It's about time for Leon to be getting back. I'd like to know what it costs to ship a barrel of crude to the refineries on the Coast. More than Mr. Atlas will be willing to pay, I'll wager. That is, if we had an oil well."

Dennis was pulling for Genevieve to buy Atlas out. Everyone in the company was pulling for her—those that knew, at least. Nobody liked Atlas, and they especially didn't like Atlas and Leon. Joe Cairo said, "It's like he's got a pit-bull dog ready to go for your throat."

Atlas hadn't brought Leon along to have him liked, and he had succeeded beyond his greatest expectations. Joe Cairo had let a few of the men know that I had whacked Leon and they had all congratulated me.

I didn't believe that Dennis truly understood what Genevieve had in mind if she was able to buy the drilling contract. I told Dennis again about the water but he'd just shrugged. "As long as I can make a hole in the ground, there is always the chance I can strike oil. If she gets that bastard off my back, I'll be the happiest driller you ever saw."

I went to bed that night with the feeling that something was going to happen the next day. I didn't know what it was going to be, but I felt that things would never be the same after tomorrow. I didn't know if they were going to be better or worse, I only knew they'd be different.

Teddy Atlas must have felt the same, for, as he got in the plane, he said, "This is going to be one of my last plane rides." He was carrying a small briefcase.

I was about to spin the prop. I stopped and said, "Does that mean we're going to crash?"

He gave me one of his patented superior looks and said, as if he were talking to a worm, "If we crash, that will be your fault. I meant that I am going to close this business one way or the other, that this would be one of my last trips in this rickety kite. I cannot imagine I was ever interested in airplanes. Hurry up!"

I started to say that he'd been interested in flying before he discovered he didn't have the stomach for it. But I didn't. If we could get shut of Mr. Atlas, that would be satisfaction enough.

We had not found out what the price for shipping crude was. Leon had come back and gone straight into Mr. Atlas's tent. He'd come out a little later, but no one had asked him anything. Leon wasn't the type you went up to and inquired about matters.

I would have expected him to tell Dennis but he didn't, and Dennis had declined to ask. "It may have been something I was supposed to know. That's one sleeping dog I'm going to let lie."

But from what I'd seen of Atlas, the news couldn't have been good. He looked like a man who'd just discovered he had a good four-card hand in a five-card game. I didn't ask any questions, either.

I landed and went up the street with Mr. Atlas. As we passed the judge's office he came popping out, announcing in a loud voice that Mr. Atlas could consider himself under arrest within the next few days. He said, in his bullying, burly booming voice, that the authorities in Austin had been alerted and the state militia would be along shortly.

Atlas never paused to answer. He just trudged along with his eyes on the street, and said, in a strangled voice, "I have got to get out of this hellhole!"

I ducked into the Mex cafe and let him go on ahead to the sheriff's house. He might have thought I'd be waiting in the cafe, but he was going to be wrong. I was going to be watching.

I gave it ten minutes and then I slipped out of the cafe and circled around to an old ramshackle building that gave me a clear view of the sheriff's parlor. I could see Genevieve sitting on the settee. She rose and extended her hand when Mrs. Wallace showed Teddy Atlas in. They shook, after a fashion, the way that men and women shake, and then they sat down—Atlas in a big, overstuffed chair, and Genevieve back down on the settee. Atlas immediately opened his briefcase and

360 ❧ Giles Tippette

pulled out some papers and put them on the table beside him. Then he leaned forward and started talking.

It was a little slow going since I couldn't tell what either one was saying.

I saw Genevieve shake her head and then shake it again. Mr. Atlas said something, and she shook her head with vigor. Whatever it was he'd said, she did not agree. After a few more minutes Atlas got up and began pacing back and forth, raising his finger now and then to make a point.

Genevieve kept shaking her head no. Finally Mr. Atlas turned to her and put out his hand as if he was inviting suggestions. Genevieve sat up straighter on the settee and said something that caused Mr. Atlas to take a step back like he'd been struck a blow. Now it was his turn to shake his head no. He went back to his chair and sat down. He said something and she said something and he threw his hands in the air like it was hopeless.

I watched with puzzled interest as the play went back and forth. It was clear they were both after something but neither appeared willing to give in to the other's demands. Finally, after about a half an hour, Teddy Atlas got to his feet and began stuffing the papers back in his briefcase. It looked like the game was over. Genevieve rose as he finished his packing, and took a step toward him, holding out her hand. I was glad to see she was wearing gloves, even if they were mostly lace. They both looked resigned and I had to conclude that the deal had fallen through.

Atlas walked to the parlor door, opened it, and paused for a moment. He said something to her and she shook her head. He shrugged and started through the door. My heart sank. All of this effort for nothing. I could have told her in advance that Teddy Atlas was the kind of boy who didn't care to lose. He'd take a bath on that oil well before he'd let you beat him in a business deal. And, Lord knows, Genevieve had tried. Tried every trick any woman could think of. But it was all for naught.

Then, when he was all the way through the door and about to close it behind him, he stopped again. He said something to Genevieve, and this time she nodded. Atlas came back into the room and stood talking for a moment. At first she nodded as he talked but then she started shaking her head. As if in a gesture of finality, she sat back down on the settee like all had been said that could be said. He stood there staring at her for a moment. My heart sank. I thought it was all over and that we had lost.

But he kept standing there, one arm crossed across his chest, studying her. Finally, he appeared to ask her one last question. I could see her distinctly form the word *no* with her lips, and shake her head.

It took him about ten seconds, but then he put his hands up like a man surrendering and started taking the documents out of his brief-case and putting them on the table by the chair where he'd been sitting. Genevieve got up and went to a desk up against the wall, the kind called a secretary, and opened a drawer and took out a big, old-fashioned commercial checkbook, the kind that had about six checks showing. I hadn't seen one since my days with my father. All the cattlemen and horse traders carried them. It suddenly made me suspicious. Her daddy was a preacher in east Texas. My aunt and uncle were in the horse business in east Texas. Could Uncle Warner have given her his checkbook to trade off of? As a way for my daddy not to know he'd had a hand in it?

Or maybe, I thought, it was her ex-husband's and she'd just kept it. Probably she'd brought it along to make it look like she meant business.

She sat down at the little desk and got a pen inked up and wrote for a moment and then tore out the oversize business check. She stood up, waving it in the air for the ink to dry. I was scared to hope it was over. Teddy Atlas was still hunched over the papers, signing this one and that. Finally, he straightened up, capped his fountain pen and put it in his pocket.

They stood side by side, close together, while he showed her the papers one by one. She took them with one hand, keeping the check in the other, and gave them a good studying. Finally she read the last one and nodded. She handed him the check.

The deal was done. We were through with Mr. Teddy Atlas.

Except he wasn't quite through with my girl. Without warning he put his arm around her and pulled her to him. She'd been looking at him so her face was toward his. He very nearly kissed her. At the last second she pushed him away with her free hand. She wasn't quite strong enough to push him free so he came back for another try. A fury even worse than that I had felt toward Leon rose in me. If I could get my hands on him he'd never be mistaken for a pretty boy again.

But before I could move, the door to the parlor opened and the sheriff's wife came in. Teddy Atlas jumped back, looking guilty, and fumbled the check into his pocket. He put out his hand toward Genevieve to shake over the completion of the deal, but she ignored it, giving him a stiff nod and sweeping out of the room.

I figured I'd better be someplace else so I hotfooted it over to the Mexicans' cafe. I didn't go in, but stood at the corner and watched Atlas come out of the sheriff's house and walk in my direction. I watched him, working on my temper, trying to calm down. I wasn't supposed to know anything and I didn't want to act like I did. I didn't want Atlas to see me angry or even think I might be angry. Not until the right time.

I stepped out in the open so he could see me, and smiled cheerfully as he came up. I said, "Well, you're done early. Or you still got some to go?"

"No. We're through."

I said, "You want to get a beer or something to eat, or head straight on back?"

He looked back at the sheriff's house. He said, "Let's get back to camp. The quicker I get packed, the quicker I get back to civilization."

We were starting to walk toward the edge of town where the plane was. I said, trying to sound surprised, "Why, what do you mean? You ain't leaving us, are you?"

"Oh, yes!" He gave me what he thought was a smile. "You got a new boss now, a new backer. It ought to be a laugh a minute."

I said, still sounding astounded, "You don't mean you sold your drilling contract on my acreage?"

"Sold it? Well, I'd have given it away pretty soon just to get out from under the damn thing. Wait'll she runs into that crazy judge. And wait'll she finds out the railroad charges to ship crude oil to the Coast. Hah!"

"It's high?"

"Higher than you've ever been." He suddenly laughed. "I ought to be feeling pretty damn good." Then he got a mean expression on his face. "But that damn woman. I—" He stopped.

"She give you trouble?"

"She got hers. She thinks she's something on a stick. I've seen better in a cheap whorehouse."

I had to take myself in hand. It was a moment or two before I could speak. I tried to switch it around. "You mean she tried to hold you up on the price?"

He gave me a look of derision. "Hold *me* up on the price? Hell, I skinned her alive." He reached in his pocket and took out the check and waved it around. "She's lucky I let her off as light as I did. You should have seen her fluttering her eyelashes and stroking my hand and rubbing up against me, trying to get the price down. All that got her was a push. That one is no lady."

Little drops of sweat were forming on my forehead. I was holding myself as tightly as I could. We were nearly to the airplane. I said, "So you'll be leaving us? You and Leon?"

"Just as fast as we can get packed and you can fly us back into town. I don't know what possessed me to ever get into a drilling venture in this hellhole. I hope that bitch enjoys herself. What do you suppose a woman wants with a drilling operation out here? She told me she was divorced from some big-shot with Texaco. Maybe that was part of the settlement, that she go off and hide herself."

We were at the plane now. I lifted the tail and swung the airplane around into the wind, making sure it was exactly lined up for takeoff. Once I started my takeoff roll I didn't want to stop. By the time I had pulled the prop through and set the switches, Mr. Atlas had climbed in the front cockpit and strapped himself in. I spun the prop so that the engine caught. I stopped before climbing aboard, to make sure that

Mr. Atlas was correctly belted in. It was the first time I'd ever done it, and he gave me a strange look. I said, and smiled, "Don't want you falling out."

"We can get to the camp and have time to be back in town before the train comes, can't we?"

I said, "Don't you worry about a thing."

I climbed into the cockpit and gave the prop enough throttle so that we rolled into position. Just when I was ready to take off, I eased off on the power so that it was quiet enough to talk. I reached forward and slapped the flat of my hand on the fuselage between me and Teddy Atlas. He turned around to see what was the matter.

"What? What do you want? Let's go."

I said, "Mr. Atlas, I was watching you through the parlor window today. I saw you try to grab the lady you have described as 'that damn woman.' I saw her push you away. I saw you grab her again."

His face got angry. He said, "What the hell business is it of yours?"

I said, "That lady you described as a bitch is the woman I'm going to marry." It took it a second or two to soak in, for him to comprehend something that didn't have him in the starring role. By the time he realized my implication, I had shoved the throttle home and we were bumping over the ground at thirty miles per hour. Just as he started to yell, I pulled the stick back and lifted the airplane into the sky. I kept full power on and the nose tilted up. I was heading for altitude. He was half turned in his seat, yelling back at me, a pleading expression on his face. Because of the wind and the roar of the engine I couldn't understand his words, but there was no mistaking the fear in his eyes. He very much did not look like the man in authority, the man about town, a man of the world, a force to be reckoned with, a young man in a hurry to be on top. He didn't even look very egotistical or self-satisfied. But he needn't have worried about being on top; I was fixing to put him on top.

CHAPTER 20

I KEPT the nose of the airplane up, climbing steadily on the course I had taken off on. It didn't matter what direction I was headed since my destination was ten thousand feet. It took quite a few minutes for the underpowered Wright Cyclone engine to struggle its way upward in the high, dry air. Mr. Atlas had made some bleating noises and waved his hand around trying to convey some sort of information to me. It didn't matter. My mind was made up about what was going to happen and nothing he could say or do would change that. After we passed through about six thousand feet he seemed to give up. He'd slumped lower and lower in his seat until I could barely see the top of his head.

Then, finally, the altimeter was winding up to ten thousand feet. I needed that kind of altitude for what I was about to do. I watched the gauge and, as the big arrow passed the zero, signifying I had reached my goal, I pulled the nose up sharply in a hammerhead stall. The plane hung suspended for a second or two and then fell off on its left wing and went into a left-handed spin. I made no attempt to correct it and the revolutions began to turn faster and faster. The nose was now pointing straight down at the desert below. Mr. Atlas could have had a good view if he'd cared to look, but he'd disappeared down into his cockpit. Out of the corner of my eye I could see the oil camp off in the distance; or I could see it out of my left eye for a flicker of an instant because the airplane was spinning so fast—it was on my left and then my right and then my left again.

It was a scary maneuver, to let a plane spin out of control. Most of the time you would control the rate of spin by easing in a little opposite rudder. But I wanted the fast spin. It made even my stomach feel the slightest bit queasy. I had no idea what it was doing to Atlas. Nothing good, I hoped. I had once used the maneuver in France to shake a German fighter off my tail. When I had corrected the spin and went into a shallow pullout, he'd kept going and crashed into the hard ground below us.

The desert was rushing up at an alarming pace. I was feeling the gravitational force pulling at my body. It would be much worse when I pulled the airplane out of the dive.

First I stopped the spin by shoving in opposite rudder. When I had the plane in a simple dive I could see we were coming up on four thousand feet of altitude. Our airspeed was a little over a hundred fifty miles an hour. If I wasn't careful I could peel the wings off like that German had done so long ago in France.

Very gently I started pulling back on the stick. It didn't want to respond because of the terrific force on the wings, but I kept urging it gently, trying to bring the nose up from the dead vertical. I could have cranked in some flaps to slow the airspeed, but the airplane was going too fast. It would likely have ripped the flaps off.

By the time we were down to thirty-five hundred feet I had managed to get the stick back enough so that the nose was slowly coming up and airspeed was dropping. I didn't want to lose all that airspeed, though, because of some further maneuvers I had planned for Mr. Atlas.

As we slowed, the stick came back easier. At thirty-two hundred feet the airspeed was down to one hundred twenty miles per hour and I felt that the plane was fully under control. I leveled off at three thousand feet and, using rudder and ailerons, immediately went into a series of snap rolls. The airplane really wasn't designed for that, but it handled it well enough. I exited from my last roll in a dive. But I only held the nose down long enough to build speed and then I brought the plane back up and began a series of swoops such as you might get on a roller coaster. After that I snapped the plane around in a tight Lufberry circle, then went into an Immelmann turn and finished off with a shandelle. By then I was fairly certain the airplane needed cleaning up, so I flipped it over on its back and flew along parallel to the ground at about five hundred feet. Sure enough, some material came falling out of the forward cockpit that I think had once been in Mr. Atlas's stomach.

It was when I rolled out of the upside-down flight that I saw her. It was her again, golden hair and gray gingham dress. She was just standing out on the prairie, sort of shimmering, and shading her eyes to watch the airplane. I had convinced myself she existed only in my head, but she was very much there, and I was in an airplane and Mr. Atlas was in the same airplane, so there could be no mistake. She was real, though what kind of real, I wasn't sure about. I felt it odd that she should suddenly turn up on the very day that Genevieve had completed the deal with Atlas.

When I was past her I turned hard to the right. Off in the distance I could see the little cluster of rocky mountains and the ranch house in among them. I couldn't see the neat fields but I knew it was the place I'd seen her before, standing on the porch, the place where the oxen had come from.

I made another pass past her, flying low and looking over the desert floor. It seemed flat enough and clear enough for a landing. I turned into what little wind there was and made a slow, careful approach, flaring out about five feet above the ground so that I was doing no more than twenty miles per hour when I touched down. I had feared the plane would frighten her, but she stood stock-still, watching with great interest. I taxied as close to her as I could and then, leaving the prop just ticking over, set the brake and jumped out of the cockpit. I glanced at Atlas as I walked by. He was slumped to one side of the cockpit, not even half-conscious. I swung my attention back to the girl. She stood there watching me walk up. You'd have thought it was an everyday experience for her to have an airplane set down in her front yard, so to speak. I walked straight up to her. She looked up into my face. She had golden hair and golden skin, but she was not as finely featured as I'd thought. She was also thicker through the body and there was a good sprinkling of freckles on her arms and face. But I'd waited a long time to ask her a question and I was determined to do it. I said, "Are you an angel?"

She answered me in the broadest, most nasal Texas twang I'd ever heard. She said, "Naw. My name be Saddie May Merkins."

"And you haven't been watching out for me?"

"Lawdy, mistuh, I don't be knowin' who you be. I ain't watchin' out fer nothin' 'cept my daddy's livestock and crops." She pointed behind her. "We be hired to run that farm back thar', but they ain't much left to do. Daddy rented out them last eight oxen was on the place."

I said, looking past her, "There never was an angel. Except in my head."

She was frowning at me. "What's that you say, mistuh?"

I shook my head. "Nothing. Listen, I'm going to drop a fellow off here. He's not feeling very well. Wants to get out of the airplane. If you've got some water you might give him a little, but I'd stay away from him. He's kind of messy."

I went over to the plane, and indeed Atlas was kind of messy. He had vomit all down the front of his white silk shirt, which wasn't so white anymore. I got some rags out of the tool compartment and used them to unbuckle his harness. His head was lolling around and he was moaning and making heaving sounds, but they were dry heaves. He didn't have anything left to give.

I protected my hands with the rags and got him by the shirt collar with both hands, and heaved and tugged him until I had him over the side of the airplane. Finally gravity took over and he fell to the ground. I looked down at him, lying in the dirt and sand. He was white as a sheet and drool was coming out of a corner of his mouth. I resisted an urge to kick him in the ribs and instead climbed back into the rear cockpit. The girl was still watching intently, as if all this was being done for her benefit. I gave her a little wave and then I shoved the throttle forward and rolled across the desert floor until I attained flying speed. After I was in the air I made a low circle, flying right over Atlas. He hadn't moved. But the girl looked up, shading her eyes and watching as I disappeared. She'd come over and was standing by Atlas, looking at him curiously. Had I been her I'd have wanted a snake stick to pin his head to the ground before I got too close.

I wasn't quite satisfied with my work. I'd have much rather beat his face in with my fists for what he'd said about Genevieve, and for putting his hands on her. But as things worked out, the use of the airplane was perhaps a little more poetic.

I was aware of being very tired when I landed back at the drilling camp. Dennis was on the rig when he saw me taxi up. He immediately shut the rig down and came running for the airplane. I didn't bother to shroud the engine with the canvas. All I did was tie the plane down as protection against any sudden gusts of wind. I was planning on leaving as soon as I could get my gear together. I badly wanted to see Genevieve.

Dennis caught up with me before I could get inside the tent. He said, puffing a little, "What the hell happened? Where's Atlas?"

I made him wait until we were inside the tent and I could get a drink of water before I told him anything. I said, "She bought it. You've got a new backer. Atlas is out."

He was very excited. He said, "Well, did she say her plans? What does she want me to do? Teddy Atlas come back with you, or stay in town?"

I sat down on my cot and slowly told him everything I knew, even including Atlas trying to put his hands on her after the deal was struck. I did not go into much detail about the aerobatics I'd flown for Atlas's benefit, but I knew I didn't have to for an old hand like Dennis. I finished by saying, "Last I saw of him, he was lying on the ground with that golden-haired girl you said I'd imagined watching him."

He stared at me in openmouthed wonder for a long second or two. Then he swallowed and said, "Judas Priest, Willis, you can't leave the man alone out there in that desert, he'll die."

"That girl is with him."

"For all you know, she is a halfwit. She could walk off and leave him to die of thirst or worse out there on that desert."

"The farm or ranch her father sharecrops is not quite a mile from there. If he walks north he would see it."

"What if he doesn't walk north, and she ain't there to guide him?"

I shrugged. "Then I guess he's in a lot of trouble. Listen, Leon is now trespassing on my land. I want him off."

Dennis was still staring at me. He said, gently, "Willis, I know you are plenty angry at Atlas for what he done. And I don't blame you. But you can't leave him out there in the middle of the desert without food or water and the only help an addle-headed girl. This ain't you, Willis. Think on it."

I did for about a minute and a half. Then I said, "Look, I'm anxious to get back to town and see Genevieve now that I can see her openly. I want to find out what the deal was and what her plans are."

"You mean her drilling plans.

That wasn't what I meant, but I didn't say anything to the contrary. I said, "Look, go tell Leon that Teddy Atlas needs him. Tell Leon he is supposed to fill up a tow sack with some grub and get as much water as he can carry. And tell him to get some rags and clean out the forward cockpit. Tell him that is where he'll be riding. Tell him I'll meet him at the airplane in half an hour."

Dennis got up. He looked doubtful. "I'll go tell him, but I ain't sure how he's gonna take it. You want him to carry a sack full of grub and water to his boss. He's gonna want to know why."

I said, "Tell him Mr. Atlas is scouting a new drilling site and it's going to have to be done on foot."

Dennis shrugged. "Sounds pretty thin to me. But maybe he'll buy it."

"Tell him Mr. Atlas is expecting us back within the hour. And where is that pistol you stole from the Army?"

"It's in my suitcase, under my cot. But be careful. It's loaded with a full clip and one in the firing chamber. All you got to do is cock it and it will damn near go off."

"I've fired the famous Army Colt forty-five. Remember, a half an hour. I'm going to drop Leon off and get into Pecos to see Genevieve."

Dennis had been wrong. Leon was at the airplane ahead of me. As I walked up he was busy wiping the forward cockpit clean. He turned and looked at me, but didn't say anything. I had the Colt .45 in the back waistband of my pants so that Leon couldn't see it. I went about the business of untying the airplane and then pulled the prop through a couple of times to prime the carburetor. Then I went around to the rear cockpit and set the ignition. I looked at Leon. I said, "Get in and strap down your shoulder harness."

He threw the gunny sack in first and then hoisted himself up and sort of fell into the cockpit. The engine was still warm so it only took one spin to bring it to life. I ran around the wing and jumped in and was in the air in a matter of moments.

I found the spot in which I'd left Teddy Atlas in about fifteen minutes. The girl was gone and Atlas was staggering around in the searing heat, going in exactly the wrong direction. He was headed west which would bring him nothing but miles and miles of desert and salt flats. I buzzed down low over him, but he didn't even glance up. He was stumbling like a drunk man. I didn't know why the girl had left; likely his appearance and condition had scared her. Leon had his head over the side of the cockpit, looking down. It should have been clear, even to him, that Atlas wasn't in the best condition.

I dropped a wing and pulled throttle and settled gently onto the desert floor. I taxied to where I was only about fifty yards from Teddy Atlas. I looked at Leon. He had turned in his seat to look at me. I said, "Get out."

His eyes were flat. He said, "The boss don't look so good. We better take him to the town or the camp."

I pulled out the big .45 and rested my hand on the barrel. I cocked the hammer. I said, "My daddy made his living for twenty years as a gunman and a bank robber. I'm a better shot than he ever was. You want to help your boss, you take that food and that water and go help him. Now get out. Last warning. Next sound you hear will be this pistol blowing a hole in you."

He moved slowly, but he moved. Halfway over the side of the plane he said, looking at me with hate in his eyes, "It's a lucky thing for you you've got that gun."

I said, "Luck had nothing to do with it, Leon. I brought it for just this purpose. Now move it."

He dropped to the ground with his gunnysack of provisions. The moment he was out of the airplane I gunned the throttle and made a rapid, bouncing takeoff over the rough ground. I circled once.

Atlas was still walking like a drunk and Leon was hurrying to catch up with him. He glanced up as I went over, and I could imagine what he was thinking. I didn't know what their chances were. Town was fifteen miles away. A good two- or three-day walk. Camp was about the same. Their best bet was the ranch house where the golden-haired girl lived, but I doubted if Atlas had understood about it from the girl, and Leon wouldn't know. But they had water and provisions and Leon was strong. I felt sure they'd put other people in worse spots. I felt no remorse about leaving them in the wilderness. My only regret was that I had neglected to tell Leon it was me that had hit him in the back of the head with the two-by-four. I turned the plane toward town and Genevieve.

We didn't make any attempt to talk until after dinner, even though she was bursting to tell, and I, to listen. The sheriff and his wife very graciously turned the parlor over to us after a few moments of polite talk, and went upstairs, leaving us to our privacy. The first thing I said was, "You bought it?"

Her eyes were dancing. "Didn't he tell you?"

I was on shaky ground. I didn't want her to know all of what Atlas had said. "He implied he got the best of you. In fact, I think he said he skinned you."

She threw her head back and laughed. "Oh, that phony son of a bitch. I could have had his shirt if I'd held out a little longer. After the judge and those freight rates, he was dying to sell."

"What did you have to give? Tell me, I got a right to know."

"He had seventy thousand dollars in cash in that drilling contract and I bought him out for forty-five thousand." She laughed again, putting her head back so that her wonderful neck showed to good advantage. "And the bastard started off by declaring he wouldn't take a cent less than ninety thousand for his end. Well, his end got half that."

I was excited for her success and amazed at the way she had played Teddy Atlas. But I felt awkward having her be the buyer. I said, "Honey, all this is great and you've saved Dennis's rig and string of tools, but you ain't really bought anything. There's no more oil out there than there is in the crankcase of that old truck we've got. I can't believe you've got forty-five thousand dollars just to throw away."

She took my face in one of her hands, squeezing my cheeks until my lips almost pursed, and shook my head back and forth. "I didn't buy it for the oil, sweetheart. We have already talked about this. I bought it for the water. You wanted the water, don't you remember?"

"Yeah, but not forty-five thousand dollars' worth. Hell, this makes me feel like a leech or something."

"No, no, it's a wonderful investment. It will do good but it will also make money. Atlas was too stupid to see that. But then, he didn't own the land."

I gave her a slow, sly look. "Neither do you."

She gave me the look right back. "Yeah, but I got influence."

I frowned at a sudden thought. "Boy howdy, this leaves Dennis out in the cold. I don't know what he's going to do."

She gave me a disbelieving look. " 'Do'? He's going to stay right here and drill at least two more water wells. That is, if he wants the whole contract paid off. Remember, I bought a drilling contract in total and that total is one hundred twenty-five thousand dollars. Dennis has received seventy thousand. He's got another fifty-five thousand coming."

"Dennis wants to drill for oil."

"He can drill for all the oil he wants to but he's going to complete two more wells into that artesian spring. You do think two more flowing wells will fill up that lake?"

I said, unwillingly, "Yeah, I guess so, but that was back when I was dreaming. I had no idea this would come true."

"Do you think Dennis will drill where and how you tell him?" I shrugged, "To quote Dennis, he's happy just making a hole in the ground. We might be looking for water, but he's going to be hoping for oil."

She tried to make a face but she was too pretty for it. She said, "Wouldn't that just be our luck? Strike oil and lose about twenty-five cents a barrel shipping it to a refinery. I hope there's no oil down there. But we've got to go and see Dennis in the morning and make sure he understands. I hope that horrible Mr. Atlas isn't there."

Of course, I wasn't going to tell her what I'd done, because I didn't want her to think I'd been spying on her or to know how brutal I'd been to the two men.

But there was another subject that had to be covered and even though I shied away from it, it had to be brought into the open. I said, "The other day, when you had me mention the freight rates to Mr. Atlas, I flew back over the town. I saw you leave the sheriff's house and go over to the hotel." We were sitting side by side on the settee, but now I turned to face her. I said, "Don't tell me it ain't none of my business, because it is. What were you doing going to that fleabag hotel?"

Her eyes widened. "You spied on me? You *spied* on me! How dare you!"

I shook my head. "No, get off that horse because he ain't going to buck. This ain't my first rodeo with you, lady. I wasn't *spying* on you, I happened to see you while I was flying over the town. You had on a bright yellow dress so you were a little hard to miss. Now, give me an answer I can understand."

She said, "I don't like this, Willis. It shows a lack of trust in me. I'm shocked. Shocked."

"That horse still ain't going to buck."

She said, in a cool voice, "I had left a small valise at the hotel. If you must know. The sheriff and the maid must have overlooked it. If you must know, it contained my—my undergarments."

That brought a dry laugh from me. I said, "Come on. You want me to believe you are embarrassed about your underwear? Ha ha."

"I resent your laughing."

I leaned over and kissed her on the corner of the mouth before she could react and pull back. I said, "I thought it was something like that, I'm just impressed to see you blush like a schoolgirl talking about your unmentionables. I thought you were too sophisticated for that. What are you making all the fuss about?"

"Never mind. You've embarrassed me. Now, let's get back to the well-drilling business, and how we're going to turn that into the farm-and-ranch business for a whole town."

"Look," I said, "I can't let you put another fifty-five thousand dollars into this thing. If the money has to be found, I'll find it."

"I hold the contract."

I threw up my hands. "You may be the most stubborn woman in the world. You have gone far beyond what any disinterested party could have been expected to do. My word, Genevieve!"

She looked at me in a tender way and asked, softly, "Do I seem like a disinterested party to you, Willis?"

There wasn't much answer to that, not without taking a good deal on myself. But I didn't like her spending her money on my interests. I stood up. It was going on for nine o'clock and I still needed to speak to the sheriff. I said, "We will have time to talk about these matters in the near future. Right now we'd better let them lie."

I kissed her good night in the outside hall and then she went upstairs to call the sheriff down for me, and to go to bed.

The sheriff was very nearly ready for bed himself, but we walked outside and I told him about two men that had gotten lost in the desert due north of town.

He said, as we walked, "You'd guess about ten to twelve miles?"

I nodded. "Yes, unless they've wandered off-line."

"I'll take my pickup and run out there first thing in the morning."

I stopped in the moonlight. "I wouldn't be in too much of a rush, was I you, Sheriff. I think both these gents could do with a little touch of afternoon sun."

"Friends of yours, are they?"

"Oh, yes. One is that Mr. Atlas been visiting in your house. The other is his bodyguard."

"Hmmph. Must not have done a very good job—of bodyguarding."

"Well, a party can't be alert for everything. But Miss Smith and I will be going out to the oil rig in the morning and then we will be flying out of here in the afternoon. I'd just as soon she didn't have to suffer Mr. Atlas's company again."

"I understand. So you'll be leaving us?"

"Just for a short while. I'll be back pretty quick. Might be longer for Miss Genevieve."

"You staying in town tonight?"

"Yeah, I'll make a bed over at the hotel. I think that would be more seemly."

"Right. Well, I'm much obliged about the tip about those lost prospectors. I'll get on it right after lunch tomorrow."

I walked to the hotel feeling better about the matter than I had been. Not that I didn't feel that Teddy Atlas didn't have something awful coming to him; I just didn't feel that it was my duty to inflict it. They'd get out of it with a bad sunburn and a little discomfort. I doubted that west Texas would ever see them again.

I had not told Genevieve what our plans were, and I did not until after breakfast the next morning. I bade her pack all her gear and get ready. I said, "We're going to fly out to the oil rig for a quick talk with Dennis and then we're going to fly to San Angelo."

"Where is San Angelo, and why are we going there? I have a vague idea where it is but no idea what out business is there."

"San Angelo is about three hundred miles east of here, on the railroad, on the route to Houston. Our business there is us. I want to get us out of here to where we can be in some comfort, and San Angelo is the nearest town of any size in that direction. I think we need to have us a talk. After that, I expect you to go on to Houston on the train and I will fly back here to see about the drilling of the wells."

I had expected her to give me an argument as she generally did about most issues, but she just quietly nodded her head and said, "All right. How long a flight is it?"

I said, "About five hours, depending on headwinds. I'll have to carry extra gas cans, so you'll have to ride in the rear cockpit with me for a time. It'll be a little crowded."

She reached up and kissed me. "I don't mind."

The amazing thing about that was that the conversation and the kiss took place within sight and hearing of the sheriff and his wife. It sort of put an official stamp on matters.

From the moment we landed and she stepped down from the airplane every eye in that oil camp was focused on her. I didn't blame the men. She was wearing a lively light-blue skirt with a blue-and-white polka-dot blouse, with a white scarf wrapped around her neck. On her feet were a dainty pair of blue pumps that never touched the mud, men ran in such a hurry to build her a board path from the scrap lumber. Her hair was glowing and so was her skin, mostly from inside her, but a little from the seventy-mile-an-hour winds she'd just faced in the airplane. Her clothes were not what I would have chosen for her to fly in, but then, she was a lady who know how and when to make an impression and she succeeded admirably as the new boss of the oil camp.

Dennis led the way, as excited and animated as I'd ever seen him. He made certain that the boardwalk was in place before she proceeded.

To me the whole camp seem different. The absence of Teddy Atlas and Leon seemed to have freed the air and removed the element of fear. There was almost an element of gaiety among the men, though I doubt any of them knew about the changes that had occurred.

Dennis led us into our tent. He bade us sit down and then sent for coffee and the fixings. While that was coming I stepped outside and had one of the roustabouts fill up four five-gallon cans with gasoline, and instructed him to take them to the airplane.

When the coffee came and we were settled I told Dennis briefly what had happened. Of course, he already knew most of it so I was doing it partly for Genevieve's benefit. Again I left out the part about dumping Atlas and Leon in the desert. There was no need for Genevieve to know about that.

I said, "In short, Dennis, this is your new boss. She's the lady with the money."

He reacted in his courtly, slow manner. Be damned if he didn't get up off his camp stool and give her a little bow. He said, "I'll do my best, ma'am, to do the work you want."

She said, "Dennis, you've got a fifty-five-thousand-dollar draw left on your drilling contract, but some matters have changed that you might not like. We want you to leave the pipe in the hole and let this water flow into that big basin that runs to the west. Our intentions are to create a lake to further the farming and ranching interests of this area."

Dennis nodded. "I can do that, ma'am. You've already bought the pipe."

"And then Willis wants two—"

I said, alarmed, "Wait a minute. I didn't buy that drilling contract. I can't tell Dennis where to drill."

"All right," she said, "you're my drilling superintendent. Now you can."

"I don't know what that means."

"But Dennis does."

Dennis smiled. "It means you are my boss, just like back in France."

I was embarrassed. I said, "I don't know about that. But if you're willing to drill for water, I got an idea or two."

"Tell me."

I pointed to the northwest. I said, "As soon as you tear the rig down here I'd like you to move it about a half a mile along the north side of the basin toward the west. The ground slopes down there and I got an idea that spring is coming up toward the surface in that direction. I'd like you to drill until you hit water and then turn that into the basin. Then I'd like you to do the same thing to the south, except I think you'll have to drill up closer to the lip of the basin because the ground slopes away to the south."

Genevieve said, "After you've got three water wells flowing, you are free to drill for oil anywhere on the property with whatever money you've got left out of your contract. Is that acceptable?"

Dennis stood up and put out his hand. He started toward me but I frowned and he switched, in midflight, to Genevieve. She shook his hand and stood up. She looked at me. "Are we ready to go?"

"As soon as Dennis can get the cook to put us some sandwiches and water in the cockpit."

"Good as done," he said. Before he went out of the tent to see to the matter he took my hand and looked into my eyes. He said, "I never thought I'd get this lucky. Even back to those days in France. Boy howdy, you was the right one to hook up with."

It embarrassed me, but I shook his hand back. I said, "No, I was the lucky one. Without you I wouldn't be standing here."

He said, "Your water wells will get done. I saw from the first that you were serious about the business. I was just trying to make money. You was after something far greater."

I was a little startled. I said, "Wait a minute. You got the wrong idea."

But he was already gone. Genevieve turned around and looked at me. "I doubt it," she said. "I doubt he has the wrong idea."

Not long afterward we flew out, her cuddled in the rear cockpit with me, her hair blowing in the wind. We flew over the oil camp and I waggled the wings of the airplane and those on the ground waved back. Then I located the railroad tracks and turned on course. We had food and water, full tanks, and twenty extra gallons of gas in the front cockpit along with my little dab of baggage and Genevieve's considerable ensemble.

I had chosen to fly us out of Pecos because I wanted to avoid any unpleasantness with Atlas, but mainly because I wanted to get us to a place that was nearly civilized where we could have some comfort and convenience for a talk that was way overdue. Also, I needed a spot more near the center of things to go looking for the money I needed to pay back Genevieve.

I followed the railroad track just east of town and went up to fifteen hundred feet and began flying on a direct line toward San Angelo. I didn't know if it was an omen but, looking at the telltales in the wing struts, I could see we'd picked up a tailwind.

CHAPTER
21

SAN ANGELO was a thriving town of about five thousand souls, its commerce built on farming and ranching and the U.S. Army's outpost, Fort Concho. One of the reasons I had chosen it was because of its accommodations in the Hotel Bluebonnet, a four-story modern hostel with elevators and refrigerated air. Its dining room was said to have the best food in Texas west of Austin, and they even had champagne in their bar.

A taxicab took us and our luggage into the city and to the hotel, where bellboys descended to take our burdens out of our hands and into the hotel. I engaged a suite for us, signing us in as "Mr. and Mrs. Willis Young." The luxury accommodations cost $35 a night, and it tickled me slightly to think that I was paying for them with the money Atlas had given me.

The suite contained two bedrooms, one bath, and a sitting parlor. I let the bellboys distribute our luggage as they saw fit and then I gave them a dollar apiece and closed the door to the rest of the world. While I was signing us in Genevieve had never said a word, nor had she asked for separate accommodations. She now stood in the center of the sitting parlor with her head down, twisting her neck scarf in her hands. To that moment she and I had never done more than exchange passionate kisses. I think we both knew the time had come either to commit or not commit.

The flight had tired both of us out. I could see the fatigue in her face and I knew I felt the same. I'd had to land twice to put more gas in the tanks and the wind had shifted from our tail to a quartering breeze. It had added an hour to the flight. I said to her, standing there, looking so vulnerable, "Why don't you take over the bathroom and have you a full bath and refresh yourself? I'll go down the hall and get me a quick shower and put on some fresh clothes. But you take your time."

She nodded. "All right."

Before I left the room I called room service and asked them to send up a bottle of champagne and some ham sandwiches in half an hour. They said they'd do it, and I left the room.

I didn't take much time with my shower, maybe fifteen minutes. When I got back to the room I put on a pair of clean jeans and carried a fresh shirt out into the parlor and sat down. They brought in the champagne and sandwiches and I signed for them, still without putting on my shirt, though I did give the boy who brought up the stuff a dollar. For some reason I was gave out. I didn't feel like I could raise a foot to don a sock and boot, much less a shirt.

So I was sitting like that when she came out from the bathroom. She was wearing a robe made out of a kind of light, shiny material. She stood about five feet away from me, studying me with her eyes. Finally she said, "You look pretty good without your shirt, though I expect you know that, that being the reason you haven't got one on."

I stood up and went over to her. I said, "You know you got to marry me." She looked at me for a second and said, "How old are you?" I said, lying, "Twenty-eight."

She put her head back and laughed. "Yeah, about like I'm nineteen."

I said, "And you don't look a day older."

"Stop." She put her hand up. "If I've got to rob the cradle I'd like to know by how much."

"You going to marry me? I never wanted anything very much in my life—never cared—but I seriously want you to marry me. I can't say that I know what it is, exactly, so I'm not very free with the word, but I think I love you. I can say for certain I wouldn't swap you for anybody else in the whole world."

She smiled up at me with a tenderness that went deep into her eyes. "Do you care more about me than flying?"

I put my arms around her waist and pulled her to me. I said, "Yeah. And I'm old enough to be your husband. Is that good enough for you?"

She pulled back a little so she could see into my face. "Willis, there are a lot of differences between us. We have traveled different roads to get here. For instance, I am a Christian and I don't think you are."

"I've been exposed more than you think."

"I know you are a good man. I know you are kind and that you think of others, but being a Christian involves a great deal more than being good."

I felt my heart kind of sink. I said, "Are you telling me you won't marry me if I'm not a Christian? Because I ain't going to lie about something that important."

She shook her head. "No, I'm not saying that. I'm just asking if you will keep your mind and your heart open."

"Of course I will do that. That's easy to say. But this proposal is starting to get into overtime."

"We don't know much about each other. If you think for a moment, we have not spent all that much time together."

"Then why did you, of all the people in the world, come to my rescue in Pecos? Must have been something there beside a casual meeting in Galveston."

She put out her lower lip but it wasn't a pouty gesture—more thoughtful. She said, "That's true. Yes, it seems like there was something between us from the very first. I feel like I've known you for a long, long time." She looked up at me. "I think I love you, Willis. In fact, I'm almost certain I love you. Yes, I love you."

She raised up on her tiptoes and we kissed, long and deeply. It was the kiss I had been aching for, much longer that I'd realized.

We forgot the champagne and sandwiches and went into one of the bedrooms and took off our clothes and made love. I had heard the expression "made love" before, but I hadn't known what it meant until that hour with her in that bed in that hotel. When it was over I was as spent and yet as satisfied and fulfilled as I'd ever been in my life.

We didn't either one say anything for a good long time, just lay there, naked on the bed. Finally I rolled off and went into the parlor and popped the cork on the champagne and got some extra glasses and the tray of sandwiches and brought them back into the bedroom. She sat up and I sat on the side of the bed and we sat there, drinking champagne and eating the sandwiches, which had gotten slightly stale, and not talking much. Conversation didn't seem to be called for.

Finally I set the empty champagne bottle and the tray on the floor and said, "I don't have a real good idea right now how much I'm going to support us, but if you'll live like I can afford, we'll make it somehow."

She stroked my bare arm. "We don't have to worry about that. What are we going to do tomorrow?"

I had not told her, not really, why we'd flown to San Angelo. I said, "I'm going to put you on an eastbound train for Houston and I'm going to get in that airplane and go and try and find the money to pay you back."

She sat up, looking alarmed. "Oh, no. You'll do no such thing. It's not necessary."

"It is for me. Honey, I love you but I'm a man, with a man's pride of responsibility. I've got to do this myself."

"But you have," she said, sounding a little frantic. "By writing all those letters. By telephoning your uncle. You made it all happen, don't you see?"

"A while ago you talked about being a Christian. Well, I knew that before you ever said a word, because I knew you were the angel that Dennis kept saying we needed."

"I'm not that angel, Willis. Please believe me."

"But you are. Who was it showed up to save us? You."

She looked into my eyes for a long moment. She seemed to be

debating with herself. I couldn't imagine over what. She said, "Willis, please let this alone. I'm asking you as a favor to me, to us, to drop it."

I had to laugh. She sounded so serious. I said, "I'll admit I don't like using your ex-husband's money. And I ain't going to like living in his house. But I'm not going to make you suffer by being a hardhead about it. I want this to be my money. You're still the angel, I just want to buy your wings."

"Oh hell!" she said. She fell back flat on the bed. "You are going to ruin everything."

I gave her a frown. "How? What's the matter with you?"

"If you try to raise money, you'll go to some of your relatives and it will get back to your father and then what will he think?"

I frowned deeper. "What in hell are you talking about, girl?"

She sat up swiftly and jabbed a finger at my chest. "You were the angel, Willis. You! You and nobody else. You were the one cared about those poor people. You were the one wanted to get the cup of water for them so they could finally hold their heads up. Nobody else thought of that except you."

"That don't make me the angel."

"Yes it does."

"How?"

"Because your uncle called your daddy and your daddy got on the train and headed for Pecos, and my daddy knows your aunt and uncle and they told him your daddy was coming and I met him in San Antonio and by the time we got to Pecos, we knew what we were going to do. He wanted to back you. Said you had the money coming. That was his checkbook I was trading out of." Her eyes were big and a little frightened.

I was stunned and a little confused. "Your daddy knows my uncle Warner and Aunt Laura?"

"I told you that. Everyone in town knows my daddy. But when I was missing you and you were writing me and I was too stubborn to write back, I called him on the telephone and he told me what they knew and I decided to go and see what I could do. I was so touched about the water. So you see, you were the angel. You kept looking for the angel but it was you all the time."

I said, slowly, "My daddy bought out that drilling contract?"

She nodded. "Yes. It was not my ex-husband's money. It was yours."

"No it wasn't, it was my daddy's."

"That's not what he said. He said he owed you that much and more, for going your own way. He said that you'd only done what he would have done if it had been the other way around. He said he had made it hard on you but he wanted to make it up. That was why he was going to put up the money. Said it was yours anyway." She suddenly got up on her knees on the bed so she could look me right in the eyes. "But he doesn't want you to feel like he was trying to buy his way out. You've got to respect that."

I hung my head and got thoughtful. I looked off into the corner, still thinking. I said, "Well, I am mighty thankful it is not your ex-husband's money. That part is good, anyway."

She said, "Are you going to be jealous of my ex-husband?"

I looked at her like she was having to repeat first grade. "You betcha! Hell yes, and forevermore. And the less said about him, the better off you'll be. You get me?"

She was a little taken aback. "That's not very reasonable."

"Then call me unreasonable." I reached out and pulled her to me. "I don't want to even think another man has ever touched you. Call me selfish if you want. I don't care."

"But what about your father? Willis, I promised him I wouldn't tell you. He wants you to have a fair start and he thinks he was unfair, but he's a proud man."

"You don't have to tell me that." I mused to myself, considering, thinking of what it must have taken for him to make such a gesture. He didn't often admit he was wrong. It suddenly made my feel very close to him.

She said, "So you own the drilling contract. He wants it to be his gift to you—no, he wants it to be your due. So he doesn't want you to thank him. And I promised."

I put an eye on her. "Glad to see how well you keep your promises."

She put her nails into my forearm. "Don't you torment me. Tell me now you won't tell him."

I leaned over and kissed her. "I can't promise you that. But now I've got to go see him."

"What for?"

"Because he's my father and I haven't seen him in a long time. Just to say hello. And I want to see my mother. You want to get married in Del Rio or Houston or Pecos? We can get Judge Crater to perform the ceremony."

"Good heavens, not Pecos!"

All of a sudden we both got quiet. This was getting down to the real crux of the matter. We sat there, me on the side of the bed, her in the middle with her legs crossed. She put her hand on my back and rubbed it back and forth. She said, "Willis, do you realize what you've done?"

"About what?"

"The water. But not just the water—all of it. All that it says in Matthew twenty-five."

I looked around at her. "Are you talking about the Bible? *That* Matthew?"

She was lying on her side, absently rubbing my back with the tips of her fingers. She said, " 'Jesus said to them, "I was hungry and you gave Me food. I was homeless and you gave Me shelter. I was thirsty and you gave Me water." And they said to Him, "When did we do that, Lord?" And He said, "When you did that for the least of these, my brothers, you did it for Me." ' "

It startled me. "I never did anything like that, Genevieve."

She said, "Yes you did, honey. I saw those men gathering around that well, watching that water rise up out of that pipe. These were the 'least of these' if there ever were a 'least'. Nobody else cared about those poor people, but you did."

I thought about it for a moment, but I was troubled. I said, "Yeah, but look here, Genevieve, I'm planning on developing that lake. True enough, it's open range and that water is free to all who want to water their stock. But if you want to farm or irrigate, you'll have to deal with me."

She laughed softly. "That has nothing to do with it, honey. I've already found out you're easy to deal with."

I looked around at her. "And Mr. Atlas found out you weren't easy."

She sighed and rolled over and sat up on her side of the bed. "Mr. Atlas was so damn easy I feel guilty. He already wanted out of a bad deal and I kept making it sound even worse with those tricks. And when he'd try to make a good argument I'd simply cross my legs and he'd forget where he was."

That made my mouth drop open. "You did what! Listen, I nearly killed that poor man for touching you. And you were leading him on. Genevieve, you are going to make it hard to learn to be a Christian."

She put her hand to my mouth. "You don't *learn* to be a Christian. Jesus comes into your life and chooses you and that is it. After that, you look back and wonder how you could have been so blind for so long."

I wrinkled my nose. "*He* chooses you? I thought you had to choose him. I remember all the invitations in church and all the people who would feel the calling. We had one old man used to feel the calling every other week."

"You don't worry about how it works. Jesus will see to it."

We ate supper that night in the hotel dining room. We were both a little subdued knowing we were going to be parting on the morrow. She was going to take a train for Houston and I was going to fly to Del Rio to see my parents. We would not be apart very long, but right then, in the tender stages of the growth of our love affair, we didn't want to be apart at all.

Halfway through the meal I said, "I suppose getting married in Houston would be the best. But not in that house."

She gave me a severe look. "Listen, Willis, that is not *his* house.

He doesn't live there. And other people lived in it before he bought it. It's my house. And when we are married it will be your house, too. I want you to stop this silly jealous foolishness."

I did not feel chastised. I said, "Nevertheless—let's get married in a church. Let your father do the ceremony. Houston will be better because it will be about the same distance for my parents as yours. I think we ought to get married in Del Rio so I could take you to Mexico for a honeymoon, but I know you won't like Mexico."

"I love Mexico."

"Yeah, where?"

"Acapulco."

I laughed. "That's not Mexico. That's Galveston South. I'm talking about places where they never even saw a tourist."

"All right. You pick it and I'll go."

A little later, over coffee and dessert, I looked off into a corner of the dining room and shook my head. "I can't believe my father bailed me out. He was never the most open-handed of men, especially with me. But I guess when you rob banks for a living you figure you ought to teach your son the value of a dollar."

She said, reproachfully, "Oh, Willis, he is a real gentleman. And he thinks the world and all of you. If you'd've needed a million dollars he'd've got it."

"You mean I now have the money to take care of Dennis?"

"Well, not exactly. It was not planned that you would know, so that checkbook I have of his, will only honor my signature. He took a sample and fixed it up with his bank back home." She hesitated, looking embarrassed. "If you need some money, we'd better go to the bank in the morning and let me sign a check."

I looked at her and shook my head. "Wilson Young does it to me again."

"But he didn't want you to know! He was afraid you wouldn't take it. He said the only thing harder-headed than you was an anvil, and a hard anvil at that. He said you killed a mule, too, by letting it kick you in the head."

"That," I said dryly, "is some joke Wilson Young bends like a crowbar. There are mountains that have moved before he has."

"Yes, but he is terrifically good-looking. I see where you get it, now."

I flushed. "Listen, there's one good-looking party at this table and it ain't me."

"Quit saying 'ain't.' It's common."

That night, we lay in the dark and I looked upward and said, "I don't know how all this happened. All I can tell you is that I am happier than I've ever been."

She hugged me hard. "It's only going to get better."

"It's going to last," I said.

Her train was due at three o'clock the next afternoon. It was the express, which had come thundering through Pecos like it didn't exist. She would ride that to San Antonio and then change trains for Houston.

But I had to leave earlier if I was to make Del Rio before nightfall. There was some rough terrain between the two cities and I didn't relish flying over such country in the dark and having the engine die. I was going to get away about ten o'clock.

We had breakfast and then went to a bank where she cashed a check for five thousand dollars and gave it all to me in hundreds. I said, feeling a little funny, "I don't want to make a habit of this."

She said, "It's your money, honey. Though, once we get married half of it will be mine. This is a communal property state, you know."

"Does that mean that half—" I stopped. I said, "We been doing way too much talking about money."

She rode in the taxicab with me out to the airfield where I had the Jenny tied down amid a clutch of larger and more modern planes. Some of them could carry twelve passengers. I had been taking note of that trend in aviation, but I didn't say anything.

I had the taxi wait while she said good-bye to me. She asked me if I was going to write to her. I said, "Hell, woman, I'm not going to be gone that long. I'll damn near beat you back to Houston. But I will call you on the telephone."

We were leaning against the fuselage, and she hugged me. "You be careful."

"Listen, there is one thing—" I hesitated to bring it up because I didn't want to make it seem as if I were testing her. I said, "Not long after we're married, if Dennis is successful in drilling the other two wells, there will be a lake. I'm going to have to go to Pecos and stay awhile to develop the land around that lake. There's not going to be any quick money in it because those people don't have any money. I guess you'll prefer to stay in Houston for that time. I figure to build a little cabin. It's going to be a kind of rough life, but I can make some money if I do it right, and I can also do some people some good."

She hugged me. "I hate Pecos, but I'd rather be with you. Besides, I'm a better businessperson than you are."

"You will? You'll really come to Pecos with me?"

"Of course."

I looked at her and then I shook my head. "I don't think so. After about a couple of weeks of that kind of life you might not care for the faithful wife life so much. No, I think I'll leave you in Houston with your maid."

She hit me fiercely in the chest with her fist. "Don't you be deciding for me what I'm going to do, mister." She suddenly grabbed me and kissed me hard. "You are the first man in my life. I intend to be wherever you are."

I looked at her and blinked, overcome with her emotion. I finally said, "Hell, okay."

Not too long afterward my wheels cleared the turf of San Angelo airfield and I was airborne. I circled the airport once, looking down. I could see her standing by the taxi, waving up at me. She'd finally confessed why she'd been running over to the hotel while I had been flying over Pecos that day. She'd been going over to give my daddy a report on the oil deal. Well, he'd fooled me, and fooled me bad. But that was all over. We were father and son, and we were going to get along as such or there would be hell to pay. He might not approve of some of the things I'd done, but then, neither did I approve of all his actions.

I turned the airplane southeast toward Del Rio. I had a hard flight ahead of me.

My father said, "How come you wearing them stovepiped, slick-leathered, polished-up low-heel boots? Them ain't riding boots. How come you can't get yourself a proper pair of high-heeled boots?"

I said, calmly—as calm as I'd tried to keep my visit—"Because they ain't riding boots, Dad. They are boots worn by aviators. Which is what I am. I'm a pilot."

"I guess them funny-looking pants go along with the boots."

"Jodhpurs? Yes. But I understand that you wore a pair of these when you tried to steal a quarter of a million dollars in gold from the United States Government."

That brought a moment of quiet. He said, "What right do you have to speak of that?"

It was an opening, but I let it pass by. I said, "The right that you are my father and that you were doing something you thought was right, and I admire you for that."

He looked covertly at me out from under his eyelids. "You do, eh? What do you know about it?"

"Word gets back," I said succinctly.

We were sitting in his office, a fair-sized wood-paneled room with a bar at one end and a shelf of books at the other. The whiskey I would have easily believed, but not the books. Yet Mother had told me he was reading everything from Mark Twain to the Bible. She'd said, "Son, your father has undergone a tremendous transformation. Don't disturb it."

It was my second day there. We had killed the fatted calf and pig and welcomed home the reluctant transcended son. I would not think of myself as the prodigal son because I had not gone away in bitterness nor had I hit bottom. At least not emotionally.

My mother and I had had a very tender time and she had been reduced to tears to understand that I was beginning to understand that my life depended on Jesus Christ. I don't believe I'd ever seen her happier. It was a good feeling for me to finally give her what she had so long sought—and probably had never expected to see come about in her lifetime. I let her know that Genevieve was no small part of my new feelings.

But there was Wilson Young sitting across from me and a lot of words hadn't been said. Maybe they didn't need to be said, but I felt like they did. I said, "Dad, we ain't talked about this before, but I defied you when I went off to fight in a war you didn't believe in."

He was sitting there in his boots and his hat and his starched jeans. He nodded slowly. "Yeah, you did defy me. Slammed me in the face as a matter of fact. But that was your choice. And you done it."

I said, "What was it you done when you took me out on the train to west Texas and showed me two hundred thousand acres of dust and sand and rocks and cactus? To tell me that was all I could expect if I enlisted in the French Air Forces? What was that?"

He smiled a little thinly. "I reckon that was a fistful of sand right in the face. About what you was doing to me."

"But you told me that patch of sand was what I was worth."

"At the time that was what I felt."

I said, "I'm leaving in the morning. I need to know how you feel now."

He seemed to draw himself up, which was no mean feat for Wilson

Young since he generally looked drawn-up. He said, "I've had occasion to revise my opinion."

"Why?"

He looked uncomfortable. He said, "Maybe by the way you comported yourself in the war."

I said, "Bullshit. Tell the truth, Dad."

He writhed in his chair. "Well, just on general reasons. That good enough for you?"

I got up and walked across to him. I said, "I'm about to break a promise, but I do it in the best of interests. I thank you for backing my worthless two hundred thousand acres. I thank you for backing me. I will not disappoint you. Jesus will not let me."

He stood up. "Your mother been talking to you?"

"No."

"If she does, you might want to listen. Might be something in that stuff she believes in."

We shook hands and then we sort of awkwardly hugged. He stepped back, looking uncomfortable. He said, "Reckon it will rain?"

The day I was to leave, we sat in the breakfast room, just my dad and me. He said, "Reckon what you are going to do now, son?"

I took a drink of coffee. I said, "Well, I've told you and Mother about the wedding plans, so I guess you know I'm going to marry that girl, that lady."

He nodded. "Luckiest thing that ever happened to you."

"Then I'm going to develop that land you gave me. With that lake in the middle of it it ought to be worth some money."

"You got plenty to back you here. Up to half a million."

"Don't need it, thank you."

"Then what? After the land?"

I frowned. It was kind of hard to explain. I said, "Dad, I think there is a future in commercial aviation. Carrying passengers. They got planes can taken a dozen, fourteen passengers two hundred, even three hundred miles. It's the coming thing and I'd like to get in on the ground floor."

He gave me a half-smile. "Folks thought I was nuts going into bank-robbing when I did. Guess something has always got to be new."

He and my mother walked me out to my plane. I said, "I reckon you know you bought me this plane. I'm much obliged."

He said, "I'd rather it was a damn good horse."

"It is." I smiled. "With me in the saddle."

Then I hugged them and flew off, heading for Houston.

Some unusual things happened after that. Genevieve and I got married in a Baptist church in Houston with her daddy doing the honors. For a honeymoon we went to Pecos and I built a cabin and went into the land business. Genevieve was a great help and a non-complainer.

There was one curious afterbirth of the whole matter. Two years after Dennis gave up and shipped his rigs, after drilling us three magnificent water wells but no oil wells, three major producers came into Pecos County and quickly drilled discovery wells at three and four and five thousand feet. They drilled twelve of those on my land. In a very short time, Genevieve and I were millionaires. It made getting into the commercial airline business all that much easier.

ABOUT THE AUTHOR

GILES TIPPETTE was a Texan by birth and by choice. He began earning his living as a writer in 1966. Prior to that he had been a venture pilot, a mercenary, a diamond courier, and a bucking-event rodeo cowboy. In addition to his books, he authored over five hundred articles for such magazines as *Time, Newsweek, Sports Illustrated, Esquire*, and *Texas Monthly*. Until his death in October 1999, Tippette lived in prime quarterhorse country in Tyler, Texas, with his wife, Betsyanne.